## GET A CLUE!

Be the first to hear the latest mystery book news...

With the St. Martin's Minotaur monthly newsletter, you'll learn about the hottest new Minotaur books, receive advance excerpts from newly published works read exclusive original material from featured mystery writers, and be able to enter to win free books!

Sign up on the Minotaur Web site at:
www.minotaurbooks.com

# *PRAISE FOR JAMES D. DOSS*

## THE SHAMAN SINGS

*A *Publishers Weekly* Best Book of the Year*

"Stunning." —*Publishers Weekly* (Starred Review)

"Doss mixes an equally potent brew of crime and Native American spirituality." —*Booklist*

"Magical and tantalizing." —*New York Times Book Review*

"Gripping. . . . Doss succesfully blends the cutting edge of modern physics with centuries-old mysticism." —*Rocky Mountain News*

"Fascinating . . . impressive. . . . Like Tony Hillerman, Doss is able to combine the supernatural with the modern in a compelling and believable book." —*Woodland Hills Daily News*

"Delightful—a marvelous mixture of mysticism and murder." —Ken Englade

"Doss plots like a pro . . . an encore would be welcome." —*Kirkus Reviews*

## *. . . AND HIS OTHER CHARLIE MOON MYSTERIES*

### SHADOW MAN

"Doss likes to toss a little Native American spiritualism and a lot of local color into his mysteries. Fans of the series will be well pleased." —*Booklist*

"Fans of Daisy Perika, the 80-something shaman who brings much of the charm and supernatural thrill to James D. Doss's mystery series, should like *Shadow Man* . . . nice reading." —*Rocky Mountain News*

*MORE . . .*

THE WITCH'S TONGUE

"With all the skill and timing of a master magician, Doss unfolds a meticulous plot laced with a delicious sense of humor and set against a vivid southern Colorado." —*Publishers Weekly*

"Doss's ear for Western voices is remarkable, his tone whimsical. . . . If you don't have time for the seven-hour drive from Denver to Pagosa, try *The Witch's Tongue* for a taste of southern Colorado." —*Rocky Mountain News*

"A classy bit of storytelling that combines myth, dreams, and plot complications so wily they'll rattle your synapses and tweak your sense of humor." —*Kirkus Reviews*

DEAD SOUL

"Hillerman gets the most press, but Doss mixes an equally potent brew of crime and Native American spirituality." —*Booklist*

"Lyrical, and he gets the sardonic, macho patter between men down cold. The finale is heartfelt and unexpected, and a final confrontation stuns with its violent and confessional precision."
—*Providence Journal Bulletin*

THE NIGHT VISITOR

"The author is indeed a treasure. . . . A hybrid of Tony Hillerman and Carl Hiaasen, but with an overall sensibility that is uniquely Doss." —*Denver Post*

"The dialogue crackles, and the Southern Colorado atmosphere astonishes, especially at night." —*Publishers Weekly*

"Fans won't be disappointed. . . . Doss pulls together an archeological dig, abandoned children, and a good, old-fashioned murder to pull off his latest success." —*Chicago Tribune*

THE SHAMAN'S GAME

"Suspenseful and satisfying. . . . Doss has reproduced the land of the Southern Colorado Utes with vivid affection."—*Dallas Morning News*

"Doss could be accused of poaching in Tony Hillerman territory . . . but Doss mixes mysticism and murder with his own unmistakable touch."

—*Orlando Sentinel*

"Deft storytelling . . . compelling . . . ingenious . . . intense . . . a richness of prose and plot that lifts it out of the expected ranks of mystery fiction."

—*Arizona Daily Star*

GRANDMOTHER SPIDER

"Propelled by fast-paced action and intriguing characters . . . like something out of Stephen King . . . with snippets from Dave Barry."

—*Chicago Tribune*

"Humor crackles through pages packed with surprises."

—*Albuquerque Journal*

THE SHAMAN'S BONES

"Fans of Tony Hillerman's Navajo mysteries will find a new home here."

—*Denver Post*

"A worthy addition to a richly rewarding series . . . Doss again creates a fascinating mix of gritty police work, the spiritual traditions of Southwestern Indians and irresistible characters."

—*Publishers Weekly*

THE SHAMAN LAUGHS

"This is Hillerman country . . . but Doss is gaining . . . I hope these shaman activities go on for a long time."

—*Boston Globe*

WHITE SHELL WOMAN

"Although less well known than other Native American-based mystery series, the Charlie Moon novels are quickly rising to the top of the pack. Doss has a fine comic touch—playing off Moon's laconic wit against Daisy's flamboyant personality—and he just may be the best of the bunch at seamlessly integrating anthropological and spiritual material into his stories."

—*Booklist*

ALSO BY JAMES D. DOSS

*Snake Dreams*

*Three Sisters*

*The Shaman Sings*

*The Shaman Laughs*

*The Shaman's Bones*

*The Shaman's Game*

*The Night Visitor*

*Grandmother Spider*

*White Shell Woman*

*Dead Soul*

*The Witch's Tongue*

*Shadow Man*

# STONE BUTTERFLY

*JAMES D. DOSS*

St. Martin's Paperbacks

This is a work of fiction. All of the characters, organizations, and events portrayed in this novel are either products of the author's imagination or are used fictitiously.

STONE BUTTERFLY



Library of Congress Catalog Card Number: 2006043406

ISBN: 0-312-93665-6
EAN: 9780312-93665-5

Printed in the United States of America

St. Martin's Press hardcover edition / September 2006
St. Martin's Paperbacks edition / October 2007

St. Martin's Paperbacks are published by St. Martin's Press, 175 Fifth Avenue, New York, NY 10010.

10 9 8 7 6 5 4 3

*For*
*T. David and Nam McDonald*
*Bangkok, Thailand,*

*Morgan Norris*
*Blackwell, Oklahoma,*

*Mary and Sandra Hale*
*San Diego, California,*

*and*

*Jack Arrington*
*Mesilla Park, New Mexico*

# ACKNOWLEDGMENTS

I wish to offer my thanks to
Ralph Dahlstron, M.D.,
Silver City, New Mexico,
and
Geri Keams and James Bernardin,
author and illustrator, respectively, of
*Grandmother Spider Brings the Sun*,
ISBN: 0-87358-694-8
Rising Moon Books for Young Readers from
Northland Publishing, Flagstaff, Arizona.

# PROLOGUE

*MADISON COUNTY, ALABAMA, JUNE 29, 1922*

Mother, Daughter, Dog

*MOMMA carries freshly churned butter—a half-gallon lard can in each hand. Floppy sandals poppity-pop on the sand.*
*Little bare feet tripping after go patter-patter.*
*The trailing blue-tick hound makes no sound.*

• • •

As on all their weekly treks to town, where butter was bartered for those few necessities not produced on the Nestor farm, mother, daughter, and dog marched single file along a narrow pathway through chigger-infested blackberry bushes and broad-leafed poison pokeweed. The trail snaked along the slippery bank of the Flint River for nearly a mile before intersecting the gravel road to Sulphur Springs. It was not yet nine o'clock, and the heavy atmosphere was already steamy-hot. "Try to keep up, Daff."

"Yes'm." Daphne scratched at an itchy sore on her elbow.

Without a glance over her shoulder, she added: "And stop pickin' at that scab!"

"Yes'm." *Granny Nestor says that all mommas has eyes in the backs of their heads.* The child squinted hard to see the spot. *They must be under her hair.*

Momma rolled her visible eyes. *Lord, I don't know why I*

*even bother—it just goes in one ear and out the other.* She cast a nervous glance at the brackish, slow-moving waters. *This place is alive with cottonmouths and copperheads and God only knows what else.* What Else was approaching her left ear. The target of the assault heard the tiny engine whine, felt the fat black mosquito land on her neck. *Well, I ain't gonna put a bucket down to smack you, so you might as well go ahead and get it over with.* The stab came swiftly, was followed by a victorious drumroll of thunder. Momma frowned at a somber shroud of low-hanging cloud. *There's rain in that; enough to soak us to the skin.* She quickened her pace. "Get a move on!"

"Yes'm." It seemed that no matter how fast Daphne's chubby legs chugged along, she was always a dozen steps behind. This, she reasoned, was mainly on account of *Momma walks too fast* and *My legs is too short for me to keep up.* But there was more to it than that; the inquisitive child often felt compelled to stop and pick up a pearly fragment of mussel shell, or pluck a pretty brown-eyed Susan, or make an ugly face at a daddy longlegs. She was a busy little pilgrim.

The young mother shuddered at a sinister wriggle-rustling in the grass. "Watch out where you're steppin', Daff. And don't touch *nothin'*—no fuzzy worms, no ugly-bugs—you hear me?"

"Yes'm." But even as she spoke, the child spotted a temptation. *Oh! Pretty—pretty—pretty!* Pink as a wild rose, glistening with pearly dew, it glittered like a jewel fallen from heaven. But most striking of all, a network of crimson veins webbed its translucent wings. Daphne poked her big toe at the exquisite apparition, expecting it to fly away. It did not. *Poor thingy—you must be sick.* The child squatted, gently picked it up, whispered: "I'll take you home to Granny Nestor—she'll make you all well." She thought it best not to mention that Granny's prescription for every ailment—be it toothache, dizzy spell, or painful boil—was a tablespoon of castor oil, followed quickly with a soda cracker. With a furtive glance at the back of her mother's head, the ardent collector slipped this latest acquisition into her apron pocket with an assortment of other treasured objects—like the shiny silver dime Grandpa Nestor had given her for the tent meeting collection plate, a once-lively June bug (recently deceased), and the bloodred Indian arrowhead she had picked up here just last week.

Near a lichen-encrusted log, a largemouth bass broke the river's still surface to take an unwary minnow. Momma just *knew* it was a cottonmouth that had dropped off a tree branch. She prayed: *Please, Lord—fix it so we can live someplace where there ain't so many snakes and skeeters.*

The tot bent over to snatch up a small jade-green frog. The thing was clammy-cold in her hand. *I think Miss Froggy's dead.* She was about to straighten up when—

The hound (who enjoyed such sport) cold-nosed her on the behind.

"Eeep!" she yelped, and hurried to catch up with Momma.

Heavy with a second child, the nineteen-year-old turned to scowl. "What've you been up to, Daff?"

"Nothin', Momma."

"Nothin' my hind leg!" Momma raised a lard-bucket like she might take a swat at the girl. "After I told you a hunnerd times not to, did you pick up some dead thing and hide it in your apern pocket?"

"Oh, no—cross my eyes and hope to die!" Daphne's left eye focused on the tip of her freckled nose, the right one stared straight at her mother.

Momma cringed. "Please Daff—don't *do* that." She added the standard warning: "Someday they'll stick thataway."

"When they do, I won't be able to see where I'm a-goin'." Imitating Grandpa Nestor (who would get up at night without lighting a coal oil lamp), Daphne bounced off a cottonwood trunk. "Oh, Jimminy—what was that I jus' bumped into—a ellyphant's leg?"

"Now you stop that silliness!" To keep from laughing, Momma called up terrible images of pain and death, which also provided inspiration for a dire warning: "And you'd better start payin' some attention to what I tell you—you keep on pickin' up them creepy-crawlies, one of 'em is gonna bite you and you'll swell up and die!"

The eyes uncrossed, an impish smile exposed a too-cute gap in a row of miniature teeth, a chubby hand closed around the stone-cold amphibian in her apron pocket. "I only stopped to look at a little bitsy frog, but she hopped an' hopped away"—Daphne demonstrated with little arcs of her hand—"and I heard a splish-splash when she jumped inta the river and got et by a great big garfish." To illustrate how the voracious gar had chomped the frog, the girl clicked her tiny teeth together.

Momma shook her head. *This child is just like her daddy and all her daddy's folks from up yonder in Butler County—she can't open her mouth without lyin' a blue streak. I wonder what on earth will ever become of her.*

Quite a lot, as it turned out.

In time, plump little Daphne would grow up to be tall and willowy as a Texas sunflower, semi-pretty, and moderately clever.

On her sixteenth birthday, she left Alabama for the land of the Shining Mountains, entered the State of Colorado with great expectations, the state of holy matrimony with a Grand Junction banker who collected Burmese star sapphires and died—as she wrote to her mother ". . . on account of being run over by a green International Harvester lumber truck loaded with jack pine pallets." Daphne wept as Thaddeus Silver was buried in the First Methodist Church cemetery, wore black silk and a downcast expression for eleven months before drifting westerly into Utah and reciting the vows of marriage with Mr. Raymond Oates, who was building up a fine herd of Herefords by burning his brand on other stockmen's cattle. Each of these marriages produced a son, but sad to say—neither Ben Silver nor Raymond Oates, Jr. would exhibit the least manifestation of brotherly affection. Or even half brotherly affection.

• • •

This is how the troubles got started that (decades later) would plague Southern Ute Tribal Investigator Charlie Moon, an upright and amiable citizen, and his aunt Daisy Perika, who is anything but. (Amiable and upright, that is.) How does one describe the tribal elder?

Conniving is a word that comes to mind.

Irascible is another.

And then, there is her little eccentricity: *Daisy talks to dead people.*

# ONE

*COLORADO, SOUTHERN UTE RESERVATION*

In the Shadow of Three Sisters Mesa

THIS being his weekly visit to his aged relative, Daisy Perika's long, lean nephew was seated at her kitchen table. It was evident that his entire attention was focused on the tribe's weekly newspaper, more particularly a column by a Granite Creek astrologer-psychic, wherein the seer predicted that (following an earthquake of unprecedented magnitude) the Lost Civilization of Atlantis would surface in the South Pacific! Though it was absolutely certain that the calamity would occur on February 10 at 9:15 A.M. Mountain Standard Time, the stars and planets were somewhat foggy on the precise year of the event—which might be 2007, or perhaps 2077—depending upon whether or not Saturn decided to visit the House of Uranus whilst that latter planet was in diametric juxtaposition to the Twenty-sixth Planet, which had not yet been discovered. The whole thing was a sham, of course.

(*Clarifying note:* Reference is not made to the astrologer's immodest prophecy—but rather to the more unpretentious sham currently being committed by Charlie Moon, whose apparent interest in the newspaper was a pretense.)

As it happened, Moon had heard the tramp's shuffle-footed approach when the intruder was a good hundred yards away, and the full-time rancher, part-time tribal investigator thought it would be entertaining to see how his aunt would deal with this unwelcome guest. In happy anticipation of the fireworks to come, he turned another page of the *Southern Ute Drum* and waited for the fun to begin. In about six seconds, he estimated. And began to count them off. *One thousand and one. One thousand and two.*

If Daisy had not been concentrating all her attention on the preparation of a morning meal for herself and her nephew, she might have been aware of Yadkin Dixon's arrival. Or perhaps not—the hungry man was intentionally making a stealthy approach.

*One thousand and three. One thousand and four.*

The way Mr. Dixon saw it, a hard-hearted old woman who kicked at chipmunks and heaved stones at pretty, flitting bluebirds could not be expected to deal kindly with a self-educated economist who firmly believed in the concept of a free lunch. Or free breakfast, as the case might be.

*One thousand and five. One thousand and six.*

The first evidence of his unwanted presence was the tap-tap of a knuckle on the kitchen window—and his long, horsy face gawking at her through the glass. After a startled twitch, the Ute woman quickly turned away. In Daisy's Book of Bad Things, this particular pestilence fell into that same insufferable category as the dull ache that plagued her left hip on a rainy day. Her remedy was: Ignore the hateful thing, it would eventually go away.

Her attempt to pretend that Dixon did not exist was wasted on the thick-skinned beggar who camped out somewhere in the vicinity of her home. The persistent fellow was not about to leave without some nourishment to occupy that hollow space betwixt the Coors pewter belt buckle and his spine.

Shamming on unashamedly, Moon pretended to be engrossed in an article entitled "Treating Hemorrhoids with Acupuncture." *Ouch.*

After ignoring the beggar for a full two seconds, Daisy gave up the game. Like death and taxes that were here to stay, Mr. Dixon was not going away. She wiped her hands on a polka-dot apron, jerked the back door open.

Before she had a chance to say something uncivil, Dixon tipped a tattered slouch hat. "Good morning, ma'am—and God bless you." Though a greeting of this sort tended to disarm his ordinary marks, he might as well have expected a cheerful "Howdy-do" to charm a grinning-skull tattoo off the hairy hide of a whiskey-soaked Hell's Angel.

Daisy marched outside, wagged a finger in his face. "Don't you start ma'am-ing me, you two-legged coyote." *Ugh—he smells like last week's fish.* She glared at the filthy white man. "What d'you want this time?" *As if I don't know.*

Charlie Moon also knew. And unseen by those outside, he had made his way to the cookstove, plopped several fat sausage links into a cast-iron skillet.

Mr. Dixon assumed a pitiful tone. "I wondered if you could spare a poor, homeless person a few leftovers from your table." His hopeful smile exposed yellowed teeth that resembled hard little kernels of unpopped corn. "Some cold, pasty oatmeal—or a few potato peels?"

"I gave you something to eat just last week." Daisy tried to recall the details and did. "It was a cheese sandwich, big enough to choke a bull moose." Though somewhat rusty from lack of use, Daisy's conscience gently reminded her that *the months-old cheese was fuzzy with blue mold and on top of that the bread was hard enough to break a brass monkey's teeth and—* Being one who did not accept criticism gracefully, she interrupted the inner voice: *I scraped the fur off that cheese. And even if the sliced bread was a little stale, you can't expect a dirt-poor widow woman to give her last slice of fresh bread to a man who hasn't used a toothbrush since that goober-pea farmer from Georgia was president.*

Blissfully unaware of Daisy's internal dialogue, the hungry man rubbed his stomach. "Alas, I have long since digested that delectable delicacy." Dixon assumed a saintly expression he had recently seen on a stained-glass window at St. Mark's Episcopal Church in Durango, where he had also tapped the Rector's Emergency Discretionary Fund for bus fare to Topeka so that he might attend his dear old mother's funeral (while Dear Old Mother was on a Caribbean cruise with her latest husband). "I would be grateful for some broken soda crackers. Or a shriveled-up apple core."

Moon cracked three brown-shell eggs on the edge of the skillet, smiled appreciatively at the man's line of talk. It was always a pleasure to witness a highly skilled professional going about his work.

Daisy was not about to leave the subject of the white vagrant's last visit. "And after I fed you that sandwich, what did you do?" Like a well-rehearsed attorney, the prosecutor-persecutor answered her own question. "You thanked me by stealing a brand-new ax from my pile of piñon wood!"

The beggar—who was short of everything but pride—stiffened his back and lied: "I did no such thing."

Her nostrils flared dangerously. "Don't tell me that, you snake-eyed sneak-thief—I was watching you from that window." To identify the physical evidence that supported her accusation, the witness for the prosecution pointed to indicate the aforesaid window.

Little wheels turned in his head, tiny ratchets clicked and clacked, and so on and so forth. Figuratively, of course. "I might have picked up your ax." Dixon's highly plastic features effortlessly assumed the injured expression of one who—though painfully wounded by a malicious and false accusation—would not take offense. "But even if I did—all I ever intended was to borrow it for a few hours."

The hard-faced woman had a ready answer for that. "Then why didn't you bring it back?"

Having fended off many serious allegations over the years, Dixon did not miss a beat. "It is my faulty memory." He leaned forward, fixed his feisty accuser with an earnest gaze. "Ever since I was struck north of Clarksville, Tennessee, by that speeding L&N freight train that was pulling eighteen boxcars and a green caboose, I can hardly remember anything—even my name." He paused for a moment, evidently involved in an intense mental effort to recall what the initials Y-D stood for, only to be defeated by the arduous task. "But be assured that as soon as I return to my modest encampment, I shall search for your—uh—dear me, you see—it has slipped away from me already." A cherubic smile. "Tell me again—what it was that is missing—a hammer from your toolshed?"

The old teakettle was approaching a boil; she hissed at him: "You took my new ax—and it was on my woodpile!"

Dixon stared at the neat stack of split piñon. "Hmmm." He nodded as if the light was beginning to dawn. "An *ax*, you say. Well if I should find such an implement among my meager belongings, I shall bring it to you directly."

"Well I won't hold my breath." Daisy exhaled. "And there's another thing." Inhaled. "You've got no right to be squatting on the Southern Ute reservation." She pointed at her house. "My nephew's inside, and he's a tribal policeman and—"

"Is that a fact?" Dixon's poor memory had made a remarkable recovery. "I was under the impression that Mr. Moon had retired from the Ute police department several years ago, to manage his cattle ranch."

"Charlie is a tribal investigator, and if I just snap my fingers—" she displayed a finger and thumb, all cocked to snap, "—he'll trot out here and arrest you right on the spot and—"

"You called?"

Following Dixon's gaze, Daisy turned to see her nephew's lanky form in the doorway. Moon had brought with him a platter of scrambled eggs and pork sausage. These victuals were tastefully accompanied by a pair oven-hot biscuits.

Yadkin Dixon fixed a hopeful gaze on the food. "It is good to see you, sir. I have continued to follow your career for some time now—and if I may say so, I am to be counted among your many admirers."

Moon chuckled at the blatant flattery, offered the plate to his ardent fan.

The gift was gratefully accepted by the famished man.

Daisy shook her head, turned to mutter misgivings to her overly generous relative: "Now that good-for-nothing bum'll be back every day, begging food, stealing anything that ain't nailed down." Knowing her words were wasted, she elbowed him aside, huffed and grumbled her way back into the kitchen.

Charlie Moon waited patiently while the enthusiastic diner devoured the hearty breakfast. After Dixon had wiped his mouth on his sleeve and burped, the tribal investigator gave him a look that would have shaken a more sensible man. This was accompanied by an order. "You bring that ax back *today.*" As the sly fellow was opening his mouth to protest, the Ute cut him off: "And if you so much as steal a *look* at any of my aunt's property, I'll give Chief of Police Whitehorse a call. The very least he'll do is run you off the res. More likely, he'll put you up in the tribe's modern correctional facility for ninety days."

Normally such a threat would have caused Dixon to protest, or at least raise an eyebrow, but a full stomach has a calming effect on a man. He picked a pointy juniper needle off a convenient branch, thoughtfully picked his teeth, pondered the offer of a free room and three meals a day. Concluded that it would place too many restrictions on his cherished freedom of movement. "I will certainly return the lady's ax." He tossed the toothpick aside. "And henceforth, I promise not to—uh—borrow any property that belongs to your charming aunt." He raised his right hand to show Moon a soiled palm. "You have my word of honor, sir."

*Great. With that and six bits I could buy me a seventy-five-cent cup of coffee.* Moon looked up to watch a golden eagle float by. By the time he lowered his gaze, the scruffy-looking white man had ambled over to the Columbine Expedition.

The visitor caressed the Ford Motor Company product. "This is quite a spiffy motorcar."

Moon winced at the greasy streaks Dixon's grubby fingers were tracing on the glistening fender. "I just waxed it."

"And you did a fairly decent job." Mr. Dixon got that faraway look in his eye, also cleared his throat. Which is a double warning that whether the unwary listener likes it or not, he is about to share a favorite memory. "Back in Michigan, when I was just a young lad, my daddy owned a cherry-red

1963 Jaguar XKE 3.8 coupe. Pop kept it garaged, except on Sundays, when he'd roll it out and take me for a ride into Lansing." His sigh was scented with nostalgia-blossom perfume. "Talk about your fine automobiles—there is absolutely *nothing* like a Jag."

## *AUNT DAISY'S VERY BAD DREAM*

DAISY was busy at the propane range, putting the final touches on her nephew's breakfast. This amounted to one skillet filled with sizzling sausage and fried potatoes, another of fluffy scrambled eggs, plus a simmering pot of green chili stew. *Work, work, work—that's all I ever do.* As a gray mist slipped out of Spirit Canyon and settled over her mind, the cook sighed. *I bet that thieving white man'll be back here tomorrow, licking his lips and asking for any prime rib and baked potatoes that's left over from my lunch.* Recalling his whining request for an apple core, her wrinkled face crinkled into a crooked little smile. *I ought to give him a big, shiny red apple with enough pickleweed poison in it to kill a dozen smelly moochers—that'd teach him a lesson he wouldn't forget!* In Daisy's version of the heartwarming tale, this was how Snow White had dispensed with the witch, who should have known better than to trust a silly white girl who had run away from home to hang out with a truckload of dwarves. From the shaman's experience, one *pitukupf* in the neighborhood was sufficient.

Fortunately for Mr. Dixon, the cook had dismissed him from her malevolent thoughts. But Charlie Moon was not so lucky. As the broth began to froth and bubble, Daisy sensed the time was ripe to make some trouble—and commenced to stir the pot. "Charlie, there's something that's been bothering me."

Moon turned another page of the *Southern Ute Drum.* No sham this time.

"I've been having this same bad dream, over and over."

No response. She turned up the volume. "Last night, I had it again. It was so scary I woke up with the sweats."

He frowned at a full-page listing of Upcoming Events, had a great notion. *I should take Lila Mae McTeague to the dance.* No two ways about it—the long-legged FBI agent would be the best-looking woman there.

The Ute elder turned to scowl at her nephew. "Did you hear what I said?"

"Sure." *I wonder if Lila Mae's ever been to a Bear Dance. Probably not.*

"Plop, plop, plop."

Moon shook a wrinkle out of the newspaper. "What?"

"That was the sound it made."

He stared at her hunched back. "The sound what made?"

"The blood."

"What blood?"

She brought him a man-sized platter of eggs, sausage, and potatoes. "The blood dropping onto that dead man's face!"

"Oh. Right." He reached for a paper napkin, considered tucking it over his new white linen shirt with the mother-of-pearl buttons, decided to put it in his lap.

She hurried back to the stove. "You don't have the least idea what I've been talking about."

"Sure I do."

"Then tell me."

"The blood. It was going . . . uh . . . drip-drip."

"It was going plop-plop-*plop*." She turned down the ring of blue flame under the pot, tossed him another challenge. "And how was it that I happened to hear that blood going plop-plop-plop?"

With Aunt Daisy it was nine-to-one for a nightmare, so he played the odds. "You was having one of them weird dreams."

"I knew you wasn't paying no attention." She banged the wooden spoon on the stove. "What I said was—I've been having the same *bad* dream, over and over."

*Might as well get this over with.* "Tell me all about it."

She sniffed. "Oh, you don't really want to know."

"Yes I do. And if you keep me in suspense, I won't be able to eat a bite of breakfast."

*That'll be a day to remember.* Daisy brought the stew pot to the table. "I dreamed about a skinny little girl."

He watched her ladle a generous helping of green chili stew onto the mound of scrambled eggs. *That looks good enough to eat.* He took a taste. *It could use some salt.*

She reached out to tweak his ear. "You're supposed to ask me: 'Who was this skinny little girl?' "

"Consider yourself asked." He reached for the shaker.

She slapped his hand. "Don't do that—I've got it seasoned just right. I don't know who she is."

Momentarily deprived of salt, the Ute warrior raised his fork, expertly speared a sausage. "Then why should I have asked?"

"To show proper respect to a tribal elder."

"Right." He opened a steaming biscuit, inserted a generous helping of butter.

"I don't know who the girl is, because in these dreams, I don't ever see her face." She hobbled over to the stove. *Back and forth, back and forth—it's a wonder I don't wear a path ankle-deep into the floor.* "But I know she's in trouble. Serious trouble."

Behind her back, Moon snatched the shaker, added several dashes of sodium chloride, tasted the result. *That's some better.*

While preparing a plate for herself, Daisy paused to stare through the window at a diaphanous fluff of cloud floating over the big mesa. She watched it snag itself on the tallest of the Three Sisters. "In these dreams, the girl is standing over the dead man."

He took a sip of black coffee. *I forgot to put sugar in it.* He remedied this error with six heaping spoonfuls.

Daisy was silent for a long moment, watching the cloud that had become a misty wisp of gray hair on the petrified

Pueblo woman's head. "And what makes it so awful is that her little hands is soaked in blood."

As chance would have it, he had just poured tomato ketchup onto a heap of fried potatoes.

The shaman shuddered. "And that blood just keeps dripping off the tips of her fingers—onto the dead man's face."

Charlie Moon was not a squeamish diner, but food was meant to be savored. He eyed the bloody chunk of spud on his fork. *I wish she would wait until after I've had my breakfast to tell me about her nightmares.*

Daisy Perika brought her plate to the table, thoughtfully watched her nephew frown at a slice of ketchup-painted potato. "All night I could hear it, even when I was wide-awake—all that blood dripping off her hands, onto that dead man's face." She saw the indecision on Charlie Moon's face. "There was so much that it puddled up in his eye sockets."

Knowing she would finally tire of the subject, he decided the fried potatoes could wait. In the meantime, he would fortify himself with eggs and sausage and buttered biscuits.

The old woman settled herself into a chair. For a while, she picked at her scrambled eggs. After a few tentative bites, she lost interest in her meal. Fixed her gaze on a Wildflower of the Month wall calendar. Began to hum her favorite Ute ballad, which she claimed had been stolen from her tribe by the British. Then, in a scratchy-creaky voice that would have set a deaf man's teeth on edge, she sang thusly:

*In Sweet Grass Town, where I was born,*
*There was a fair lass dwellin'...*

And so on. Until she got to the good part:

*O grandmo-ther, make my bed!*
*O make it hard and narrow—*
*My sweetheart died for me today,*
*I'll be with him to-morrow.*

After the next and semifinal verse, and following his aunt's long, melancholy sigh, Charlie Moon concluded that he had won the waiting game. He could almost taste his starchy, ketchup-tinctured victory.

From the corner of her eye, the tribal elder spotted the home fry that was newly impaled on the tines of her nephew's fork. She mumbled a hastily devised and highly discordant epilogue:

*And knowin' I'll be no man's wife,*
*I'll slit my throat with a butcher knife . . .*

The crimson-dripping morsel was rising toward Moon's lips.

Her mumble rose to a mutter:

*And my blood drips down,*
*Down in the dust in Sweet Grass Town . . .*

She watched the fork slowing—possibly coming to a stop . . .

"Plop," Daisy said. "Plop-plop."

# TWO

*TONAPAH FLATS, UTAH*
On the Lonely Side of Big Lizard Ridge

HAVING no idea that he had a soul mate in an adjoining state (he would have greatly admired Daisy Perika's pepper and spunk), Ben Silver muttered under his bushy white mustache: "I hate Mr. Alexander Graham Bell. Also Ma Bell and all the little baby Bells. Plus all the Bell family's mangy dogs and flea-bitten cats." He glared at the offending instrument. "But most of all, I hate Bell Senior's infernal invention!"

And he did. Except for the thin little Indian girl who trudged through Hatchet Gap now and then to do some light housework for him, Ben Silver assured himself that he hated virtually everyone, living and dead, including persons he had never met or heard of. This was a slight exaggeration; there were a few historical figures that he admired. Mr. Silver was, in fact, not an entirely unreasonable man—there was a particular reason that he particularly despised Mr. Bell and his family and livestock and the fruit of Mr. Bell's inventive mind.

Why? Because when the telephone rang at his elbow, Ben Silver was seated comfortably in his favorite chair by his favorite window, with his favorite book. On top of that, he was rereading his favorite short story. Mr. Silver was enjoying this yarn for what he figured was maybe the hundred and eleventh time. The volume was a 1934 edition of *Guys and Dolls,* and Ben's favorite story happened to be "A Very Honorable Guy." His other favorite was "The Lily of St. Pierre," but that is another story. The phone kept right on jangling. Ben turned a yellowed page. *It's probably Doc Stump's nurse checking to see if I took my new blood-pressure pills. If I don't pick up, maybe she'll figure I'm dead and go bother somebody who's still warm.* This stratagem was not effective—whoever it was did not give up—the blasted thing kept right on ringing. For what he figured was maybe the hundred and eleventh time that month, Ben began to get somewhat scorched under the collar. *Who's so damned determined to annoy me?* He placed a two-dollar bill between pages seventy-eight and seventy-nine, set the venerable volume aside, snatched up the offensive instrument. "Why don't you go drink a bucket of lye—or stick a sharp stick in your eye!"

The gravely voice on the other end of the line was an echo of his own. "Hello yourself."

"I should've known." Ben groaned. "Why won't you let me be?"

"Just wanted to see how you're getting along. After all, I am your younger brother."

"You're my younger *half* brother, you two-bit ambulance-chasing twerp." Ben shook his head. "I cannot imagine why my sainted mother ever consented to marry your father." He paused to wonder what she could have seen in the mule-faced old crook. "But I will say this—Raymond Oates Senior—low-down, egg-sucking, cattle-stealing varmint that he was—was a lot more man than you'll ever be."

Knowing how his daddy would have appreciated this bare-knuckled compliment, Raymond chuckled. "I'm glad I caught you in a good mood."

"You don't fool me, Ray—I know why you're calling. Same reason you always do. So don't bother to waste my valuable time and your sour breath asking—the answer is still N-O, which spells get lost!"

"Look, Ben—neither one of us is getting any younger. I just thought—"

"You thought wrong, pudding-brain—you'll never get

your grubby hands on it! Not tomorrow. Not next month." There was a sudden shortness of breath. "Not *ever*—" Ben Silver gasped, waited until his wind returned, then smiled cruelly. "And as long as we're talking about your father, I think the old thief liked me better than you."

Aside from a sinister whisper of electronic hiss, the line was deathly silent.

When he did speak, Raymond's voice had taken on a flinty edge. "You're the thief, Ben. The day Daddy died—before his body was even cold—you broke the lock on his trunk and . . . and you took it."

Ben grinned. "Damn right I did—so rat-face Raymond wouldn't get his sweaty paws on it." He felt a blunt pain in his chest, grimaced. "And if I had it to do over, I'd take it again. But it wasn't stealing—what I took was my mother's property. And she always meant for me to have it."

Another silence.

"Ben, be reasonable. You've had it for all these years. And you're in poor health." The attorney had assumed his highly civilized, professional tone, which generally earned him two hundred and fifty dollars an hour plus expenses. "I know you're not exactly living hand-to-mouth, but if you had a big wad of tax-free cash I'm sure you'd find something useful to do with it. I'd be willing to pay you—"

"Stuff your money, Raymond Oates!" The pain was throbbing now. Ben ground his teeth until the ache under his breastbone subsided. "Now listen to this—I'm only gonna say it once. Just for spite, I plan to outlive you. But even if I don't, after I'm dead and buried, I'll still see you don't get it. I might go to Salt Lake and give it to a museum—or to some stranger I happen to meet on the street. Or maybe I'll bury it where nobody will ever find it!" With a fine sense of drama, Ben Silver hung up on his half brother, smiled at his image of Oates the Lesser chewing on his tongue and foaming at the mouth. *It's always such a wonderful blessing to have a heart-to-heart chat with the closest kin you got left on earth.* His round face assumed a puzzled look. *Now what was I doing when my sweet little half brother called?* Remembering, he reached for the Damon Runyon volume, found the marked page, picked up again with "A Very Honorable Guy." The feisty old man tried to read but did not comprehend the strings of words; he completely lost track of the serious business being transacted between Feet Samuels and the Brain. Finally, he laid the book aside, sighed. *I may not live another year.* He placed a hand on his chest, felt the comforting thickness of the canvas neck wallet concealed under his shirt. *If I was to drop dead right this minute, somebody would find it on my corpse and nine chances out of ten, my half brother would end up gloating over it.* That simply would not do. *Before I'm gone, I've got to do something with Momma's keepsake so Raymond won't be able to get his mitts on it.* He turned in his chair, watched a lemon-tinted sun fade to a blushing pink, fall toward Big Lizard Ridge, flush a bloody crimson before slipping into Hatchet Gap. By the time the sky over Tonapah Flats had turned dark purple, and just as the hoot-owl hooted, Ben Silver knew exactly what he'd do. He found a neat stack of business cards in a desk drawer, removed the rubber band, thumbed through the rectangles until he found the one he was looking for.

That night, for the first time in months, the old man slept peacefully.

# THREE

## *THUNDER WOMAN*

SCARCELY an hour after Ben Silver had hung up on his half brother, the curtain was about to rise on a second drama. This performance would be staged at the more densely populated end of Hatchet Gap, that narrow crevasse that had—according to a time-honored and lurid rumor—been cleaved into Big Lizard Ridge by Thunder Woman—who did it with her hatchet. According to sworn testimony, she was piqued off about something or other.

The moral here, if there is one to be discovered, is that only the most dim-witted males underestimate the inner resources of the gentler gender.

## *THE BUTTERFLY*

THOUGH the sun shone warmly on her back, Sarah Frank shivered in the slight breeze, pulled a faded denim jacket tightly around her gaunt frame. The fourteen-year-old was always cold, always hungry. Paying scant attention to the traffic, she crossed the busy highway. Mr. Zig-Zag—so named because of the jagged white lightning logo imprinted on his black head—was even more oblivious to the world than was his mistress. Sarah paused long enough to snatch up her cat, then trotted across the asphalt to evade a massive SUV that was bearing down on them like a charging rhino; the glistening behemoth did not slow. A backwash of whirlwind ruffled the cat's fur, whipped the cotton skirt around her skinny legs. She paused in the vehicle's wake, watched it vanish in a flurry of whirling dust. *Why did I hurry? I could have just stood there in the road, held my arms out, and said here I am. That big car would never have been able to stop. I would've been smacked onto it like a moth.*

She raised her gaze to Big Lizard Ridge and Hatchet Gap—and recalled the legend of Thunder Woman. *When I die, I'll fly away. But I'm not going to be a smudgy-brown moth—I'll be a beautiful butterfly.* But what she had in mind was not a fragile little rainbow thing with silken wings. Sarah's eyes narrowed. *I'll be a* stone *butterfly—and when I pass by there'll be earthquakes and thunder and lightning and whirlwinds and big trees will break and fall down!* She squeezed the cat a little too tightly. *And if somebody treats me bad, I'll make him SO sorry.* It was, if a somewhat extravagant stretch of adolescent imagination, still a rather grand vision. But in the meantime and prior to any such majestic metamorphosis, the wingless visionary was obliged to occupy her time with more mundane tasks than wreaking global havoc—such as running an errand for Marilee Attatochee, the elder cousin who provided her with food and shelter. Sarah's Papago relative served as a sort of substitute mother. Sort of.

As the girl marched robotically across the graveled parking lot toward Oates's Supermarket, her huge brown eyes gazed blankly at the flint-hard world. She had once overheard Miss Simmons (her English teacher) say that she thought the orphan's face resembled those starved, haunted visages one saw in old black-and-white photographs of Holocaust victims. Sarah liked Miss Simmons. She had mixed feelings about the children at school. The boys were mostly stupid as bugs and hardly worth a thought. Worst of all were the pretty girls in their pretty dresses and always-new shoes. Initially humiliated by their smirks and giggles at her tattered old clothes, she had burned with shame. But if the burning had charred her soul, it had also ignited embers of hatred. For months, this had been enough. Hating them. Hating them to death! After a while, the little fire had gone out—the enmity crumbling into cinders. But there was a small something left among the ashes. Something hard, like a diamond. No one could make a scratch on her. The silly, cruel children could no longer hurt her. Sarah had almost ceased to care—at least during the harshness of day, when one was forced to see things as they really were.

There were other times though, during the long, lonely nights, when spring rains pelted the steel roof over her cot, or when west winds hummed sinister hymns in the chokeweed vines. This was when she drifted away, dreamed her dreams. Often, Sarah's parents would come to embrace her, praise her, whisper encouraging words in her ear. Mommy and Daddy were young and strong and full of love and consolation. Sometimes, she would see bright visions of *Cañón del Espíritu* and Three Sisters Mesa. Daisy Perika was always there near the canyon's mouth. Sometimes the wrinkled old Ute woman was standing in the door of her little house trailer saying "Come right in, Sarah—my goodness how you've grown up!" Or Daisy would be at her gas stove, stirring a pot of steaming posole. In these dream-fantasies, the Ute elder was always smiling, always eager to welcome the child she had sheltered before. And then there were the most special of all the dreams, even better than the ones with her parents. Charlie Moon would appear out of nowhere. Charlie tall as a tree, Charlie with his big cheerful smile, scooping little Sarah up in his arms, hugging her, teasing her, telling her silly stories about how "mink trout" in the cold Piedra grew their winter fur during the Month of Dead Leaves Falling and shed it during the Month of Tender Grass.

In these honey-sweet dreams, the aged teenager was as she had been in those olden, golden times—sometimes a mere toddler, or perhaps she would be six or seven years old. Whatever her age, she was always happy. Always perfectly safe and secure. As the amber-tinted dreams would fade to black, Sarah would drift up toward consciousness and think blissful thoughts. *Someday, I'm going to have a closet full of pretty new dresses. Strings of silver and turquoise to wear around my neck and yellow ribbons in my hair. Seven pairs of shoes, a different color for every day of the week. And plenty of good food to eat. But not enough to make me fat.* She would smile at that. *I might even grow up to be pretty. Pretty enough that Charlie would want to marry me.* Then she would awaken, stare at the dirty little window above her bed, promise herself that as soon as her cousin had gone off to work and Marilee's boyfriend had wandered off to some bar, she would call the Southern Ute Police on the telephone and ask them to find Charlie Moon wherever he was, tell him to come and get her at Tonapah Flats, Utah. She had no doubt he would. In all of Sarah's gray, uncertain world, Charlie was the one bright constant that she could depend on.

But always, the sun would rise over Frenchman's Butte. And when it did, the pitiless white rays would evaporate the wispy remnants of her girlish hopes and dreams. Sarah's mother and father had been dead for years and years. Dead as the whitened cattle bones in the Little Sandy Wash, dead as her hopes for a little happiness. The sunlight would also remind Sarah that Daisy Perika was a gruff, penny-pinching old woman who didn't like anybody. Especially not children. Come to think of it, the old woman was a lot like Ben Silver—who was *so* grouchy. Anyway, Daisy might be dead and gone after all this time. And Charlie Moon would probably be married by now, to a smart, pretty wife who wouldn't want a stupid, gawky girl in the house. Especially not one who was madly, madly in love with her husband. That would make things tense.

• • •

UNNOTICED by Sarah Frank, a sleek, black Lincoln Town Car pulled into the parking lot behind her. The driver eased along the graveled surface, just keeping pace with the girl.

• • •

BEFORE she did the grocery shopping, Sarah was compelled to follow the dual ritual.

Her first stop was in front of the Cactus Rose Pawn Shop. Showing no interest in hunting rifles, bone-handled sheath knives, or the various musical instruments on display behind the shatterproof window, she fixed her gaze on the single object capable of catching a young lady's eye. The stunning pendant on the coin-silver chain was the most lovely thing she had ever seen. The oval of Australian opal was as large as a hen's egg, and from deep inside, a thousand iridescent stars glittered with fire of every radiant hue. In the child's fantasy, these were the fragments of a rainbow that had frozen over a snowcapped granite peak, fallen to earth, shattered at a Ute wizard's feet—to be assembled into the present jewel by a flick of a red-willow wand, a muttering of magical commands. But never, not even in the wildest flights of her imagination, did the girl dare to imagine that she might wear such a piece of heavenly glory.

Her eyes filled to overflowing with opalescent radiance, she hurried away, pushed through the door at Canyon Country Newsstand and Magazines. Feigning a slightly bored expression, she went up and down the aisles, idly glancing at enticing titles on paperback books, occasionally removing a volume to admire a lurid picture on the cover. Most of these featured an astonishingly beautiful woman and a ruggedly handsome man. Sarah finally approached the children's section, ran the tips of her brown fingers along the colorful volumes, finally stopped at the one she loved the most. On the cover, there was a cunningly painted picture of a tiny little bug-woman with eight legs. Well, only two legs really; Grandmother Spider used six of her appendages for arms. When Sarah was certain the clerk at the counter wasn't looking—the fourteen-year-old was embarrassed to be reading a book meant for small children—she thumbed through the few pages, became a companion of those archetypal animals from long, long ago, when the world was young and the little spider-woman stole the source of warmth and light from the monstrous Sun-Guards. As on all of her previous visits, she whispered the words, imagined herself to be Grandmother Spider, standing in the center of the circle with all the happy animals dancing around their heroine. Lost in the dream world, the young reader felt secure in her privacy. But of course, she was never alone in the store.

Today, the clerk was busy with a meek-looking man who was purchasing this month's copy of *Guns & Ammo*. A chubby, freckle-faced little boy was sitting cross-legged on the floor, reading *The Skateboard Life*. A forty-six-year-old woman with stringy hair, stone-hard eyes, and a lout of a husband had selected a steamy romance *(Young and Passionate Nurses)* plus a pair of instructional volumes: *How to Assume a New Identity* and *Common Poisons and Antidotes*. She had no interest whatever in antidotes.

In addition to these few customers, someone was watching Sarah Frank. And with considerable interest.

Having finished with the charming little book, Sarah placed it back on the shelf, promised Grandmother Spider she would be back as soon as she could. *And when I've saved up some money, I'll buy you and take you home.* Noting the clock on the wall, she left Canyon Country Newsstand and Magazines with Mr. Zig-Zag tucked under her arm, trotted along to the supermarket.

•••

THE heavyset man approached the clerk, placed the book on the counter. "Thelma, would you gift wrap this for me?"

The young woman smiled at the familiar face. "Certainly, sir. Won't take a moment."

•••

SARAH pushed the supermarket cart along with Mr. Zig-Zag perched up front, as if he were in charge of navigation. She selected two cans of tuna so there might be some left over for her cat, three fifteen-ounce cans of store-brand pinto beans because they were the cheapest, a loaf of sliced pumpernickel rye because Marilee liked dark bread.

• • •

THE man in the blue suit and red power tie watched the Ute-Papago girl move purposefully along the aisles stocked with canned goods, was pleased to see that the skinny child performed her shopping with an intense concentration that was unusual in one so young. For what he had in mind, it would help if the kid was smart. He grinned. *But not too smart.*

• • •

SARAH pushed her cart to the fresh produce section, paused to eye shiny apples and purple grapes, passed these by to select a half-dozen red potatoes. Her shopping completed, the girl looked around to make sure none of the children from school were nearby to witness her poverty. But even as she showed the cashier Marilee's voucher from the welfare office, Sarah Frank's face was warm with shame.

The redheaded woman rung up the sale, stamped the voucher, gave the little Indian girl a pitying look, said what she always said. "How's your cousin and Mr. Harper getting along?" Thought what she always thought. *Not that I care a damn about that bottom-feeder Al Harper. But Marilee's a good egg.*

The girl shrugged, mumbled her usual "Okay, I guess," hurried away with her bag of staples. The cat followed his scarecrow mistress through the exit, into the parking lot.

Blue Suit was waiting outside. He emerged from a long, black automobile, removed a cigar from his mouth, presented the sort of frozen smile worn by used-car salesmen about to make their pitch. "Hey—ain't you Sarah Frank?"

Startled to hear her name spoken aloud, she stared up at the clean-shaven white man, noticed that he had a shiny red parcel tucked under his arm.

Mr. Zig-Zag rubbed up against the man's immaculate trouser leg.

The owner of the leg cringed, gave the cat a scowl, then reset the smile as he searched the thin girl's face for some sign of recognition. "D'you know who I am?"

Sarah shook her head.

"I'm Raymond Oates." He saw a flicker of interest in the Indian girl's eyes. "I believe you know my brother Ben."

A slight hesitation, then a nod.

"Well, ol' Ben's actually my *half* brother. We had the same momma, but different daddies." He tapped off a clump of cigar ash, which landed on the cat's head. "From what I hear, you do some housework for the old sourpuss."

Sarah managed another nod.

Oates didn't notice the nod; he had fixed his gaze on the Tonapah Flats Truck Stop, atop of which a twelve-foot-tall neon facsimile of a shapely Indian woman wielded an electric-blue tomahawk. (A passing tourist from Paducah—who had a half-dozen pink plastic flamingoes stuck in her flower bed and a husband who listened to every word she said—had offered the frank opinion that the sign was "garish.") Oates looked down to smile upon the girl. "If you're not in a great big hurry, why don't we go into the café. I don't know about you, but I could do with a bite to eat."

Sarah glanced shyly at the huge sign blinking on the peaked roof.

THUNDER WOMAN CAFÉ—OPEN 24 HOURS

Having no sense of propriety, her stomach growled. "I don't have enough money."

"Hah!" Oates stuffed the cigar back into his mouth, it wobbled as he spoke. "You don't need any money. Whenever me and my friends eat at the Thunder Woman, they don't charge us a copper dime."

She stared. *He must be lying. Or maybe he's crazy.* Searching for an excuse to refuse the unsettling invitation, Sarah pointed at Mr. Zig-Zag. "I don't think they'd let him in." It was common knowledge that the café manager, a disreputable person (whose parents had named him Groundhog!) hated cats and dogs and what he called "snotty-nose kids."

"Don't give your kitty cat a second thought." Oates tilted his head back, blew a fair-to-middling smoke ring, watched the wispy donut drift upward. "Fact is, I own the café and bar and the liquor store. And for that matter, the whole truck stop. Including the gas station, the Laundromat, the video store, even the ladies' and gent's toilets."

She heard herself say: "Really?"

"Dang tootin'. I am what the common folk call stinkin' rich." He pointed the cigar over her shoulder. "I also own the Oates's Supermarket. Which is why it's named after me—Oates, don't you see?"

Sarah gave the Thunder Woman Bar and Café a hopeful look. "Could I have a cheeseburger?"

"A-course you can, little lady. *Double-meat* cheeseburger. And crispy-curly cheese fries and a great big chunk of coconut-creme pie. Plus a soda pop."

She stared at the man in the blue suit and red tie, watched him launch another smoke ring into the sky. Only this one wasn't really a ring—it was a triangle. *Maybe he's the Devil.* She wondered what he'd want her pitiful little soul for.

# FOUR

## *THE PROPOSITION*

RAYMOND Oates ushered Sarah Frank to his reserved booth in a corner, between a potted palm and the cigarette vending machine. The owner of the establishment gave his super-sized manager a drop-what-you're-doing-and-come-here-right-now look. All 268 pounds of Groundhog came lurching and heaving toward the boss. He offered his employer a sly, submissive smile, but as soon as Oates's eyes were focused on the menu, the manager of the Thunder Woman Café shot the skinny Indian girl a flat-eyed look that made Sarah's skin prickle. If she had known about the occasional "odd job" Groundhog did for Boss Oates, the child would have certainly lost her appetite.

Oates ordered black coffee with a tablespoon of vanilla extract, a ham steak, three eggs scrambled with sautéed onions, a side of biscuits and white gravy. After consulting with the girl, he ordered Sarah Frank a large Cherry Coke, a Momma Bear cheeseburger, and medium crispy-curly cheese fries. Oates selected a fish and chips plate for the cat, hold the chips and tartar sauce.

Groundhog scribbled on his order pad, ambled away.

Sarah half-listened to the white man's incessant chatter, which was mostly about how he and Ben had come to be half brothers, how Daddy Oates had made his money on land and cattle. Raymond also bragged about going off to the university where he got his law degree and made lots of important friends—which was how he got to be "stinkin' rich" and now owned half of Tonapah Flats. The best half.

His narrative was mercifully interrupted by a sleepy-eyed, footsore waitress who nodded deferentially at Oates, unloaded her tray without comment.

While the feline and the famished Indian girl attended to their meals with civilized delicacy, Oates attacked his ham and eggs with savage enthusiasm—but between bites he stole furtive glances at his potential business partner. As she put away the final morsel of burger, the last greasy cheesy potato, he asked: "You ready for some pie?"

Sarah shook her head. "I'm too full, but thank you."

"No matter, you can take some home." He shouted an instruction to the manager.

Groundhog opened a refrigerated display case, removed a whole banana-creme pie. Once again, he gave Sarah the eye. *Wonder what ol' Oates is up to now. Whatever it is, there must be some money in it for him.* After delivering the boxed pie to the boss, he began to wipe the counter at a location within earshot of his employer and the skinny girl.

From an inner jacket pocket, Ray Oates produced a fresh cigar and a fourteen-karat gold-plated lighter. Being a man who always focused on the work at hand, he went slightly cross-eyed as he touched a flame to the tip. "You like living with your Aunt Marilee?"

"She's my cousin."

*Okay, Little Miss Correct-Your-Elders, so she's your damn cousin.* He tried again: "Are you happy living with Marilee and Al Harper?"

Amorphous concepts like *happy* surfaced only in Sarah's dreams, melted away with the dawn. The orphan opened her mouth, closed it—stared at her enigmatic inquisitor.

Undeterred by her silence, Oates took a puff on the ten-inch stogie. "Way I hear it, Marilee works all day to support her live-in boyfriend." He removed the *Arturo Fuente* Curly

Head Deluxe from his mouth, pointed it at the girl. "Did you know Al was a sneak thief and a jailbird?"

The girl maintained her blank stare.

"Well he is." He returned the cigar to its rightful place between his lips. "And they both drink too much. Don't take no offense, Missy—I'm just a straight-talker. And I'm here to tell you—those two are a couple of losers." He exhaled a cloud of smoke, stared deep into her brown eyes, as if he saw something there. "But you ain't no loser—you're just down on your luck." Without the least effort, he assumed a foxy expression. "And I'm also here to tell you—your luck is about to change for the better. You and me are gonna conduct some business."

Having never encountered anyone remotely like Raymond Oates, Sarah was hanging on every word.

Aware of his advantage, Oates forged ahead. "Like I already said, I know about how you do some chores for my half brother Ben—like running a little errand now and then." He affected a significant pause. "How much does he pay you?"

Sarah shrugged. "Fifty cents for making his lunch."

Oates snorted.

She felt a sudden need to defend grumpy old Ben Silver. "He gives me a dollar if I bring him some groceries from the store." It was a very long walk from the supermarket, across the highway, down behind Marliee's house and through the brush around the Little Sandy Dry Wash, then up the trail through Hatchet Gap, which was the only way through Big Lizard Ridge. And if you didn't go through the gap, you had to walk a long, long way down the highway, and take the dirt lane that went around behind the ridge, and that was also a long, long walk.

While she performed this mental review of the local geography, Oates produced another snort. "A measly dollar—what an old cheapskate!" He pushed the pretty red package across the table. "This is for you."

She gave the parcel a wide-eyed stare. "What is it?"

"Just a gift from one friend to another."

She shook her head. "But I couldn't accept a present from—"

"It's just a little book." His mouth twisted into a knowing grin. "And there's some bookmarks in it." He glanced around the café to make certain some Nosy Parker wasn't eavesdropping. Didn't notice Groundhog, who was scrubbing at an invisible spot on the countertop. "But don't open it up until you get home and you're all by yourself. And don't tell Marilee or that crumb-bum Al Harper I gave you a little present." Oates tapped his nose in a way he had seen Paul Newman do in an old movie. "This is just between you and me, see?"

Of its own accord, her hand reached out. Sarah's fingertips caressed the shiny paper, her eyes looked wonderingly at the generous man. "Thank you."

"You're welcome as warm sunshine in January, kid." Oates pointed his chin at the brown paper bag in the seat beside her. "Them groceries for Ben?"

Sarah shook her head. "That's for Marilee."

Satisfied with slandering the girl's Papago relative, the attorney had no further words to waste on Marilee Attatochee. "How often do you go to see my half brother?"

"Now that school's out, almost every day."

"Do you and Ben get along okay?"

Sarah frowned, shook her head. "When I don't do something right, sometimes he yells at me."

"Oh, don't think nothing about that—grumping about anything and everything, that's just Ben's way." *You may be the only soul on earth the nasty old bastard can stand to have around him.* Oates leaned across the table, gave the girl a goggle-eyed look. "What's he say about me?"

"Not very much." Little Miss Frank lived up to her name. "Except that he's going to dance a jig around your coffin and sing 'Happy Days Are Here Again.' " The Ute-Papago girl assumed this must be some kind of white-person funeral ritual.

"And he will if he gets the chance." Raymond Oates's plump torso shook with chuckles. "Ben and me don't get along. Never did." As he slipped back five decades, the half brother's eyes took on a glassy, faraway look. "It all started over that stupid lizard he caught and put in a shoe box. Made a reg'lar pet of it—even gave it a name." *Lonnie Lizard. Now is that dumb, or what?* "After it turned up with its head chopped off, he claimed I was the one that killed it."

Stunned at the thought of such a reprehensible crime, Sarah was unable to keep the question in her mouth. "Did you?"

The lawyer glared at the girl, saw the accusation in her tight lips, quickly looked away. "There was never a smidgen of proof."

• • •

BEING busy eavesdropping on the boss's conversation with the Indian kid, Groundhog was distracted by a husky truck driver who demanded "some service over here." The manager of the Thunder Woman Café flipped a grimy dish towel over his shoulder, approached the customer—who shoved an empty coffee mug across the counter. "Gimmee a refill."

Groundhog nodded. "You got it." *But coffee won't be all you'll get in your cup.*

• • •

A shadow of her appetite having returned, Sarah eyed the white cardboard pie box. She wondered whether it would be all right to have a piece before she took it home. Just a small one.

Oates looked through the fly-specked window, at what he could see across the busy highway. Above the peaked roofs of dismal frame houses, faded façades of failing businesses, and intermittent clusters of scrub pine, the long, jagged spine of Big Lizard Ridge dominated the skyline. Brother Ben's place was on the far side of the ridge, at the mouth of Hatchet Gap. *Well, it's time to stop beating around the bush, get down to brass tacks.* His brow furrowed. *Beating around bushes, getting down to brass tacks—why do we say stuff like that?* The intermittently intellectual fellow rolled a few possibilities over in his mind, terminated the process when his head began to ache. He focused his gaze on the girl. "Sarah, my half brother has something I want. And I'm ready to pay a pretty penny for it. But every time I bring the subject up, the old snapping turtle bites my head off." The wheeler-dealer assumed an optimistic expression. "But I think maybe you could help."

This unexpected request made her feel very important. "How?"

"By acting as a go-between."

Sarah watched Mr. Zig-Zag lick grease off his paws. "What's a go-between?"

*This kid gets right to the point.* Another scowl. *Right to the point—point of what?* Another thudding ache in the brain. He clenched his teeth on the cigar stub. "A go-between is a person who arranges a business transaction between two other parties—who for one reason or other, can't or won't talk directly to one another." The attorney tried to think of just the right way to say it. "Ben has this . . . this *pretty* thing." He described the family heirloom in some detail.

Having never heard of such a wonderful treasure, Sarah Frank wanted to see it. Hold it in her hand. *But Mr. Silver would never show it to me . . .* The half brother's booming voice jarred her out of the reverie.

"It belonged to my old man, but the day Daddy died, Ben made off with it and I ain't seen it since. If you could talk him into selling it to me, I'd pay him a pile of cash." He grinned at the girl. "And you'd get a commission."

"What's a commission?"

*I like the way she cuts right to the bone.* "A commission's a piece of the deal. I'd pay you ten percent of whatever the pretty thing cost me."

Sarah thought she was beginning to get the gist of it. "How much would it cost you?"

Oates grinned ear-to-ear. *This is my kind of kid.* "Hard to say. It'd be up to you to talk Ben into the deal. But just for starters, let's say we're talking ten thousand dollars for Ben. That'd mean a thousand to you."

Her entire body went tingly numb. "A whole *thousand dollars*?"

"That's the least fee you'll get." He leaned across the table. "Here's the way it'd work, Sarah. Let's say I put up eleven thousand bucks. The cut would be ten thousand for Ben, one thousand for you. But if you manage to buy it from my brother for a lower price, that's fine with me. You'll still get your thousand, and keep the difference."

Sarah crinkled her face into a frown.

*Looks like 'rithmetic ain't her best subject. I gotta make this simple enough so's a oyster could understand.* "Let's say you talk Ben into selling for five G's. You'd get your one plus five more. Which would make six thousand for you."

The puzzled expression was stuck on her face.

*I'm gonna have to spell it out.* "Okay, just for the sake of argument, let's say Ben likes you so much, he decides to *give* it to you. I wouldn't know that, and I wouldn't care. Soon as you deliver the pretty thing to me, you get the whole eleven thousand." He raised an eyebrow. "Just *imagine* what you could do with that much money."

A certain clarity of understanding began to dawn on the poverty-stricken girl.

Seeing a hint of avarice glinting in her eyes, Oates hurried on. "I know that sounds like a huge pile of cash to a little kid like you, but it's pocket change to me. But don't think you wouldn't earn it." *Now for the ticklish part—I sure hope she gets my drift.* "See, what makes this go-between job hard is that Ben don't want me to have the pretty thing. If he knew I was the buyer, he'd never sell it. Not for a *hundred* thousand. The deal you set up would have to be . . . well, whatever you can think of." He looked up at the acoustic-tile ceiling. "But consider this as a for-instance—maybe you could convince Ben that some other person wants to buy it on the Q-T. Like say, some rich out-of-towner who's a good friend of yours—somebody who'd give you the money to buy it." Oates stuck the cigar stub into his coffee cup. "First of all, you'd have to find out where Ben keeps the thing—just to make sure he still has it in his possession. And you'd have to get a good look at it." His bleary blue eyes became hard as glass marbles. "Work it out any way you want, but here's the bottom line—when you bring me the pretty thing, you'd get eleven thousand bucks. All in twenty-dollar bills." His face flushed rosy pink. "How much of that wad you take back to Ben—well, that's entirely between you and him."

Sarah Frank stared at the attorney. *He wants me to steal it.*

Raymond Oates saw the flash of fear in her eyes, "Think it over, kid. You decide to help me on this, and over and above any cash you earn—I'll give you a *real* nice present." He jutted his chin at the crimson-tinted, ribbon-tied parcel at her elbow. "Something worth a damn sight more than what's in that little package." He read the question in her eyes, removed a black velvet pouch from his jacket pocket, pushed it halfway across the table. "Want to take a peek inside?"

Again, her hand moved as if it had a mind of its own. When she saw the opal pendant, Sarah's mouth gaped—her heart stuttered, seemed as if it might stop.

The chubby tempter attempted a Santa Claus smile; what he produced was a hideous leer. "Pretty bauble, ain't it? Should be—set me back nine hundred bucks!" He snatched her heart's desire away, stuffed the pouch back into his pocket. "You want to hang this geegaw around your neck, all you got to do is come up with a workable plan for getting me what I want. I have my lunch here at high noon, almost every day of the week." He pointed toward the parking lot. "If you see my Town Car out front, come inside and tell me what you've got in mind. If I like your plan, the pendant's yours to keep, and I'm talking up front—before you deliver the property that's rightfully mine. And when you bring me what Ben stole out of our house before Daddy's corpse had time to get cold—then you get the cash money." The piggish man's right hand doubled into a hamish fist, hammered the table just hard enough to make the stainless flatware rattle. "But whatever happens, kid—don't you *ever* say anything to anybody about this." His final words came slowly, floated between them like balloons about to pop. "You—understand—what—I'm—telling—you?"

Sarah Frank felt her head nod.

• • •

LATE that night, shortly after Marilee Attatochee and Al Harper had gone to bed, Sarah switched on a tiny plastic flashlight. Ever so carefully, she untied the blue ribbon on the shiny red package. Unfolding the paper, she could hardly believe her eyes. How could he have known. . . .

There on her lap was *The Book. Grandmother Spider Brings the Sun.*

It was like an impossibly wonderful dream. Almost as good as those sleep-visions where Charlie Moon showed up in a gold-and-white limousine and drove her back to Colorado where they would get married in St. Ignatius Catholic Church and then live ever-so-happily together in a three-story redbrick house on the banks of the Piedra.

One by one she turned the pages, whispered the written words. When she got to the page where the little spider lady was dancing by the clay pot she had brought the warm light in, all the smiling animals in a circle around her . . . Fox and Wolf and Moose and Bear and . . . Sarah wept. Her tears fell onto the charming picture.

She was closing the book when, tucked in between the last page and the cover, she found the "bookmarks"—five twenty-dollar bills! After staring wide-eyed at the most money she'd ever had in her hands, Sarah switched off the flashlight, hurriedly slammed the book on the greenbacks, stuffed it under her pillow. The thin girl sat on her bed, nervously curling and uncurling her numbly cold toes. *With a hundred dollars I could buy a bus ticket to Durango, and even have some left over.* The desire to leave for Colorado on the first eastbound bus out of Tonapah Flats was intense enough to make her entire body tingle. The thought of the magnificent fire-speckled opal, suspended from her neck on the silver chain, made her shudder with anticipatory delight.

*But until I got to Aunt Daisy's home, I'd have to keep it under my dress so nobody would see it.* Still another but: *But unless I can come up with a good plan for getting that pretty thing from Mr. Silver, Mr. Oates won't give me the opal pendant. And if my plan works, he'll pay me thousands of dollars.* For a child who had always been so wretchedly poor, the urge to stay and give the seemingly impossible task a try was compelling. Sarah made her decision. *First, I'll try talking to Mr. Silver.* She sighed. *He'll get all red in the face and yell at me. No, he'll never give the pretty thing up . . . so what can I do?* She knew, of course, and blushed with shame. Like lying, stealing was a dreadful sin.

Instantly, it was as if someone whispered in her ear: *Mr. Silver stole it from Mr. Oates's father, so returning it to the rightful owner wouldn't really be stealing—it would be a good thing to do.*

Thus justified, Sarah Frank snuggled into her small bed, was pleased when Mr. Zig-Zag cuddled himself behind her head. She yawned. *I should never have thought Mr. Oates was the Devil. He's more like an angel.* As she was slipping off to sleep, a troublesome thought floated along with her: Wasn't the Devil also some kind of an angel . . . a very *bad* angel?

# FIVE

## *COLORADO, SOUTHERN UTE RESERVATION*

WHILE a spray of stars still sparkled overhead, Daisy Perika groaned and grunted her way out of bed. She dressed herself with the patience necessary for one whose arthritic joints protest when flexed. As a final touch, she pulled a woolen shawl around her stooped shoulders, stepped outside on the porch. Aside from the rhythmic sigh of her breaths, and the barest whisper of a breeze in the junipers, there was not a sound. Though summer was only days away, the pearly-gray dawn blooming over the black ridges filled her with a shuddering chill. The warm comfort of her bed pulled at the sleepy woman, but having made up her mind, she went back inside, pulled on a heavy overcoat that had belonged to her third husband. Wanting an early start for the journey that got longer with every passing winter, the tribal elder had decided to take her breakfast with her. She stuffed a foil-wrapped egg-and-pork-sausage sandwich into one of the spacious coat pockets, a pint jar of honeyed coffee into the other. Thus prepared, she slung a hemp bag over her shoulder, got the sturdy oak staff in hand—and left her cozy home behind.

Daisy felt uneasy about venturing along the particular path she had in mind. Father Raes Delfino had issued several stern warnings that she should stay away from the dwarf, whose hole-in-the-ground dwelling was in *Cañón del Espíritu.* Unlike other *matukach*—and even some of the younger tribal members—the Catholic priest did not disbelieve in the little man's existence. On the contrary, it was Fr. Raes's view that the *pitukupf* was real—and potentially dangerous. It was his concern for Daisy's immortal soul that led the Jesuit to counsel this reckless member of his flock to avoid any communion with the deceitful creature. But since the priest's retirement as pastor at St. Ignatius, Daisy rarely saw him and so his influence in her life had gradually diminished. When Fr. Raes wasn't off gallivanting around some foreign country, he spent his days in that little cabin on Charlie Moon's ranch. Which reminded Daisy of another reason she felt guilty about today's errand—her nephew also strongly disapproved of her walks into Spirit Canyon. Charlie's objections had nothing to do with the *pitukupf*—he was one of the younger generation who dismissed the dwarf as a tribal myth. He worried that his elderly aunt would take a bad fall, break an ankle or hip. If that happened, she would be stranded in the wilderness between the walls of Three Sisters and Dog Leg Mesa, where only cougars and coyotes would hear her calls for help. By the time he came looking, it would be too late.

As far as the priest's objections, the aged Catholic maintained a tolerably clear conscience. *After all, I haven't brought any gifts along for the little man. And anybody who knows anything about the dwarf knows that he never gives away his secrets for free; he always expects some food and a trinket or two.* One well-crafted rationalization led to another. *And Charlie Moon shouldn't worry about me falling and breaking a bone. I know the canyon like it was my own backyard, and I'm careful where I put my feet.* And another. *And even if I was to die up here, that's lots better than wasting away in a [expletive deleted] nursing home while some freckle-faced white girl spoons me [another expletive deleted] mashed squash from a baby-food jar and tells me how nice I look today.*

Thus justified in her mind, Daisy made her way happily

along the winding path that took her into the gaping mouth, down the sighing throat, deep into the shadowy bowels of Spirit Canyon. As she hobbled along the deer trail, the elder's eyes searched the ground for those medicinal herbs necessary to stock her singular pharmacy. The primary object of this particular quest was a plant known to botanical science as *Corydalis aurea,* to local folk as Golden Smoke, and to traditional Utes as Stick That Gives You Nosebleeds. Loaded with alkaloids, including protopine and corydaline, it was a very dangerous weed indeed. Daisy had a secret recipe, which combined the herb with Skullcap and a few other bits of this and that. The process of preparation was quite tedious, requiring several days of boiling, drying, mixing, a touch of this and a dab of that, additional boiling, further drying, and so on. The end result was a sedative that was useful for treating twitching and nervous tics. So far (by the Grace of God, Father Raes believed) none of the Ute shaman's patients had died from her medications. Daisy was certain that several of her customers had enjoyed significant benefit from her chemotherapy. The self-taught herbalist had certainly benefited—to the tune of twenty-five dollars per dose. Cash money, if you please.

As Daisy was approaching a place where she had stopped many times before, she averted her eyes from the spot the *pitukupf* called home—a badger hole long-abandoned by the original tenant. During dozens of dreamlike trances (or trancelike dreams?) she had found herself inside the little man's underground dwelling. Straggles of roots hung from the ceiling, and resinous piñon wood always burned and popped in his fireplace—where a rabbit's carcass might be seen roasting on a juniper spit. More than this was difficult to recall.

Now, from the corner of her eye, she noticed a wispy something rising from the burrow. It might have been a smoke from his fire, or perhaps it was merely early morning mist. For once, Daisy really did not want to see the little trickster. *I'll stop a little farther up the canyon and have a couple of bites of my sandwich and some coffee.* And she would have done just that. Except for what she saw close to an aged, pink-barked ponderosa.

A cluster of Golden Smoke.

Forgetting about the dwarf, the enthusiastic pharmacist unslung the hemp bag from her shoulder, headed straight for the bonanza. On hands and knees, she used a short, heavy-bladed knife to dig up each plant root-and-all, place it with due care into her herb bag. When this work was completed, Daisy got hold of her staff, pushed herself to her feet with a groan. Doing so, she felt a sharp pain at the small of her back. *Maybe I should rest awhile.* She seated herself by the ponderosa, leaned the hemp bag against its trunk. A gray ocean of weariness washed over her, each wave pulling her in deeper . . . deeper. *Oh my goodness. Maybe I'm getting too old for these long walks—and this digging is awfully hard work . . .*

The shaman slipped into that shadowy corridor between *Here* and *There.* It was a dim place, but she could still see the daylight side. And what she saw unnerved the old woman.

The *pitukupf* was standing by her left foot. Grinning. Like she was something to be made sport of.

It was irksome. Onerous. Also aggravating.

*I'll find me a rock, throw it at the little imp.* But bound by the cords of an altered state of consciousness, Daisy was unable to wiggle a toe, much less lift her hand to cast a stone. The last thing she remembered was the dwarf reaching into her coat pocket, removing the egg-and-sausage sandwich. As she drifted even further away, the shameless little thief was unwrapping the foil. It was perhaps just as well that the shaman did not see the *pitukupf* eat her breakfast; she might have died from an attack of impotent fury. But whether she was better off or not is debatable. The visionary had fallen into that dark, noisome void where nightmares and madness are made. The dream was one Daisy had suffered through several times during her recent slumbers.

*The skinny girl with the club in her hand leans over the old man's body.*

*As before, as always, she has his blood on her hands.*
*The blood falls. Plop.*
*Falls on the man's face. Plop. Plop.*
*Falls like it will never stop. Plop. Plop. Plop.*
*The girl seems to be mesmerized by the horror on the floor.*
*Until someone appears at a window, casts a long shadow.*
*Startled, the gaunt child raises her head.*
*Sees the living, breathing personification of her worst fears.*

*For the first time, the shaman-dreamer sees the girl's face.*

*Recognition jars Daisy Perika like a sudden thunderclap—completely stopping her heart.*

*After missing a half-dozen beats, it will restart.*

# SIX

## *THE FOREMAN AND THE OUTLAW*

It was almost noon when Charlie Moon stepped off the Columbine headquarters west porch, onto the hard-packed earth. The owner and boss of the outfit was trailed by Sidewinder, who had simultaneously emerged from underneath the porch. The man and the hound approached the rancher's favorite mount. Paducah was nothing much to look at—which is such an exaggerated understatement as to pay the horse a huge compliment—but Moon knew the animal to be reliable; the very soul of good temper and sobriety. *Not like somebody else I could mention.* Though he had her in mind, the Ute stubbornly refused to acknowledge the presence of the small brown mare that had followed him from the porch (where she had been waiting patiently for his appearance) and now stood with her head over his shoulder, eyeing his every move with intense equine concentration—as if she was a first-year medical student viewing of the magical hands of Dr. Moon, world-famous brain surgeon.

What the Indian cowboy was doing was packing Paducah's saddlebags, which does not require quite so much dexterity as the art of splicing subminiature cerebral arteries after having removed a clot the size of something a flea might cough up.

Nevertheless, having the right stuff in the saddlebags is no small matter, and Moon was focused on his work.

The horse who went by the name of Paducah also paid no attention to Sweet Alice, but there was no particular significance in this. Mr. P treated pretty much every creature and effect of nature with equal disregard, be it a rattler coiled at his feet, a snarling cougar crouched on a shoulder-high boulder, the roaring approach of a flash flood, lightning striking a pine snag a few paces away—to name just four. Most of the Columbine cowboys allowed as how this was because Paducah was stupid, which (they claimed) was on account of the fact that his head was solid bone except for a walnut-sized cavity which contained his so-called brain which was actually a peach pit. Charlie Moon did not accept this view; he had no doubt that Paducah was both highly intelligent and completely fearless. Being an uncomplicated man, he saw no need to reconcile these apparently conflicting personality traits.

Whatever the case, the impassive beast stood motionless under a drooping cottonwood, and in the company of the two other horses Moon had saddled earlier that morning. Paducah would occasionally condescend to whisk his brushy tail in a futile attempt to swat the one creature even the most standoffish gelding cannot ignore—a pesky horsefly.

Though her nose occasionally nudged the brim of his black hat, the Ute studiously ignored this equine alien who dared trespass on Columbine territory. For a moment, the ploy seemed to be working—the curious little mare turned away from the human being, fixed a benign gaze upon the Columbine hound.

Apparently unaware of the boss's foreign policy, Sidewinder exchanged friendly nose-sniffs with the pariah horse.

Apparently unaware of the dog's unseemly behavior, Moon tended to his business, which was making sure nothing of importance was left behind. As he placed an item into a saddlebag, he would make a mental note. *Port bag—two pounds of coffee. Percolator. Three tin cups. Pound of sugar. Three Idaho potatoes. Two yellow onions. Bottle of olive oil. Salt and pepper shakers. Cornbread makings. Two cans of baked beans. Can opener. Forks and spoons.* With the bad little mare matching him stride-for-stride, he sidled around to the opposite side, where the inventory began again. *Starboard bag—knife for filleting the fish. Cast-iron skillet. Chives. Garlic powder. Can of red worms. Velveeta cheese for bait in case the worms don't work. Chunk of beef liver in case the cheese don't do the job. Box of fishing gear.* The rods and reels were already packed in saddle holsters designed to carry rifles. *I don't think I left a thing out. Now all we need is the fish.* Lake Jesse would provide.

These happy thoughts were interrupted by the scuff-scuff of the Columbine foreman's boots coming down the lane from Too Late Bridge, which (as might be expected) spanned Too Late Creek, on the far side of which was the foreman's house. To Moon's dismay, the foreman (as might be expected) was in his boots. Not in the mood for any of the cranky old stockman's grim forecasts or whining complaints, the Ute cinched up his saddle. What he had in mind was placing Pete Bushman in the same category of nonentity as Sweet Alice.

The newcomer stopped a yard away from the boss. Waited for the Ute's customary greeting.

Sidewinder regarded the bushy-faced Bushman with the kind of gaze that did not invite a "hello-old-dog" greeting from the uppermost member of the hired-hand food chain.

Being in practice from shunning Sweet Alice, Moon pretended not to see the man. *I know what I forgot—something sweet for dessert. What should I take?*

The foreman cleared his throat.

*Two cans of peaches and a jar of fried apples.* The Ute nodded to agree with himself. *That'll be just the thing after pan-fried trout.* Tasteful anticipation made his mouth water.

Upping the ante, Pete Bushman coughed.

The taciturn Ute was deaf to this throaty remark.

"Nice mornin'," Bushman observed. A yellow-toothed smirk split the hairy place at the bottom of his face. "Thought I'd drop by and cheer you up."

Moon muttered. "That'll be the day."

"Well, as a matter a fact—"

"Stuff a sock in it, Pete."

The foreman's eyes bulged. "Do *what*?"

"It's a colloquial expression—means I don't want to hear no bad news." The boss sang in a resonant bass voice: "No-time, from no-body!"

"Well I just wanted to—"

"If we've been invaded from the north and the government of the United States of America is attempting to beat back a swarm of armed-to-the-teeth Canadians, just keep it to yourself. If there's a rip-snortin' tornado twistin' up the lane, I don't want to know about it 'til sometime next week. If the price of beef has dropped fifty percent, you can write me a letter. If the Columbine's entire herd of twelve hundred and forty-one head of Herefords is dead or dyin' from some mysterious ailment, that is a matter for you to deal with." In case his foreman might not have gotten the drift of this, he added: "Don't you bring up *nothing* that might ruin this fine day."

"Okay. Whatever you say." Pete Bushman bit off a plug of Red Man chewing tobacco, tongued it into the hollow of his jaw. "But just to keep the record straight, only eight hundred and ten a them white-faced cattle are on the Columbine." The hairy-faced old troublemaker chewed with gusto. "The other four hundred and twenty-eight are over yonder on the Big Hat." He spat onto a flat rock.

Charlie Moon counted up his stock. The foreman's numbers added up to twelve hundred and thirty-eight. Which suggested that three bovine citizens were missing since the Columbine's last census. He was about to demand an account of those that were unaccounted for when he realized Bushman was up to no good. *He's given me a short count just to get me to ask. Well he can stand there waiting until doomsday before I do-die-do!* He winked at his hound, threw back his head, and belted out a line of "Old Blue."

Sidewinder—who was a good dog too—joined in. On the chorus, of course.

Bushman yelled over the racket: "If you're interested in what happened to them three steers that come down with a bad case a the—"

Without taking the bait or missing a beat, Moon shook his head.

The foreman was not discouraged. If Bushman's middle name had not been Clarence, it might well have been Persistence. And though his wrinkled forehead did not protrude from the pressure of excess frontal lobe tissue, Pete C. Bushman always had another trick up his sleeve. He smiled at the sight of the outlaw horse, who was close enough to Charlie Moon to nibble at his ear. Sweet Alice had crippled up a half-dozen good men before the Ute had tried to ride her last year, and the final big Hoo-Ha had occurred over at the Big Hat—and on a bet of course. Mr. Moon had come within a gnat's whisker of getting himself killed dead. He'd taken that in good humor, like any real cowboy would—but something had happened *after* that to turn him sour on the animal. There were rumors that Moon had tried to ride Sweet Alice a second time, and she'd done something *really* bad that made him plenty mad—but if any of the hired hands knew what it was, they weren't talking, which meant that none of those cowboy gossips had the straight scoop. And of course, the Indian wouldn't say a word about it, but it was a known fact that the soft-hearted fellow had decided to turn the animal loose rather than send her to the dog-food factory over at Pueblo. At first, it had looked like things would work out fine for all concerned. The mare had fallen in with a herd of wild mustangs that wintered on the Big Hat's north pastures. A Mexican fence-rider claimed she'd taken up with a pie-eyed pinto stallion. Maybe the pinto got more than he'd bargained for, or maybe the mean-eyed little outlaw mare decided she didn't like spotted horses. Whatever it was, come spring, Sweet Alice had crossed the Buckhorn Range onto Columbine land, and started socializing with the work horses, passing the time of day in happy horseplay, plus helping herself to several bales of unearned hay.

As if that wasn't more than enough, she'd started hanging around Charlie Moon. In fact, she followed the Ute around like a lost puppy. It was a running joke amongst the f[illegible] dozen cowboys plus the foreman, who had a forty-[illegible] dollar pool on how many days it would be before the Ute completely lost his temper and shot the annoying animal right between the eyes with his .357 Magnum revolver. Bushman had reached in the bucket, drawn the scrap of paper that Little Butch had penciled "6 Days" on, and as four days had already passed by with the horse's skull still intact, he had decided to agitate the waters.

While Moon crooned and Sidewinder howled, the foreman chewed on the wad of Red Man, polished up his plan of attack, spat a second time, barely missing a scuttling black beetle who was working hard with all eight legs to get to some urgent appointment. After the final verse, he made an observation: "Looks like you've got some serious ridin' in mind."

Relieved at this change of subject, Moon nodded his fine John B. Stetson hat.

Bushman's face was as innocent-looking as a face such as his could possibly be, which was somewhere between Gabby Hayes and Fidel Castro. "Expecting some company?"

"Yes I am." Moon stared at the saddlebag. *Still seems like I've forgot something.*

Though he had been fully informed of the upcoming event by his wife, the foreman pretended ignorance. "Well, let me see if I can guess who." He chewed with thoughtful enthusiasm. "I'd expect one of 'em must be that pretty FBI lady. What's her name now—Molly Fay?"

"Lila Mae." Moon could not contain the smitten-idiot grin. "Miss McTeague to you."

"Oh, right." The foreman effected spit number three, hit a knobby root on the cottonwood tree. "Now let me see. Who's the second guest? Hmmm." Rapid chewing seemed to vitalize the gray matter. "I bet it'll be that tough copper from Granite Creek—Scotch Parrish."

"Scott Parris," Moon said. *I know what I forgot—tartar sauce. I'll bring along a king-size jar.* All fishermen are optimists.

Bushman pulled at his scruffy beard. "But I can't figger who your *third* guest might be. Guess I'll just have to be satisfied with guessin' two of 'em."

Moon looked over Paducah's saddle at his peculiar foreman. "There's just the two of 'em and me, which adds up to exactly three." He nodded to indicate the other saddled horses. "Count the mounts, Pete."

*Ha—he walked right into it!* Pointing his finger at each equine in turn, Pete Bushman counted the saddled horses. "One. Two. Three." He aimed an impertinent digit at the nag's head that was hanging over Moon's shoulder. "Four."

The Ute's dark face might have been chiseled from stone. "There ain't but *three* horses here."

Bushman managed to look startled—like a foreman who has just discovered that his employer has lost his senses. "Excuse me, boss—but maybe you ain't noticed that Sweet Alice has been follerin' you around like you had your pockets fulla apples—"

Charlie Moon cranked up the glare to nine hundred watts. His words came out in that no-nonsense monotone the Ute reserved for very serious business. "Pete, if I say that there ain't but three horses here, that's the way it is."

The crusty foreman shrugged. "All right. I'm just the old, feeble-minded straw-boss a this here outfit. You're the Man. Hey, if you say two-plus-two is three, that's fine by me."

Moon buckled the straps on the saddlebag. "I'm glad we got that straight."

Affecting a hurt expression, the foreman turned on his boot heel and stomped away. With his back to the Indian, Pete Bushman felt free to let a smile warm his face. *That outlaw hoss has the boss right on the hairy edge. I wish I'd a drawed* five *days instead a six!*

## *THE CALL*

On his way back from the pantry, Moon was passing through the enormous parlor with two cans of peaches in his left jacket pocket, a jar of fried apples in the right, a sixteen-ounce bottle of tartar sauce in his left hand, a couple of extra Idaho potatoes in the right. On the list of the Ute's Top Ten

Culinary Proverbs was—and he lived by such sage sayings—You Can Never Have Too Many Spuds. He heard a pickup door slam outside. *That'll be them.* The telephone rang as he was passing it. Having two too many spuds, Moon paused, secured the pair of root vegetables snugly under his left arm, picked up the receiver. "Columbine Ranch."

"You don't have to say that every time I call—I *know* which ranch it is."

Moon smiled at Aunt Daisy's caustic response. "Who's calling?"

"What do you mean who's calling—you know as well as I do who I am!"

He heard a familiar knock on the door, yelled: "Come in."

"Come in? Where do you think I am—standing outside under a tree?"

Moon waved the jar of tartar sauce at his friends. "No, that was somebody else I was telling to come in."

"Who?"

Moon was in a whimsical mood. "Scotch Parrish and—"

The voice screeched in his ear. "Charlie Moon—have you been drinking hard liquor?"

"Uh—no," the AA member said. "Not even soft liquor." *Not for thirteen years, seven months, and four days.* "Actually, it was Pete Bushman that said 'Parrish'—"

"That wasn't Bushman, I know that fuzzy-faced white man's voice."

"—and I guess it just got stuck in my mind." The drowning man treaded water for a time. "Hasn't that ever happened to you?"

"No it has not." The line went dead for a few heartbeats. "You've got me so mixed up I've forgot what I called about."

Moon smiled at his friends. "Have a seat over by the fireplace."

"I'm already sitting by the fireplace," the tribal elder grumped.

"I didn't mean you." He grinned. "You can stand up if it suits you."

"Well it *don't* suit me!" Quite suddenly, the tribal elder

recalled the purpose of her call. "I wanted to talk to you about something important."

"I'm listening."

"Remember that dream I had?"

The old woman had five or six dreams every night and told him about most of them. And the majority of these sleep-fantasies fell into the same category. The semicompulsive gambler went with the odds. "Uh—was this that dream about something scary?"

"Yes." *He* did *remember—will wonders never cease!* "Well, I had it again." Daisy would not mention that she was napping in Spirit Canyon. "And I saw the little girl again."

*What little girl?* "Well, I'm glad to hear it."

In a wasted but necessary gesture, Daisy shook her head. "Well, you shouldn't be glad—it's bad news." She paused for dramatic effect. "*Seriously* bad news."

Prepared for a pleasant afternoon with his best friend and his drop-dead-gorgeous sweetheart, Charlie Moon was not in the mood even for so-so news, and certainly not the seriously bad variety. Having already informed his foreman about his state of mind, he now proceeded to discourage his aunt from sharing her worries. "Uh, look—I have some guests here right now and we're about ready to ride off on a combination fishing-picnic, so how about you tell me about this later?" *Like sometime late next year.*

His aunt assumed her I'm-the-closest-thing-you've-got-to-a-mother tone: "Charlie Moon, forget about picnics and fishing. You've got no business having a good time when someone we know is in trouble."

Good-Time Charlie knew when he was whipped. "Okay. Who's in trouble?"

The tribal elder heard a woman laughing in the background. "Who's that?"

Moon's head was starting to ache, but he strained to sort this out. "You said someone was in trouble. I asked you who. Then you said 'who's that?' "

"When I said 'who's that,' I wanted to know who's with Scott Parris."

He chuckled. "You mean Scotch Parrish?"

Daisy's silence spoke volumes. Volumes that would not be shelved in the children's section at the Quaker Day School library.

Reading her meaning, Moon cleared his throat. "Lila Mae's here with Scott. We're going to ride over to Lake Jesse and drown some worms, then have us a fish fry and then we'll—"

"Lila Mae—you mean that FBI woman?"

The planner of the picnic reset the potatoes under his arm. "Yup. That's the one." The "FBI woman" looked his way. Moon winked at her, as if to say: *You're my main squeeze.*

Miss McTeague winked back, as if to say: *I'd better be your* only *squeeze, Big Boy.*

"Oh." This was Daisy speaking in his ear.

"Oh, what?"

"Never mind."

"Never mind what?"

"About the little girl in my dream."

It was coming back to him. "Are we talking about the kid with you-know-what dripping from her hands?"

"I told you to never mind!"

"Plop." Moon felt entitled to a satisfied smirk. "Plop-plop."

"You—" his aunt informed him with the assurance of one who had reams of data on the subject, "—are a big jug-head."

"Sorry. I tried, but I just couldn't hold it back."

"Well try harder!"

"So did you see the kid's face yet?"

A brief silence. "Maybe I did, maybe I didn't."

In his mind, Moon carried a snapshot of his aunt. He grinned at the wrinkled, feisty-eyed face. "Well if you did, maybe you'll tell me who she is so I can—"

"So you can tell that fancy-pants FBI hussy you're all hootchy-kootchy with? Hah!" There was a click in his ear.

*Hussy? Hootchy-kootchy?* Moon wondered where his elderly aunt picked up language like that. *Probably watching old movies on TV.*

Being in the off-duty mode, Lila Mae approached the object of her affections with hips swinging, spoke over her shoulder to the man she'd rode in with. "Turn your head, Scott."

"Yes ma'am." Because his neck was stiff, the Granite Creek chief of police turned his entire body, and watched their reflections in a window. "It's not like I'd care to witness whatever disgusting displays unchained lust might lead you two to." He squinted to see better. *Charlie needs to wash that windowpane.*

Being off-duty, Lila Mae was not packing. Her 9-mm Glock automatic, that is. Off-duty, she packed a .32. She wrapped a pair of arms around the tall Ute, planted a kiss on his mouth.

Parris, who was a widower, sighed at the scene in the window. *I should've brought my girlfriend along. Except that Theresa don't like horses or fish or being out-of-doors.*

Lila Mae gazed at her man. "What was that all about?"

"If you don't know," Moon grinned, "I guess we'd better do it again. As many times as it takes you to figure it out."

"I was referring to the telephone call from your aunt."

"How'd you know it was my aunt?"

"The look on your face. Like you'd just stepped on a two-by-four with a rusty nail in it. Pointy end up." She flashed a smile that made his head spin. "That and the fact that you mentioned her by name."

"Oh. Right." He held her closer. Wondered where she was packing the off-duty .32 automatic. *Must be in her boot.* "Aunt Daisy calls me whenever she's got something on her mind."

"Well of course she does. Because you're so sweet. And lovable. And full of empathy."

"That's all right as far as it goes," Moon said. "But you forgot to mention my sterling qualities of modesty and humility."

"No I didn't." *Charlie is* so *cute.*

"Okay," Parris muttered. "You two break it up. I'm hankering to hook me a yard-long trout." *Or three foot-long ones. Or six six-inchers. No, that's going too far downscale.*

*Anything less than ten inches, I'm throwing back. Well, maybe less than eight inches.*

McTeague gave Moon a worried look. "Charlie, would you mind if I asked you a personal question?"

"Not a smidgen. Go right ahead."

"Okay. Why do you have two potatoes tucked under your left arm?"

"Because three wouldn't fit?"

Lila Mae McTeague shook her pretty head.

Charlie Moon gave it some serious thought. "Okay, try this. These dudes were kind of cold when I got 'em outta the box in the cellar, and it's not a good idea to drop a chilly spud into hot ashes; that'll split and pop 'em quicker'n you can say 'who fired that shot!' Under the arm is a good place to do a pre-warm."

Scott Parris nodded his hearty agreement.

McTeague turned up her nose.

Minutes later, the men and the woman rode off to the south of the ranch headquarters, up a rocky ridge, through a small forest of spruce and pines and ferns and vines, past a sturdy log cabin where a retired, reclusive priest was spending his twilight years, onto a high prairie where a glacial lake was set like a jewel on the Columbine's grassy gown.

The hound came along for the fun. And the outlaw horse, of course.

• • •

CONSIDERING all the possibilities that might have marred their afternoon, such as tangled lines, broken rods, rattlesnake bites and the like, the outing went tolerably well.

After losing a race with a cottontail, Sidewinder trotted off after a striped lizard.

After watching Charlie Moon unpack the saddlebags, Sweet Alice began to munch the lush grass along the shore.

Scott Parris, who was an inveterate fly caster, toiled and sweated like a coal-mine mule for three hours and reeled in a matched pair of nine-inch cutthroats. Being of that peculiar

Midwestern culture which believes that one must work hard to have the least bit of fun, he was gratified with the results of his labors.

The Ute preferred red worms to Parris's fuzzy little artificial lures, and a working majority of the finned creatures cast their votes in favor of the live bait *du jour.* He would affix the wriggly creature to a hook, cast it upon the waters and wait. Which gave him ample time to gaze at the lady's fine form.

As she worked with her bait.

No, fish bait.

Parris watched the lady too, as Lila Mae awkwardly made her first cast of a beef-liver chunk. It landed within a yard of the shore. *The woman simply don't know how to fish.* Though her second cast was only a marginally better attempt, she snagged something. A sunken log, the experienced angler surmised. Parris surmised wrong.

Special Agent Lila Mae McTeague had hooked a famished trout. Sad to say, it was the only fish she subtracted from the vast community inhabiting the alpine lake. Sad from Scott Parris's point of view, that is. There were two reasons for his ill-concealed dismay. First, because—remarking that this was really "too easy"—the rank amateur terminated her effort after making the catch of the day. Second because her rainbow was, as Moon whooped, a real "Jonah." According to the Trusty Buddy spring scale, Mr. Jonah was a couple of ounces in excess of seven pounds.

Parris grumbled under his breath about *beginner's luck.*

To add to his misery, Lila Mae set the magnificent trout free.

And for each of the white man's trout, the Ute caught three.

The fishes were duly filleted and fried in the iron skillet. The picnic was uniformly appreciated by all partakers of the feast. But what with the trout and the baked beans and baked potatoes, none of the diners—not even Charlie Moon—were ready for dessert.

As a rouge-faced sun fell low over the Misery Range, the trio mounted up. The horses, who seemed to have caught the carefree mood of the late afternoon, proceeded in a slow, ambling walk. The Ute—who never passed this way without paying a courtesy call on Father Raes Delfino—led the party toward a modest log cabin that was half-concealed in a grove of spruce. Of all of God's servants, the priest was Daisy Perika's favorite. And for that matter, Charlie Moon's too.

Having perceived their approach while they were still far away, Fr. Raes had put a bookmark in his leather-bound *Imitation of Christ* and set it aside. When he heard the horses' hooves, he opened the door before they had a chance to knock.

Having tied their mounts to an oak hitching post, the trio approached the saintly man, whose white hair formed a snowy halo around his head.

Sidewinder sallied off to inspect the aromatic carcass of a ground squirrel.

Sweet Alice followed Charlie Moon to the door.

The horse's peculiar attachment to the Ute had not gone unnoticed by the FBI agent. Neither had Charlie Moon's apparent disregard of the animal's fondness for his company. On top of that, the horse looked oddly familiar. *I know I've seen that animal before.* Lila Mae McTeague could no longer contain her curiosity, but knowing her man, she avoided the direct question, and went for the query-designed-as-a-comment. "Charlie, I think it is so *cute,* the way that horse follows you around." She barely heard his muttered response.

"There ain't no horse followin' me."

"I suppose she is a pet."

He repeated himself, loud enough for her to hear clearly.

Mildly chagrined at his dismissive tone, she pointed at the animal. "If there's no horse following you, then what do you call that?"

Moon set his jaw.

Scott Parris gave McTeague a cautioning look, and a whisper. "Let it drop."

She did, with a shrug. *Men can be* so *peculiar.*

Parris whispered again. "That's Sweet Alice."

The name, as names often will, instantly rang a bell. McTeague recalled where she had seen the homely little mare—it was only last year, in the corral over at the Big Hat, when Sweet Alice had used Charlie Moon to bust up a rail fence. *Oh, so that's it. The big, bad cowboy's still mad at the horse he couldn't ride. But the poor creature just* adores *him.* She wanted to laugh, but well-bred ladies avoid unseemly displays of mirth.

At the door, Parris and Moon exchanged greetings with the priest, who—having heard about Sweet Alice and Moon's aversion to the four-legged man-killer—tactfully ignored the beast's presence at his door. The woman was another matter entirely. Having not yet met the apple of Moon's eye, and hoping the Ute might marry someday, Father Raes was delighted to be introduced to the strikingly handsome young woman, and thought: *This is a very intelligent person.* He invited his guests in, brewed a pot of black tea, another of coffee, produced a tin of Italian vanilla cookies, offered thanks to God for the food and drink, felt especially blessed to share the canned peaches and fried apples provided by his drop-in guests.

While they ate, Sweet Alice stood at the window. Stared at the back of the Ute's head.

After the dessert and hot beverages, the elderly priest had a sudden recollection. He reached into his shirt pocket, removed a folded piece of paper. "Ah, I almost forgot. Your foreman stopped by this afternoon, left this message for you. I suggested that he deliver it to you on the lake shore, but Mr. Bushman intimated that he did not wish to disturb your picnic with your friends." He offered it to Moon.

Moon eyed the paper warily. "What's it about?"

"I have no idea." Father Raes raised an eyebrow. "I naturally treated it as a private communication."

The owner of the Columbine mulled it over. *Pete Bushman never brings me any good news. And I'm not in the mood for the other kind.*

Guessing what was going through his friend's mind, Parris grinned. "I think he wants you to read it to him."

Being a serious-minded fellow, the priest misunderstood the jest. "Shall I?"

Unable to say yea or nay, Moon simply shrugged.

Taking this as a yea, Father Raes unfolded the paper, adjusted the rimless spectacles perched on his nose. "Ah—it appears to be a transcription of a telephone message." *The foreman's handwriting is atrocious.* He cleared his throat and began: "Tell Charlie don't worry about what I called about this morning. I'll take care of things myself." A frown. "Mr. Bushman gives no indication of who the caller was." Father Raes passed the slip of paper to Moon.

The Ute glanced at the message, stuffed it into his shirt pocket. "It's from my aunt Daisy." It was the last line that bothered him—whenever Daisy Perika made up her mind to *take care of things myself,* she was likely to stir up all kinds of trouble.

Scott Parris was inordinately fond of the grouchy old woman. "Auntie-D doin' okay, Charlie?"

Charlie Moon nodded. The sensible part of his mind insisted that this whole business was nothing more than an old woman's bad dreams. But a dark corner of the Ute's imagination was chilled by the possibility that somewhere out there, a skinny little girl was in serious trouble. Maybe she did have blood on her hands. Or soon would. *But until Aunt Daisy tells me who she is, all I can do is wait for the hammer to fall.*

He would not have long to wait.

# SEVEN

## *TONAPAH FLATS, UTAH*

AFTER soul-searching her way through a long and mostly sleepless night, Sarah Frank had made up her mind to do what must be done. First, she would make her final trek to the far side of Hatchet Gap. After that, she planned to purchase a one-way bus ticket to Durango, Colorado, which was very near the Southern Ute reservation. And one way or another, she would make her way to Aunt Daisy's home in the remote canyon country. She happily imagined that from time to time, Charlie Moon would drop by and take them to Ignacio for lunch at Angel's Café. But a worrisome thought, always in the background, troubled the fourteen-year-old: *I hope Charlie isn't already married.*

Shortly before dawn warmed the barren land, Sarah was out of bed and fully dressed. Not wishing to attract her cousin's attention, she did not switch on the bare, sixty-watt bulb suspended from the cobwebbed ceiling. While Mr. Zig-Zag watched with intense feline interest, she used a small flashlight to pack her black canvas backpack. There was not that much to take. She folded her other dress (the blue one that wasn't torn), some tattered underclothing, a pair of white socks, a well-worn pink plastic toothbrush, a small bag of wrapped peppermint candies, a zippered diary marked TOP SECRET, and the *Grandmother Spider Brings the*

*Sun* book Mr. Oates had given her. Switching off the flashlight, she removed a manila envelope from under her mattress. Inside were a half-dozen treasured photographs of her dead parents, and Sarah's birth certificate.

Now every girl must have her cherished secrets, and there was a certain *Something* Sarah had solemnly sworn not to mention to a living soul . . . *cross my heart and hope to die . . . on my mother's grave . . . and if I break my promise a big tree will fall on me and break my back!* The oath was in force *as long as my flesh is warm*—which might be but for the briefest of seasons, and intertwined in this mystery were both rhymes and reasons.

This treasure would not be packed with her other possessions; day and night, the Utmost Secret would be suspended from her neck, touching her skin . . . *as long as my flesh is warm.*

With admirable stealth, and leaving her cat inside, she slipped out the back door. Minutes later, Sarah had deposited her canvas backpack in a clump of sage near the Little Sandy dry wash. The girl had just returned to her bedroom when she heard the plop-plop of her cousin's bare feet coming down the dark hallway. Hurrying to get into bed, Sarah stubbed her toe on something in the dark—but she squelched the yelp, and managed to slip under the covers just as the door opened.

Marilee Attatochee stuck her head in the tiny bedroom. The day's first cigarette dangled from her lips, the red-hot tip bobbled as she spoke. "Sarah?"

The fully dressed girl faked a yawn. "What?"

"Thought I heard something back here." Marilee gave the aged cat an accusative look. "It was probably Mr. Ziggy rustling around."

Sarah responded with exaggerated politeness. "His *name* is Mr. Zig-Zag."

"Oh, right." Distracted from her original mission, Marilee groaned, stretched her chubby, stubby arms. "I'm gonna make some breakfast for me and Al. You ready for somethin' to eat?"

"Yes, thank you." Sarah knew it might be a long time before she had another meal. "Some eggs, please. And fried baloney. And biscuits."

"We're fresh outta biscuits." Marilee noticed the edge of a collar showing on Sarah's neck. *She's dressed herself already. Wonder what she's up to?* "There's only two eggs left and Al's got dibs on those. But I can make you some oatmeal."

"Okay. Can I have a fried baloney sandwich too?"

"Sure."

"With three pieces of baloney?"

"You got it, Snookums." The woman turned her back, padded down the hallway toward the kitchen. "But don't feed no baloney to Mr. Ziggy—tell him to munch on somma these mice I keep trippin' over." As an afterthought, she added: "Money for food don't fall outta the sky, y'know."

When Sarah showed up in the kitchen a minute later, the cat trailing behind, her cousin arched a penciled eyebrow. "My, my—you sure got dressed in a hurry. I guess the thought of some oatmeal must've gonged your chime." Getting no response from the girl, Marilee stirred the watery gruel, shook in another measure of the wholesome Quaker's product. *I guess all kids have their secrets.*

Al Harper slunk into the steamy kitchen with the enthusiasm of a half-drowned man dragging himself ashore. He was wearing corduroy pants, a dirty undershirt, a three-day beard, a bad smell, and a scowl. His right eye was clear and mostly blue, the left orb resembled the white of an egg.

Marilee gave him an amused glance. "Gracious me, Alphonse. You are lookin' mighty pretty this morning."

"Go suck a sour crab apple, squaw-woman," he growled, and plopped into his customary chair, propped his arms on the table. "Where's my breakfast?"

She put a cup of black coffee between his elbows. "The eggs are still in the shells. You want 'em to show up in your plate, try sweet-talking the cook."

"Hah!" He winked the working eye, grinned across the table at the girl. "You're up early."

Marilee plopped a bowl of oatmeal in front of Sarah. "Here you go. I put some brown sugar on it."

"Thank you." Sarah added in a mumble: "Don't forget the baloney sandwich."

The smelly man sneered. "You don't need no baloney, kid—what you need is a good—"

"Shut your mouth, Al!" Marilee swatted his face with a pot holder, smiled apologetically at her cousin. "So what'll you do with yourself all summer, now that school's out? Aside from working for Ben Silver, I mean."

Sarah shrugged.

Suffering under the comical delusion that he was the Man of the House, Al Harper was determined to dominate the breakfast-table conversation. He sipped at the scalding coffee, gave Sarah some advice. "You oughta find yourself some kinda full-time job. There's no future in doin' odd jobs for old Sourpuss Silver."

It was Marilee's turn to "Hah!" and she made the most of it. Her lip curled in a sneer. "That's a good one, comin' from you, Mr. Unemployed. When's the last time Alphonse Harper brought a greenback dollar in the door?"

Harper put on a piteous look, rubbed at the small of his back. "I'm blind in one eye and can barely see outta the other. And I've been severely and permanently disabled ever since I fell offa that loading dock over at the furniture plant—I'm not able to do reg'lar work." He added, with a hint of mystery: "But I'm onto something. Something that'll put us in the chips. Just wait, you'll see."

Marilee looked at a cobwebbed corner of the ceiling, which was about three notches more attractive than her pallid-faced boyfriend. "He's always 'onto something,'" she said to the clump of dusty filaments. "What a laugh." But deep inside, she continued to hope.

While his wisecracking girlfriend cracked eggs into the skillet, Al muttered: "I still say the kid oughta get a full-time job and help pay for her keep."

"I've tried everywhere," Sarah explained with exquisite patience. "The supermarket, the Dairy Queen, the Tip-Top Laundromat. They all say I'm not old enough."

His expression relaxed into the natural leer. "You're old enough to—"

"Shut up, Al. One more crack outta you, I'll poke this Lucky Strike in your good eye." Marilee took a long pull on her cigarette, addressed her next remarks to the girl. "Sooner or later, some kinda regular job will turn up for you." As an afterthought, she added: "You won't be able to do any housework for Ben Silver this morning. I got to go pick the old man up, take him to the clinic for his doctor appointment." Now Marilee addressed herself: "That'll take a big chunk of my day, but he pays me seven dollars and fifty cents an hour, so I ain't complaining." The thought of all the chores she had to do today made the woman weary. "After I bring Silver home, I got to go to the welfare office and see about Al's disability. They still haven't approved his application." She glanced at her boyfriend. *Maybe if I really did put his good eye out so he was altogether blind, the welfare'd come through.*

"I'd go with you," Al said. "But I got to go see a man. About some business."

She flicked cigarette ash onto his plate. "Just make sure it's a *man,* Alphonse. You mess around with me, I'll get the butcher knife and cut off your—" She glanced at her younger cousin. "You want anything else, Snookums?"

Sarah nodded. "The baloney sandwich." She paused. "Three slices, please."

Marilee put four slices of Oscar Mayer's best between slices of white bread.

Unseen under the table, Mr. Zig-Zag licked lips that had never tasted mouse-flesh.

# EIGHT

## *CROSSING OVER TO THE OTHER SIDE*

THERE were a number of things Sarah Frank did not like, ranging from certain obnoxious persons and disgusting foodstuffs to a variety of painful sensations and unpleasant circumstances, and she kept a list in her diary which at last count numbered one hundred and four. Among the top ten was being alone in the house with Al Harper. Therefore, before Marilee departed in her Dodge minivan, the girl slipped out the back door. She had a brown paper sack clutched in her hand. Mr. Zig-Zag tagged along with his nose in the air, sniffing hopefully at the grease-stained parcel. She addressed her cat without looking down. "I'm sorry, but you can't have any baloney right now." *There's something I have to do first, and then we have a long, long way to go.*

She crossed a backyard littered with windblown trash, stepped over a drooping chicken-wire fence, picking her way among pieces of discarded lumber, clumps of greasewood, and golden rabbit bush. Sarah counted off her steps in the sand. It was fifty-four paces from the fence to the dry wash, 121 more to the big salmon-colored rock that stood like a sentinel at the entrance to Hatchet Gap—her shortcut through Big Lizard Ridge to Ben Silver's house.

• • •

THE moment Marilee drove away (she was leaving early to fill the van with gas and pick up some things at the pharmacy) Al Harper hurried back to Sarah's cubbyhole-sized bedroom, looked out the rear window, watched the girl's thin form turn left, gradually disappear into an undergrowth of prickly thorn trees and yellowed willows that thirsted for the next flow of rainwater that would trickle down the Little Sandy. *Wonder where the little Indian bitch is goin'?* He considered the evidence. *She's not headed toward the Gap and Ben Silver's place to do some chore for the old goat, which she naturally wouldn't a-course, 'cause Sarah knows ol' Ben won't be there 'cause Marilee's takin' him to the doctor.* The noxious man scratched at his belly, belched up an odor of breakfast. *Maybe she's headed down to the Dairy Queen.* Another, more interesting possibility occurred to him. *I bet Sarah's got herself a feller. Sure, she's goin' to meet some hairy-legged pimple-face in the bushes.* Another belch. *Well, what the hell do I care where she goes or what she does. I got my own business to take care of.*

Rubbing at his blind eye, Harper went into the kitchen, squatted to open the door under the sink. He reached behind a gallon jug of bleach, removed Marilee's plastic toolbox that still had the Wal-Mart bar-code sticker on it, reflected that the woman could fix most anything, from a leaky faucet to a crapped-out toaster oven. He snickered. *Good thing she don't know that I'm on to her hot little secret.* He opened the toolbox lid, found the Do-It-All screwdriver with the dozen interchangeable bits. Al unscrewed the base of the egg-shaped handle. Nine of the bits were inside, along with Marilee's cache of spare cash. He unrolled the small cylinder of bills, counted up eighteen dollars. There was also a half dollar, a dime, and a nickel. Pocketing the proceeds of his meager theft, he sighed at the pitiful state he had come to, how low he had sunk since he'd walked out on Betty-Lou, who was chief cashier at the supermarket. *This is no way for a man to live. I need to find me a woman who's got a full-time job—somebody with a stash worth stealing.*

•••

KNOWING that Al liked to spy on her, Sarah paused among the rustling willows, pushed down a spindly branch, took a long look at her bedroom window. *If he was watching me, he must've given up and gone.* Crouching, she backtracked along the wash, stopped to make sure her backpack was where she had left it, then set her face toward Big Lizard Ridge. *Now I can go through the Gap without Al knowing.*

•••

DURING the passage of a day, sunlight would not penetrate into Hatchet Gap for more than six hours, and there were thousands of dark, lichen-encrusted, spider-infested nooks and crannies that had never felt the warm touch of solar rays.

Sarah made her way briskly along the familiar deer path that wound around great chucks of gray sandstone, beneath shadowy overhangs, through patches of prickly pear cactus and clusters of pearly flowers she called snowdrops. At one point, alerted by a warning hiss from Mr. Zig-Zag, the thin girl stood still as a post. Barely a yard away, an enormous corn snake slithered across the path, disappeared under the bristly corpse of a tumbleweed.

When her cat was ready to proceed, she followed.

Halfway through the Gap, and at the highest point in the arched passage, Sarah paused to gaze in awe at the outlines of several human hands on the smooth sandstone walls. She could not pass this special place without musing about time's lost mysteries. These ancient markings in the crack in the back of Big Lizard Ridge were the color of blood. But it was not blood. According to the tale a toothless old Paiute man had told her, the people who had lived in this land long, long ago would fill their mouths with a coarse mixture of water and powdered red ochre. The young man who was privileged to perform the ritual would place his hand against the gray wall and spew out the rusty-red mixture onto his hand and the stone. This was the means of leaving the imprints, which—according to her informer—were at least three thousand years old. Sarah could not imagine anything so ancient as that, and wished she could grow up to be clever, like the aged Paiute.

• • •

SIXTEEN minutes later, Sarah Frank was on the far side of Hatchet Gap. She was within a hundred paces of Ben Silver's house when her cousin's van pulled up.

• • •

HAVING heard the urgent *toot-toot,* Ben Silver took a firm grip on his cane, headed toward the front door. *Why does the consarned woman always have to blow her horn. Don't she know I can hear her coming a half-mile away?*

"Helloooo," Marilee yelled. "Mr. Sil-veeerrr."

He stomped onto the front porch. *And why does she have to yell my name? It's not like she'd be here for anybody else—not another soul lives on this dead-end road.*

Marilee Attatochee made a wig-wag wave from her minivan, shouted again. "Ben, you oughta get somebody to run a blade over your road. There's potholes big enough to swallow a cow. And I come close to getting stuck in that muddy spot by the spring."

The irascible old man shouted back at her. "You don't have to screech, woman—I got my hearing aid turned up to a hundred percent."

The Papago woman laughed like this was the funniest thing she'd heard all year, and this annoyed him all the more. She got out to open the passenger-side door.

"I can open the door for myself, thank you very much," he grumped. "I'm not an invalid yet." He shot the plump young woman a scornful look. "In fact, I bet I could walk your chubby legs off."

"You probably could," she shouted back.

Silver winced, turned his hearing aid down. "While we're

headed to the clinic, Marilee What's-Your-Name, why don't you tell me everything you've been doing since I saw you last week. And don't leave nothing out."

She slipped under the steering wheel. *Well now I've seen everything. Mean old Ben Silver, who never acted like he cared whether I lived or died, wants me to talk to him about my dreary life.* And so she did. All the way down the rutted, potholed lane, all the way down the paved highway to the Tonapah Flats Clinic. Marilee did not leave anything out.

Silver smiled all the way. It was great fun, watching her lips move, not hearing a word she said.

• • •

KNOWING where Mr. Silver kept his spare key, Sarah removed it from under the red paint can on the bottom shelf in the woodshed. After unlocking the back door, she put the key back again. A moment later, she was in the old man's house and all alone—except for her cat.

# NINE

## *QUITE A SIGHT TO SEE BEFORE BREAKFAST*

SHERIFF Ned Popper stared at the homely, sunburned face.

It stared back at him.

When he winked, it winked.

He dipped the brush in an antique shaving mug, swiped on a generous helping of creamy suds, went right to work with the genuine George Wostenholm ivory-handle straight razor that had belonged to his maternal grandfather. With a delicacy developed by long practice and demanded by the craggy landscape of his face, he scraped off a day's growth of whiskers, taking care not to encroach on the handsome handlebar mustache, which was his chief vanity. After completing this solemn morning ritual, the Utah lawman grinned at the image in the mirror, which was obliged to return the favor. "For a man of your years," he said, "you don't look all that bad."

When the telephone rang, the widower was frying bacon and eggs in a skillet, taking care not to overcook the yolks. Annoyed at having his breakfast disturbed, he frowned at the caller ID. *What do the state police want this time?* "This is Popper, Tonapah Flats Top Copper."

This produced the expected chuckle from Sergeant Jefferson Davis Martinez. "Hey, Ned—we got us some trouble."

"What flavor, J-D?"

"Big pileup. Over on the interstate, close to the Texaco truck stop. We got one man rolling, ETA ten minutes. Next closest officer is an hour away, and she's on a call to rescue some poor bastard who's getting beat up by his wife. If you could lend us somebody to help direct traffic—"

"Say no more, señor. I'll send my on-duty deputy."

"Thanks, Ned."

Popper turned to check the black iron skillet. The eggs were brown and crispy around the edges. *And them yolks look hard as the knobs on a brass bedstead.* The superstitious man hoped this wasn't a sign that he was in for a bad day. He turned off the propane flame, dialed his office. Waited through six rings. *Why don't Bertha answer the phone? I don't know why I bother to have a dispatcher anyway.* He pressed and released the cradle switch, dialed Deputy Packard's cell phone.

## *TATE PACKARD'S COFFEE BREAK*

AFTER parking his unit in front of Dinty's Grille, Deputy Sheriff Tate Packard had taken a seat in a booth that provided a panoramic view of Big Lizard Ridge. The lawman showed more interest in the scenery than in his immediate surroundings. In Packard's opinion, Dinty's was a dump, Dinty would have to get lots smarter to qualify as a moron, the coffee was awful, the food was worse. On top of all this, it annoyed him that some temperamental artist with a knife had—for reasons unfathomable to ordinary mortals—slashed the booth's vinyl seat cover into shreds.

The alleged sub-moron was swiping wet circles on the counter. "Hey, Tate. What're you doin' over there? You don't drop in all that often, but when you do, you always sit at the counter."

"Habits tend to dull a man's life." The deputy kept his gaze on the great outdoors, which didn't look all that great through Dinty's filthy window. "From time to time, I feel the need to look at things from a different perspective."

Dinty chuckled. *That boy don't have enough work to keep a bone-lazy man occupied. Day in, day out, nothing to do but drive back and forth or sit around somewhere nursing a cup of java. I bet he's waiting for one of his good-looking girlfriends to show up, then he'll sneak off with her to some quiet spot.* The hard-working, girlfriend-deprived proprietor of Dinty's Grill sighed. *I should be so lucky.*

The cell phone in Tate Packard's jacket pocket chirped, he snatched it. "I'm here."

Sheriff Popper's voice boomed in his ear. "No you're not, Tate. You're on your way out to the junction with the interstate, then six miles west. There's been a multiple-vehicle accident near the Texaco truck stop, and the state cops need our help."

"Uh—"

"What is it—you waiting for one of your twisty-hips to show up, so you can get all cozy with her—whilst the county is paying you to do police work?"

Packard flushed pink. "Oh, no, sir. It's nothing like that. It's just—"

"Look, Tate—it's been about thirty years since I was young and frisky, but I still remember how it was. Here's what you do—on your way to the wreck, give your sweetie a call. Tell her today you have to earn your pay. Then make a date for sometime when you're off-duty."

The blush darkened to beet-red. "Uh, it's just that this is Bearcat's day off. If I go help the state cops, that'll leave us with nobody here in town to—"

"Don't worry about it, I'm coming in directly. Now get moving."

Deputy Packard heard an ambulance siren wail in the distance. "Okay, boss. I'm on my way." Seconds later, the door of Dinty's Grill slammed behind him. Cranking up his unit, he switched on the emergency lights and siren, kicked up a hatful of gravel, roared down the highway toward the interstate. Before he was out of town, Packard used his cell phone to dial the memorized number. No response. He waited ten rings before pressing the OFF button. *Dammit all.*

## A CHANGE OF PLANS

As Marilee Attatochee turned in at the clinic, Ben Silver did not hear the shrill shriek of the ambulance siren. But he did see the boxy white vehicle—red lights flashing—tearing out of the Emergency Room Only parking lot, rolling down the two-lane toward the interstate. The deaf man cranked up the volume control on his hearing aid. "Wonder what that's all about?"

Marilee shrugged as she glanced at the rearview mirror, saw Deputy Sheriff Tate Packard's black-and-white zoom by at eighty-plus miles an hour. "Whatever it is, it ain't good."

Inside the clinic, Marilee and Ben Silver found out what it was all about.

There had been a major accident out on the interstate. At least two dead, six seriously injured. All nurses, all physicians were on alert for ER duty. This included Dr. Stump, the physician Ben Silver had been scheduled to see, and his appointments for the day had been canceled. Shortly thereafter, Miss Attatochee and Mr. Silver were headed back toward his home. The old man grumbled all the way. Why didn't the clinic have more doctors? Why did those mostly out-of-state coconut-heads out on the interstate drive ninety-nine miles an hour? Why didn't the state police authorize their officers to arrest and shoot on the spot those mental defectives that drove so recklessly? And so on and so forth.

Marilee took it, but not happily. *I wish I had me one of them hearing aid thingamajigs like Ben's that I could shut off. Then I wouldn't have to listen to this dinky old man's silly prattle.* Across the road from Dinty's Grill, she turned left onto Ben Silver's private lane, followed it around behind Big Lizard Ridge. The driver muttered to herself. "I hope I can get through that mud hole at the spring without getting stuck."

Silver cranked the hearing aid volume up all the way, leaned sideways toward the driver. "What'd you say?"

Marilee repeated her statement, much louder this time.

"You don't have to yell at me! Besides, there ain't nothing wrong with this road. What you need to do is get some tires with a heavy tread. And it wouldn't hurt none if you learned how to drive this bucket of bolts!"

Seven dollars and fifty cents an hour came in handy, but Marilee had absorbed what is commonly known as *just about enough.* She slowed the van to a crawl. "Mr. Silver, you don't pay me enough to take all this guff."

"What's that?"

"You heard me."

He chuckled. "What's bothering you, Miss Okeechobee—"

"The name is *Attatochee*!"

"That's no proper kind of name." He frowned thoughtfully, also puckered his mouth. "Sounds more like a sneeze. I bet when your mother was naming you, she got too much snuff up her nose and—" He chuckled. "Well, you can see what I mean."

Her brown hands went white-knuckled on the steering wheel. *If I had a gun, I'd shoot him.*

Ben Silver was having entirely too much fun. "Now if you'll try not to interrupt for at least a microsecond, I'll frame my question again. What's the matter, Marilee Kerchoo—you hinting for a raise?" This being a purely rhetorical question, he did not wait for a response. "Okay, then. Times is hard, and even though you don't deserve it—a raise you get. Starting right now—no, don't let it ever be said I'm not a fair-minded man." He glanced at his wristwatch. "Starting when you picked me up about thirty-six minutes ago, I'm paying you—" He paused, pretended to reflect. "Seven dollars and *sixty* cents an hour."

That was enough and change. Marilee braked the small van to a neck-popping halt, which activated the plastic facsimile of a female Hawaiian mounted on the instrument panel. Hula Girl waggled her hips.

"Hey—what'd you stop for?"

"You're offering me a ten-cent-an-hour raise?" This was also a rhetorical question, but Silver did not realize it. Which is a pity, because if he had, he might not have responded, and things might have turned out better.

"I certainly am. And you needn't bother to thank me for overpaying you."

The Papago woman's eyes went stone-cold. "Get out."

He arched one of the bushy white brows. "What'd you say?"

"Don't put on your deaf-man act for me, you old fake."

He presented a derisive grin. "Oh, dear—have I ruffled your sensitive tail feathers?"

"Open the door and get out. Do it right now, before I kick you out with both feet!"

*She really means it.* "But it's almost a half-mile to my house—"

"Hey, you're the big-mouth athlete who can walk my chubby legs off."

Fuming from both ears, Ben Silver proceeded to follow orders. With the aid of his cane, he eased himself onto the earth. Before closing the door, he gave the driver a final glare. "You, madam—are henceforth fired."

"You can't fire me, you silly old billy goat." Marilee looked down her nose at the forlorn figure. "I have already resigned—forthwith!" She did not know precisely what *forthwith* meant, but she had heard a lawyer say it on TV and it sounded damned good.

Ben Silver slammed the door as hard as he could, which was sufficient to rattle Marilee's teeth and set Hula Girl a-twitching again. As he commenced to stomp along the lane, he heard her backing the van toward the highway. *Soft-headed woman, I hope she backs it right into a ditch. And what's got her girdle all twisted anyway—this is a perfectly serviceable dirt road.* Mr. Silver was not looking where he was stomping, and this is why he was startled when he stepped into a pothole, stumbled, almost fell on his face. *I'll bet she dug that there just to spite me.*

*AT THE SCENE OF THE ACCIDENT*

DEPUTY Tate Packard took a break from directing traffic, gratefully accepted a Styrofoam cup of coffee from a kindly passerby. After a few sips of the steaming liquid, he pressed the REDIAL button on his cell phone. *Answer this time.* After two rings, he was relieved to hear the familiar voice say hello.

"Hi, where're you at?" He listened. "Good. I called you earlier, but I didn't get an answer." He nodded at the explanation. "Yeah, I guess your cell phone wouldn't work there. Uh, look, I'm sorry about this—but the reason I called was Sheriff Popper sent me to a bad accident. I'm out on the interstate, about a mile from the Five-Spot Texaco Truck Stop." He listened to the sharp retort. "Yeah, I know you expected me to be at Dinty's but I can't very well be in two places at the same time. When I got here, there was people strewn out all over the asphalt, some of 'em bleeding to death." As he listened to a long list of worries and complaints, the deputy shook his head. *Some people just don't know when to shut up.*

# TEN

## *MISHAP AT HATCHET GAP*

BEN Silver trudged on, but more watchful now about where he put his feet. The elderly man anticipated being inside his cozy home, slumped into the soft comfort of his favorite chair. This welcome vision refreshed his spirits, calmed his temper. *Soon as I rest my bones for a few minutes and get back my wind, I'll call Marilee on the phone. I'll tell that fat little firecracker she never had a chance to quit—that I'd already made up my mind to fire her before she showed up this morning. Then, I'll tell her if she apologizes, I might consider taking her back into occasional employment. Not because I need her, but just so she'll have a chance to make up for being so rude.* He grinned. *Boy, that'll light her fuse!*

On a telephone pole, a brazen raven cocked its sly head, croaked at him. Mockingly, it seemed.

Silver muttered a deprecatory remark about the feathered creature's parentage, then—weary of this world's insults—he turned his hearing aid off.

### *THE GIRL*

ATTEMPTING to make herself as small as possible, Sarah Frank was squatting on the closet floor with Mr. Zig-Zag clutched in her lap. As she listened to one side of a heated telephone conversation, the musty smell of Ben Silver's overcoat and sweaters and shoes intensified her fear. While the girl prayed that her cat wouldn't make a *meow,* a circular set of questions kept rotating through her mind. *How will I get out? What if he looks in here and finds me? What'll I do then?* As if in response to this silent query, Sarah's right hand found something in the corner of her darkened cell. It was round, hard, made of wood. A baseball bat.

## *SUSPICIOUS*

BEN Silver took a long, thoughtful look at his parlor. Something was not quite right. A drawer in a file cabinet was open by about a quarter-inch. In the bookcase, three volumes of his Wodehouse collection were leaning against *The Hobbit.* Mr. Silver's hardcovers did not *lean.* The finicky man was particularly fussy about his books, which were always lined up, standing straight as a row of Air Force cadets. His sharp gaze darted about, taking in minor details all over the room. There were other small but indisputable indications that while he was away, someone had been in his home. Someone who was looking for something. He had no doubt about what they were looking for. Or who had sent them to steal it. *Raymond wouldn't have the nerve to set foot inside my house, even if he knew I wasn't here—that spineless worm would send some hired thug to do the dirty work.* The old man heard a small creaking sound, felt a sudden chill. What if the burglar who had searched his home was still inside? His imagination filled in the blanks. Perhaps he was over there behind the heavy curtain, or crouched on the floor behind the couch. Or in the corner closet. *The rascal might even be watching me.* Faced with the need to formulate an effective plan, his intellect rose to the occasion. *I can't let on that I've noticed anything amiss. I'll just sit down at my desk, casually pick up the phone and call the sheriff's office. But I'll have to figure out some way to tell Bertha that I'm in trouble without letting the burglar know that I'm talking to the police.*

### *TONAPAH FLATS SHERIFF'S OFFICE*

DISPATCHER Bertha Katcher was, by nature, an edgy person and some days were worse than others. Today, for instance, Mildly Tense had progressed to Touch Me on the Back of My Neck and I'll Jump Out of My Skin. Every time the telephone rang Bertha lurched and yelped as if stung by a hornet. As the morning progressed, her stomach had begun to flutter. Several cups of black coffee did not help matters. Neither did the continuous snacks of Cheez Curls, apricot bon-bons, and Bubba's Super-Fine Bacon Rinds. The flutter was promoted to a growl. *Oh gracious, I hope I don't throw up all over my desk.* At a critical moment in the spotty history of this backwater Utah community, the dispatcher abandoned her duty station, made a beeline for the ladies' room. She had barely slammed the door behind her when the 911 line rang. After six rings, the emergency call was automatically transferred to the sheriff's cell phone.

### *THE LAWMAN ON HIS WAY TO WORK*

NEARING the edge of town, the sheriff of Tonapah Flats glanced at the caller ID. *It's Ben Silver's number.* "Hey—what's up, Ben?"

The voice on the other end was a cold, robotic monotone. "Uh—hello, Morgan. I thought I'd give you a ring and see why you was running late for our checker game and—"

"This is Ned Popper, Ben—you got the wrong number." *Silly old goat must have Morgan and 911 programmed on buttons right next to each other.* "You need to hang up and dial again."

"You're already on the way?" A pause. "Be here in a coupla minutes? Well, that's fine and dandy. I'll go put on a pot of coffee."

Popper frowned at the highway slipping under his pickup at a mile a minute. "Ben, what'n hell's goin' on—is something wrong?"

"You bet. Soon as you get here, I'll tell you all about—"

The line went dead.

Over many years of experience on the job, the sheriff had learned not to leap to conclusions. He reasoned that there were several possibilities. Number One: *I got onto a crossed telephone line and heard Ben Silver's side of a conversation with Morgan, but Ben couldn't hear me. Then, the phone company got things sorted out and disconnected me.* Numbers Two through Four were variations on this blame-it-on-high-technology theme. Then there was Number Five: *Ben might've been trying to tell me he was in some kind of trouble, and then his line was cut.* Unlikely, but not impossible. *Well, I guess I'd best go check it out.*

## *THE CONFRONTATION*

BEN Silver stared dumbly at the dead instrument in his hand, then at the telephone line that had been yanked out of the receptacle on the wall. The connector had been damaged, and this deliberate act of vandalism outraged the thrifty homeowner. He glared at the presumed burglar in astonished disbelief. "What in the hell are *you* doing—"

The blow landed squarely on his forehead. The old man slumped in his chair, sat there tentatively as if he was trying to decide what to do. After a few weakening heartbeats, his body made the decision for him. In a macabre imitation of a life-sized rag doll, it slid out of the chair. But Mr. Silver was neither rag nor doll, and his life was rapidly slipping away.

## *UPON HER RETURN FROM THE LADIES' ROOM*

Just as Bertha Katcher got back to her desk, the dispatcher received a radio call from the sheriff's pickup. "Unit Six, Bertha."

"Where you at, Shurf Pokker?"

Wincing at the habitual assassination of his good name, Ned Popper replied: "City limits, south side of town. I believe I just got a transferred 911 that *you* should've responded to. Where's blazes were you?"

"Uh—I'm sorry, boss. I got me a upset tummy this mornin' and I was in the ladies. Who was the call from?"

"Mr. Silver."

"*Ben* Silver?"

"You know of any other Silver in Tonapah County?" Sheriff Popper immediately regretted the tart response. "After Ben mumbled a few words that didn't make any sense, the line went dead."

"Oh, no—"

"It's probably no big deal, Bertha. Maybe a tree limb fell and cut Ben's telephone line. Or maybe he dropped his phone and busted it." Across the road from Dinty's Grill, Popper made a right turn onto the long, looping lane that dead-ended at Ben Silver's house. "I'm headed out behind Big Lizard Ridge to check on him." He waited for a response. "Bertha, do you read me?"

"Uh . . . ten-four, Shurf."

*I don't know what I pay that woman for.*

Having felt another urgent call of nature, the sheriff's department dispatcher sprinted off toward the ladies' room—and barely got there in time to puke into the toilet.

Dismissing the minimum-wage employee from his thoughts, Popper tossed the microphone aside. "Damn the pestilential potholes," he muttered. "Damn the bald tires and wore-out suspension and the Geneva Convention—full speed ahead!" The captain of the four-wheel-drive craft stepped on the gas.

## *THE SCENE OF THE CRIME*

SARAH Frank was on her knees by the fallen man, the baseball bat clenched firmly in her hand. Mr. Zig-Zag circled Ben Silver's prone figure in fastidious, mincing steps, paused to sniff the fallen man's rasping breath, perceived the fetid odor of approaching death.

The girl stared at the blood on her hands. Dazed by the mind-numbing experience, she did not hear the approach of the sheriff's pickup.

## *THE UTAH LAWMAN-LINEMAN*

SHERIFF Popper had been eyeballing the telephone line that was strung along the road with the electric wires. There was no obvious sign of a break, but that didn't prove much. *It could be a bad connection in a junction box, or a wire that's come loose inside the old man's house.* As he approached Ben Silver's home, he saw nothing amiss. But feeling the hairs on the back of his neck stand up, he shifted into neutral, shut off the ignition, coasted the pickup to a rolling stop under a gaunt poplar. Unbuckling the strap on his canvas holster, he eased himself out of the F150 with the stealth of an old cougar, taking care to leave the cab door slightly ajar.

As he would tell Deputies Packard and Bearcat later: "Something told me 'Don't knock on Ben's door.'" *Something* also told him not to step onto the porch, where a board might squeak under his boot. After a life of close calls, the lawman had learned to pay attention to *Something*. He crept up to a side window and peered in, realized he was looking into the parlor, directly over Ben Silver's desk. He didn't see the old man. Or anything that seemed out of the ordinary.

Until the girl rose up from behind the desk.

The sheriff was almost as startled as Sarah Frank when she saw the shadowy silhouette of a man at the window.

But not quite.

With a shriek, the girl instinctively flung the baseball bat at the glass.

Popper cursed and ducked. The curse came off quick enough, but not the duck. He saw the Louisville Slugger shatter the glass just sixty-two milliseconds before it connected with his forehead, clipped off his brand-new, county-issue flat-brimmed hat. He landed flat on his back. The hard-skulled man had taken worse hits, and was stunned for only a few seconds. When he managed to get onto a pair of wobbly legs, Popper's top priority was picking up his hat, checking the damage, returning the handsome lid to where it belonged. "Ouch!" The sheriff winced, rubbed at the place above his left eye where a lump would soon form. When the lawman took a second look through the broken window, he didn't expect to see her. As he would tell his deputies: "While I was laid out like a pole-axed mule, lookin' up at nothin' but wild blue yonder and a cloud shaped like a nineteen-forty-nine Studebaker—I heard the back door slam."

Popper proceeded to brush a few fragments of glass off his shirt. *Crazy kid—what the hell was* that *all about?* He marched around to the back of the house to find out. The girl was already out of sight. He peered at the Gap, with all its shadows and sandstone boulders and stunted trees. *It was that Sarah-what's-her-name who's staying with Marilee and that Harper bum. When I see that silly girl, I'll sure give her a good talking-to. She could've killed me with that danged baseball bat!* He returned to the scene of the near-miss, started to pick up the wooden club, but some cop instinct made him hesitate. He squatted, had a close look at the bat. There were bloody fingerprints on the wood. He drew a deep breath, yelled through the window. "Ben—you okay?"

Silence was the eloquent response.

Sheriff Popper entered by the back door, crossed through the kitchen, into the parlor, found Ben Silver on the floor by the desk. The old man's nose had been bashed flat, there was blood all over his face, and it had pooled in his eyes. Ben's left boot was on the floor by his knee. *God in heaven—*

*what's happened here?* He knelt for a closer look. The collar on Ben's white linen shirt had been ripped open, two buttons were missing. He found a light pulse under the jawbone. *Well, at least he's alive.* He yelled again. "Ben! Can you hear me?"

Astonishingly, the old man's right eye opened. The orb was looking past Ned Popper, at something the sheriff could not see. Not even if he had turned his head.

Encouraged by the anger blooming in Ben's eyeball, the sheriff grinned. "Hey, you hard-headed old bastard—I'm glad you're still with us." *What's happened here is plain as the smashed nose on your face but I got to ask the question.* "Ben—who was it that lowered the boom on you?"

Silver's mouth opened, his lungs rattled. "Hit me . . . tried to fight but . . . it don't matter . . . it's gone . . ." He made a small gurgling sound, then: "Sarah . . . Sarah Frank—she's got it."

The sheriff lost the grin. "Sarah's got *what*?"

Slowly, slowly, the anger wilted away. Ben Silver's mouth was silenced forever. His eye remained wide open, as if staring in infinite wonder at the *unseen.*

# ELEVEN

## *A DISCREET INQUIRY*

Sheriff Ned Popper put one foot on the massive slab of sandstone that served as a doorstep, rapped his knuckles on the door. *One. Two. Three.* On the count of four, he heard a clop-clopping across the hardwood floor. The white porcelain knob turned, the clop-clopper cracked the door—just enough for one of her eyes to peer through. Recognizing the face, Marilee unhooked the chain, opened the door wide. Dressed in faded jeans and a man's western-style white shirt with pearl buttons, the Papago woman clutched a wet dishrag in her hand. "Hell's bells, Ned—what happened to you?"

The lawman gingerly touched a finger to the gauze patch he had applied to the lump on his forehead. "Aw, nothin' I won't get over."

Her lips made a small *O*, which was also the next word out of her mouth. "Oh, don't need to tell me—let me guess. It's Al, ain't it? I bet he got in another fight over at the Gimpy Dog Saloon, and you had to break it up." She squeezed the dishrag until dirty water dripped on the doorsill. "Did my idiot boyfriend whack you with a beer bottle?"

"No, Al didn't whack me with no bottle."

"Has somebody killed him?" Behind the frown, there was the faintest hint of hope.

Despite the dull pain that threatened to pop off the top of his head, Ned Popper grinned. "Not so far as I know." *But if somebody did, it'd be a benefit to the community.* He looked past her into the gloomy interior of the low-rent dwelling. "If you ain't too busy, could I come in for a minute?"

"Sure you can, Ned." As she stepped aside to let the man into her small parlor, a cloud passed over Marilee's round face. "Oh, my God—is it Sarah?" She put a hand over her mouth, as if to keep the question from coming out—mumbled through her fingers. "Has she been hit by a car or somethin'?"

"No, she ain't been hit by no car." Without waiting for an invitation to sit, the sheriff eased his lean frame onto a hideous green couch. He removed his hat, turned it in his hands. "I understand you took Ben Silver over to the clinic this morning."

*Oh, then it's Ben.* Relieved, Marilee plopped into a chair. "Yeah, I did. But we was only there for a few minutes. All the doctors was put on emergency call because of that pileup on the interstate." Trying to look like she cared, she asked the obvious question. "Has something happened to Ben?" *I bet he's died from pure orneriness.*

The sheriff's eyes narrowed as he picked a clinging skunkweed burr off his knee. "When you took Ben home, did he seem to be all right?"

Unnerved by the grim look on Ned Popper's weather-worn face, Marilee nodded. "Sure he was."

The lawman put the burr into a blue glass ashtray. "When you dropped him off at his house, did you notice whether there was anybody else around?"

Marilee looked at the dishrag in her hands. "I didn't exactly take him to his front door." Feeling more than a little foolish, the Papago woman proceeded to explain how she and Ben had had "some words," how she had "let him off a ways down the lane from his house." Having completed this highly sanitized account of the confrontation, she said: "What's happened to Ben, Sheriff? Was that long walk too much for that old man—did he have a heart attack or somethin'?"

Ned Popper was staring down the dark hallway. "Does Sarah still do chores for Ben?"

Beginning to feel miffed that her questions were so pointedly ignored, she nodded.

*She's about to clam up on me.* "Look, Marilee—I have to ask you these questions—that's what I get paid to do. But at the moment, it wouldn't be proper for me to tell you why." He leaned forward, looked her straight in the eye. "You understand what I'm saying?"

"Yeah. I guess so." She exhaled a great sigh, got up from her chair. "I'll do whatever I can to help you."

The sheriff made another probe. "If Sarah went over to see Ben this morning, maybe she could help me some."

Having surrendered, Marilee waved the dishrag like a white flag. "No, she didn't. My little cousin always tells me when she's goin' over to Ben's place. And besides, she knew I was hauling him to the clinic for his doctor's appointment." Seeing his oddly blank stare, she explained: "There wouldn't be any good reason for Sarah to go over to Ben's house when she knew he wouldn't be at home—now would there?"

"No, I guess not." *No* good *reason.*

She followed his second glance at the hallway. "I don't know where she is—out prowling around somewhere with that cat, I expect."

"Well, thank you, Marilee. I guess I'd best be getting along." Popper got to his feet, felt a sudden throbbing where the baseball bat had raised a purple lump. He closed his eyes until the pain subsided, then headed toward the front door. He put on his hat, reached for the doorknob, then—as if it was an afterthought: "Where does the girl sleep?"

"She's got a little room in the back." Marilee arched a thickly penciled eyebrow. "Why?"

The lawman hesitated. "Well, Sarah's a quiet child. She might've come in the back door while we was talking. Maybe she's back there reading a comic book."

"Sarah don't read comic books."

"When I was a kid, I read *Superman.* And *Little Lulu,* cover to cover."

Marilee smirked at the old geezer. "An' I bet your family didn't even have a TV."

"Matter of fact, they didn't." Popper removed his hat, put on his most amiable smile. "Before I go, let's make sure Sarah's not in her room." He reached in his pocket, consulted a gold-plated Hamilton pocket watch. "If I could have a couple of words with the girl, it would save me another trip back here." *But in thirty minutes flat, I'll have a warrant to search this house from one end to the other.*

Marilee shrugged. "She ain't here, but come and see for yourself."

He followed her down the hall.

The former pantry was barely able to accommodate a small cot, a pink chest of drawers that looked more like a cardboard toy than proper furniture.

The woman stared. "Well—that's funny."

Pretending to be barely interested, the sheriff did not ask what was funny. He knew Marilee would tell him.

She did. "Just look at that—her schoolbooks are stacked up on the chest. She always keeps her books in her backpack. But her backpack's gone." Marilee began to open drawers. "Well, I just don't believe this."

"What's that, Marilee?"

"Some of her clothes are gone!" Seeing the lawman's blush, she set her jaw, made a fist. "Ned Popper, if you don't want another lump on your gourd-head, you'd better tell me *right now*—what's happened to Sarah?"

The sheriff tried to shrug off her belligerent stare.

The woman held her breath until she thought she might faint. "Do you think Sarah has run away from home?"

Nodding at the stack of abandoned schoolbooks, he said: "Kinda looks like it, Marilee." He waited for her to say it.

She did. "Then you've got to find her!"

*It's times like this I hate this damn job.* Ned Popper cleared his throat. "Have you got a picture of the kid—one you could loan me for a couple a days?"

# TWELVE

## *TO FLY AWAY*

SARAH Frank ran through Hatchet Gap like a wild-eyed deer, numb with fear, often stumbling, sometimes falling, but never, ever looking back.

Delighted to participate in such exhilarating sport, Mr. Zig-Zag began by trotting along at her heels; as she slowed, he chose to lead the race.

The skinny girl dared not imagine who might be behind her, but always before her—as if etched on her retinas—was the bloody image of Mr. Silver's face. As a chill wind whipped her skirt, it seemed as if she might never emerge from the dismal fissure in the Big Lizard's spine. When Sarah caught sight of a dazzle of daylight, and saw the slender thread of paved highway neatly dividing the settlement of Tonapah Flats, she fell against a piñon snag, gasped for half-strangled breaths, felt the hurtful hammering in her chest.

*My heart's going to stop.*

From somewhere above her, came the raucous caw-caw of an impertinent raven.

*I'm going to fall over on the ground and die.*

Sarah Frank imagined that stray dogs and gaunt coyotes would gnaw the flesh off her bones; sand beetles and grub worms would consume what was left. She closed her eyes, waited for that little *window* to open in the darkness. On those occasions when it presented itself, the rectangular opening provided her with a view of tomorrow; but she expected no tomorrows. This time, she believed, it would give her a glimpse of the other side. She might see Mommy and Daddy; hoped they would not be angry with her.

What Sarah saw was Nothing. It seemed as if she was about to slip away into its infinite embrace. Indeed, Darkness reached out to touch her, hold her, enfold her—smother out the flickering flame of life, gather her into that endless gloom . . .

*But through the window, a tiny wriggling speck of light—some bright thing swimming in the night? It grew, unfolded, blossomed. Rainbow colors. Coming closer. It was a fish. Not a very large fish. But in the flicker of a silken fin, it swallowed up the vast ocean of Nothing.*

The girl-child's morbid premonition had been somewhat premature.

The black-and-white cat adjusted his miniature motor to medium-purr, rubbed a furry shoulder against her leg.

This optimistic statement had a remarkably soothing effect on the recipient of the gift. Sarah's breaths and heartbeats began to slow. The realization was startling: *I'm not going to die.* She pushed fingertips against her temples, tried to press away the fear. *But I can't just stand here—I've got to work out a plan.* When she opened her eyes, the first thing they focused on was something still far away—a pickup parked in front of her cousin's home. It was Sheriff Popper's truck. *I'd better find a place for me and Mr. Zig-Zag to hide.*

Minutes later, she had retrieved her concealed backpack, was hurrying along the rocky bottom of the Little Sandy. Though the midday sun was on her back and the day was warm, the girl could not stop shivering. With an unnerving suddenness, her knees became so wobbly that it seemed her frail legs might finally fail her. Sarah found a shady spot under a thick stand of sickly willows, and crouched there to rest. It was abundantly clear that Mr. Zig-Zag did not realize the gravity of the situation—he took the opportunity to chase after a yellow butterfly. After the aged cat had given up the hunt, she had a finger-shaking, face-to-face encounter with her pet, explained the hard facts of life. Her dire warnings terminated thusly: "... so you've got to be very, very careful, or we'll both end up dead!" The animal seemed to be appropriately sobered by the stern words, but perhaps he was merely running out of steam.

Sarah shared a portion of her food with her companion, then curled up with the cat clutched close to her chest. The hours passed ever so slowly. Nervous little naps came and went with puffy gusts of dust-laden wind. When she finally opened her eyes to see the sun settling onto a pinkish-blue horizon, the girl abandoned her hiding place. She resumed her walk along the dry wash; the cat—quite contented with his unpredictable life—ambled along behind. As the serpentine dry stream made a loop toward the rear side of the Dairy Queen, the girl who had felled the sheriff climbed the bank of the Little Sandy, crossed a trash-strewn alley, approached the building with the wary instinct of a hunted fox. Passing through clusters of tumbleweed, she concealed herself behind an odorous green Dumpster.

A Chevy low-rider parked out front of the Dairy Queen thump-thumped with vulgar gangster-rap. Merle Haggard's lonesome wail floated up from a rusty old pickup.

Fat black flies buzzed around Sarah's head, a horrid mix of stale-food smells made her stomach churn. Leaving the concealment provided by the Dumpster, she slipped along in the eastern shadows of the cinder block structure, gazed across the highway at the Greyhound bus station, which was a small, square building between the Pancho's Cantina and the Pizza Hut. A Trailways bus was puffing black diesel smoke. A uniformed driver was loading large cardboard boxes in a luggage compartment. Best of all, the destination sign over the front window said DENVER! *This is our chance.* She reached for the cat.

But wait—pulling up slowly through the easterly shadow of the big bus, was a low-slung black-and-white sedan. As it came into the light, Sarah could see Tate Packard's face behind the steering wheel. When he seemed to look directly at the spot where she was standing, Sarah's heart almost stopped. But the deputy evidently did not spot the terrified runaway. He was responding to a call on his radio, and in lulls between the roar of passing cars and trucks, Sarah could make out a few words.

"Roger that dispatch . . . no sign of . . . setting up a roadblock . . ."

There was a whuff-whuffing as an owl passed overhead. Sarah looked up at the gathering twilight, wished very hard. *If I had wings, I would fly away to some secret place where nobody could ever hurt me or Mr. Zig-Zag.* She closed her eyes, hoped, wished ever so hard—but the power of flight was denied her. Having had many bitter disappointments, she was not surprised. The fugitive retreated back into the dry wash, away from the noisome rush of motorized society. As she plodded along toward the darkening horizon, a pale yellow moon cast Sarah's crisp shadow on the sands. It suddenly occurred to the girl that she was not real. *I am a shadow. If the moon goes behind a cloud . . . I'll fade away and be nothing.* She would have been quite satisfied to enter a state of nonbeing.

But there was no cloud for the moon to go behind.

And so, the shadow-girl kept putting one foot in front of the other. The dry wash was wider now, and there was more sand than rocks.

Not far ahead, she saw a pickup throw up a cloud of alkali dust as it crossed her path. Sarah knew that was Tulane Road, a gravel lane that intersected the paved highway at the Shamrock gas station. Instantly, she had an idea, and thought it only right to share it with Mr. Zig-Zag. She scooped up the aged cat, whispered into his ear. "I know a good place where we can stay for a little while."

The whisper tickled his ear, which reflexively flattened against his head.

She didn't put the animal down until they were at the culvert under the road. She knew that during flash floods, the big concrete pipe would fill with a roaring torrent of muddy water. *I hope it don't rain tonight.* The girl scanned the darkening sky, saw a few stars prickling through the fabric of night. She crouched, made her way halfway along the circular cement hallway, laid her thin body down in a pile of brush and trash, made up her mind to stay wide awake. As she immediately drifted off to a light sleep, Sarah's mind shifted to dark thoughts. *Maybe I won't ever wake up. Maybe there will be a big storm upstream, and the water will come roaring down here and carry me away to another . . .*

When she did awaken, Mr. Zig-Zag was mewing, licking her nose with his sandpaper tongue. Having no timepiece, Sarah did not know that it was well past midnight, but at the end of the gray tunnel she could see bright moonlight. *I must have slept a long time.* She got up, brushed leaves and dirt off her skirt.

After a short walk on Tulane Road, she cut off behind the Shamrock station, stubbed her toe on something she could not see. The moon passed behind a thundercloud, casting the back of the gas station into inky darkness, but the business side was lit up like noonday. At this small hour, there was a single vehicle at the pumps—a massive green pickup, with an equally green horse trailer attached. Sarah took a deep breath, summoned up all her courage. She emerged from the shadows, pretended to be interested in the Coke machine. The big, rough-looking man who owned the green pickup was pushing a credit card into a slot, selecting 87 octane, mumbling that "the damn gas prices just keep goin' up and up." His plump wife was headed for the ladies' room, calling back: "Now, Buddy, don't you drive off and leave me, like you did up in Reno last week when you thought I was in the backseat asleep!"

Busy grumbling about money-grubbing Arabs and big-oil price gougers, Buddy gave no sign that he'd heard a single word his helpmate had said. Which was his normal mode of behavior.

Sarah noted that the pickup was pointed toward the interstate. Once it got there, it could turn either east or west, which was a chance she was willing to take. But she had noticed the Colorado license plate on the pickup—and a little chrome logo on the tailgate proclaimed that the vehicle had been purchased from the La Plata Ford Dealership in Durango. Besides that, this man and his wife had been in Reno last week. And Sarah—who loved to study maps—knew that Reno was in Nevada, and Nevada was to the west of Utah. So they must be going east, back to Colorado—probably to someplace not far from Durango, and that town was very near the Southern Ute reservation. And aside from her knowledge of geography, the runaway felt certain these weary-looking people were going home. Despite her few hours of sleep, Sarah was still very weary, and if she had a home, that was certainly where she would go. And stay there forever and ever.

While the gas was flowing into the pickup tank, Buddy went into the station to purchase candy bars and beef jerky.

Sarah picked up her cat, approached a few steps closer.

A fierce-looking black horse with a white star on her forehead was looking out of the trailer. She eyed Sarah and her cat, as if to say, *I know what you're up to. You'll never find a place where you can hide. They'll find you and put a rope around your neck and hang you on a tree limb while you choke and kick. That's what they'll do. And if you try to get in here with me, I'll stomp you to death.*

That is what Sarah imagined the horse would say, if horses could talk. But she was beyond being afraid of the big mare. After what she had been through during the past few hours, she was not afraid of anything—except getting caught by the police. In the glare of ten kilowatts of overhead lights, she walked up to the rear of the horse trailer and looked the sole occupant straight in the eye. "Me and Mr. Zig-Zag are getting in there with you. And if you step on me—or hurt my cat," she made a small fist and showed it to the placid beast, "I'll punch you right in the eye!"

The mare—who adored children and cats—responded with a friendly whinny.

# THIRTEEN

## *THE FED*

FBI Special Agent Lila Mae McTeague parked her car in the reserved space the Bureau had leased from the Cattleman's Bank, opened the rear door to the narrow stairwell, clicked her heels up the twenty-four steps, entered the long hallway, counted off five paces to her corner office door. The recently installed electronic combination lock displayed three light-emitting diodes, all in a row. If during her absence the dial had been turned as much as six degrees in either direction, the orange light would be on. If the microwave motion detector inside the office had been tripped, a red light would be flashing. The high-tech lock was showing a comforting green; all was well. She twirled the dial four times to enter the combination, pressed the black button at the hub, turned the shiny brass doorknob, entered her two hundred square feet of work space. The time was precisely seven A.M.

McTeague was one of the federal government's most dedicated and efficient employees. Within minutes, she had called the Durango field office to notify a computer of her arrival in the "temporary" Granite Creek office, made a pot of coffee, checked sixteen e-mails, trashed all but three. At half past the hour, she logged onto the Bureau's official site, typed in her password, clicked on the DAILY CRIME REPORT icon. When the window opened, she went to the Region menu, clicked on Southwest. The first report was on last night's Indian casino robbery just north of Santa Fe. The second described a kidnapping of a woman in Flagstaff. McTeague had heard reports on the ten o'clock news, and gave the briefings a quick scan. It was the third report that piqued her interest.

DEPT OF JUSTICE RKK 2006/6-21/99803AADC

PRELIM RPT 2:22 AM EDT—TO BE UPDATED THIS PM

PAGE 1 OF 2 PAGES

HOMICIDE/ASSAULT/BURGLARY

TONAPAH FLATS, UT

JURISDICTION: TONAPAH FLATS SHERIFF'S OFFICE

CONTACT: SHERIFF NED POPPER [SEE CONTACT INFO P 2]

VICTIM/Homicide: BENJAMIN SILVER/ WH MALE/ AGE 74

(NO PHOTO/NO SS)

VICTIM/ASSAULT: NED POPPER/ WH MALE/ AGE 67

(NO PHOTO/NO SS)

SUSPECT: SARAH FRANK

FEMALE NAT AMERICAN/ S-UTE/PAPAGO[TOHONO O'OTAM]

[JUV]/AGE 14

(NO PHOTO/NO SS/NO PRINTS)

APPARENT MOTIVE: TO BE DETERMINED

SUSPECT'S CURRENT LOCATION: UNKNOWN

SUSPECT LAST SEEN: TONAPAH FLATS UT/SILVER RESIDENCE

SUSPECT RELATIVES:

FATHER: PROVO FRANK [S UTE/DECEASED]

MOTHER: MARY [MN: ATTATOCHEE] FRANK [PAPAGO/DECEASED]

SIBLINGS: NONE

GRANDPARENTS: NO INFO

COUSIN: MARILEE ATTATOCHEE/FEMALE NAT AMERICAN/

PAPAGO[TOHONO O'OTAM]/ TONAPAH FLATS UT

SUSPECT FRIENDS: NO INFO

SUSPECT CONTACTS: JUV S FRANK HAS BEEN LIVING WITH

MARILEE ATTATOCHEE (SEE RELATIVES—ABOVE)

McTeague scanned the second page, then read the terse report two more times, hoping to glean something beyond the sparse information contained in the few words. *There is something familiar about the father's name.* She selected the DEPT JUSTICE Database menu, clicked on General Search, typed PROVO FRANK into the SEARCH rectangle, watched a miniature hourglass fill with electronic sand. The file, including color images, was 155 megabytes. She transferred it to her hard disc. *I'll read it later. What I want to know right now is . . .* She typed in CHARLES MOON, initiated the document search. More sand sifting through the hourglass, then—*Bingo!*

The FBI agent downloaded several other confidential files, made a call to a talkative contact in the Bureau's Salt Lake office, another to the Tonapah Flats Sheriff's Office. After this flurry of early morning activity, the lady sat behind her desk, mulling over what she had learned. There was a final call to make. She hesitated.

• • •

WHEN the telephone interrupted his morning routine, Charlie Moon was washing his breakfast dishes, singing "Good Morning, Sun" loudly and slightly off-key. He strode down the hall, into the parlor, picked up the instrument on the third ring. "Columbine Ranch." The voice that vibrated the membrane in his right ear canal made him smile.

"Charlie, I'm sorry to call so early, but I picked up something in the Bureau's Daily Crime Report that might interest you."

He leaned against the chinked-log wall. "Aside from cattle rustling, why would I be interested in crime?"

"Well, for one thing—your name popped up."

"Whatever it is, I didn't do it. And even if I did, I've got a dozen hired hands that'll swear I was playing straight poker with all fifteen of 'em when it—"

"Shut up and listen."

"When you sweet-talk me like that, I can't help but do whatever you say."

Agent McTeague read the report verbatim. After completing the recitation, she waited. Nothing.

The Ute was gazing through the parlor window. All the joy of the morning had slipped away. *I should have kept in touch with Provo's little daughter. Made sure she was all right. How many years has it been since I last saw her—*

"Charlie—are you there?"

"I am." He wished he were not.

"When I saw the father's name, I realize you were acquainted with him."

"Provo Frank was my close friend." The Ute sounded older than his years.

"I see." *That wasn't in the file.* "And his daughter Sarah—I assume you must have met her."

He nodded at the woman who was some forty-odd miles away in Granite Creek. "Yeah."

From the leaden tone, McTeague knew the answer to her next question. "I suppose you'll be going to Tonapah Flats."

"That's right."

"Mind if I come along?"

"I don't mind," Moon mumbled.

The highly organized federal employee checked the time, estimated how quickly she could shut down the computer, lock the file cabinet and hall door, get to her Ford sedan. "I'll be there in fifty-five minutes. An hour at the outside."

"Don't break any speed limits, McTeague." *There's no big hurry. Whatever Sarah's done is history.* Charlie Moon hung up the telephone, hung his head, stared at the varnished oak floor as if he had never seen it before. The long-legged man cocked his right boot. His earnest intention was to kick a wicker trash basket across the parlor. He hesitated. *That would be a dumb thing to do. And I don't want to start off the day by doing something dumb.* He kicked it. Hard.

• • •

CHARLIE Moon called his elderly aunt. Told Daisy Perika where he was headed. And why.

As her nephew unloaded his bad news, the tribal elder listened with uncharacteristic patience. *I knew it. Sarah has killed that old man.* Making no reference to her series of bad dreams, Daisy muttered: "Soon as you know something, call me."

• • •

THOSE privileged few who are accustomed to riding in the comfort of a luxury automobile, such as a Rolls-Royce Silver Seraph or Mercedes-Benz SL65 AMG, may be interested to know that designers of horse trailers do not invest excessive attention to the issue of suspension. Indeed, these conveyances are apt to bounce and buck like some of the more spirited equine stock transported therein. Furthermore, the interiors tend to smell a certain way, and it is not like the sweet essence of wild roses in late May, but more like the terminal end of a herbivorous quadruped which processes hay—despite the fact that horse trailers are usually well ventilated. This is relevant, because the early morning hours of Sarah Frank's journey were bitterly cold. It was the most awful ride she had ever had in her life. When the green pickup finally pulled to a stop, the girl was very angry at having been so abused for so many hours. Sarah also harbored serious doubts that she would ever be able to walk again, but using the horse's tail for assistance, she got up onto stiff legs, made her way to the rear of the stinky trailer, unlatched the double gate. She paused only long enough to address the host passenger. "I'm sorry for saying I'd punch you in the eye. I didn't really mean it. It's just that . . ." She sighed. "Well, yesterday was a *really* bad day for me." She patted the mare's neck. "Good-bye." *I wish you were my horse.*

As she latched the steel gate, the owner of the pickup and trailer and horse happened by. Maintaining his customary form of speech, Mr. Bigbee yelled, "Hey, Half-Pint! What're you doin' there—messin' around with my livestock?"

Since yesterday morning, Sarah was a changed girl. Bold

as a week-old colt, she gazed brazenly at the big rancher, pointed at the black mare. "Is she for sale?"

Lapsing into a thoughtful silence, he gave the unlikely buyer a cursory once-over. "She might be—for the right price." The rough old horse trader snorted. "How much you got in your sock?"

Sarah heard her mouth say: "You mean money?"

"No, kid—I mean pop-bottle caps." He grinned at her puzzled expression. "A-course I mean money. So how much *diñero* d'you want to spend on a bronc?"

The girl in the tattered dress smiled hopefully. "Would five hundred dollars be enough?"

*Like you got five hundred bucks.* "Not while there's a breath a life in my body, Small-Fry." He jerked his chin to indicate the animal under discussion. "I would not even think a lettin' go a this fine piece a horseflesh for a dime less than . . ." He scratched at the stubble of two-day-old beard. "Than twelve hundred."

Sarah's voice was hoarse. "Twelve hundred *dollars*?"

"No, Missy. Twelve hundred *porky-pine ears.*" Highly amused with his inimitable wit, "Buddy" Hank Bigbee leaned backward like a willow in a hard wind, let out a bray-ish "Haw-haw-haw." Straightening his spine, he glared at the girl. "Tell you what. You throw in that fleabag of a cat, I'll knock off—maybe thirty-two cents from the price." Another string of haw-haws. He also slapped his thigh, and tears rolled down his leathery cheeks.

The girl's dark eyes flashed. "Mr. Zig-Zag don't have any fleas!"

He regained just enough composure to reply: "Zig-Zag, huh? That's a funny name for a cat."

Sarah was about to offer a response when Mrs. Bigbee showed up. The woman gave her husband The Look, which took all the wind out of his sails. "Buddy, are you teasin' this sweet little girl?" The Look made it clear that he damn well better not be doing no such thing.

The sly look slipped off Buddy's face and down his collar. "Oh no, Sugar-Cake—I was just trying to close a deal."

He cleared his throat, pointed a wiener-sized finger at Sarah Frank. "Tillie, this kid wants to buy Clara Belle."

Tillie Bigbee shook her head at Sarah. "No you don't, honey. That black mare is blind in her left eye and she's had a bad stomach ever since she et a little piece a bob-war that was in a bale a hay." She shot a poisonous glance at her husband. "In fact, if'n Buddy here was to offer you a brand-new twenty-dollar bill to take Clara-B off'n his hands, you should laugh in his face." To demonstrate how, Tillie "ha-ha'd" him a good one, then turned a motherly smile on the child. "What d'you want with a dumb ol' horse anyway, sweetie? All they do is chomp hay and make manure and run up vet'nary bills."

"I could ride her."

*What a little darlin'*. "Ride her where?"

Sarah hugged Mr. Zig-Zag closer to her chest. "Where are we now?"

The middle-aged couple stared at the enigmatic girl.

"I mean, what town?"

The kindly woman frowned. "Why, we're in Cortez." Tillie added: "That's in Colorado."

Knowing quite well where Cortez was, Sarah did a quick mental calculation. "I could ride Clara Belle all the way to Aunt Daisy's home." She estimated that it would take three days, maybe four.

Tillie Bigbee found her smile again. "And where does your auntie live?"

The runaway realized she had made a tactical blunder. "Oh, off that way." She pointed to where the sun was coming up.

*Poor little thing.* "Well, you find yourself a good horse that can see outta both eyes. And don't you ever buy nothin' that walks from my husband—Buddy'd cheat his own mother in a horse trade, if she was still alive and had two dollars in her apron pocket." Her Christian duty done, Tillie grabbed her man by the shirtsleeve. "C'mon, let's go get some breakfast before I faint from hunger and fall back in it."

Much saddened, Sarah watched them go. *I would have*

*been glad to give five hundred dollars for Clara Belle, even if she don't see too well. I could've rode her all the way to Aunt Daisy's trailer-home and then into Spirit Canyon and up the trail onto Three Sisters Mesa . . .* Her thoughts drifted back to a splendid world that had been filled to the brim with happy times.

# FOURTEEN

## *THE JOURNEY*

FOR the past hundred miles, Charlie Moon and Lila Mae McTeague had not exchanged a word. Time seemed to have stalled somewhere along the way, but of course it had not—the cosmic clock had not ceased to tick and tock, and the rocky third planet continued its ponderous spin—presenting that most compelling illusion of the sun sailing serenely across the pale blue sea of heaven. Having peaked at an infinitesimally brief high-noon appearance, the neighborhood star had fallen into that inevitable decline which is the destiny of even celestial luminaries. Aside from following the golden disk on its illusory westerly course, the Columbine Expedition did not participate in the deception. This solid chunk of reality had been assembled by skilled United Auto Workers at the sprawling, noisy plant in Wayne, Michigan. Driven by the silent Ute, powered by a throbbing eight-cylinder internal combustion engine, it rolled along on a hot ribbon of asphalt.

Seeing a particular mile marker flash past, the FBI agent consulted her map, shattered the brittle silence. "Take the next exit."

The tribal investigator slowed, eased the automobile off the interstate onto a two-lane blacktop that bubbled and steamed in the midday sun. Moon's mind was occupied with thoughts of Provo Frank's daughter. *Sarah has gotten herself into some deep trouble. I hope I can do something to help. But how do you help someone who beats an old man to death with a baseball bat, assaults the sheriff—and then makes a run for it?* Life was an enigma wrapped in a mystery, and like those Greeks who came to see Jesus, the Ute was seeking wisdom.

Being of a more Semitic disposition, McTeague was looking for a sign.

Behold—one appeared at the side of the road. Though perforated with sixteen rusty-ringed bullet holes, the mangled steel rectangle had obstinately refused to die; it clung to the post by a single bolt. Having persevered to do its duty, it did—informing the passing motorists that Tonapah Flats was 6 MI down the road. Presently, there was a second, home-brew sign, presumably provided by a local with tendencies toward paleontological humor:

**CAUTION!**

Carcharodontosaurus Crossing

"The reference is to a North African carnosaur of the Cretaceous period," McTeague said. "Which was about a hundred million years ago." She flicked a glance at the driver. "If you would you like to know more, I will be happy to oblige."

No response.

She was happy to oblige anyway. "The Carcharodontosaurus had a head the size of a kitchen refrigerator, a massive tail for knocking enemies about, short arms with three-fingered hands. These fingers came equipped with extremely sharp claws." The lady examined an immaculately manicured array of lethal-looking fingernails. "Momma Carcharodontosaurus used these claws to rip the eyes out of moody male acquaintances who refused to carry on a civil conversation."

This would normally have produced a smile, but it was one of those rare days when Charlie Moon's mind—

troubled as it was by guilt and regret—was fairly afire with sinister images. Right on cue, Nature provided fuel, and fanned the flames. As the breeze pushed aside a curtain of low-hanging clouds, a sinuous torso appeared on the sandy flatlands. Its knobby spine was armored with jagged plates, the wrinkled gray hide bristled with thick, close-cropped hair. It appeared to be the fossilized corpse of a miles-long reptile. Moreover, the stone beast was split neatly in half—as if an angry giant had laid a mammoth cleaver onto its back. As they drew closer, it became apparent that the plates were merely extruded basaltic flow, the "hair" stunted juniper, thirsty scrub oak, and other such hardy flora as manage to survive in arid wastelands.

Though not without an interest in local geography, McTeague was focused on more recent additions to the topography. Such as a pauper's collection of shabby, sad-faced homes scattered along the two-lane. "Tonapah Flats," she muttered, and indulged herself in a delicious stretch. "We have arrived."

The driver took note of a 35MPH sign, slowed to the legal limit. *No point in getting a ticket right off*. "Now to find the sheriff's office."

"It's on the right." She pointed a pointy fingernail that glistened with Crimson Passion. "About two hundred yards past the Stop-and-Shop, and if you get to the Oates' Supermarket you have—and here I quote: 'done passed it.' "

He frowned at the Stop-and-Shop. "You called ahead for directions?"

"Certainly. While on my way to the Columbine, I spoke with a deputy who calls himself Bearcat. The name on his driver's license is Leland Redstone. In case you're interested, he happens to be a Choctaw from Chickasha. I refer to the Chickasha in Oklahoma."

"This Utah cop told you all that?"

"Some men like to talk to me." She flashed a splendid smile at the Ute. "But to be perfectly honest, prior to shutting my computer down I pulled up some Bureau data on the Tonapah Flats sheriff's office."

"Must be nice to have access to FBI files. While you were snooping around on your computer, I bet you found out what's the best restaurant in this burg."

"The Bureau does not keep data of the culinary sort. But Deputy Bearcat informed me that it's a toss-up between the Thunder Woman Café and the Gimpy Dog Saloon. But he said stay away from Dinty's Grill."

"Know what I don't think?"

"Of course I do, Charlie. But if it would make you feel better, tell me."

"I don't think you called the sheriff's office, or talked to a Choctaw who calls himself Bearcat—you're making all that stuff up. Just to see how gullible I am."

"Don't think whatever you wish." The stunningly attractive FBI agent put on a saucy little smirk, touched it up with just a hint of Crimson Passion lipstick. "Anyway, I already know how gullible you are." She dropped the waxy cosmetic back into a black leather purse, where it found a cozy hideaway with her 9-mm Glock automatic and such other necessities as a working woman must carry with her when she is out and about her business. "And I won't mention that unlike a part-time lawman I will not name, we full-time professionals prefer to know precisely where we are going—and what we are going to do when we get there." *That ought to make him smile.*

It did not.

The tribal investigator estimated they would be there in about a minute, but he had no idea what he would do when he arrived. *Except stand there like a fence post, listen to this Utah sheriff roll out nine yards of serious bad news.* He stifled a sigh. *Well, at least I'll find out if they've picked up Sarah during the past few hours. Ask to talk to her if they have. Make sure she's got a first-class lawyer. And then, I'll give Aunt Daisy a telephone call—let her know what's—* These dismal thoughts were interrupted by a siren's keening wail, the urgent flashing of red-and-blue emergency lights. Both were emanating from an oncoming, low-slung automobile that was growing larger at twice the posted speed limit.

Moon slowed, pulled toward the edge of the highway. "It's thoughtful of the sheriff to send somebody to meet and greet us."

The oncoming unit screeched almost to a halt, skidded across the lane barely twenty yards away, came to a lurching stop in front of an establishment whose sign proclaimed it to be the Gimpy Dog Saloon.

"Probably taking his lunch break," Moon said.

A muscular man in a khaki uniform emerged from the vehicle, popped a tan Smokey hat onto his burr-cut head, checked his holstered sidearm, assumed the determined look of an *hombre* who has come to conduct some important business. He barged through the swinging doors and into the sour-smelling bowels of the Gimpy Dog.

Her brow furrowed, McTeague thought: *This could be just the diversion Charlie needs.* She offered the opinion that perhaps they should provide some assistance.

The tribal investigator shook his head. "That hardcase cop don't need any help. If you want to assist somebody, go lend a hand to the poor devil he's come to butt heads with."

She glanced at her partner. "Do you intend to just sit here?"

"Nope. I intend to put Mr. Ford's machine in gear and motivate right on down to the sheriff's office."

"Then I'll have to go in the saloon by myself."

Moon stared at the woman. *She's got to be kidding.*

McTeague got out of the car.

*She's bluffing.*

She slammed the door. Hard.

*The woman can't fool me. She's double-bluffing.*

McTeague marched off toward the Gimpy Dog. When she heard the Ute's boots crunching gravel, the fed allowed herself a fleeting smile. She cast a haughty look over her shoulder. "So—you've decided to back me up?"

"My momma didn't raise no fools." In three long strides, Moon was at her side. "But if you're going to create some havoc, I intend to have me a ringside seat."

As the tall man passed her by, McTeague hurried to catch up.

Upon entering the dimly illuminated space, the first thing they noticed through the smoke and artificial twilight was the husky deputy. From the BEARCAT tag on the lawman's shirt, it was apparent that this was the Choctaw deputy from Chickasha.

Moon sized him up as about six feet, two-hundred and eighty pounds, maybe one ounce of that fat. *This cop's a real woolly-booger—not a fella I'd want to get into a rasslin' match with.* He muttered to McTeague: "It don't look like he'll need your assistance."

The lady could not disagree, but she had no particular interest in the deputy or his duties. *Charlie is already enjoying this.*

Having come to play the only game in town, the two-yard-high, yard-wide Choctaw had drawn a pair of jokers. What he confronted was a red-faced, middle-aged man outfitted from the top down in a battered Golden Gate cowboy hat, green felt shirt, faded Levi jeans, scuffed Roper boots. The second party was a highly agitated blond woman whose tattooed biceps bulged from daily workouts with twelve-pound dumbbells. Miss Uncongeniality came equipped with form-fitting orange slacks, a fire-engine-red blouse, and a temper to match.

The local lawman had his palms raised in what was intended to be a calming gesture. The big man's bullfrog voice was calm as a Mississippi bayou on one of those days when not a breeze stirs. "Bettie Jean—Cowboy—I want botha you to calm down. And tell me what's goin' on here."

Hurricane Bettie Jean was not in a mood to be calmed. Her intentions were more along the line of aggravated manslaughter and feeding entrails and other leftovers to the hogs. And Cowboy Roy—the derisive nickname had been hung on the unfortunate fellow because he was deathly afraid of cattle—was the very man she intended to slaughter and disembowel. She shrieked her accusation—pointing at the sheepish-looking fellow. "That no-good bastard jerked it right offa my neck."

Moon had found a table with an excellent view of the floor show.

McTeague (with feigned reluctance) took a chair beside him.

Bettie Jean continued to shriek: "And then he stuffed it inta his shirt!"

Imitating a black woolly worm about to pounce on whatever black woolly worms pounce on, the burly constable's left eyebrow arched. "Stuffed *what* in his shirt?"

Bettie Jean screamed a spray of spittle. "What do you think—my squash-blossom necklace, o'course."

Turning on an invisible neck, Bearcat's pumpkin-shaped head rotated over the buffalo shoulders. He fixed his eyes on the counterfeit cowboy. "Izzat right?"

"So what if I did?" Roy vainly attempted to puff up his twenty-six-inch chest. "By rights, it's my proppity."

"That's a dirty rotten bald-faced lie—it is *not* yours!" Bettie J. clenched her hands into fists, shook both of them in Roy's face. "You gave me that squash blossom last year on Valentine's Day."

"Well, I'm takin' it back." Roy regarded the deputy with one of those man-to-man looks that expects understanding from the brotherly gender. "I had to, Bearcat. See, my little wifey found out about me givin' a Valentine present to Bettie Jean, and I said Baby it was just for old times' sake and wifey she says Cowboy if you don't get that necklace and bring it home to me before dark, I'm goin' to kick your butt up between your shoulders and put scorpions in your boots and poison your food so you die a horrible death, and after that I'll make your life sheer hell." The man who feared large livestock and his little wifey paused to take a breath. "And you know my old woman'll do exactly what she says." Roy set his jaw. "Besides, I laid down my own hard-earned cash for that joolrey at Coyote Joe's Pawn Shop down in Gallup, and that makes it mine." He patted a lump in his shirt, which clanked exactly like silver joolrey.

The deputy turned his head another ten degrees, addressed a bald, bespectacled bartender who was, quite sensibly, keeping the Gimpy Dog bar firmly between himself and the combatants. "Mike, did you see what went down?"

"Not all of it. I heard some yellin', then I saw Cowboy jerk that necklace offa Bettie Jean's neck." Mike shrugged. "I woulda just let it ride, but when she whipped out that big knife and made a slice at Roy, and he grabbed a beer bottle and told her to back off or he'd knock her head alla way down into her gullet, I thought I oughta call 911." He used his snow-white apron to polish a shot glass. "I wasn't sure who'd kill who, Bearcat—it was a kind of Mexican standoff 'til you showed up."

The deputy's head reverse-swiveled on the unseen axis. He offered the blonde a look of mild disapproval. "You pull a knife on Cowboy?"

"Damn right I did." She gave the bartender a poisonous look. "And if Mealy-Mouth Mike hadn't a called the law, I'd a used it too!"

"What'd you do with the weapon?"

Bettie Jean thought this was none of his business, but under the deputy's hard stare, she finally murmured: "It's in my purse."

"Gimmee the knife." Bearcat put a meaty palm out for the offering.

The outraged woman regarded the Choctaw as if he had asked for her to render up an embroidered undergarment. "I certainly will *not*." She explained: "My momma gave me that knife on my sixteenth birthday."

Not being the sort of lawman who messes around, Bearcat took a step forward, snatched the woman's purse off a table.

Bettie Jean screamed. "You leave that alone!"

The deputy fumbled through the thing, produced a folding Buck knife with a five-inch blade. "That's a concealed weapon." Not being a stickler about rules of evidence, the deputy dropped the exhibit into his jacket pocket.

Blondie addressed a plea to her boyfriend. "Roy, don't let him steal my knife what my momma gave me!"

Cowboy Roy still had the beer bottle in his hand, and he

knew just what to do with it. And because it was cows and such that he was afraid of—not sheriff's deputies—he laid the thing squarely across Bearcat's brand-new Smokey hat. The amber glass fractured, the hat was flattened.

McTeague was getting up from her chair when Moon put a hand on her shoulder. "Easy, now. Don't let's make a federal case out of a bar fight."

Seeing the sense in this, she settled down.

Bearcat looked up at the edge of his deformed hat, the effort rendering him temporarily cross-eyed. A few drops of warm beer were dripping from the brim. With all the solemnity of a chief justice of the United States Supreme Court appearing on national television to swear in a president, the Choctaw from Chickasha removed the damaged lid. While Bettie Jean and Cowboy Roy held their breaths, the deputy inspected the ruin. Pushing out the crown with a ham-sized fist, he addressed a thoughtful comment to the man who'd had the poor judgment to break a bottle over his skull. "Cowboy, you shouldn't've done that."

"I know—I'm sorry as hell, Bearcat." Cowboy Roy gulped. "I just don't know what come over me."

The deputy placed the forlorn-looking headpiece back on his head. "Roy, I'm gonna tell you just one time." He focused flat black eyes on the man. "You take that necklace outta your shirt."

"Yes!" Bettie Jean clapped her hands. "That's right, Bearcat—make him give it back to me!"

Bearcat clarified. "He's gonna give it to *me.* I'm gonna impound it as legal evidence, along with your pig-sticker. You and Roy can tell Judge Lujan your stories, and he'll decide who gets the necklace and who gets ninety days."

Bettie Jean glared in turn at each of these heartless men, tried to decide which one she hated the most, called it a draw.

Having sized up the massive deputy sheriff, Cowboy Roy was about to render up the squash blossom—when he recalled his wife's unequivocal threat. A man does not look forward to having his butt kicked up between his shoulders, having his victuals poisoned, finding scorpions in his boots, et cetera and so on. He straightened his spine, set his jaw like a vise. "No."

Bearcat's surprise was evident. "What'd you say?"

Cowboy repeated the two-letter word the deputy found so painful to hear. Emboldened by this rebellious act, he emphasized the negative response by shaking his head.

Realizing that the time for polite conversation had come to an end, Bearcat reached out, grabbed the man by his shirt collar, raised him off the floor. "I want that necklace. Cough it up, Roy."

"Awwrk!" This remark was no doubt an attempt by the choked man to suggest that the deputy had chosen a clumsy—not to say highly inappropriate—metaphor.

Unaware of the stifled literary criticism, Bearcat began to shake his victim.

Cowboy's head bobbled around like one of those plastic figurines with suction cups which certain discriminating road scholars are apt to mount on dashboards of classic Chevrolet Impalas. The effect was made even more comical by the way his legs and arms wobbled.

"Way to go," Bettie Jean shouted. "Shake it outta him!"

McTeague had had about enough. Turning her ire on Charlie Moon, she informed him: "I have had about enough."

Wanting some service, the tribal investigator waved a signal to the barman. "Enough of what, Lila Mae?"

The lady gave her companion a wide-eyed look. "We have witnessed an assault on an officer of the law." She began to count on her fingers. "Also unlawful search. Unnecessary use of force. Violation of a citizen's right to—"

"Right. And the amazing thing is that Officer Bearcat has only just got started." Moon addressed Mike the bartender, who had arrived with an order pad and an urgent desire to retreat to his sanctuary behind the bar. "I am not sure what the lady wants, but I could use a man-sized mug of black coffee. And don't forget to bring a quarter-pound of cane sugar. If you are out of sugar, honey will do nicely—especially if it's from Tule Creek, Texas." He turned to his pretty companion who was pretty fed up with his disinterest in How the Law Was Enforced in Tonapah Flats. "Coffee, Agent McTeague?"

She shook her head.

"Tea?"

The woman was not in the mood for a beverage, or any sort of refreshment. Her entire attention was focused on Deputy Bearcat, who was shaking Cowboy Roy.

Moon followed her gaze. "Like a terrier with a rat in his mouth," he mumbled. "Or a bulldog with a pork chop?" It was difficult to find precisely the right image. As he pondered this issue, Cowboy's left boot fell to the floor with a dull thud.

"This is not acceptable," McTeague muttered between clenched teeth.

"This is none of our business," the Ute pointed out. "Or in our jurisdiction."

"Speak for yourself," the fed said. "The Federal Bureau of Investigation has jurisdiction everywhere in the United States of America. And its territories."

Moon looked doubtful. "I'm not sure that applies to Utah."

The shaken man's dentures popped out of his mouth, skidded across the filthy floor.

"Oh, really!" McTeague was getting to her feet.

"Leave it alone," Moon advised.

Cowboy Roy's right boot landed near the left one.

"That does it." McTeague fumbled in her purse, found her ID.

The squash-blossom necklace, which had slipped from under Roy's shirt to under Roy's Levis, slipped down his left pant leg, spilled out like a long-lost silver-turquoise treasure.

Bearcat grunted with pleasure, discarded his victim, bent to reach for the necklace.

Like an NFL linebacker attempting to recover a fumble, Bettie Jean had already made a dive.

The muscle-bound deputy was not a man who flexed well at the waist. Seeing that the frantic woman would get her hands on the evidence before he could scoop it up, Bearcat put his heavy foot on the item in question.

"Nooooo!" Bettie Jean wailed. "You're squashing my squash blossom!" She tried without success to tug it from under his boot heel.

For the first time in days, Bearcat smiled. He was of the opinion that he had finally gotten control of the situation.

Not so.

Unable to retrieve the ornament one brutish man had nabbed and another had stepped on, the lady had but one option. She must get the second brute to remove his foot. Toward this end, she grabbed the deputy by the leg, opened her mouth wide, chomped down on his fleshy calf.

This was exceedingly painful. A low, foghorn moan escaped from Bearcat's innards.

"Oh, no," McTeague muttered. "Now he'll hit her. I've got to do something."

"He won't lay a hand on her." Moon added in a tone meant to soothe: "Just stay put."

She was not the least bit soothed, certainly didn't like to be told to "stay put" and emphasized this by stamping her foot.

Moon was the soul of serene self-control. "He won't lay a glove on her, McTeague."

"How can you be so sure?"

"Code of the West. No self-respecting frontier lawman will hit a woman. Not even if she chews his leg off at the knee." Seeing her doubtful expression, he explained: "Not while there are witnesses present."

McTeague watched the deputy grimace. *Charlie's right. He won't lift a hand against that vicious female!* Ignoring Moon's pleas to leave the brawl to the local constabulary, McTeague approached the deputy whose attacker was entwined tightly around his leg. With all the authority she could muster, the fed presented her official ID. "FBI." She gave the woman a stern look. "Let the officer go."

It would be hard to say who was the more surprised—Deputy Bearcat, AKA Leland Redstone—or Bettie Jean.

The deputy stared at the federal officer.

The woman took the opportunity to get a better bite on his leg.

Bearcat repeated the forlorn foghorn moan. Louder this time.

McTeague got a grip on the woman's ear, rotated it a good half-turn.

This twist in the plot came as a painful surprise. When Bettie Jean opened her mouth to screech and raised a hand to pull at McTeague's hand, the deputy took this opportunity to jerk his leg free.

The FBI agent released the ear, gave the woman on the floor the patented glare that had, on so many previous occasions, made it entirely clear who was in charge here. "Now get up."

Ever so deliberately, Bettie Jean got to her feet. Having clenched her right fist, the muscular woman prepared to take a roundhouse swing at the interfering federal officer.

This was an error.

Before Bettie Jean was half-cocked, McTeague dropped her with a smart left hook.

Having materialized at McTeague's side, Moon gave his favorite lady cop a frankly admiring look.

Having retrieved the silver-turquoise necklace with one hand, Deputy Bearcat was rubbing his injured leg with the other. He had regained his calm demeanor. "You the FBI agent that called the sheriff's office early this mornin'?"

Keeping a keen eye on Bettie Jean, whose gaze was fixed on the squash blossom, McTeague nodded. *I hope she gets up and tries something. So I can knock her off her pegs again. And I'll break her jaw this time!* Adrenaline is potent medicine.

Bearcat eyed the tall Indian. "This that Ute cop you said was comin' with you?"

Charlie Moon admitted that he was, and introduced himself.

The deputy sheriff offered a huge, hairy paw. "Welcome to Tonapah Flats."

Moon shook the hand that had shaken the boots off Cowboy Roy. "Speaking for myself, and Agent McTeague, we are glad to be here." He was, for the first time since breakfast, feeling fine.

Having given up the necklace as lost, Bettie Jean was contemplating two things: revenge and Lila Mae McTeague's leg. Like a starved hound stares at a meaty ham bone.

*Go right ahead,* McTeague thought. *Try to put the bite on me and I'll kick your teeth all over the floor.* Though more or less aware of the Code of the West, the Easterner could not in any sense be considered an adherent to the Rules.

Glancing up at the fed's stern face, Bettie Jean read her thoughts. And had second thoughts.

Bearcat cuffed the blond woman to a brass bar rail. There was no need to apply restraints to Cowboy Roy, who remained flat on his back, toothless, staring blankly at the saloon ceiling.

When the bartender arrived with Moon's coffee, the three officers of the law took this opportunity to seat themselves at a moderately clean table. The Ute had a taste. Then another. *That coffee has character. But not the kind you'd want to meet in a dark alley.*

Bearcat ordered a cup for himself.

McTeague did the same.

The pair of hot beverages arrived in nothing flat.

McTeague had a taste, almost gagged, pushed the mug aside.

After expending a minute or so to exchange pleasantries, Lila Mae McTeague asked whether the local authorities had picked up Sarah Frank.

Bearcat added a powdered nondairy creamlike substance to his coffee. "Nope. And Sheriff Popper and Deputy Packard and some volunteers from the community has been lookin' for her all night and most of the mornin'." He tasted the brew. *That must be the worst coffee north of the Mississippi.* Geography was not his best subject. "But she'll show up sooner or later." He looked over the cup at the attractive federal agent. "She's just a little girl—how long can she stay out there by herself?" He poured in another dash of whitish powder, added two spoons of sugar. Took another taste, made a horrible face. "When Miss Frank's belly starts to growlin', she'll come a-knockin' on her cousin's door."

Not being particularly impressed with the deputy's professional qualities, or the stimulant beverages offered in the Gimpy Dog, McTeague tactfully suggested that perhaps she and Charlie Moon should pay a call on the sheriff.

Moon took the hint, tossed off the final swallow of soul-jolting coffee, said a hearty good-bye to the spunky deputy.

# FIFTEEN

## *BAD NEWS*

THE sheriff's office occupied the west end of the Tonapah Flats Municipal Center, a rugged construction of Paul Bunyan–size pine logs capped with a corrugated steel roof.

Charlie Moon and Special Agent McTeague entered a smallish outer office. A large, heavyset woman—obviously the dispatcher—was seated in a glassed-in enclosure. She was close enough to bite an old-fashioned microphone that had been salvaged when the local AM-FM radio station had died from lack of interest. The sign on her desk notified all who cared that the moon-faced person with the painted-on eyelashes was Bertha Katcher. The woman shifted her wary gaze from the tall, slender Indian to the *Cosmo* cover lady. Miss Katcher pressed a button, her voice rattled a speaker mounted in a cobwebbed corner above the door. "You that FBI lady that wants to see Shurf Pokker?"

McTeague hesitated, then nodded.

Another button was pressed, the electric door latch clicked like a 30.06 rifle bolt slamming a big one into the chamber. "Go right on in."

Moon and McTeague entered a considerably larger space. The vaultlike door snapped shut behind them.

The antithesis of massive, muscle-bound Deputy Bearcat rose from behind a gunmetal-gray desk. The slightly built, good-looking young man resembled a teenager who hadn't yet hit his growth spurt. He cocked his head, flashed a boyish smile at the attractive woman who was a full head taller. "You must be Special Agent McTeague."

She reflected the smile back at him. "If I must, there's no point in denying it." McTeague reached into her purse, flashed her picture ID. "And you must be Deputy Packard."

"That's me all right, as you can tell by reading the label on the package." He jerked a thumb at the TATE PACKARD patch stitched above his shirt pocket, stuck out a hand.

She shook it. "My somewhat taciturn colleague is Mr. Charles Moon—special investigator attached to the chairman's office, Southern Ute Tribe."

The deputy nodded, offered his hand to the seven-foot man. "Mr. Moon's reputation precedes him." *He's that tough Indian cop that nobody messes with.*

Moon gave the pleasant man's hand a firm shake.

An older, taller, lean-as-longhorn-jerky lawman emerged from a private office. His weather-beaten face was decorated with a waxed handlebar mustache. A fresh gauze pad was taped on his forehead.

Tate Packard flashed the little-boy smile. "Hey, boss—we've got some distinguished visitors."

The FBI agent and the tribal investigator introduced themselves to Sheriff Ned Popper, who invited them into his inner sanctum. Once they were seated, he pointed to the coffee percolator. "You guys—uh, excuse me, ma'am—you folks in need of some caffeine?"

Never one to turn down a free cup, Moon allowed as how he could do with a shot.

McTeague demurred with a "No, but thank you." Her taste buds had not yet recovered from the Gimpy Dog brew.

Ned Popper poured black liquid into a Styrofoam cup, watched the Ute add six spoons of sugar. "I'd love to have a dose myself, but if I start drinking coffee after I've had my breakfast cup, I'll end up wide awake all night." The angular man opened a miniature refrigerator, removed a quart of buttermilk, poured three fingers into a heavy crockery mug that had POPPER THE COPPER printed on it. He hated the thing, but it was a birthday present from his eight-year-old granddaughter, who had made the mug at school and so that was that. He took a sip, wiped his mouth with the back of his hand, fixed his appreciative gaze on the lovely woman. "Deputy Bearcat told me about your telephone call, Agent McTeague." He cleared his throat. "I s'pose the FBI wants to find out what's happening with the missing Indian girl."

The canny fed saw the jurisdictional bullet aimed at her head, neatly sidestepped the missile. "As you know, Sheriff—the Bureau's interest in crimes involving Native Americans is generally restricted to those which occur on reservations, or involve the crossing of state boundaries." Knowing the "generally" would pique the Utah lawman's curiosity, McTeague glanced at her favorite man in the entire world. "But as it happens, Tribal Investigator Moon is a friend of Sarah Frank's family. When I became aware of his intention to visit your office and inquire about the missing girl, I accepted an invitation to accompany him."

As he turned his attention to the Ute, the old lawman's eyes glinted with a new spark of interest. "I didn't know the kid had much family left. Aside from her cousin Marilee, I mean."

Moon responded in a flat monotone a cemetery passerby might hear if dead men conversed amongst the tombstones. "I was a friend of Provo Frank."

At this reference to Sarah's father, the sheriff put a pair of rimless reading spectacles on his nose, opened a folder. He silently mouthed a few words as he read, then looked over the glasses at Moon. "Both of the girl's parents died about eleven years ago, within weeks of one another. And it says here you were involved in the investigation." The grizzled old lawman glanced at the homicide report, barely suppressed a shudder. "I can't hardly believe what was done to that poor woman."

Not wanting to discuss any of that grisly business, Moon abruptly changed the subject. "We met Deputy Bearcat down at a local saloon."

The sheriff clasped his hands into a massive, knobby fist and sighed. "I hear there was a dandy rhubarb down at the Gimpy Dog—wish I'd been there to see it."

The federal agent delivered a terse report of the fracas, winding up with: "It appeared that your deputy could have used some backup."

"I don't doubt it, but we're a little short-handed." Popper slyly eyed the attractive female, wished he was three decades younger. "My dispatcher likes to send that big Choctaw on the ugly calls, like shootouts and brawls. No matter how nasty the job is—you can always depend on Bearcat to get it done."

McTeague decided to leave the bar fight behind. "Deputy Bearcat informed us that you do not yet have Sarah Frank in custody."

"That's right enough." Popper stuffed the spectacles back into his shirt pocket, shook his head. "Late yesterday, me and Deputy Packard scoured the brush country on both sides of the ridge and didn't find nothing but some footprints, most of which could've been a week old. This morning, the state police and some local volunteers helped us search the Gap. We didn't find no sign of her. Which in and of itself don't prove nothing, because the Gap is mostly all rocks, so there wasn't many places for her to leave a footprint." For a moment, the old man wilted; weariness seemed to almost overwhelm him. "She could still be up there, layin' low as they say. There's a thousand little nooks and crannies where truckloads of full-grown persons could hide, much less one skinny little kid like Sarah."

Moon had guessed what the Gap was.

McTeague had not. She asked.

"Oh, excuse me, ma'am." The sheriff offered an apologetic grin. "Ain't it always the way with us locals—we talk like folks'll understand what we don't take time to 'splain to 'em." He pointed to a window and began to 'splain. "Across the highway yonder, that long, rocky mountain you see is what we call the Big Lizard Ridge." Popper continued with a glassy-eyed stare at the long-dead reptile. "And that narrow,

V-shaped notch, where it looks like somebody has chopped down on the lizard—that's what we call Hatchet Gap. There's an old Paiute tale about how, about eleven zillion or so years ago, before there was any people on the earth, Thunder Woman got right ticked off at Big Lizard because of somethin' or other—I don't remember what—and she gave him a big whack on the back with her flint ax." Popper paused long enough to look mildly doubtful. "At least that's what they say."

Dead silence from the visitors.

He twisted the left tip of his impressive mustache. "I guess you want to hear about what happened."

Moon wasn't entirely sure he did, but McTeague nodded.

"Okay, here's some family history." The sheriff looked far past Big Lizard Ridge, into the faded pages of his memories. "Ben Silver has lived here most of his life. About sixty-some years ago, not too long after Ben's father died in Denver, his mother moved here and married Tom Oates." *I can't imagine why Daphne did such a silly thing—woman must've had corn-mush for brains.* "Ben's half brother Raymond was born a coupla years after that. Few years later, their momma died, but Raymond Oates Senior didn't die until nineteen-eighty-five. The brothers went their own ways. Ben bought himself a place on the other side of Big Lizard Ridge, and minded his business—which was managing the Chevrolet dealership out south of town. Raymond, he went off to the university and got himself a law degree, and as they say, he made good—built himself a big three-story brick house on ninety-six irrigated acres. He also owns a dozen local businesses, which amounts to about half the commerce in town." Popper swiveled his chair so he could get a better look at the woman. "Neither one of the half brothers ever got married. And Ben and Raymond never got along. As they got older, Raymond kept on getting richer and Ben kept on getting grumpier. About six years ago, Ben sold the Chevrolet dealership and retired." Popper paused for a sip of not-so-cold buttermilk. Made a face. *More I drink of that stuff, the worse it tastes.* "Last three or four years, Ben's health has begun to go downhill. He's had a dozen or more women come to fix him meals and do some cleaning-up around his house, but none of 'em could stand him for very long." The sheriff's eyes twinkled at a passing memory. "Simple fact is, Ben was a mean old bastard." *The kind of mean old bastard that a man just can't help liking.* He chuckled. "Last winter he said he'd die cold and naked and let the rats gnaw all the flesh off his bones before he'd have any more females messing around in his house. But Marilee Attatochee—that's Sarah Frank's Papago relative—talked him into giving her cousin a try, and Ben did. It surprised everybody, but Ben and Sarah seemed to get along okay. Which don't necessarily mean Ben actually *liked* the girl—only that he could tolerate her. I imagine it was because the kid was always so quiet. It must've been female chatter that unnerved the old grouch." He glanced at Moon. "You want a refill on that coffee?"

The Ute shook his head.

"That's too bad. I like to smell it when I pour it out of the pot."

"Then I'll have a cup."

"That's very decent of you." The sheriff dispensed the brew, sniffed gratefully at the aroma. He began to rock in the chair, which accompanied his monologue with a creaky squeaking. "Last several months, Ben's been going to see his doctor every Tuesday at ten A.M. Half the folks in town probably knew that, and Sarah did for sure because her cousin Marilee was the old man's taxi driver." He looked quizzically at a passing fly, as if he might recognize the particular insect. "Ben had sold his car and wasn't in any shape to drive one anyway." He made a grab, barely missed the pesky creature. "Yesterday—which was a Tuesday—Marilee had some other stuff to do before she picked up Ben, and as soon as she left in her van—which was a few minutes after nine that morning, Sarah left by the back door. Marilee's live-in boyfriend saw the girl go."

McTeague, who had been taking notes, interrupted the narrative. "Who's the boyfriend?"

"Al Harper." The sheriff shook his head. "Harper's the kind of bum who gives parasites a bad name, but I s'pose it's Marilee's business if she wants to support him." He eyed the impertinent housefly as it made another pass. "Sarah always went to Ben's place through Hatchet Gap. Yesterday morning, she might have showed up at Ben's house after he was already gone with Marilee, or she might've watched 'em drive away. Point is, Ben never left his house without locking it up tight. But somehow or other, Sarah got inside. And she did it without breaking a window or a lock."

Moon seemed to wake up. "Any idea how she managed that?"

"I expect she must've pilfered his spare key." Popper's shrug stretched his red suspenders. "Or maybe last time she was there, she undid one of the window latches." He took a tentative sip of the tepid buttermilk. "But there's no doubt she planned to steal stuff from his house. And if there hadn't've been a bad accident out on the interstate, I expect she'd of been in there and out in a few minutes, and Ben would be alive today and mad as a stepped-on rattlesnake because he'd been burgled. But when Ben's doctor appointment was canceled because of the pileup out on the four-lane, Marilee drove him right back to his home." Popper picked up a manila file, laid it down again. "And if Sarah had heard Marilee's car coming, she'd have took off and Ben wouldn't be dead. But then another one of them funny things happened that changed everything. Marilee and Ben got into a shouting match—it was about his private driveway and what a sorry shape it was in—and Marilee kicked him outta her car and made him walk the rest of the way home. That chunky little woman sure has one helluva temper." Popper paused to chuckle, then frowned at the picture forming in his mind. "Point is, Ben was *walking* along his lane, which is why Sarah didn't hear him coming. But she must've heard him step onto the porch, or maybe put his key into the front door, and then she hid somewhere. And once Ben got inside, he must've realized somebody was in his house, because he tried to make a 911 call. My dispatcher was in the ladies' room and didn't pick up, so the call was transferred to my cell phone. Ben wasn't on the line long enough to say more than a few words to me, because Sarah yanked the phone cord outta the wall."

McTeague had her pen poised above a small notebook. "What did he say?"

The sheriff closed his eyes. "It didn't make much sense—at first I thought we had a crossed line and he was talking to somebody else. But I guess he didn't want whoever was still inside his house to know he was calling the police."

She made shorthand notes. "Could we listen to the 911 recording of the conversation?"

"There ain't one for Ben's call." The sheriff ducked his head and blushed. "We've just had a new phone system installed. Incoming calls that get forwarded to my cell phone don't get recorded." He swirled the bluish-tinted buttermilk in the glass. *That looks like goat puke.* "After Sarah yanked the cord, Ben probably cussed a blue streak, told her how he'd see that she got put in jail. I doubt the kid thought very much of being jugged, which is why she bopped him on his bean with the baseball bat. I expect she must've commenced to searching his pockets, because when I showed up and took me a look-see through the window, she was hunkered down behind Ben's desk—where he was laid out on the floor, but of course I didn't know that at the time. But I hadn't no more than got my nose close to the glass when she happened to raise up and saw me and squalled like a scalded wildcat." He grinned. "She heaved that damned baseball bat right through the window and took off like her team was two down in the bottom of the ninth and she'd just knocked a line drive and there was runners on second and third." He rubbed the lump under the gauze, winced. "Danged kid came within a whisker of cracking my noggin open like a eggshell. Matter a fact, I was pretty well scrambled for a minute or two; couldn't quite figure out whether I was Ned Popper or his cousin Henry the half-wit. By the time it come to me that I was the duly elected sheriff of this here county and had me a job to do, the skinny kid was roundin' third and makin' a hard run for home." He shook his head. "Only she didn't go home—not to Marilee's place, anyway." The sheriff had a bitter taste in his mouth, but not from the buttermilk. "When Sarah left Marilee's house that morning, she never intended to go back. The kid'd already made up her mind to run away somewheres, maybe down to southern Arizona, to her Papago folks."

"Tohono O'otam," McTeague murmured.

The sheriff did not hear the correction. "But the kid's poor as a church mouse on welfare who also has a gambling habit, and she would've needed some cash money for a trip." He thumped his knuckles on the desk. "So there's her motive for the burglary."

The tribal investigator and the FBI agent shared a melancholy silence.

Popper felt a pang of pity for Provo Frank's Ute friend. "If it'd make you feel any better, I don't believe for a minute that girl intended to *kill* Ben Silver. These kids nowadays are raised on a diet of TV and movie violence—how many times has a girl like Sarah seen some actor get knocked cold with a club and then wake up with nothin' but a little bump on his head?" The bump on his head throbbed. "No, I expect she just wanted to knock Ben down so she'd have time to get away and—"

There was a knock on the door.

*Why can't I have a moment's peace.* Popper scowled under his bushy eyebrows, barked at whoever it was. "What is it?"

Deputy Packard opened the door, stuck his little-boy face into the sheriff's office, flashed a modest smile at the Ute, a super-size version at the lady.

Smiling back, McTeague thought Tate Packard was incredibly cute. And suitable material for a toothpaste commercial.

Ned Popper thought his deputy was a damned nuisance.

Seeing the sour look on the sheriff's face, Tate Packard lost the smile. "Sir, there's somebody here who wants to have a word with you."

Popper set his lantern jaw. "Tate, in case you ain't

noticed—I am *already* having a word with somebody. In fact, I am having a serious conference with a couple of professional peers." He sneered like a fox about to bite a rooster's head off. "The point, Deputy—is that I do not wish to be disturbed."

"Yessir, I know that. But this may be kinda important." Packard swallowed hard, bobbling his Adam's apple. "Thing is, while I was outside for a minute, talking to one of my friends—"

Popper snorted. "One of your *girl*friends."

Packard blushed. "Well, yes sir. Anyway, while me and Nancy was having us a little chat, who walks up but Raymond Oates. Sir, Mr. Oates is very anxious to see you." The deputy looked like a dog about to be whipped. "I just thought I ought to tell you."

The sheriff got to his feet, gave his subordinate a squinty-eyed look. "You give Mr. Oates a cup of that so-called coffee Bearcat makes for our jailbirds, and tell him soon as I'm finished talking with Agent McTeague and Mr. Moon, I'll give him a coupla minutes of my time."

The deputy glanced at the visitors. "Sir, I think Mr. Oates wants to talk to you while your visitors are present. He claims he has some important information." After two heartbeats, he added: "About Ben Silver's death."

The sheriff stared at his pint-sized deputy, then at the ceiling. *This is one of those times when no matter what I do, I'll wish I hadn't.* "Okay, Tate. Send him in."

Raymond Oates stuck his head over the deputy's shoulder, grinned around the ever-present cigar. "Why thank you, Ned."

# SIXTEEN

## *MORE BAD NEWS*

THE sheriff closed his office door in Deputy Packard's face, gloomily introduced Raymond Oates to Agent McTeague and Mr. Moon. As there were only two seats for guests, Oates seated himself on the corner of the sheriff's desk.

Ned Popper glowered, seemed about to protest, but managed to keep his silence.

With his back to the local lawman, Oates addressed the tribal investigator and the fed. "I heard you folks had hit town, and I thought I ought to pay the sheriff a visit while you're still around. But don't worry about me talking your legs off." He was eyeing McTeague's long, shapely limbs. "What I have to say won't take a minute." The county's most prominent citizen removed the cigar from his mouth, pointed it at the FBI agent, who had produced a pad and pen. "I wish to state—and you can write this down for the record, Missy—that I am offering a fifty-thousand-dollar reward for information leading to the apprehension, arrest, indictment, and conviction of the ruthless person who murdered my half brother." The lawyer lowered his voice to a mumble. "Plus the return of any and all property that was unlawfully removed during the burglary of said half brother's residence."

"Missy" maintained a passable poker face. "That is quite a generous reward."

Oates popped the cigar back between his lips. "Ben was the only family I had left."

Popper rolled his eyes. "Are you done now?"

"Not entirely. There's one more thing."

## *THE CONFESSION*

OATES hitched his thumbs under a pair of tasteful, dark blue suspenders that matched his exquisitely tailored blue suit. "I wish to state—for the record—that I am responsible for my brother's death."

This declaration had the stimulating effect of what is commonly known in those parts as a rabid, rip-roaring, two-headed gollywampus galloping into camp at midnight, howling like a wounded timber wolf and spitting red-hot blood. With spurs on. Even among the most rugged, steely-eyed cowboys, such an event tends to cause a temporary lull in the conversation.

Just such a lull ensued.

Having years of practice manipulating juries of his half-witted clients' peers, the attorney knew how to employ such a pause for dramatic effect, and he did.

The pair of out-of-state officers of the law waited for the man with jurisdiction to take the initiative. They were required to wait for four seconds, which was how long it took for Sheriff Popper to get his thoughts together. "Turn around Raymond," he said. "And look me straight in the eye."

The man who had made the surprise confession removed his behind from the desk, rotated his rotund self, looked down at the sitting lawman. Raymond Oates met the sheriff's flinty gaze without flinching.

Finding the low-altitude perspective not to his liking, Popper unfolded his lanky frame from the chair. In his stocking feet, he had a good five inches on the local attorney. His boot heels gave him another two and a half. Now, *he* was doing the looking down. And down his nose, to boot. He was pleased to see the ambulance-chaser wilt. "You don't mean to tell me that you've come here—in front of witnesses—to confess to a homicide."

The attorney's intelligence had been insulted. "Well of course not, Ned—that would be a damn fool thing to do!"

Popper removed the antique Hamilton timepiece from a vest pocket. "Then you've got about thirty seconds to tell me what'n hell this is all about."

Oates clamped down on the cigar. "A half-hour or so ago, while I was viewing my poor dead brother's body, I recalled something that might well be germane to his death by violence." Avoiding the sheriff's face, the shifty lawyer shifted his gaze back to the strangers. "Two or three weeks ago, right in front of Oates's Supermarket—which is one of my prime properties—I happened to meet that skinny little Indian girl who's being sought in connection with Ben's murder. I didn't realize who she was, but the kid—Sally What's-her-name, she—"

"Sarah Frank," Popper muttered. Realizing the long-winded man was all wound up, he eased himself into his seat.

"Oh, right. Sarah What's-her-name buttonholed me, told me how she'd been doing some household chores for Ben. I guess he must've been talking to the girl about our family, because the kid knew quite a lot about me—including the fact that I own the Thunder Woman Café. Anyway, she claimed she was half-starved, and hit me up for a free lunch. Well, I felt sorry for the pitiful little waif, so I took her inside and bought her a burger." He paused to smile at a pretended memory. "I happened to have a wrapped gift under my arm—a cute little animal book I'd bought for my niece in Montana, but I kinda took a liking to Sarah, so I gave it to her." He shook his head. "That big-eyed girl could charm the socks right off your feet."

Popper was drumming his fingers on the desk. "I hope this tale don't run on too long; I got a dentist appointment middle a next week."

Ignoring the critic, Oates continued his narrative: "While Sarah's feeding her face with a three-dollar wedge of banana creme pie, she tells me how Ben'd been bragging about taking some of my daddy's things. Turns out Ben told her that I'd offered him a sizable sum of cash money for their return—which is true enough." He assumed the injured expression of one cut to the quick. "I can forgive Ben a lot of things—even petty theft. But talking to strangers about private family business—well, that was going a mite too far."

McTeague did not wait for the sheriff to ask the question. "Mr. Oates, it would be helpful if you provided a list and detailed description of the items that were allegedly stolen by your half—"

"There ain't no *allegedly* about it, ma'am. And no I won't, because it wasn't nothing but some little baubles and bangles my mother had left—"

Popper interrupted: "You said it was your father's stuff."

"Well it was, dammit! But when Momma died, everything she had became Daddy's property." He gave the sheriff a pitying look. "You never heard of community property laws?"

Somewhat subdued by this counterattack, Popper withdrew into his leathery shell.

Oates addressed the lady. "Would you like to hear the rest of the story?"

"Yes. Please continue."

He rolled the cigar on his tongue. "Where was I?"

McTeague checked her shorthand notes. "Sarah Frank was revealing her knowledge of the disputed property currently in your half brother's possession."

"Oh, right. Then, bold as brass, the Indian kid says to me: 'Mr. Oates, if you'd pay me what you offered Mr. Silver for the stuff he stole, I believe I could get your daddy's belongings back.' Well, I was surprised, of course—you coulda knocked me over with a canary's tail feather. But you know how cute these kids can be, so I said: 'And how would you manage that?' " Oates locked eyes with McTeague. "Young lady, are you ready for the show-stopper?"

The federal agent nodded.

"Sarah said she'd find out where Ben was hiding the stuff, and *steal* it—and she expected ten thousand dollars on delivery!" The accomplished actor paled with feigned outrage. "Well, you can imagine what a highly respected attorney such as myself would say to a felonious proposition such as that!"

Ned Popper chuckled. "You tried to talk her down to twenty bucks."

The lawyer sniffed. "Ned, under the current melancholy circumstances—I refer to my half brother's corpse, which is barely cold—your attempt at humor is in poor taste."

The sheriff's face flushed like a hothouse tomato, but Popper did not apologize.

Within an instant, Oates got over his indignation, returned his full attention to the FBI agent. "Naturally, I gave the kid a good talking-to. Explained the difference between what is right and what is wrong—from a legal perspective." A listless sigh. "I thought I'd gotten through to her, but looking back, I guess I was wasting my breath. What I should've done was report the kid's proposal to Sheriff Popper right away." He gave the lawman a sideways glance. "But I expect he'd have made a big joke out of it." Cutting off a retort from the lawman, he continued: "The point is, the girl was a thief. And I'm convinced she burgled Ben's house to find that stuff he'd stolen from my daddy, figuring she could sell it back to me." He exhaled, seemingly deflated with the knowledge of his guilt. "If I'd been more stern with the girl—made her understand I'd never pay a dime for stolen property, even when it was mine—maybe Ben would still be alive. It'll weigh heavy on my conscience 'til I draw my last breath." Palms raised, he got to the bottom line: "That's the reason I'm offering the humungous cash reward. Maybe somebody who knows where Sarah is will come forward and give the police some help." He stuffed the enthusiastically chewed cigar into an inner jacket pocket. "If you folks have any questions, I'll be spending the afternoon in my office." He launched a saucy grin at McTeague, tipped a make-believe hat. "I will also be preparing a statement for the media about the reward." Raymond Oates turned the knob, opened the door, and was gone.

The ceiling fan rotated oh-so-slowly.

On the wall clock, a second hand rotated around its circular path.

Somewhere in the neighborhood, a lonely dog howled a mournful lament.

"Well," Popper said with a weak smile, "that's a hard act to follow."

Charlie Moon got to his feet, thanked the sheriff for his time.

McTeague followed his lead.

Moon opened the door for his lady friend, followed her into the outer office.

Bearcat, AKA Leland Redstone, had returned in the interim to deposit prisoners Cowboy Roy and Bettie Jean in the Tonapah County Detention Facility, which was the same lockup as last year's Tonapah Flats Jail, but had a much better ring to it.

Moon and McTeague ignored questioning glances from Deputies Leland "Bearcat" Redstone and Tate Packard, who were semi-busy with feigned paperwork.

The fed muttered: "Do you believe Oates's story?"

The Ute did not know what to believe. "I'd like to hear what Sarah has to say."

"As would I." McTeague clamped the purse under her arm. "But as the girl is not available, I suggest we pay a call on Miss Marilee Attatochee."

"Good idea." Moon baited the hook. "I'll get some directions."

She bit. "That will not be necessary."

Moon presented a wide-eyed expression. "You already know the way?"

"Of course." *Charlie is so cute when he thinks he's put one over on me.*

Mr. Cute laid it on thick. "No matter how fast I go, you're always a couple steps ahead of me."

Flashing a saucy smile over her shoulder, the FBI agent wondered whether she should tell Moon about what she had discovered in Bureau files about Sheriff Ned Popper's various and sundry (alleged) misbehaviors—which included a report of a brutal physical assault on a burglar caught red-handed. The incident had occurred a dozen years ago and the Tonapah Flats district attorney had not filed any charges. Lila Mae McTeague wrinkled her pretty nose at the recollection of a particularly odorous detail: the DA at the time had been Ned Popper's godfather. And there was that Bureau rumor she'd picked up, to the effect that someone in the Tonapah Flats Sheriff's Office was on Raymond Oates's payroll. The insider was (so the story went) fixing traffic tickets, passing confidential police information to Oates, even destroying records that might prove embarrassing to the county's most prominent citizen. The prime suspect was Ned Popper. But McTeague paid little attention to rumors and could see no useful purpose in passing this one on. Charlie Moon had worries enough.

# SEVENTEEN

*CORTEZ, COLORADO*

HAVING tied a yard of cotton string onto Mr. Zig-Zag's collar, Sarah Frank entered a convenience store. Going up and down the aisles, she selected a few necessities for the final leg of the trip: a bag of gummy bears, a package of sliced baloney, a small box of crackers, a twenty-four-ounce bottle of Pepsi-Cola. Having paid for these purchases from her change purse, the customer shyly asked the cashier for directions to the bus station.

Though reluctant to expend more than the minimum effort his job required, the sallow-faced youth was touched by the hopeful expectation shining in the girl's big brown eyes. Feeling more than a little manly, the little man advised the customer that "there ain't been no bus terminal in Cortez for years and years." Glancing at her cat, he asked: "Where're you two headed?"

Having said too much to the people who owned the horse, the little fugitive was cautious. "On the other side of Durango." Sarah added quickly: "I have family there." Family. That was a sweet, heartwarming word. Like *home*.

Assuming an older-brother attitude, the clerk propped his elbows on the counter, gave the skinny girl a thorough inspection. "You look kinda young to be traveling by yourself."

She bristled at this. "I'm older than I look."

"Yeah, right." A crooked grin exposed an excessive display of gums. "Whacher name?"

She hesitated. "Sarah."

"I'm Otto." A sly pause. "Otto Palindrome." If the girl got the joke, there was no evidence he could see on her face. "Otto is what you call a palindrome, see—you spell it backward, it's the same." To demonstrate, he spelled it. Backward. "o-t-t-O."

The Ute-Papago girl stared at the peculiar young man until Mr. Palindrome blushed pink. "Tell you what, kid—you head down thataway—" Otto pointed to the south, "—until you get to the intersection where Route One-sixty veers off to your left. You oughta be able to catch a ride that'll take you to Durango, which is about forty-five miles." He scratched at a thin growth of peach-fuzz on his chin. "A friend of mine makes a run to Durango almost every day. I'll tell him to be on the lookout for you."

Sarah thanked him and departed. As she tugged Mr. Zig-Zag along on the end of the string, she considered the task ahead. Though never having hitchhiked, she was of the opinion that sticking your thumb out and actually asking for a ride would be a lot less effective than sneaking into a horse trailer. And more dangerous. *Some bad person might pick me up and murder me and cut my body up in little pieces and feed it to . . .* The girl shuddered, closed her eyes, and for just an instant—the *little window* opened and through it she could *see* her corpse being pecked on by hideous buzzards. But she just had to get to Aunt Daisy's home, and difficult times demand that a person take risks. She sucked in a bracing breath of the crisp morning air, called up a positive thought. *Maybe somebody nice will stop.* She imagined a kindly man and his pleasant wife, who would have a three-month-old baby in her arms. The woman would call Sarah "Honey" and offer her a dozen oatmeal-raisin cookies, but she would accept only one. Or two. Or maybe three if they were not so large. The nice lady would pet Mr. Zig-Zag and say, "That's a pretty cat, and it sure is a fine day to be hitchhiking." *I'll probably be at Aunt Daisy's before dark. And even if she's in a grumpy mood, she'd never turn me away.* As Sarah passed a home-appliance store, she was astonished to see her face in the window. And it was not a reflection, this was an old black-and-white snapshot. In the still image, she was holding her cat and (with the sun in her eyes) trying to smile at Cousin Marilee's camera. Sarah could hear the TV announcer's voice booming through the open door.

"—Frank is being sought by the sheriff's office in Tonapah Flats, Utah as a 'person of interest' in connection with yesterday's homicide."

When Ben Silver's scowling face flashed on the screen—staring straight at *her*—Sarah dropped her small bag of groceries.

The unseen announcer continued: "After being brutally assaulted, Mr. Benjamin Silver was found in his home by Sheriff Ned Popper. The victim died shortly after naming the girl, who has not been seen since."

Sheriff Popper's weather-beaten face appeared on the screen, talking into a SkyNews microphone. "We have reason to believe Sarah Frank has important information about Mr. Silver's death." Ned rubbed at the bandaged bump on his head. "She's most likely still in the vicinity of Tonapah Flats, but it's possible she managed to get out of town, or even out of Utah. So if anyone sees a young lady matching the description we've provided, we hope they'll call the sheriff's office and let us know." He went on to give a toll-free number, which wormed its way across the TV screen and under his chin. Popper faded and Sarah's photograph appeared again. The announcer stated that "The family of the deceased is offering a substantial cash reward for information about Miss Frank's whereabouts. Anyone who believes they have such information may call the toll-free number, which will connect them to the sheriff's office in Tonapah Flats." The same 800-number inched across the screen again.

When she realized that her mouth was hanging open, and a red-faced man in the store was looking through the window at her, Sarah scooped up her cat, stuffed him in her backpack. She zipped the cover almost shut—leaving the startled creature just enough of a slit to breathe through. At this moment, a police car pulled into the parking lot between the small strip mall and the busy highway. She picked up the plastic grocery bag, did her best to look as if she had nothing at all to do but stroll along and window-shop. More than anything in the world, her thin legs wanted to run—carry her away like a leaf in the wind.

Sarah's heart did not stop racing until she had put almost a mile of Route 160 behind her. *If a police car stops and they ask me what I'm doing, I'll just say I went shopping and I'm walking home. If they ask where home is, I'll just point east and say over there.* She had put her thumb out twice, but to her dismay, both vehicles had zoomed past as if she was invisible. Sarah had considered praying for help, but decided it would be better not to take the chance. She reasoned that when you've done something *really* bad, like run away from home without telling Marilee (not to mention lots of other stuff she didn't even want to think about) God was bound to be mad at you. Leaving Him alone seemed more sensible than taking the risk of getting zapped by a stroke of lightning. As she was thinking these thoughts, the girl was trudging along beside the highway, paying no particular attention to the traffic.

A heavy cloud-curtain slipped between earth and sun. A treetop-high dust-devil sucked up a cubic yard of sand from a construction site, tossed a cardboard box across the road, swished her skirt around her knees, spit grit in her face. Mr. Zig-Zag let out a pitiful yowl. She pulled the elderly cat from her backpack, clutched him to her chest, attempted to soothe him with comforting words. She also whispered a few words to herself and, despite the presumed risk, to someOne else. *God—I'm sorry for the bad things I've done.* This was, of course, merely a preamble to an urgent request. She dared not make her petition out loud—that would be far too bold—but she dropped a mental hint that it would be helpful if *somebody nice would stop and give me a ride.*

The miniature twister sauntered off to rattle awnings in a trailer court.

A dozen more paces along the shoulder, then . . . Sarah heard an enormous SSSHHHH, as if the Cosmic Librarian were calling for silence.

The sound of air brakes was followed by a double-creak as a huge bus came to a stop beside her.

Sarah turned to stare at the magnificent coach, all silver except for a long blue stripe beneath a row of spotless windows. Seeing the door open, she caught her breath. *Someone must be getting out here.*

No one emerged.

The inside of the bus was filled with a soft, violet light. She could see the driver, a large, barrel-chested black man. He wore a short-sleeved white shirt, black bow tie, black razor-creased trousers, shiny black shoes. He turned his head.

Sarah could *feel* the penetrating eyes behind the opaque sunglasses. And then she remembered the pale-faced boy in the convenience store. "Are you Otto's friend?"

This inquiry produced a wry grin. "Yes, I am." The voice was deep, like (she imagined) a whale speaking from the bottom of the ocean. "You rather ride than walk?"

She felt herself nod.

"Then get on board, child."

Without a thought of disobeying, she managed to get her foot onto the first high step. It was easier after that. She had barely gotten inside, when the driver pulled on the crank handle, slammed the door behind her. "Sit anywhere you want."

All the seats were plump, plush red velvet. All were empty. After a glance at the long, narrow aisle, Sarah Frank chose a spot right immediately behind the driver. She could see his face in the mirror mounted above the broad windshield.

He released the brake, stepped on the accelerator. Like a great ship leaving harbor under full sail, the massive craft slipped away effortlessly, and without a sound. "Where're you and that spotted cat headed to?"

Her voice was a mousy squeak. "To Aunt Daisy's. She lives on the far end of the Southern Ute reservation, not far from Chimney Rock and right next to Spirit Can—"

"I know where she lives." He sniffed. "In these parts, I know where *everybody* lives."

*He sounds like a braggart.* And braggarts were not to be trusted. *I hope he doesn't murder me and cut my body up into little pieces.* Another thought occurred to her. Sarah fumbled with her change purse.

The face in the mirror put on a disapproving frown. "You don't need no money to ride on *this* bus!"

She stared at the startling visage. "I don't?"

"Huh-uh." The back of his black head shook, and the face in the mirror dutifully did the same. "This here's a special *charter* bus. And when-so-ever I'm not on a partic'lar job, the boss lets me pick up whom-so-ever I want to. And if I don't choose to charge 'em a solitary dime, that's up to me!" The big mouth smiled, presenting a dazzling display of pearly white teeth. "But it'll be 'leven dollars for the cat."

"Oh, yes sir. I can pay—"

"That was a joke, young lady." The frustrated comedian rolled his eyes.

"Oh." *He's a big smart aleck.* She wanted to ask, "Where are *you* headed to?", but did not dare.

The driver began to sing:

*O Beulah Land, sweet Beulah Land*
*As on thy highest mount I stand*

The bus was picking up speed. Little white houses flashed by. Also sunflowers. Big signboards. Tall pine trees. The driver shifted gears. The engine hummed the hymn along with him.

*I look away across the sea*
*Where mansions are prepared for me*

It seemed very odd, but by and by, as miles and minutes slipped past the windows, Sarah began to feel comfortable. Even cozy. And for the first time since those bright days before her parents died—safe. She thought it over and corrected herself: *No, it wasn't quite that long ago. When I was a little girl and Charlie Moon gave me a piggy-back ride—I felt like I was where nobody can hurt me.* She considered praying again, offering thanks. But a troublesome thought nagged at her. *Maybe God doesn't know where I am.* She decided that it might not be prudent to attract the Almighty's attention.

For no apparent reason, the driver laughed out loud.

Sarah smiled, found the various sensations very curious and also appealing.

Big wheels rolling faster and faster, droning . . . *nnnnnnnnnnnn*

Big engine humming . . . *mmmmmmmm*

This cavernous chariot carrying her somewhere.

Ever and ever nearer to . . . *Beulah Land?*

# EIGHTEEN

## *THE COUSIN*

As Moon pulled his Eddie Bauer/Triton V-8 Expedition to a stop, the heavy automobile's seventeen-inch all-terrain tires crunched pleasantly on a bed of white gravel. The tribal investigator and the federal agent took their first look at the place Marilee Attatochee called home. The peaked roof perched atop the shotgun house was shingled with a varied collection of corrugated steel sheets; most were rusty-brown and loose as week-old scabs, a few were shiny as newly minted silver dollars and nailed down tight, the ones nearest the chimney were sooty black. In stark contrast to the decaying gray clapboards, the front door and window frames were freshly painted and looked new and blue as a robin's egg in June. In one of the windows, a round brown face appeared between a pair of white plastic curtains. Dark tufts of coal-black hair sprouted out this way and that, suggesting one of those indestructible cartoon characters who had recently experienced a hundred-kilovolt electrical shock.

"That must be Miss Attatochee," McTeague murmured. *She looks like a tough cookie.* The fed was eager to probe Sarah Frank's cousin with a few pointed questions, but deferred to the Ute. "Would you prefer that I wait outside? The lady may feel more comfortable talking to you if I'm not present."

"Because you're a blue-eyed devil and I'm a sympathetic Indian?"

"Blue-eyed *what*?"

"It was what we Utes refer to as a 'figure of speech.' "

"Do you Utes like my blue eyes?"

The dark man was able to blush without showing it. "They're more . . . violet."

Lila Mae studied his craggy profile. "You're very sweet, Charlie."

"I'm glad someone has finally noticed the sugary aspect of my character."

She offered up a smile. "But you're also full of guile."

His innocent expression was a question mark.

She explained: "You evaded my question."

He watched the other woman, the one in the blue-framed window, who was watching him right back. *This Attatochee gal looks like she's mad enough to bite somebody's head off at the neck, chew it up, and spit it right in his face. I'd better take McTeague in for protection.* "Fact is, Lila Mae, you evaded *my* question."

"What question was that?"

"D'you think the Papago woman would feel more comfortable with me because you're a blue-eyed devil and I'm a sympathetic Indian?"

"In my considered professional opinion, a stressed-out member of the Tohono O'otam tribe is more likely to share a confidence with another Native American than with someone of a more—shall we say—European persuasion." The FBI agent pursed her lips. "Now it's your turn."

He took a deep breath. "I like your eyes too much, McTeague." *Not to mention everything else.* Which he did not. Mention it, that is.

"Thank you, Charlie. I like your eyes too."

His face split in a grin. "You do, huh?"

"No. I was merely toying with you." Resorting to unfair tactics, she batted long lashes over the violet orbs.

Despite the fact that his mind had suddenly melted into

mush, Charlie Moon tried his best to come up with a witty response. When he opened his mouth, nothing came out.

The vampish woman was delighted to observe her devastating effect on the helpless male. *Treetop-tall Charlie's such a little boy at heart—such a* darling *little boy.* She did a quick sidestep. "Besides being a sympathetic Indian, you're also a friend of the family. I refer to Sarah Frank's father, not the Attatochee clan."

Moon cleared his throat, found his tongue. "We're partners, McTeague—from here on in, it's just you and me." He paused to let that sink in. It did. Her peculiar expression—as if she were about to say something that would shake the earth—rattled the man. He returned his gaze to the Attatochee window. The Papago woman's face had vanished. "And I imagine she'd like to talk to another woman."

Twice in rapid succession, the Ute musician had plucked just the right chord.

"Very well." McTeague consulted her compact, found the reflection satisfactory. "If it will make you more comfortable, I shall tag along. But only to show you how wrong you can be."

"Having read somewhere or other that humbling experiences build strong character, I will appreciate the soul-searing humiliation."

"This is your territory, and I expect you to conduct the interview without any help from me." She slung the black purse over her shoulder. "At the appropriate moments, I shall smile and nod. But I will not have a solitary word to say."

Moon swallowed a smirk. *That'll be the day.*

This issue seemingly settled, they abandoned the comfort of the Ford Motor Company product, approached the dreary dwelling.

Marilee Attatochee was waiting, her hand clenched on the cold porcelain doorknob. As Moon's knuckles made the first rap, she jerked the door open, looked the slender, seven-foot Ute up and then down and then up again, all the way from the horsehide boots to his John B. Stetson hat. *He's just as good-looking as the last time I saw him.* When the object of her close inspection was about to open his mouth, she barked: "You don't have to introduce yourself—I know who you are."

Moon returned a blank stare.

*He don't remember when we met at Provo and Mary's wedding in Ignacio.* But Marilee remembered the Ute. And his cranky aunt Daisy. Not wishing to refer to that ancient history, she said: "Sarah talks about you all the time." The tough little woman shot a suspicious glance at his long-legged, well-dressed companion who looked as if she'd just stepped off the cover of *Glamour* magazine. "Who's this?"

Charlie Moon removed his expensive black hat. Opened his mouth—

After having waited for an eternity that lasted barely one tick-tock of the clock, the woman at his side forgot her solemn Vow of Silence, and took up the slack in the conversation.

"I'm Special Agent McTeague, Miss Attatochee." She presented her ID. "I'm with the Federal Bureau of Investigation and—"

"FBI!" Marilee flung her arms in the air. "I don't believe it—some mean old white man gets killed and my little cousin runs away from home and all of a sudden it's a *federal* case?"

"I'm not here on official business," McTeague said. *Not yet.* "I'm a friend of Mr. Moon, who happens to be a Southern Ute tribal investigator, and as you know, Sarah Frank is—"

"Sure, I know—half Ute, on her daddy's side." The Papago woman stepped back into the dusty, musty gloom of her ten-by-twelve living room. "You want to come inside?"

They did. And did.

The air scintillated with a curiously incongruous mix of Glade air freshener and ingrained-in-the-carpet cigarette smoke. In a corner, a television with the sound turned down displayed a snowy picture of a chubby middle-aged man concealed behind a painted clown's face. The program was

*Uncle Jiggs' Children's Hour.* Uncle Jiggs was mouthing words to the kiddies: ". . . so stay tuned for good ol' Bugs Bunny and that nasty Daffy Duck."

Marilee pointed to a worn-out couch that was sway-backed as a thirty-year-old plow horse, the bile-green tint of that fluid that passes for blood in grasshopper veins.

Without a qualm, her visitors seated themselves on it. There was a protesting groan, an ominous creaking, a slipping toward the middle which brought them closer together.

The woman of the house plopped down on the best piece of furniture in the room, which happened to be a cushioned maple rocking-chair. Staring at the astonishingly pretty, immaculately well-groomed white woman, Marilee unconsciously reached up to smooth her unkempt hair. When that task proved impossible, she thought it best to divert attention from her so-called hairdo, and did this by addressing a curt remark to Charlie Moon. "I know why you're here."

Though the reason for their visit seemed obvious enough, the sworn officers of the law waited to hear from the self-proclaimed oracle.

As if attempting to see a path into the future, Marilee examined the back of her hand, where a network of blue veins looped over taut tendons. She stole a glance at the Ute. "You want me to tell you where you can find Sarah." *You figure you can sneak her back to the res, stash her out in the boonies where nobody'll find her, not even this slick-as-snail-spit FBI agent.* "But I don't know where my cousin is." She made the hand into a fist, erasing the tangled map. "Sooner or later, Sheriff Popper and his deputies will track her down. And when they find her, they'll turn her over to the juvenile authorities and they'll lock Sarah up 'til . . ." Her words trailed off like tiny sparrow tracks in a twilight snowfall.

As if he had read the Papago woman's thoughts, Charlie Moon wondered why he was here. To find Sarah—spirit her off to some safe hiding place? No. That was not an option. If, by some off chance he did encounter the missing teenager, he would be duty-bound to turn her over to the legally constituted authority. Which, in this jurisdiction, was either Sheriff Popper or the state police. After turning the question over in his mind, the tribal investigator concluded that he was in Tonapah Flats so Sarah would not be without a friend. A friend who would comfort her, listen to her side of the story. After which he would get Oscar Sweetwater on the telephone, tell the tribal chairman straight-out that the tribe had an obligation to hire a top-notch attorney to defend Provo Frank's daughter. *And if the penny-pinching old politician balks, I'll go to see Walter Price, who is the smartest lawyer west of the Pecos.* He remembered that Price was also one of the most expensive. *But I'll work something out. Even if it takes the rest of my life to pay it off. Even if I have to put up the Columbine for collateral.*

The fact that neither of these people had said a word since entering her house was beginning to nag at the feisty Papago woman. A terrible thought occurred to her. "What is it—you come to tell me they've found Sarah? Is she—" Both fists clenched. "—all right?"

Again, McTeague responded before the Ute could get a word past his lips. "As of a few minutes ago, when we were conferring with Sheriff Popper, Miss Frank had not been found. And we have no reason to believe she is not perfectly fine." *Of course, for all we know she could be perfectly dead.*

"Oh, thank you." *It's so nice to talk to another woman.* "It's such a relief—to know Sarah's not hurt." *Or dead.* "Or anything."

Realizing that she had gained a small advantage, the federal agent continued: "Charlie—Mr. Moon and I—are merely here to see if we can be of any help." She paused to smile at the missing girl's older cousin, and used sleight of hand to plant the first seed. "Is there anything at all we can do for you?"

As Marilee Attatochee thought about it, her brow furrowed into the sort of dark ridges that gaunt, overalled Tennessee sharecroppers used to plow behind sweating mules. "Once they find her, they'll put her in the lockup for sure. Can you make sure she gets a really good lawyer?"

As the fed was about to assure her on this point, Moon finally found his tongue. "Consider it done."

The Papago woman raised an eyebrow at the taciturn man. "So. You're an Indian who *can* talk. I was beginning to think maybe you was a mute Ute."

"By tribal law—you can look it up—Section Sixteen, Paragraph Twelve, 'Women and children can talk all they want, but adult males are limited to twelve dozen words a day.'" Moon grinned. "I save 'em up 'til I have something important to say."

"Sarah thinks you're the finest man in the whole world." Marilee looked him straight in the eye. "But she's just a dumb kid—what does she know?"

"Hmmm."

The Papago woman actually smiled. "Did that count as a word?"

He shook his head, presumably to conserve precious syllables.

"I don't think them Ute laws apply here in Utah." Marilee made this observation with a judicial air. "This is your chance to run off at the mouth."

He mulled this over. "You might be right."

The special agent decided on the direct approach. "Miss Attatochee, have you had any communication whatever from Miss Frank since Mr. Silver was assaulted?"

"You can call me Marilee." She began to rock in the maple chair. "And no, I ain't heard a single word from Sarah." Miss Attatochee pointed at the floor. "For all I know she could be holed up under the house with the pack-rats and polecats"—she aimed the finger at the ceiling—"or up in the loft with the vampire bats," she rocked faster, "or she could be up yonder in Montana or even in Canada. But if you was to ask me—" She was interrupted by the sound of tires on gravel. The slam of a pickup door. The crunch of boots on the white stones. A thumpity-thump on the door.

Marilee frowned and asked herself: "Now who could that be?" Wanting an answer, she got up to see. Which required looking out the window.

# NINETEEN

## *JOHN LAW COMES CALLING*

It was Sheriff Popper who had pecked his knuckles on marilee Attatochee's door. He offered the face in the window a bashful grin, raised his hand in a halfhearted salute.

Marilee opened the door, fixed him with a mean-as-a-scalded-pit-bull grimace. And just in case he hadn't noticed her teeth, she barked: "What're *you* doin' here, you beady-eyed old son-of-a-bachelor?"

The lawman's grin faded. "Well, I just thought I'd drop by and—"

"When I loaned you that snapshot of Sarah and her cat, you never told me you'd give it to them TV vultures." She pointed at the antique RCA console. "Now almost ever time I turn the tube on, I see my poor little cousin—and hear them so-called news reporters talking like Sarah was wanted for some kinda horrible crime."

After having subsided to a barely noticeable tremor, the throbbing ache in Popper's head started quaking in the neighborhood of seven-point-six on the Afflictor Scale. He rubbed at the patch of bandage above his eye. "I'm sorry, Marilee—but I was elected to do a job for the county—"

"If you run again, you damn well won't get my vote!"

"—and I hafta do it the way I see fit." He tried to look past her. "Mind if I come in for a minute?"

She cranked her malevolent glare up to gale force. This had about as much effect as throwing marshmallows at a brick wall. "Oh, no. I don't mind. In fact, of all the Tonapah County sheriffs we got, you're just about my favorite."

The stream of abuse rippled over the thick-skinned old alligator's back. Knowing it would annoy her, he tipped his hat, winked. "Why thank you, ma'am."

As he mounted the sandstone-slab doorstep, the lady of the house stepped aside and tried again. "Maybe you'd like a cup of gourmet coffee I made with hand-ground Hawaiian beans—and how about a big piece of strawberry shortcake with whipped cream?"

"Oh, I'll take a rain check on the shortcake—strawberries make me break out all over." Ned Popper removed his hat, waved it at Moon and McTeague. "And I've already had my limit of coffee for the day. But if you've got a cold bottle of soda pop, I wouldn't say no to that."

Marilee muttered something rude under her breath, stomped off to the kitchen.

Easing himself into Marilee's fine rocking chair, Popper addressed the out-of-towners on the couch. "I hope you folks don't mind me dropping in."

Speaking on behalf of Moon and herself, McTeague made it clear that they did not mind in the least.

"After you're through talkin' to Marilee, I figured you two might like to take a run over to Ben Silver's house."

McTeague appreciated the local lawman's invitation, and said as much.

"After this business is finished, let 'em go ahead and elect someone else—I'm getting tired of this line of work." The old man closed his eyes, rocked back and forth. "After I hang up my spurs, this is how I'll spend every day of the week." He exhaled a deep, satisfied sigh. "Except for now and again, when I'll bait me a hook, drop it in Plumbob Creek." *And while the bobber drifts on downstream, I'll lean my head on a willow stump and drift off to sleep.* The rocking chair went squeak-squeak. Then slower. Squeak . . . squeak . . .

The disgruntled woman in the kitchen picked this tranquil moment to begin banging percolator parts. Pots and pans. A coffee can. The cacophony suggested a demented drummer.

The sheriff sighed. "What that feisty little spark plug needs is a day off to rest." *I'd be glad to take her fishing.*

Presently, Marilee Attatochee appeared with a tray, plopped it on a wicker coffee table. She described what could be clearly seen: "There's two cups of coffee and a Diet Coke for Ned. And some packets of sugar and non-dairy creamer. And a box of little sugar donuts."

Special Agent McTeague took a cracked mug of the black liquid, thanked her host, performed a discreet one-sip taste test. *This is really excellent.*

Reading her face, Marilee said: "I put half a dozen ground-up piñon nuts in every pot. And some little pieces of eggshell."

Ned Popper helped himself to the carbonated beverage. "Thank you kindly, Marilee." He took a fizzy sip, presented a sly grin. "Come next election, you wouldn't actually vote against me?"

Glowering at the man who had taken her rightful place in the rocking chair, the registered voter seated herself on a stool. "I may *run* against you."

The sheriff winced at the threat.

Noticing that no one among those present was showing any interest in the tiny tire-shaped pastries, Charlie Moon took the box of Little Debbie's finest and balanced it on his knee. He also helped himself to all the packets of sugar, emptied them into his coffee cup.

Halfway through the soft drink, the sheriff cleared his throat. "There's no word yet on Sarah." He dared not meet the Papago woman's stony gaze. "But I wouldn't worry. She'll turn up." He rolled the aluminum can between his hands. "And soon as she does, I'll make sure—"

This statement was interrupted by a scritchy-scratchy sort of noise, such as beady-eyed vermin are apt to make.

## THE INTRUDER

MARILEE and her guests sat very still, listened.

The sounds came from the yonder end of the shotgun house.

The was a rusty creaking as the doorknob turned.

The Papago woman and the three officers of the law waited.

A sinister screee-eeek as the back door opened on rusty hinges. As it closed, a metallic clickety-clatch of the latch.

Floorboards squeaked as footsteps approached.

A pause, as if the intruder was having second thoughts. Then third ones.

Then, more squeaks on the oak floor.

Marilee got to her feet, the expression on her face speaking louder than words. She knew who this was.

Alphonse Harper approached the dimly lit parlor blinking, muttering to himself. "Tubby must be off somewheres."

Now her words were heard: "No she ain't!"

To say that he jumped two inches off the floor and swallowed half his tongue would be but a slight exaggeration. He also made a sound which can only be described thusly: "Eeeow-wah!" When Mr. Harper had regained some small portion of his composure, he frowned at his girlfriend. "Whatta you mean—scarin' me half to death?"

"Hah!" she replied, and added for clarification: "Halfway is not what I had in mind."

The sometimes man-about-the-house noticed the other visitors. Sheriff Popper, with whom he had from time to time had "professional encounters," was no stranger to Al Harper. He jerked a thumb at the strangers. "Who're they?"

Marilee Attatochee parried this inquiry with one of her own. "Where've you been—hanging out with your boozed-up, half-wit friends?"

Being a man with considerably more pride than substance (as quite a few women believe is common among the hairy-legged gender) Alphonse Harper straightened his back, gave the short, stumpy woman a comical, cross-eyed look that was intended to be stern. "I comes and goes as I please." He hiccuped. "So don't you be callin' on me to do any . . . any . . ." The word he was vainly searching for was "explaining."

The Papago woman caught a whiff of his breath. "You've been drinking."

Mr. Harper attempted to hold his breath as he replied, which is well-nigh impossible. "I ain't not."

Though not a grammarian of the first water, Miss Attatochee had her standards. "You ain't *what*?"

As the fascinated audience watched, her boyfriend began to wilt. "Well, maybe a beer or two."

"You stink like a six-pack or two." In preparation for laying down the law, she squared her shoulders. "You want to drink yourself pie-eyed, that's your business, Al—but don't come home drunk. And buy what you drink with your own cash." She pointed in the general direction of the kitchen. "Don't go stealing my hard-earned money out of my toolbox."

His good eye bulged with righteous indignation. "Did not."

"Yes you did."

Another hiccup. "No I didn't. Swear on my momma's gravy—" *No, that wasn't what I meant to say . . .*

"Then who took it?"

There are times when a man should keep his mouth shut. Or, if he is bound to speak, avoid outright lying. The petty thief would have been better off if he had simply admitted to the petty theft, thrown himself on the mercy of the court. But Al did what came naturally. "Sarah stole it."

The tough little woman seemed to expand in all directions. Until she was approximately the diameter of a fifty-five-gallon drum. A drum full of explosive material. "What did you say?"

Mr. Harper did not notice the sign on the drum, which clearly warned of the DANGER of making sparks in the immediate vicinity. Indeed, he was of the opinion that this conversation was going his way. "Hells bells, it's all over town—everybody in Tonapah Flats knows the kid's a burglar." He shrugged. "It was Sarah that took your piddlin' eighteen dollars and sixty-five cents."

Neither Moon nor McTeague could suppress a smile.

Ned Popper opened his mouth and laughed out loud.

Considerably offended that the sheriff had dare cast aspersion on his well-honed falsehood, Harper gave the gray-haired old copper a haughty look. "Well, she did."

Marilee Attatochee had a strange look in her eye. It was one that her boyfriend had never seen there before. The expression was not merely one of unabated hatred. Not simply white-hot anger. Nor could it be summed up as signaling a serious intent to do him grievous bodily harm. It was more like a combination of all three.

Enhancing the illusion, her voice was calmness itself. "That does it."

He grinned at the little woman. "Does what, Poopsie?"

She pointed at the back door. "Go."

The brevity of her command confused him; this verb needed a subject. "Where?"

"Outside."

"Oh." Mr. Harper believed he was beginning to get the gist of the plot. "You want me to go for a walk so you can talk to these folks—"

"Hit the road, Al. Make tracks. And do it right now."

He did not appreciate her tone. No female was going to talk to him like that, especially not in front of witnesses. A man had his reputation to think of. He looked down his crooked nose at the pushy Papago woman. "I'll go when I'm damned good and ready."

She approached in quick stomps that came very near to punching holes in the hardwood floor.

Alphonse Harper's feet contained about sixty more IQ points than his brain; they backed him into the dark hallway, barely keeping him out of her reach.

A moment after he backed into the kitchen, his voice was heard again. "Hey—what're you doin' with that skillet." A brief silence was followed by an answer to this pertinent question. It presented itself as that sort of soft, thudding sound such as might be produced if a husky person smacked a ripe pumpkin with a heavy, cast-iron object. This was immediately followed by an "Ow!" and the sound of clomping boots beating a hasty retreat, which was matched by the woman's heavy steps. Plus two more thuds on Harper's pumpkin. "Ow! Ow!"

In alphabetical order, the visitors in the parlor offered comments.

McTeague (alarmed): "She is assaulting the man!"

Moon (looking askance at the television—where a furious Elmer Fudd, armed with a stubby double-barrel shotgun—was chasing Bugs Bunny through an apple orchard, firing both barrels sixteen times each without reloading): "Sometimes I am inclined to agree with those folks who say there is too much violence on TV."

Popper (disappointed at hearing the back door slam): "Dang. Sounds like Al's got away."

Approximately one minute of heavy silence ensued, during which McTeague glared at those callous lawmen who showed not the least interest in whether Citizen Harper lived or died. Such unprofessional behavior irked the fed right down to the marrow.

Precisely eighty-nine seconds after the last "Ow!" Marilee Attatochee returned. Wearing an immaculate pink apron and a big, pearly toothed smile, she was obviously much refreshed—even to the point where an astute observer would have concluded that the harried soul had assumed a bright new outlook on life. It was true. Having rid her home of the pesky nuisance, the five-foot female was, in short, a new woman. She paused by the rocking chair, patted the local sheriff on the shoulder as if he was her favorite brother. "Any of you cops want your coffee heated up?"

• • •

As the barge-like bus drifted slowly down a Durango avenue, Sarah's nose was pressed against the window. She was *so* close to home now. Or, since her parents had died, the closest thing she'd ever known as home.

Soon, the town was behind them.

The girl gave up a sigh that was transformed into a yawn.

The driver began to sing, oh so softly.

His honeyed baritone drifted off to conjure up a faraway yesterday:

*Hush, my child*
*Lie still and slumber*
*Holy angels guard thy bed*
*Heavenly blessings without number*
*Gently fall upon thy head.*

This was the lullaby her mother used to sing to her . . . *when I was oh, so small.* Sarah's head fell back onto the downy back of the velvet seat. Her soul fell into a deep, peaceful sleep.

# TWENTY

## *THE GAP*

AFTER receiving a call to transport an elderly asthmatic to the clinic, Marilee Attatochee shooed the cluster of cops out of her home. Her teenage cousin was missing, mountains might crumble and Wall Street tumble, but it was a hard world and a woman had to earn herself a living. As she cranked up her van, the zealous entrepreneur instructed Sheriff Ned Popper to arrest Al Harper: "—if you see that cross between a one-eyed snake and a beer-guzzling gutter-skunk skulking around my home."

Straining not to smile, the lawman leaned on the Papago woman's taxi and requested some legal advice. Like what offense should he charge Mr. Harper with.

Marilee spat a response right back at him: "For impersonating a grown-up man!" Her dander up and dancing, she pointed to the nearest tree and added: "And hang him from that cottonwood limb so I can watch him kick and gag and turn blue in the face!"

The sheriff solemnly promised to do whatever Utah statutes allowed, but in Harper's case he doubted hanging would be called for. "Not unless he steals a horse. Or insults a sworn officer of the law."

Sensing that this was the annoying man's notion of a jest, and fresh out of varmints to compare her ex-boyfriend with, the outraged woman departed, her vehicle kicking up a spray of gravel in its wake.

• • •

BEHIND Marilee's modest home, Charlie Moon, Special Agent Lila Mae McTeague, and Ned Popper gazed at Hatchet Gap.

"That's the shortcut Sarah Frank always took over to Ben Silver's place," the local lawman said. "It's only about two miles from where we're standing. Not many of the locals go into the Gap—it's supposed to be a spooky place." To make it clear that he gave no credence to such superstitions, Popper produced a raspy snicker. "There's an old Paiute who hunts all over these parts, but he won't set foot in the Gap. Claims it's 'a bad place for an Indian'—says some old spirits still hang about in there. But I guess them tales never bothered Sarah much. Anyhow, Marilee was usually too busy to drive her over to Ben's place, so the kid didn't have a helluva lot of choice. The only other way to get there is around Big Lizard Ridge on Ben's private lane, which is a five-mile walk from here, maybe six." A gauzy cloud slipped away to unmask the midafternoon sun. Popper pulled his hat brim down to shade his gray eyes. "If she's still up there, a hundred men might search for weeks and not find her." The canny old sheriff gave the Ute a quick sideways glance, tried a long shot that was coated with subtle flattery. "But one man who was a sure-enough tracker—the kind who could follow a panther across a mile of solid bedrock—he might find her in a few minutes."

Moon heard the message loud and clear, as if Popper had shouted in his ear. *He wants me to search that canyon, see if I can flush Sarah out of her hiding place.*

The sheriff watched the Indian's eyes. *He won't do it.* Popper heaved a weary sigh. *Well, it was worth a try.* "You folks want to take a drive over to Ben Silver's place?"

Every day holds a surprise or two. Popper's popped up quite unexpectedly.

Charlie Moon offered his Expedition keys to the FBI agent. "Maybe you'd like to follow the sheriff." *Unless you already know the way . . .*

McTeague was not surprised. "While you take the route through Hatchet Gap."

The tribal investigator nodded. "I'll show up in about an hour. Maybe two." He pushed his hat brim back, basked in the warmth of the sun. "I intend to take my time."

Barely suppressing his satisfaction, Sheriff Popper concluded that he had misjudged his man.

• • •

FROM Marilee Attatochee's backyard, the Gap had appeared to be no more than a crack in Big Lizard's back. As Charlie Moon entered the fissure in the long, sandstone ridge, it was apparent that Thunder Woman had given the unfortunate reptile a truly earth-shaking whack. It was natural that he should compare this crevasse to *Cañón del Espíritu*, whose wide mouth opened near Aunt Daisy's home. There were stark contrasts. Compared to the ruffled mesa-skirts that formed the sloping walls of Spirit Canyon, the cliffs in Hatchet Gap were almost vertical. The largest canyon on the Southern Ute reservation boasted a year-round stream, but what little rain fell from the arid skies above the Gap would instantly slip between the jumble of crumbled rocks, percolate down through porous pebbles and sand. Moon tried to imagine fourteen-year-old Sarah making this long, lonely walk, just to earn a few dollars working in the old man's house. *She must've needed the money pretty bad.* A few paces ahead, a rock squirrel poked its black head from under a clump of spiny hopsage. The *Spermophilus variegatus* fixed beady eyes on the long, lean intruder. The rodent's face reminded Moon of Al Harper's pinched features. *Or maybe it wasn't entirely about the money—Sarah may've just needed to get away from Marilee's house for a few hours.*

With no continuous path through the rubble of fragmented stone, it was a slow, tedious hike. The bowels of

Hatchet Gap did not make for a picturesque place. Photographers from *Western Scene Magazine* would not haunt its quiet space. Happy families would not come here to picnic. The Ute watched a prairie rattlesnake slither under a wedge of sandstone. The walls were fractured with minor fissures, stained with a residue of a dark brown lichen that suggested coagulated Big Lizard blood. The stale air was sour-smelling and musty, the featureless shadows oppressive in this desolate space where the cleansing power of direct sunlight had never touched and never would.

Halfway through the Gap, Moon reached the high point in his journey. He could see a vertical slit of light at the far mouth of the crevasse. *From here on, it's all downhill.* He took a half-dozen steps, paused to pick up a fragment of hand-chipped obsidian. *Looks like a hide scraper.* As he straightened his back, his gaze locked on a remarkable display.

On a flat panel of the sandstone wall, there was a seemingly random array of human handprints. No, he corrected himself—not prints. These were *outlines* of hands. They might have been placed on this hard canvas a mere few hundred years ago, or ten thousand. They seemed to gesture to the Ute. To call to him.

*We are here forever*
*You are of us*
*Come close*
*Put your hands on ours*
*Be here forever*

Mesmerized by these sinister whispers, stunned by what *seemed* to be taking shape before his eyes, Charlie Moon was unaware that the obsidian artifact had slipped from his fingers . . .

*The solemn procession of elders was led by an Ancient-of-Days grandfather who wore a snarling wolf pelt on his back, a fluffy owl-feather apron suspended from his waist. On the heels of the Maker of Spells—eyes bright with an exhilarating mixture of bone-quaking fear and breathless anticipation—was the boy about to become a man. The initiate carried a leathery bladder crafted from a bull elk's intestine; this contained a thickish mix of spring water and powdered red ochre.*

This scene slipped by in bits and pieces, like a choppy old motion picture assembled from scraps strewn across Dream-Time's cutting-room floor.

*After an extremely painful but essential ritual—which involved piercing the boy-man's tongue with a porcupine spine, smearing the blood on his cheeks and chin—he was ready to be initiated into the secret Turtle Smoke Clan.*

*The youth raised the leather pouch to his lips, filled his mouth with the rusty-hued brew.*

*The shaman raised his arms in supplication to some unknown and unnamed power-spirit; the solemn retinue chanted in a guttural monotone.*

*The young man pressed a trembling palm onto the cliff wall, spewed out the brownish fluid onto his fingers and thumb. There was a murmur of approving grunts from the assembly of elders, a long, eerie wolf-wail from the shaman.*

*The act had been duly sanctioned.*

*The thing was done.*

The obsidian hide-scraper struck the ground.

Charlie Moon snapped out of the spell.

From a tuft of scrub oak jutting improbably from a finger-wide cleft in the sandstone cliff, an oversized raven cackled a rattling chuckle, ruffled her dark wings.

After taking thought, the rational man blamed the embarrassing episode on a serious head injury he had suffered several years earlier at Chimney Rock Archaeological Site. The neurosurgeon had warned Charlie Moon that he would never completely recover from such a serious concussion. *And I haven't. From time to time, I still see things that aren't there.* Add to that, the remarkable power of suggestion—Sheriff Popper's remark about Hatchet Gap being a "spooky" place had certainly helped things along. Having serious work to do, Moon shook his head—hoping this might keep the unwanted vision from returning. But something he could not shrug off tugged at the shadowy underside of his mind. Before leaving this extraordinary place, the Ute felt compelled to count the handprints. The sum was thirteen. And all but one represented *right* hands.

• • •

AFTER watching Sheriff Ned Popper turn a shiny brass key in the front door lock, Special Agent McTeague followed him into Ben Silver's house. Even after he switched on the lights, the parlor seemed to harbor a murky residue left over from the preceding day.

Clomping his cowboy boots over to a varnished oak desk, the local lawman pointed to a spot where the medical examiner had placed strips of masking tape on the hardwood floor. Popper said unnecessarily: "That's where I found Ben." He aimed the same finger at a window over the desk. "And that's where I was lookin' in when the girl tossed that baseball bat through the glass." He winced at the lump on his forehead, which had a peculiar way of double-throbbing whenever he recalled the unpleasant incident.

Taking care not to step on the spot where the victim had been found, the FBI agent approached the desk. She frowned at the broken window, now sealed from the outside with a freshly cut square of plywood. "And you have no doubt whatever that the person who threw the bat at you was Sarah Frank?"

He stared blankly at the fed.

"I mean," she added quickly, "it couldn't have been another girl—of similar age and height?"

"I guess we can't completely rule that out." The sheriff pulled at his mustache. "If Sarah had an identical twin."

McTeague blushed, changed the subject. "It's fortunate the victim was still alive when you arrived. As I recall, when you asked Mr. Silver who had bludgeoned him, he named Sarah. In a homicide, that's a nice piece of luck."

Popper took a hard look at the broken window. "It's also a lucky thing Sarah didn't crack my head open when she tossed that damn bat at me." The throbbing shifted into triple-time.

• • •

CHARLIE Moon did not know how he knew, but know he did. *Sarah isn't here.*

But being a professional lawman and an experienced poker player, he felt compelled to play the cards in his hand. Before descending from the pinnacle of Hatchet Gap, the tribal investigator cupped hands around his mouth, bellowed out a summons.

Echoes ricocheted off the stone walls like ghostly cannonballs. A startled black-tailed jackrabbit materialized from behind a cluster of snakeweed, skip-hopped along the narrow canyon floor, disappeared into a dark cleft. Simultaneously, a brownish gray mourning dove erupted from a thirsty juniper, fluttered away to some uncertain destination. After this, silence. Moon called out again. Louder, this time.

• • •

STARTLED from a dreamless sleep, Sarah Frank shuddered, jerked her thin body erect. "Here I am!"

The bus driver observed her startled reflection in the yard-wide rearview mirror.

Sarah looked back at him. "Somebody called my name." The half-awake girl was immediately embarrassed by this revelation.

"Wasn't me." The driver, who had a schedule to keep, checked his pocket watch.

The cavernous coach chased its long shadow. Ever eastward.

After a few heartbeats, the passenger drifted off toward her dreams. Ever homeward.

• • •

THE panel of handprints now behind him, Charlie Moon set his face toward the lonely end of Hatchet Gap, where an old man had returned home only yesterday—to encounter a violent assault, an untimely death.

• • •

SPECIAL Agent McTeague's willowy silhouette was neatly framed in the open back door of the house recently vacated by Ben Silver. While a reddening sun fell inexorably toward its nightly destination, she kept her gaze fixed on the Gap. *Why is Charlie taking so long—could he have found some trace of Sarah?*

After generously helping himself to the contents of the dead man's pantry, Sheriff Ned Popper was enjoying a steaming cup of cocoa and a box of stale Fig Newtons. All things considered, he was satisfied with the aloof woman's company and the simple snack. He was not, he mused, a hard man to please. Reaching for his umpteenth hard cookie, he shattered the comfortable silence. "Caught sight of him yet?"

Having almost forgotten his presence, McTeague twitched at the sound of the lawman's voice. "No," she mumbled. "Not yet." A west wind, fragrant with the scent of sage, whispered in the willows. "Wait . . ." She held her breath, squinted to focus on a distant speck. "Yes. I think I see him." She did not realize that her lips had parted in a smile—as if this was *her* man, coming home . . .

Popper stuffed the last surviving member of the Newton clan under his mustache, munched it. "Soon as he gets here, I'll do the crime scene dog-and-pony show again and then—" The sheriff's cell phone warbled, and he jammed the thing against his ear. "Popper here." He listened impassively. "Okay, I'm on my way." He got up from his chair at the kitchen table, tossed the house key to the fed. "After you show Mr. Moon where Ben got knocked off his pegs, you can lock up the place. If your Ute friend wants to know something I ain't already 'splained to you, he'll have to catch me later. Right now, I've got to get back into town." He stuffed the miniature telephone into a shirt pocket. "There's been a big knock-down drag-out at the Gimpy Dog. Deputy Packard needs an extra hand and Bearcat's out on another call." As he went clomping down the hall and through the parlor, McTeague heard the crusty old lawman muttering. "Day in, day out, nothing but domestic disturbances, car wrecks, and bar fights. I should've been a barber, like my daddy."

When Moon arrived, McTeague showed him around the Silver residence. The fed repeated everything Sheriff Popper had told her.

The tribal investigator stared at the taped outline on the floor. Mr. Silver had evidently been a small man. *Small enough to be felled by a fourteen-year-old girl with a baseball bat.*

# TWENTY-ONE

## *THE WAY DAISY SEES THINGS*

As it happened, the tribal radio station was broadcasting two hours of bluegrass Big Names. Flatt and Scruggs. Doc Watson. Ricky Scaggs. The Dillards. It was quite lively stuff, and if the year had been 1930 or thereabouts, Daisy Perika might have been kicking up her heels, clapping her hands, making plans to mail Sears & Roebuck six greenback dollars for a five-string banjo—With Complete Instructions Included!

But time had done its cruel work on her bent frame. Seated on the sofa, the weary woman was only half-listening to KSUT FM. Having just finished a snack of walnuts and prunes, she was hunched forward, squinting intently at the work on her lap. What she was doing was sewing tiny blue-and-white beads onto a miniature pair of goatskin moccasins. These were for Myra Cornstone's most recent baby boy—which made four in a row, and the young woman wasn't even married to the *matukach* truck driver who shared her bed. Not that this was altogether Myra's fault, of course. The way Daisy saw things, Charlie Moon was mostly to blame. Just a few years back, when Myra had only one baby, Daisy's nephew had an opportunity to marry the nice-looking young Ute woman—but what did Charlie do? Why the big jug-head muffed his chance, of course. When it came to women, all Charlie did was chase after those blue-eyed, white-skinned *matukach* hussies! In her anger, Daisy poked the needle all the way through the soft leather sole—and into her thumb.

"Ouch!" She also muttered a few other expletives, which shall remain unreported.

Daisy sucked a droplet of blood from the puncture wound, blamed the painful injury on Charlie Moon, and made herself a solemn promise to have yet another talk with her nephew. ("Having a talk" meant giving him a finger-shaking-in-your-face lecture, under which circumstances he was expected to sit and listen and not open his mouth except to say "Yes ma'am.") In Daisy's view, it was high time Charlie settled down with a nice Ute girl. Or—if it came to that—even an uppity Navajo, or one of those shifty-eyed Pueblo Indians. But not an Apache, thank you. That would be going a tribe too far. The point was, if Ute women and men kept marrying up with the whites, why in another fifty or sixty years the whole tribe would be a bunch of pale-faced, yellow-haired so-called Indians who wouldn't know a bow-and-arrow from a willow basket. The more the aged woman pondered the grim situation, the more she was convinced that this was a devious plot by those devilish *matukach* to get control of tribal lands and gas leases and the casino. Daisy knew exactly how they went about it. It started with all those flashy movies and TV shows about rich white people who were always having such a fine time. That Hollywood propaganda was what got the younger, softer-headed Utes to thinking about—

She jumped when Alexander Graham Bell's invention rang. Ben Silver's soul mate glared at the offensive thing. *Depend on a dead white man to come up with an infernal machine that scares a peaceable old woman out of her wits.*

It did it again.

Setting her work aside, Daisy put the receiver to her ear. "If you want to sell me something, you'd better hang up before I forget I'm a lady and tell you where you can stick your telephone—"

"It's me."

"Charlie?"

"Last time I looked."

"Don't you get sassy with me." She recalled that he had bought her the new telephone. "This blasted thing rings too loud. When it goes off, my old heart just about stops."

"Turn it down."

"What?"

"There's a little switch on the side that sets the ringer volume. You can switch it to low."

"I don't like to mess with switches and knobs and whatnot. Next time you're here, you can set it for me." She got a fresh breath. "And why're you wasting our time talking about stupid telephones? I've been waiting all day for you to call and tell me what you've found out about Sarah Frank."

"Uh—that's what I called about."

"Well then get on with it!"

"We've been in Tonapah Flats, met with the sheriff. They're still looking for Sarah."

Daisy tried to decide whether this was good news or bad. "Where could she be?"

"Don't have any idea." A pause. "But there's a chance she might head for Colorado."

The old woman's heart raced. "You think she might come to my place?"

"You're the only person she knows on the res."

Daisy shook her head. "It's a long, long way for a girl of her age to travel alone."

"If she knocks on your door, I hope you'll let me know."

Evading the subtle question, she said: "What do you mean 'we'?"

"Beg your pardon?"

"You said '*We've* been in Tonapah Flats.' Who's there with you?" Scott Parris, she hoped.

"Special Agent McTeague."

"Oh." Disappointment fairly dripped from Daisy's lips. "That tall, skinny white FBI woman." She heard Moon's chuckle in her ear. *He don't understand nothing.* "Myra

Cornstone's had another baby." A pause. "And I know for a fact that you're not the father!"

Moon could not come up with a defense against this charge.

"I'm making some moccasins for it." Daisy added acidly: "When the whites take control of the reservation, don't say I didn't warn you."

"Uh—right." *What in the world is she talking about?*

Daisy shifted gears again. "I just can't believe Provo Frank's little girl would actually murder somebody."

"We don't know exactly what happened yet," the tribal policeman said. "So let's not jump to conclusions." There was a roaring sound as a cattle truck on the westbound side of the interstate made a not-so-close encounter, rumbled off toward the looming sunset. "If I hear anything I'll give you a call."

"Don't call—come by and see me." Her tone was softer now, almost pleading. "We could go into town. Maybe have some lunch at Angel's."

"It's a date." The cell phone signal was starting to break up. "I'll talk to you tomorrow."

Daisy returned the instrument into its cradle, picked up her needlework, stared at the tiny pair of moccasins. *Seems like half of the Indian children I know end up dead or in jail before they have time to grow up.* She got up, hobbled off into the kitchen to make a fresh pot of coffee—and as she would tell Louise-Marie LaForte during her next telephone conversation with the elderly French-Canadian woman: "I almost jumped out of my skin!"

What almost made Daisy shed her wrinkly epidermis was Yadkin Dixon. Or more explicitly, Mr. Dixon's homely face—which was peering in through the kitchen windowpane. Daisy Perika was in no mood for nonsense. The enraged woman hit the back door like an antique locomotive with a full head of steam. Before the slab of oak had slammed behind her, she shook a fist and screamed: "What d'you think you're doing, you big Peeping Tom!" This was more insult than inquiry—she had not the least interest in what the white man thought he was doing.

Undaunted by this affront to his dignity, the unflappable Mr. Dixon tipped his tattered hat. And offered her a short-handled ax. "I believe you wanted this returned?"

Daisy snatched her property from his hand, pitched it onto a pile of kindling wood. "Thanks for nothing." She pointed in a direction that was away from her home. "Now get going before I lose my temper." The bottom of her face split into a froggish grin. "If you ain't out of sight by the time I count to three, I'll go get my twelve-gauge and pepper your behind like it was a fried egg!"

"Woman, I am impervious to your blustering threats." The superstitious vagrant produced a peculiar-looking object from his shirt pocket. It was a tiny portrait of a famous Indian warrior encased, along with a few grains of blue corn pollen, in plastic. "In case you do not recognize this object, it is a powerful magic amulet given to me by an Apache medicine man. It protects the owner from buckshot, bullets, and arrows—none of these things can hurt me."

"Is that right?" The Ute woman squatted to pick up a peach-sized stone. "Let's see if Big Chief Geronimo can protect you from this!" Before Yadkin Dixon could dodge, she made an overhand throw, which went low, landing a few inches below the buckle on his belt.

From the man's yelp, it may reasonably be concluded that it hurt.

## *STILL A LONG WAY FROM HOME*

As if in response to some subtle subliminal signal, Sarah Frank floated up from a deep sleep, surfaced into a dream-like consciousness. What she saw—through the windshield and down the road—was an enchanting picture from the pages of her memory book. There in the slanting light of the late-afternoon sun, just as she remembered it, was the sturdy bridge. Under it, the Piedra—swollen with foamy snow-melt—roared its boisterous way south toward Navajo Lake. She knew that a few miles on the other side of the tumultuous river, at the end of a rutted dirt road, Aunt Daisy's cozy little trailer home was nestled among a cluster of juniper and piñon. In hopes of seeing it, the girl closed her eyes. But what the visionary perceived were shadows from the past. Sarah shuddered, dismissed these troublesome ghosts. "You can let me out at the bridge," she shouted, and scooped up her backpack.

Mr. Zig-Zag stretched his neck to see what all the fuss was about.

Slowing, the driver glanced at the long, narrow mirror above his head. "This line don't leave passengers with miles and miles to walk before they get to their destination."

The frail little girl was at his elbow. "If you crossed the bridge, right away you'd have to turn off the gravel road"—she pointed—"and onto a narrow dirt lane. You couldn't drive this big bus on it."

Braking to a stop by the roadside, he arched a brow with justifiable pride. "I'll have you know—I can drive this vehicle wheresoever I wants to."

"No you can't." She used the firm tone of a stubborn young woman who has made up her mind. "I'll get off here."

"Well . . ." he sighed, "okay." One of the Rules of the Line was that when a passenger wanted off, no ifs, ands, or buts—the driver must comply. He pushed the crank to open the door. "But it's way too far to walk." He pointed. "You and Mr. Zag go over yonder to the far side of the bridge and wait for your next ride." Seeing she was about to open her mouth, he raised a finger to his lips: "Shush! And listen to what I'm tellin' you. There's a nice young lady I know who's got a summer job up at Chimney Rock Archaeological Site. Mary generally gets off earlier, but today she had to work late, so she'll be by in her Jeep—" he consulted the trusty pocket watch, "—in about twenty minutes. You just give her a big wave—Mary'll be glad to take you the rest of the way to Daisy's place."

Sarah thanked the peculiar man, who seemed to know everything about everybody. After watching the bus pull away, she crossed the bridge over the Piedra. While Mr. Zig-

Zag stalked some unseen prey, the girl stood in the shadow of a mushroom-shaped willow. After what seemed to be a terribly long time (almost three entire minutes!) she began to wonder whether the black man really knew a young lady who worked at Chimney Rock. And even if he did, how would he know she was coming home late today? Off to the northwest, the sky was darkening. A sudden breeze rippled through the willow branches, chilled her thin legs. *Nobody's going to show up.*

•••

BARELY sixteen minutes later, Mary Hale's mud-splattered CJ-5 rumbled onto the Piedra bridge. The driver saw no one standing on the other side.

Sarah Frank's small form was far down the dirt road—and quite out of sight.

# TWENTY-TWO

## *DEPUTY TATE TAKES THE CALL*

IMMEDIATELY after various Salt Lake, Phoenix, and Denver television stations had begun broadcasting the lurid description of Ben Silver's murder and the Tonapah Flats Sheriff's Office's urgent request for information on the whereabouts of Sarah Frank, calls started trickling in at a rate of about one every ten minutes. But aside from a report from Leota—a small settlement on the Uintah and Ouray reservation in northeastern Utah (which was being checked out by tribal police)—not a single breathless report of a "Sarah sighting" had been worth following up. After Ben Silver's surviving sibling sweetened the pot with his offer of a fifty-thousand-dollar reward for "information resulting in the recovery of certain Oates family property—"which is believed to be in the possession of Sarah Frank"—the rate of calls had tripled, but the already dubious quality of the reports deteriorated even further. Greed does indeed accomplish wondrously wicked works with the sickly human psyche. Exhausted from fielding calls, the dispatcher complained to Sheriff Ned Popper, who assigned a portion of the thankless task to his two deputies—who would take all the out-of-area calls. Grateful for this respite from chatting with well-meaning citizens and various kooks, Bertha Katcher switched the 800-line to the complicated new telephone console on the duty desk in the outer office.

It was precisely 3:54 P.M. and Deputy Sheriff Tate Packard was watching the Seth Thomas wall clock. His four-hour shift manning the 800-number would be up in six minutes. He squinted suspiciously at the second hand, which seemed to have slipped the clutch, shifted down to slow motion. *Maybe the battery's running down.* The telephone rang, he picked it up. "Hello, Tonapah Flats Sher—"

"I heard about that little girl on the TV." An elderly woman's voice squeaked in his ear. "I think I may've spotted her."

Packard noted the number on the caller-ID readout, poised his ballpoint above the NAME blank on the report form. "Who's calling, please?"

"Oh, I don't intend to reveal my identity—not 'til I'm sure I can collect the reward."

"Ma'am, the county is not offering a reward, that's a private—"

"But the man on the TV station said—"

"Why don't you tell me what you know." Tate Packard blinked eyes that felt like they'd been salted and peppered. "If your information leads to something we can use—"

The woman interrupted. "Say, are you recording this call?"

Packard barely stifled a yawn. "No ma'am. But I am filling out a form—"

"A form—are you some kinda government agent?"

"No, I'm a deputy sheriff—"

There was a loud click in his ear.

The amiable man hung up, shook his head to loosen the cobwebs. He heard the heavy clomp of size-fourteen boots, the deep voice of a bull moose–sized man.

"Wahoo!" Bearcat yelled. "Hide your fair-haired daughters and your kegs a beer—the hairy-chested, hard-drinkin' Choctaw is here!" He waved at Bertha Katcher in the soundproof dispatcher's booth, she returned the sort of wan smile a kindly mother reserves for a mischievous child. The oversized boaster continued his chant: "I eats granite boulders for breakfast and swallers live alligators for lunch. I washes it all down with muddy water and I picks my teeth with a bowie knife!"

Despite his weariness, Tate Packard grinned. "Then you're just the man I'm looking for." He pointed at the new telephone, which featured a dozen lights and twice as many buttons.

"It's not my shift yet." Bearcat pointed at the clock on the wall. "There's still almost two minutes to go."

"There won't be another call."

The Indian snorted. "Betcha two bits there will."

"You're on."

"Better make sure you've got some loose change in your pocket." Bearcat lumbered across the room to the open closet they had dubbed "the canteen." Helping himself to steaming water from a six-quart stainless steel coffee urn, cocoa from an economy-size box, miniature marshmallows from a plastic bag, and pure cream from a pint carton, he proceeded to concoct himself a seriously rich hot chocolate.

Packard fixed his gaze on the hateful chronometer. It seemed to be licking up every fragment of time, taking ever so long to savor it. *It's got to be the battery. Twenty seconds. Fifteen. Ten.* He grinned. *Eight. Seven. Six—*

The telephone rang.

*Dang!* Pretending to ignore Bearcat's snide chuckle, Packard snatched up the instrument. *I am so tired of talking to these nutcases. Please, let this be somebody who's actually seen something worth calling in about.* "Tonapah Flats Sheriff's Office," he barked. "Deputy Packard speaking."

"Hey, podner—this here's Buddy. Buddy *Bigbee.*" The inflection suggested that the caller expected his name to be familiar to any adult residing in the lower forty-eight.

"Yes sir." The deputy stifled a groan. "What can I do for you?"

"Negatory, son—this is about what *I* can do for *you.*" There was a quite audible belch. "But first of all, me'n the little woman—that's Tillie—we want to know whether anybody's already cashed in on that big re-ward."

*It's nine seconds past my shift, I oughta hand the phone to Bearcat.* "Not as far as I know."

"Fine. 'Cause me'n Tillie—we've seen that girl."

*Right. You and every other fruitcake within six hundred miles.* Packard had not even bothered to pick up his ball-point. "When and where was that?"

"Why, it was early this morning, in Cortez. That's in Colorado."

Packard dutifully went through the motions. "Sir, can you describe the person you believe to be—"

"Well o'course I can. Skinny little brown-eyed gal—and she looked *exactly* like that runaway kid we saw later on the TV. And when we spotted her in Cortez, she was totin' a cat."

"Can you describe the animal?"

"Sure. It was an old black-and-white. Had a jaggedy little mark on its head." There was a noisy interruption, while the chain-smoker coughed. "Which was why, at first, I thought the girl'd just sidled up to mess around with our mare—'cause the cat and the horse had the same kinda jaggedy marks on their heads."

Packard reached for the blown-up print of Sarah's photograph, took a careful look at her cat. The jagged imprint on the animal's head reminded him of a petroglyph he had seen in Paiute Canyon. *It's probably just a coincidence.*

Buddy Bigbee cleared his throat, pulled another drag on his cigarette. "Later on, after Tillie and me saw the little gal's picture on the TV—we figured she must've hitched a ride in our horse trailer late last night, while we was passin' through Utah on our way back to Colorado." He added: "It had to be when we stopped for gas at that Shamrock station in Tonapah Flats."

The deputy's fingers tightened on the telephone; he lowered his voice to barely above a whisper. "Did you speak to the—uh—person whom you assumed to be the missing youngster?"

"Damn right we did!" "Buddy" Bigbee went on to describe the high points of his encounter with Sarah Frank, capping it off with: "The kid said she wanted to buy my horse—and acted like she had the cash to do it." He effected a dramatic pause, then dropped the bomb that almost blew the deputy out of his chair: "And we even know where she's headed."

The outer office was silent as a Sunday morn following a deep snowfall. Deputy Packard felt Bearcat's gaze stinging the back of his neck. "And where would that be?"

"Kid told us she was going to see her Aunt Daisy—and I did me some checkin' around and found out there's a Daisy Perika on the Southern Ute res. And according to the TV, the runaway kid's half Ute." The wily rancher cleared his throat. "Now do me and Tillie get the re-ward or don't we?"

The deputy forced a tone that suggested a bored disinterest. "I'll keep a record of your call, sir—just in case something develops from it." He produced an artificial sigh. "But you might as well know—we've had a few hundred reports of girls—several of 'em with cats. They all more or less match the description of Miss Frank, and several of 'em are a lot closer than yours. It'll naturally take quite a lot of time to check out every call, but if the girl you encountered should turn out to be the one we're looking for, you'll certainly be notified."

The caller was more than disappointed; he was downright melancholy. When the Colorado rancher responded, he sounded like another, much older man—who was destined to cash in his chips without ever making the big score. "Well, I s'pose she might've been just some ordinary kid with a black-and-white cat." Mr. Bigbee's sigh was the genuine article, his question hopeful. "I s'pose you want my phone number."

"Certainly, sir." Deputy Packard closed his eyes while "Buddy" Bigbee named the nine digits that had already been captured on the caller ID. "Thank you. If anything comes of this, we'll be in touch with—"

"Oh, now that you mention it, I almost forgot something. Might be important."

"Yes sir?"

"The cat had a funny name. Kid called it 'Zig-Zag.' "

Packard clenched his teeth. "Anything else?"

"No, that's about it."

As he was hanging up, Packard heard Bearcat's heavy footsteps approaching, quickly pressed the CLEAR button to wipe the caller's telephone number off the screen.

The massive deputy looked over the small one's shoulder, sucked up a noisy slurp of hot chocolate. "Had any decent leads?"

Packard snorted. "Don't I wish." He pushed himself erect, effected a stretch. "But what really frosts me is I took most of that last call on *your* shift." He grinned at his huge partner, pointed at the still-warm chair. "You owe me two minutes."

Bearcat grinned back. "You owe me two bits."

Packard flipped the Choctaw a shiny Oklahoma quarter.

• • •

MARILEE Attatochee's supper of baked beans and fat-free turkey wieners was interrupted when the telephone rang. "Yeah?"

"Hi, Marilee. This is Deputy Packard and I—"

"Is this about Sarah?" *Oh, God—please don't let her be dead.*

"Uh, in a way. I just need some routine information."

"What?" She wiped her mouth with a paper napkin.

"Does Sarah have any birthmarks?"

"No. Not that I know of." She was tapping her foot on the floor. "Anything else?"

"Uh, just one more thing—does her cat have a name?"

"Sure." *What a dipstick.* "All pet cats have names."

The deputy waited a few heartbeats, then realized she was going to make him ask. "Well, it might help if you happened to remember—"

"Sarah calls him Mr. Zig-Zag."

"Oh." *That cinches it. The kid is on her way to the Southern Ute res in Colorado. To see a Daisy Perika.* "Thanks,

Marilee. That's all I needed to know." The vacuum-like silence pulled a few final words from his mouth. "Just fillin' in some blanks on the forms."

"Tate, if you hear any news at all—" The Papago woman was talking to a dead line.

# TWENTY-THREE

## *MEMORIES*

YEARS ago when she had first come to visit Aunt Daisy, the bumpy ride along the rutted dirt lane had been a delightful adventure, and it had not seemed like such a long way—the sparse forests of juniper and piñon had fairly flown by the truck window. That smaller, earlier version of Sarah Frank would walk only the few paces from Charlie Moon's parked pickup to the squeaky-creaky steps of a wooden porch attached to the Ute tribal elder's trailer home.

Now, as the fourteen-year-old trudged along on the lonely road, gnarled trees stood like sullen sentries, staring suspiciously, whispering breezily among themselves about the unwelcome stranger in their midst. The familiar forms of the Three Sisters were oh, so far away—practically on the other side of the world! And no matter how fast she walked, the petrified Pueblo women on the distant, misty mesa seemed to get no closer. Worse still, the sun—glowing a dull cherry-red behind wind-carried dust—was sinking behind the distant mountains, preparing to settle in for a long night. *Me and Mr. Zig-Zag will be all right.* She jutted her chin. *There's nothing in the dark to be afraid of . . .*

But that, of course, was a lie.

Sarah's thoughts drifted off to memories of her aged Papago grandmother, who would brighten early evening twilight by telling hoary old tales about how the Rattlesnake People slithered up from Mexico on their bellies, how Jackrabbit stole seed corn from the Pima, or how (and this one always chilled Sarah's blood) Trickster Coyote lured a little Papago girl into the brush and ate her for supper! Granny would spin these lurid yarns while coiling cunningly crafted baskets from such meager resources as were available in the bone-dry Sonoran solitude. The hues the Papago elder used were of the desert. For white, Grandmother would tediously split-stitch sun-bleached yucca stalk fibers over a grayish-brown bear grass filler. When the self-reliant artist required black, she would harvest fibers from the sinister-looking seedpod of devil's claw—and for red she spilled yucca-root blood! And every example of the old woman's craft featured a special image—a horned toad, a stroke of dry lightning, a claret cup blossom. Each of these archetypal forms suggested something mysterious and magical, but those secrets had not been shared with the half-Ute girl.

Every season, the old woman would use new baskets for the gathering. In late June, they would walk miles along the shallow Jojoba Arroyo to an isolated stand of saguaro cactus, where Grandmother would use a long stick to knock the pungent fruits off the pinnacles of the towering plants. When the season was right, they would gather agave leaves (but only from the north side of the plant) or mesquite beans. Whatever the task, after the long day's work, the walk home with the loaded baskets always seemed twice as far as the morning's joyful journey. When little Sarah lagged behind, Grandmother would bark good-naturedly at her: "Step-step-step. Keep on putting one foot in front of the other. Do that, child—and you can take yourself anywhere!" And so Sarah had.

And so she did.

## *SNIFFING THE NOSTALGIA BLOSSOM*

HAVING prepared a bubbling pot of green chili stew (with extra-generous measures of beef and potatoes) Daisy Perika ladled out a modest helping and seated herself at the kitchen table. The aroma rising up from the greasy, brownish broth was deliciously tantalizing. She rolled a buttered flour tortilla into a narrow cylinder, dipped her tablespoon into the brew. But as she consumed her meal, Daisy barely tasted it. *I wonder where Sarah is right this minute?* Probably in southern Arizona, she thought—hiding amongst her peculiar Papago relatives, whose brains (in the Ute elder's opinion) were probably almost useless after all those years of baking in the sun. Was it actually possible that Provo Frank's daughter could have killed a man—just because he'd caught her stealing something in his house? Well, of course it was. For one thing, Sarah was half Papago, wasn't she? *And even if the girl was a full-blooded Ute, our children today aren't like we was when we were their age. When I was a little girl, we respected grown-ups and did what we were told. But now the young people talk back to the elders, even laugh at them—right to their faces! And they watch all those shoot-'em-ups on the television. But worst of all, they pop pills like we used to eat peppermint and licorice sticks.* As she pondered these dreadful changes in her world, the hot stew was transformed to merely warm, then tepid, and the old woman's heart grew cold. Daisy took a final spoonful, made an ugly face, pushed the bowl aside. *I don't seem to be able to make that stuff as good as I used to.*

## *THE TRICKSTER*

KNOWING that Darkness was creeping up behind her, busily sweeping away what was left of day, Sarah Frank didn't dare glance over her shoulder. The child kept her gaze fixed on the uncertain path ahead. Mr. Zig-Zag trotted along like the free spirit he was, occasionally pausing to sniff at a tender sprig of rabbit bush or slash a paw at a passing moth. As the first wave of dusk rolled over them, hurried on ahead to shroud mesas and canyons in a dusky cloak, the girl heard the first mutterings of a nameless dread. Fear spoke to her not by means of words; the sinister syllables were tingly skin-prickles, shivery shudders, a sour lump in the stomach. She translated: *Nobody but Aunt Daisy lives out here. And I don't know how far it is to her trailer. It might be around that next bend or behind that big ridge or—what if I took the wrong dirt road and I'm going . . . nowhere.* Nowhere was not where she wanted to go, but it was too late to turn back. She called up optimistic thoughts: *Even if I took a wrong turn, it's not necessarily all that bad. I've got food in my backpack, and a Pepsi, and a little blanket. Me and Mr. Zig-Zag could find a place to sleep until morning.* Despite the fact that spring was fading into summer, she knew it would be a long, cold night. Uncomfortable, certainly. *But it's not like we might get hurt by something.* The frail little girl tried to push the thought of several potential *somethings* out of her mind. Like rattlesnakes. A freckle-faced boy at school had told a horrid tale about how, in search of precious warmth, these deadly vipers would wriggle into a sleeping person's bedroll, snuggle up to them—and fang them as soon as they moved! According to this same authority, there was *nothing* that hurt so bad as a rattlesnake bite. She also refused to consider tawny mountain lions that would snatch up spotted cats (and children!) by the neck, drag them off somewhere and eat them alive. Hadn't that nice little Mormon boy over by Mossy Butte been killed and eaten by a cougar? There were other *somethings* she also refused to think about, such as black bears and stinging scorpions and scuttling centipedes and huge, hairy-legged tarantulas and—

Up there, hanging on the edge of a small bluff, she saw a horrid, twisted cottonwood. It was the tree Daisy called Old Ugly. "It's all right, Mr. Zig-Zag, we're on the right road. Everything's going to be fine." The cat did not reply, but the girl heard something that made her heart leap, and miss a beat. *What was that?*

Whatever it was, there it was again.

A dry, scuffing sound in the bushes.

The girl stopped, stood still as one of the dead junipers.

Mr. Zig-Zag instantly self-petrified, a front paw frozen in midstep.

Sarah blinked at her pet—all she could see were his white spots. By the fractured magic of twilight, he had become a jigsaw-puzzle cat, missing half his pieces.

While both human and feline barely breathed, Sarah whispered to her pet. "Whatever it was, it's gone." And so, picking up their pace, they started once again.

Almost immediately, there were light, padding sounds off the edge of the dirt lane.

When Sarah stopped, the movement in the mesquite also paused.

Could it be an echo? No.

When she resumed her walk, the unseen creature resumed the stalk.

Darting looks at the brush, the cat mewed a pitiful whine.

She tried to sound brave. "Don't worry, Mr. Zig-Zag, it's probably nothing."

But it was definitely not *nothing* and Mr. Zig-Zag certainly did worry. He kept himself as close as possible to the girl, brushing against her legs as she hurried along.

And then—the frightful sounds ceased.

Sarah forced a hollow little laugh. "See, I told you not to worry. It was probably just a silly old raccoon."

It was not. And like so many evils that we would wish away, it had not departed.

A woolly-black cloud drifted off the face of the moon; now there was light to illuminate the threat.

The gaunt figure appeared in the center of the lane, perhaps a dozen paces ahead. Toothy mouth open, tongue lolling.

Mr. Zig-Zag arched his back, hissed like a punctured tire.

Sarah saw the hungry look on the coyote's face, understood what he wanted. "No!" she snapped, and snatched up her cat. The girl unslung her backpack, stuffed the terrified animal inside. On this occasion, the creature did not resist. But once the pack was back on her back, Mr. Z-Z popped his head up to look over her shoulder. And hissed again. This time, with more confidence.

The coyote stared at the skinny child. Licked his black lips.

The Ute-Papago girl stared back. "Go-way!"

The coyote took a couple of ambling steps forward. Grinned wolfishly at his intended victims.

"Aunt Daisy's house is down this road," she said. "And that's where me and Mr. Zig-Zag are going."

Mr. Coyote took another step. Bared his teeth.

To Sarah, the carnivore's message could not have been more plain if he had been speaking perfect English. *He's telling me to give him Mr. Zig-Zag. Then I can pass.* Such an outrageous proposal was beyond consideration; it was insulting. The girl picked up a knotty little branch that had fallen off the tree called Old Ugly. It was reassuringly heavy in her hands.

She stood eye-to-eye with the coyote. The canine made no sound, but his eyes spoke eloquently. *I don't believe you'll stand and fight. You are bluffing.*

Sarah understood her precarious position. *I can't run, he'd catch me and pull me down. And I can't just stand here, hoping he'll go away.* This left but a single option, and it was one that must be exercised immediately. With an ear-splitting shriek, she raised the stick over her head—charged the coyote!

The predator was so startled by the unexpected attack that before he managed a swerving retreat, Sarah landed a stinging blow across his neck, another on his hindquarters. As the animal disappeared into the brush, the child was startled to hear a long, piercing war cry, followed by a shouted taunt at the defeated enemy—which was delivered in a volatile mixture of Papago, Ute, and English. It was, of course, her own voice.

• • •

Barely a mile away, Daisy Perika was washing up some supper things while listening to Mule Skinner Blues on KSUT tribal radio. As usual, Daisy was no mere spectator—she was deep into the spirit of the thing, tapping her heel, bellowing for Little Water Boy to bring his buck-buck-bucket round—and if he didn't like his job he could dang well fling his bucket down. "Eee-haaa!" she screeched, and flung a soapy saucepan across the kitchen, where it banged against the stone fireplace chimney with a resounding *WHANG!*

• • •

BECAUSE such conduct on the part of a tribal elder might suggest a childish impetuosity bordering dangerously near unseemly behavior, a few words of clarification are deemed necessary. Here they are: Though the Ute song-stylist admittedly preferred the lively 1960s Fendermen version of the ballad to the venerable Jimmie Rodgers "Blue Yodel #8," Daisy's raucous screech and flippant tossing of metal cookware did not reflect an intent on her part to enhance the Singing Brakeman's composition—her boisterous contribution was an *involuntary innovation.* Which calls for a physiological explanation. Here it is: The enthusiastic ad-lib occurred because the *flexor carpi radialis* and *pronator radii teres* muscles in her left forearm went into a sudden spasm. Much more could be said about the various nerve fibers and their connections to muscles and the central nervous system, but the explanation provided is considered sufficient.

• • •

WHILE rubbing the tingling left elbow, Daisy cocked her head. *What was that yelping?*

(No, she does not refer to her own yelping—the tribal elder is elderly, but not senile. What Daisy's thought alludes to is the coyote-chasing girl's war-whoop, though she does not realize that Sarah is the whooper in question, or even that the girl was chasing a coyote.)

Daisy had not heard Sarah's shout with her ears, but the shaman was gifted with seven other ways of sensing startling events. Number five (not her favorite) was initiated when Daisy's elbow flashed red-hot, her arm jerked with an unpleasant sensation identical to an electric shock—and the alarming sound appeared in her mind.

• • •

SARAH Frank stepped smartly along, the rising full moon at her back, Mr. Zig-Zag securely in her backpack, the sturdy stick in her hand. The skinny girl was no longer weary. She was, in fact, fairly bursting at the seams with pent-up energy—enough to run all night, chasing the cowardly coyote over rocky ridges, through patches of brush, down into deep arroyos—all the while shouting insults and threats. Exultant in her newfound powers, she promised herself that from this time forward, she would never, ever be afraid. Not of anything.

Bless her soul. The valiant little girl had not the least notion of the terrors awaiting her. The first (and least) of them was only sixteen seconds away, when she turned off the rutted dirt road into what passed for a driveway. She followed the almost invisible pair of tire tracks through the small forest of piñon and juniper, into the clearing.

There was no trailer house.

It was as if Daisy Perika's familiar home had been snatched away, the old woman with it. The venerable Airstream had been replaced by a solid-looking little house, constructed mostly of stones, and wearing a cocky pitched-roof hat that glistened brittle in the moonlight.

A single, dreadful possibility presented itself: *Aunt Daisy must be dead. They've taken her old trailer away. There's no telling who lives here now, probably some mean old Indians who hate children and if I knock on the door, they'll probably call the tribal police and—*

Though she had not made a sound, the front door opened. It framed an elderly, stooped figure. "Who's out there?"

A flood of relief washed over the girl. "Aunt Daisy—it's me!"

# TWENTY-FOUR

## *RX: VITAMIN P*

DAISY Perika's mouth gaped. *My Lord in heaven—it* must be *Sarah—half-grown and looking like a scarecrow draped in a feed sack.* "Who's 'me'?"

"Sarah. Sarah *Frank.*" She wrung her hands. "Don't you remember me?"

Daisy appeared to think about it. "Hmmm. Yes, I guess maybe I do." She cocked her head. "You're Provo Frank's orphan daughter. Your mother—she was one of them desert Papagos from down yonder at the bottom of Arizona—what *was* her name . . ." This, she actually had forgotten.

"Her name was Mary. Mary Attatochee, before she married my father."

"Oh, right. Good ol' Mary What's-her-name. I remember her now." Daisy looked the skinny girl up and down. "Since the last time we met, you've grown a couple of feet."

Sarah straightened her back as she approached the porch. "I'm going on fifteen."

"As old as all that," the tribal elder muttered. "Isn't this a big surprise—you showing up at my place." She tilted her head back, looked past the girl. "I didn't hear a car pull up."

The footsore pedestrian slipped off her backpack, released the cat from its confinement. "I walked."

"Walked?" *Surely not all the way from Utah.* "From where?"

"I had a ride to the bridge over the Piedra."

*Pitiful little thing footed it all that way—and by herself.*

Sarah stooped to rub her finger along the cat's spine.

The animal fixed its amber eyes on the aged woman, emitted a thin whine.

*How about that—uppity Mr. Zig-Zag still remembers me.* The Ute woman frowned at the gaunt-looking feline. "So—how's old Rag-Bag doing?"

Though knowing Daisy's game, Sarah pretended to be unaware of the devious old woman's mischievous machinations. "I guess it's hard for you to remember." Her pitying tone suggested that being old as Moses's great-grandmother might have something to do with it. "His name is Mr. Zig-Zag."

"Zag-Zig, is it?" Daisy snorted. "That's a funny name for a cat." She waited for a correction that didn't come, then: "I never cared much for cats. Or dogs. All they do is eat and—"

"You don't have to worry about feeding Mr. Zig-Zag. Or me." Sarah reached for the small parcel hidden under her blouse, quickly lowered her hand. "I've got some money."

The old woman arched a doubtful eyebrow. "Have you now?"

The uneasy guest nodded. "I'll pay for our food." Her stomach growled. "And we don't eat much."

*I can believe that—you're skinny as a garter snake.* "Come on inside. I'll fix you something that'll stick to your ribs."

A wide-eyed Sarah Frank followed the tribal elder into her home. "It looks brand new."

Daisy closed and bolted the door. "It's not quite a year old."

"What happened to your little house trailer?"

"Child, that's a too-long story, and I'm way too tired to gab about it tonight." She switched on a floor lamp. "Tomorrow, we'll have plenty of time to talk about what's been happening in my life." *And in yours.*

In the parlor, a particular piece of furniture caught the runaway's eye. "That's a *really* big TV set."

The old woman nodded. "Yes it is." *And I know what you're thinking.* "From time to time I watch some of those other educational shows, like *Oprah*—but nothing much else." She added slyly: "The news is all so bad that I hardly ever turn it on."

Relief flooded over Sarah. *Then she doesn't know anything about what happened back in Utah.*

Practically reading the girl's mind, Daisy cut her a slashing sideways glance. "So how's things back in Arizona?"

The little fugitive shrugged her shoulders. "Oh, okay I guess."

"So what are your Papago kin up to these days—sittin' around chompin' cactus-apples and dried lizard and whatnot?"

Sarah sniffed a delicious odor. "They mostly eat hamburgers. And pizza."

"Well, you'll get none of that junk food here." Daisy waddled over to the stove, lifted the lid on a charred pot. "Everything I serve up is rich in vitamin P."

Sarah knew she was expected to ask which vitamin *that* was, and so she did.

"It's the best of 'em all." Daisy made this assertion with an utterly serious expression. She stirred the leftovers, watched plump chunks of beef float up through the greasy brew. "It sharpens up the brain and strengthens the liver—but most of all it gives a person that's slow lots of get-up-and-go." She lifted the cedar spoon to her lips, tasted the frothy broth. "Mmmmm—it's a good thing those lazy Papagos never discovered vitamin Perika." Daisy winked at the recent arrival. "Why they might have come up here and stole all the Utes' horses, and chased us off to North Dakota!"

While the famished girl consumed two bowls of green chili stew, and the cat lapped up a saucer of milk, Daisy and Sarah chatted about scary encounters with coyotes, about how a little dab of flour thickened stew or posole just right, about how to keep squirrels and bats out of your attic, what foods one should never feed a cat, and so on and so forth. But the old woman—who was a long way from being a fool—did not press the girl about the reason for her unexpected arrival on the Southern Ute reservation. When Provo Frank's daughter was ready to talk about her recent troubles, she would. The way Daisy saw it, there was plenty of time to wait. The tribal elder was mistaken.

After Daisy had switched off the lights and tucked Sarah Frank under a colorful Pendleton blanket on the couch, the weary little girl waited until she could be absolutely certain the old woman was asleep. After considerable ticking and tocking of the clock, rhythmic snores began to drift from Daisy's bedroom. Sarah reached under her blouse, put her hand on the canvas wallet that was suspended from her neck on a nylon cord. She checked to make sure the zipper was firmly fastened, then pressed her fingertips on the packet to make sure the precious object was still inside. It was, of course. Plus some cash money.

The cat curled up by her pillow, purred like a small, precision motor.

Sarah removed her hand from Ben Silver's neck-wallet, reached out to stroke Mr. Zig-Zag. "Don't be afraid," she whispered, and made her pet a solemn cross-my-heart-and-hope-to-die promise: "Whatever happens, we'll *never* be poor again." In no mood for sleep, the runaway mulled over what had happened since yesterday morning. Finally wearied of thinking, she willed the moonlight spilling in the window to fill up her eyes. This was quite pleasant, but such rapturous sweetness visits only briefly, then slips away.

It was not so very long before a horde of bison-clouds came thundering across the sky-prairie; the silver satellite was trampled under flinty, spark-kicking hooves. When a light rain began to patter against the glass pane, she drifted off into that shadowy domain . . . where dreams and insanity abide side by side.

# TWENTY-FIVE

## *ALREADY TOO LATE*

A bright tide of sunlight streamed over the sleepy land, washing away the clinging residue of night. The rain-cleansed air was tonic enough to raise the sick from their beds, the sparkling symphony of birdsong sufficient to cheer the most dismal soul. Except for Daisy Perika.

The tribal elder grunted and groaned her way from under the Amish Lone Star quilt (a Christmas gift from Charlie Moon), slipped a blue flannel robe over her nightgown, gave the sleeping girl a glance as she passed through the parlor, padded into the kitchen (the most important room in the house) where Mr. Zig-Zag was sniffing at the floor, in search of a tasty tidbit that some thoughtful human being might have left there for a famished creature of the feline persuasion.

The old woman made a halfhearted kick at the cat. "G'way, Rag-Bag." Well aware that there was no danger, the animal rubbed against her ankle, whined hopefully.

"Don't go cuddling up to me, you spotted-face, flea-bitten moocher." Daisy measured out two heaping tablespoons of Folgers' finest into the perforated basket, then—remembering her guest—added two more. *I guess Sarah's old enough to drink coffee.* She held the stainless steel percolator under the tap until icy-cold well water reached the four-cup level. Then another quarter-cup for the pot.

The fourteen-year-old subject of Daisy's thoughts appeared in the kitchen, rubbing at her eyes. "Are you making breakfast?"

*Food, that's all children and cats think about.* "Not yet." Daisy went to the propane range, placed the coffeepot on a back burner, turned a knob to ignite a cheerful ring of blue flame. "Coffee first, then food." She shot a gimlet-eye look at Provo Frank's presumptuous daughter. "That's the way I've always done it, that's the way I'll do it 'til the day I die." The maestro's tone made it abundantly clear that even the slightest variation on this theme was unwelcome in the extreme.

Stifling a yawn, Sarah came to stand by her side.

In silence, they waited. Time passed so terribly slowly, as time always does while one awaits and anticipates some desired end. But watched pots do eventually boil, and by and by, the water under the hollow base began to bubble, thence to surge up through the stem, whence the percolator proceeded to do its work, which is to perk.

Blip.

Long pause.

Blip.

Shorter pause.

Blippity-blip.

Blippity-blip-blip.

Daisy closed her eyes, sniffed. As she had become aged and jaded, most of the ordinary pleasures had faded. A few had vanished altogether. But every morning that God gave her, that first aroma of fresh coffee was a special blessing. Well worth forcing her old bones out of bed for.

Sarah had her coffee as Charlie Moon preferred, which is to say—excessively sweet.

Half an hour later, they were seated at Daisy's kitchen table.

The guest did not speak until she had cleaned her plate of the last scrap of scrambled egg, the final morsel of pork sausage. Sarah wiped her mouth with a paper napkin. "That was very good. Thank you."

Despite her grumpy self, the cook smiled.

The spotted cat, who was under the table working on the remnants of a can of tuna, added a whining comment which might have been a compliment.

Sarah thought so; she wiggled her toes at her pet. "Mr. Zig-Zag thanks you too."

Busy adding blackberry jam to a hot buttered biscuit, Daisy responded with a dismissive "hmmph."

The girl was pleasantly surprised when the Ute elder offered her the biscuit. She accepted the treat, began to eat as if she had been starved for weeks.

The wily old woman watched. "Next time you want to visit, you might give me a telephone call—let me know you're comin'." She added: "I might have been away when you showed up."

"If you had been, we'd have stayed in Spirit Canyon 'til you got back." Sarah offered the furry half of the team a quarter of the biscuit.

Being a roughshod product of the Great Depression—and having intended to eat the tuna herself—Daisy cringed inwardly at this additional extravagance. But letting it pass, she repeated last night's question: "So how're things amongst your Papago folks on the res?"

"I don't know." Sarah looked her inquisitor straight in the eye. "I've been staying with one of my cousins who moved off the reservation. Her name is Marilee."

"Marilee Attatochee?"

The girl's eyes popped. "Do you know her?"

The old woman nodded. "She was at your parents' wedding in Ignacio—at St. Ignatius." *Tough-looking little woman—and meaner than a pit bull with a nose full of porcupine quills.* Daisy had instantly taken a liking to Miss Attatochee. For a moment, Daisy couldn't think of anything else to say. But like other moments, this one would pass. *I can't just up and ask her if she came here because she stole some stuff from an old white man in Utah and killed him.* "Everything all right at your cousin's house?" After a wary glance from the child, she added: "I hope you and her was getting along okay."

Sarah twisted a paper napkin into a tight little rope. "Marilee's nice." *But Al Harper is horrible.* "And school wasn't too bad." She looked out the window, where a mountain bluebird had landed on a spindly juniper branch. "But I decided I'd rather be in Colorado."

Daisy nodded. "Colorado is lots better than being in—" She barely caught herself before she said *being in jail.* "Better than most places." She reached for the pot. "You want some more coffee?"

Sarah, who had rarely touched the stuff, was feeling very grown-up. "Yes." She smiled. "Thank you."

*Well, at least she has nice manners.* She poured the girl a half-cup of the potent black brew. *But from what they say, so did John Dillinger and Baby-Face Nelson and lots of them other cold-blooded murderers.*

• • •

As has been mentioned, the front windows of Daisy Perika's home provide a spectacular view of the mouth of *Cañón del Espíritu.* That long, meandering, and rather deep canyon is defined on one side by the stately form of Three Sisters Mesa—which serves as a pedestal for the trio of petrified Pueblo women—and on the other by another, somewhat less distinguished mesa known simply as Dog Leg, so-called because of an abrupt bend about halfway along its length which, if one's imagination leans toward anatomical analogies, might well suggest a canine leg joint.

Now, consider what may be seen *behind* the Ute elder's home, where she seldom bothers to gaze. The earth in her outback is cut with red arroyos, bulging with rocky ridges, dotted with piñon, juniper, and prickly pear cactus, plus an occasional cluster of pointy yucca spears. The distinguishing feature of this otherwise common-as-dirt vista is a flat-topped pillar of sandstone which, for some obscure reason, is known locally as Mule Shoe Butte. There is no record of a shoe, mule or otherwise, having ever been associated with the spot. Such are the mysteries of rural place-names. The more relevant point is this: While Daisy and Sarah were enjoying their breakfast, a determined young man had attempted to conceal his automobile among a cluster of red willows that had found root in a shallow arroyo about fifty yards off the dirt road. He was now atop Mule Shoe Butte, stretched out on his stomach, watching Daisy's house. The stranger removed an antique brass telescope from his coat pocket, did a squint-eye at the Indian woman's home.

The spy in the prone position was Deputy Sheriff Tate Packard, who had driven all the way from Tonapah Flats in hopes of finding the Ute-Papago girl who was wanted for questioning in connection with the Benjamin Silver homicide. A less intelligent, not-so-experienced deputy might have simply walked right up to the Ute elder's door, knocked, smiled at the woman of the house, introduced himself as a representative of the Tonapah Flats Sheriff's Office, inquired whether Daisy Perika had any notion of the current whereabouts of one Sarah Frank. But Tate Packard was, as Sheriff Popper had often said, an uncommonly clever young man. And having served seven years with the BIA police, Packard knew his way around the Navajo and Hopi reservations, and though the differences in culture and character of the various Native American tribes was more remarkable than their similarities, the deputy sheriff had concluded that the various groups had certain characteristic in common, two of which particularly applied to the situation at hand. (1) They mistrusted outsiders (especially lawmen) and (2) they protected their own (especially from lawmen). And so here he was, watching the old woman's home, hoping Sarah Frank was inside, waiting for the runaway to show her face.

• • •

WHEN the astonishing thing happened—and it had not occurred with such force since she was a little girl—Sarah was putting away the breakfast dishes. At first, what she saw was merely a small, clearer-than-air spot on a varnished cabinet door. A spot that was *not* really there. The better to see it, she closed her eyes. The phantasm was much brighter now, and took on a rectangular shape, resembling a window—a portal into those dark places where ordinary mortals cannot see. For the oddly "gifted" girl, this not an unfamiliar sight. Much of the time, the picture was a blank canvas. Just as often, she would see an amorphous form that was hard to identify. This morning, it was different.

What she saw was an enormous *eye.*

The eye was staring at her.

Daisy, who was storing an iron skillet in the oven, started when the child dropped a heavy platter on the floor, where it shattered. *She's standing there with her eyes shut—no wonder she dropped the plate!* She waited for the girl to mutter an apology.

Sarah watched the huge eye blink. "I have to go."

Daisy bent to pick up pieces of the platter. "Go where?"

She opened her eyes, stared at the knotty-pine wall as if she could see through it. "Away."

Daisy cocked her head at this. "Why?"

The girl scooped up her cat. "There's a man. He's come to get me."

"What man—who is he?"

The girl clutched Mr. Zig-Zag to her neck. "I don't know. But I have to go away." She turned an oddly calm face toward the old woman. "He's got a gun."

The tough old Ute straightened her back. "So've I." There was a double-barrel 12-gauge in her closet. "And I know how to use it."

Sarah knew this was true. Several years ago, when the elderly woman lived in the metal-skin trailer, she had watched Daisy empty both barrels at a UFO which had been within a few yards of her front porch. "It's not you he's after. If I leave before he gets here, maybe he'll go away."

A stubborn person herself, Daisy recognized the determination that had hardened the girl's thin face. She made an instant decision that would shatter lives in ways that could not be repaired. "Go hide in Spirit Canyon. When you get to that pointy red rock on the Three Sisters side—the one that looks like a stubby carrot—take about a dozen more steps until you see a deer trail going up the slope. Up near the top, in a place where the rock is dark brown, there's a shelf along the cliff—and a little cave. When I was a little girl, I used to hide up there." She put the leftover biscuits into a plastic bag, gave this to Sarah Frank. "If you've got to go, do it—don't stand there gawking at me like some pie-eyed heifer!" Daisy waved both hands. "Hurry, now."

• • •

THE deputy saw the pair of figures emerge on the far side of the Ute woman's home, adjusted the focus on his telescope. Though Tate Packard knew it was bad luck to boast—even to oneself—he couldn't help smiling, and whispering: "I knew it—just wait long enough, and she'd have to show herself." He watched the girl wave good-bye to the elderly woman, then hurry away toward the mouth of the big canyon. A man with less self-control might have gotten up and followed her immediately. Deputy Packard did not move. He watched Sarah Frank through the telescope as she entered the chasm. Only when she had begun the trek up the rock-strewn slope did he get to his feet, brush the dust off his jeans. *Five'll get you ten the kid's gone to hide what she took from old man Silver's house.* A smug, little-boy grin lit up his face. *I bet she'll be plenty surprised to see me.*

# TWENTY-SIX

## *THE DEAD-END KID*

As Tate Packard paused to wipe beads of sweat off his forehead, he could feel the pulse throbbing in his neck. The slightly built, boyish-looking young man was breathing hard from his ascent up the steep, rocky trail. *Must be the altitude.* The Utah cop smiled at this cop-out. *Whatever it is, I need to get into shape.* After ascending another few paces, he found himself on a narrow shelf that appeared to be about fifty paces long. Above his head, a sheer cliff wall rose up to the crest of the mesa; it was streaked rusty-brown from seeping rainwater. Below his boot heels was a hundred and fifty yards of rocky slope. He marveled at his good fortune and the teenage girl's poor judgment. *Aside from the trail, there's no way out—I've got her cornered.* After these self-congratulations, there was a moment of misgivings. *But where is she?* After a long, thoughtful look at the shelf, Packard decided there was only one possibility. His gaze rested on a spot near a dead ponderosa with sooty-looking bark. Almost hidden by a tuft of sage, there was a small, vertical slit in the sandstone wall. *There's no other place she could be.* A sigh of resignation. *Might as well get this business over with.* He approached the miniature cavern, cleared his throat. "Sarah, it's Deputy Tate Packard—from the Tonapah Flats Sheriff's Office." He flashed the disarming grin.

"You remember me—I'm the good-lookin' one. Bearcat, he's the Choctaw deputy that looks like Alley-Oop's big brother." He waited in vain for a response. "Look, kid—I know you're in there. You might as well come on out."

Above him, a fresh breeze swept across the mesa top, through the piñon trees. A pungent fragrance spilled over the edge of the vertical cliff.

"And I know you're scared." He inhaled an invigorating whiff of the descending pine scent. "Hey, if it was me on the run, with a thousand cops and all the wild-eyed gun-totin' bounty hunters in a half-dozen states lookin' to collect a big reward for my hide—I'd be scared too." Assuming she could probably see him from her hidey-hole, the deputy squatted so he wouldn't look so scary to the fourteen-year-old. "But listen—and this is the honest truth—I'm not here to take you back to Utah on a murder charge." He maintained the grin. "Fact is, I'm not even on official duty. I took a few days off work so's I could track you down on my own time. See, all I want to do is collect the reward from Ben Silver's half brother. And all Ray Oates wants is what you took from ol' Ben. As far as Oates is concerned, you can hide out 'til doomsday." He stared hopefully at the dark cleft in the wall. "So whatta you say, kid?"

The kid didn't say anything.

He heard a low roll of thunder, glanced uneasily at the graying sky. "I sure hope you ain't gonna make me hang around out here and get rained on."

Still no response from the girl.

But there was a whining *meeeooow* from Mr. Zig-Zag.

An urgent *sshhhing* sound.

Sarah made an ineffective grab for her cat.

The curious feline came strolling out of the slit in the wall.

"Well, well," Packard said. "What've we got here?"

Mr. Zig-Zag approached the off-duty lawman, rubbed his head on the squatting man's knee.

From her place in the darkness, Sarah watched the deputy pick up her cat, get to his feet.

He rubbed a finger along its knobby spine, felt a returning ripple of feline pleasure.

Barely above the mesa top, a flash of lightning illuminated a black cloud's soft underbelly. This unseemly display was quickly followed by a cracking of thunder that threatened to split the earth. An acrid scent of ozone charged an atmosphere already tingling with hair-raising electricity.

The deputy's eyes narrowed. "Sarah, I ain't gonna stand out here all day long, waitin' for you to make up your mind. So listen to me. Here's the deal—you come out, give me what I come for, and I'm gone."

Another flash of electric fire, an almost simultaneous crash of thunder.

When he was eleven years old, Tate Packard had seen his cousin Teddy get struck by lightning. That had been almost twenty years ago, but some nights he still dreamed about blackened skin, sinew stripped from bone, and worst of all—the sweetish smell of cooked human flesh. The young man's jaw tightened; he wrapped his fingers around Mr. Zig-Zag's neck. Having lost the boyish grin, his lips were hard and thin. "You come out or I'll come in. But not before I've pulled this mangy old cat's head off!"

Sarah Frank hesitated, but only for a heartbeat. She shot out of the cave, a cannonball with flailing arms and legs.

*She's makin' a run for it!* The startled deputy dropped the cat, made a desperate grab for the girl—

## *FLIGHT*

A half-hour later, Deputy Tate Packard's blue-and-white Bronco was lickety-splitting it along the rutted lane through a driving rain, kicking up mud in its wake, putting miles and minutes between *here* and *back there.*

The driver's white-knuckled hands gripped the steering wheel as if the hard plastic circle was a life-preserver in a storm-tossed sea. Under his breath, the unrepentant sinner alternately cursed and prayed. Above his head, the heavens flashed and grumbled.

Guilty thoughts were a heavy yoke on his neck. *Maybe I shouldn't have done it but I did. And what's done is done—there's no turning the clock back.* A deep breath as he considered the bright side. *I've got what I wanted. Nobody saw me come, and nobody saw me leave.* He smiled grimly, nodded. *And there's no way to go now but straight ahead.*

Alas, as the heavy vehicle approached the Piedra bridge, straight ahead was not its manifest destiny. There was a sudden skidding, a vain attempt to brake, an impotent turning of the steering wheel, a gut-twisting realization—*I'm going into the river.* The driver-become-passenger closed his eyes, gritted his teeth so hard the enamel cracked. *I'm a dead man.*

The Bronco went sliding inexorably toward the steep, slippery bank.

And down it went, tumbling end-over-end.

Into the roaring waters.

• • •

HAVING received a 911 call from a passing trucker, the Southern Ute Police Department immediately dispatched the officer nearest to the scene of the incident. Danny Bignight—a Taos Pueblo man—had been with the SUPD for almost thirteen years. Unless he discovered a mangled corpse in the wreckage or someone who was severely injured, an auto accident rarely caused his pulse to rise over its normal resting rate of sixty-eight beats per minute. Bignight prayed he would not encounter a grisly scene. He prayed even harder that there would be no children involved. By the time he arrived at the Piedra bridge, a gathering of motorists had stopped to gape.

Oblivious to the peppering rain, a big-shouldered truck driver approached the SUPD unit, introduced himself as Sosteno Martinez.

Bignight grabbed a five-cell flashlight, got out of his unit. "Did you witness the accident?"

Martinez shook his head. "I got here right after it happened." The good Samaritan pointed at a soaked-to-the-skin man who had gratefully accepted a blanket from a kindly passerby. "But that guy saw it happen. He even tried to rescue the driver, but no dice."

Bignight trotted down the highway, aimed his flashlight at the half-submerged automobile, made mental notes. *No headlights or parking lights on. Internal dome light on—probably because both doors are open. No sign of anyone inside.* The Bronco was bumping its way downstream with lurches and jerks.

Returning to the bridge, the SUPD officer approached the eyewitness. "What's your name, sir?"

"Yadkin," Blanket-Man mumbled, and coughed.

Bignight had pad and pen in hand. "First name?"

"Yadkin *is* my first name. Last name's Dixon." In case the uniformed cop could not put this together, he explained: "Yadkin Dixon."

"I understand you were first on the scene."

"That's a fact."

Bignight jerked his chin at an old Chevy pickup parked nearest to the bridge. "That your vehicle?"

Yadkin Dixon shook his head, raised a dirty digit. "This thumb—and my feet—that's how I get around."

"So you were hitchhiking?"

"Trying to." The chilled vagrant shivered. "I'd walked all the way down from that little pond up by Route one-sixty—"

"Capote Lake?"

"If you say so. Back where I come from, a lake is something you can launch a sixty-foot yacht in." Y. Dixon noted that his audience showed no particular interest in how big lakes were back where he'd come from. "Anyway, I'd stopped here by the bridge, figuring that if somebody was to drive across it toward the main highway, they wouldn't be about to break the sound barrier." Seeing the bewildered expression on the Indian cop's face, the experienced hitchhiker explained: "If they're going slow, you get a chance to look 'em straight in the eye. And once you make eyeball contact with the driver, five times out of four, he—or she as the case may be—will stop and give you a lift."

Bignight liked the 125 percent odds. *I'll have to remember that.*

Dixon pointed in the general direction of the Bronco, which was still moving downstream. "But when I saw this car coming, it must've been doing a good sixty miles an hour. What with it being so dark from the thunderstorm and all, I s'pose he didn't even see the bridge—not until it was too late. Poor devil ran right into the river." He wiped a corner of the blanket across his mouth. "I did my best to get him out, even managed to grab his hand in mine." The almost-hero shuddered. "But you can see how the water's rippin' right along—it pulled him loose, swept him away." Dixon clasped his hands, closed his eyes. "Until the day I die, I'll hear those awful screams."

Bignight grimaced. "Aside from the driver, were there any other passengers in the vehicle?"

"Nope." Yadkin Dixon looked at the churning river and blinked. "If there was, I didn't see 'em."

"Can you describe the driver?"

"I didn't get a good look at him; it was pretty dark." After a series of hacking coughs, he eyed the cop. "You got a cigarette?"

"No." The SUPD officer made a hurried note in his pad. "Mr. Dixon—when you saw the vehicle approaching the bridge, did you notice whether or not the headlights were on?"

The eyewitness scratched at a stubbly crop of beard. "Now that you mention it, the lights weren't turned on. I'm sure of it." He grinned at the clever cop. "That must be why the driver didn't see the bridge." He stared at the distant form of the Bronco, which was now almost out of sight. "If he hadn't missed the bridge, he might've run me down—and to think that I risked my life to save his!" The hitchhiker heaved a heavy sigh. "If I ever come upon anything like this again—and I hope I never do— I won't even bother to get my feet wet!" He emphasized this decision by spitting, which—according to his ethical code—was the equivalent of engraving the oath in granite.

# TWENTY-SEVEN

## *WORRY, WORRY, WORRY . . .*

DAISY Perika had spent her day entertaining anxieties about Sarah Frank, who had fled with her spotted cat. As the tribal elder watched the mouth of Spirit Canyon swallow the slip of a girl, a thunderstorm was rumbling down the slopes of the San Juans, avalanching its way into the arid wilderness where her little home stood all alone, the last tomb in a deserted, tumbledown cemetery. All afternoon, furious winds wolf-howled around the eaves, sprightly lightning-legs danced to booming thunder-drums, windowpanes rattled. The aged woman watched and listened and wondered; is the End finally at hand? Was this deranged old world finally ripping itself asunder? She thought not, and felt a mild disappointment. *I'd like to live just long enough to see that last day.*

Though it was warm and cozy in her sturdy new home, the Ute elder pulled a woolen shawl over her shoulders. She was sitting close to the fireplace, where a few hungry flames licked voraciously at their meager supper—a half-dozen spindly sticks of split juniper. As she had done every few minutes, Daisy got up from her rocking chair, approached a window which, in fair weather, provided a magnificent view of *Cañón del Espíritu* with Three Sisters Mesa looming majestically above like a great stone battleship. Now, the trio of

Pueblo ladies were discreetly veiled behind a smoky gauze of mist, whose gray vapors spilled over the crest of the sandstone cliff, filling Spirit Canyon, flowing out of its mouth like the apparition of a long-dead river. She strained to see a particular location where the boulder-strewn slope met the vertical bluff. If Sarah had taken the old woman's advice, that's where she would be—sheltered in the small cave. The spot was marked by a black, lightning-scarred, fire-charred ponderosa that had patiently stood as decades passed. As Daisy watched, a long finger of white-hot fire reached out to touch a gnarled limb on the dead tree. The branch shattered into flinders; the remains flashed into flame, only to be extinguished by a sudden torrent of rain. After this brief display, the heavy curtain was drawn; she could see no more. She hoped the girl had sense enough to stay inside the cave, where the storm's mindless wrath could not find her.

Daisy's wrinkled face twisted into a frown that mirrored her inner annoyance. *Sarah should've stayed right here, depended on me to keep her safe. And whatever I can't handle, Charlie Moon can. If I was to call him on the phone and tell him there was trouble at my place, Charlie would drop whatever he was doing and head down here in that big car of his doing ninety miles an hour.* And if her nephew was not available, there was always the Southern Ute police. True, the officer who patrolled this section of the reservation wasn't a Ute—Danny Bignight was one of those peculiar Taos Pueblo Indians that Daisy did not entirely trust—but he was a sure-enough tough cop and all it would take was a 911 call and Danny would show up in nothing flat. Of course, even if he was in the neighborhood, *nothing flat* might amount to about half an hour.

Daisy went back to sit by the fire. Rocked in her rocking chair. Tried not to think about Sarah Frank. She was successful for about six seconds.

*Sarah went to hide in the canyon because she was afraid somebody was coming here to hurt her. Well, any fool could see she went up there for nothing. It's almost dark now, and nobody's showed up all day. And nobody will. Silly girl.* The old woman closed her eyes, sighed, cycled back into the endless loop of troubling thoughts: *I hope she's inside that little cave where she's safe from the storm. . . .*

Several dazzling flashes of lightning were followed quickly by the crispy-crackling cannonade that is Nature's way of shouting: Get under the bed, Daisy—Grandfather Thunder is about to kick your door in!

The Ute elder was in no mood for these hoary old proverbs that percolated up from her childhood memories, and stated her opinion out loud and firmly. "No he's not."

Bam!

Evidently, she was wrong.

Bam—Bam!

The old woman jumped up from her chair, turned to stare at the front door. *Maybe I was hearing things.*

If she was, she was hearing them again.

Bam—Bam—Bam!

She hurried to the closet nearest the front door. The same closet where she kept her always-loaded, double-barrel, 12-gauge shotgun. "Who's that?"

"It's me. Open up before I get blown into Conejos County!"

Thankful that her caller was not Grandfather Thunder, she flung the door open to admit Charlie Moon.

The lanky man, one hand clutching a water-logged black Stetson that was about to be carried away by the wind, erupted into her house. He removed his favorite hat, inspected its pitifully drooping brim. *I hope it ain't ruined.*

She followed as her nephew clomp-clomped a beeline to the fireplace, shrugged off a soaked denim jacket, hung it on a hook that had been screwed into the mantelpiece for just such a need. He held his soggy hat out to the drying warmth.

"What brings you out in the storm?"

Moon explained thusly: "When Danny Bignight called me at the Columbine, it wasn't storming." Not storming up at the ranch is what he meant to convey.

"Oh." She digested this tidbit, felt a tinge of heartburn. "Why'd Danny call you?"

"Some guy missed the bridge, ran his car into the Piedra." He attempted to push an unsightly dimple out of the Stetson's crown. "According to Officer Bignight, an eyewitness reported that the vehicle in question—which was going way too fast to make the turn—had just come off the dirt lane and onto the gravel road, and was heading toward the paved highway." He waited for her to absorb this information.

She did. "Which dirt road are we talking about?"

"The one to your place."

"Was this reckless driver anybody I know?"

"That's what I'd like to know."

This response puzzled his aunt, also annoyed her. "Whatta you mean by that?"

Moon tried on the hat, observed his reflection in the mirror over the mantelpiece. *Lookin' good. And Mr. Stetson don't look too bad neither.* "The population density out here is about one soul per sixty square miles, which is you. That being the case, I thought maybe this reckless driver was on his way back from paying you a visit."

"Nobody's been out here all day." With a suddenness that made her heart do a triple thumpity-thump, she recalled the fear that had driven Sarah into the wilderness of Spirit Canyon. "Did this fella have a name?"

"Everybody has a name." He made this assertion with a distinctly philosophical air.

*Big smart-aleck.* "Well, what *was* it?"

"According to the registration in the Bronco, it was Tate Packard."

Daisy shook her head. "Never heard of 'im."

"That's probably because he's not from around here." Moon adjusted his hat to a jaunty I've-got-spurs-that-jingle-jangle-jingle angle. "His complete moniker is *Deputy Sheriff* Tate Packard."

This did not sound like good news. Daisy waited for it to get worse.

Moon did not disappoint her. "He's attached to the sheriff's office in Tonapah Flats." The face under the brim of the black Stetson shot his aunt a deadpan glance. "Which is up yonder and across the border. In Utah."

"Oh, *that* Tonapah Flats." To buy some time to think, she busied herself by adding a few sticks to the waning fire. "Wonder what was he doing so far from home?"

"That's not much of a mystery," Moon said. "Deputy Packard must've been looking for Sarah Frank."

Daisy straightened her back, rubbed at a persistent ache. "Why would he think she was around here?"

"Now that's the mystery. He wouldn't have driven his Bronco all this way without a good reason to believe he'd find what he was looking for." He gave his cantankerous old aunt the hundred-watt smile. "Is she?"

*He puts on that silly grin just to aggravate me.* Daisy returned a glare, upping the ante to a kilowatt and change. "Is she what?"

Moon had not been intimidated by this crusty old woman since he was seven years old when she'd caught him with his fingers in the quart jar of her damson plum preserves that won a blue ribbon at the La Plata County Fair. "Is she here?"

The tribal elder pretended to be astonished at such a brazen question. She pointed at the floor. "You mean—here in my house?"

He nodded.

"No she's not!"

"You absolutely dead-sure about that?"

Daisy fixed him with the sort of "witching" gaze that had been demonstrated—and this was attested to by several mostly reliable witnesses—to paralyze such animals as short-horned lizards, slow-witted porcupines, and adult human males. "If she was, d'you think I wouldn't notice?"

Moon's brain was unfazed by the assault. "No. Way I see it—if Sarah Frank was in this house, you'd be bound to know." His smile wouldn't go away. "But maybe, for some reason or other—you wouldn't want to tell me."

Daisy stamped her foot. "If you don't believe me, you can search the place from top to bottom!"

The best poker player in sixteen counties generally knew

a bluff when he saw one. And he figured she was holding nothing better than a pair of deuces. If that. "You sure you wouldn't mind?"

She seated herself in the rocker. "Take it apart for all I care—as long as you put it back together again." Her mouth wrinkled into a rueful grin. "But any loose change you turn up belongs to me."

Moon called the presumed bluff. Within twenty minutes, he had searched the closets, the pantry, peeked under the bed (where the old woman stored her shoes and canned goods), the attic (accessible through a small portal in the top of Daisy's bedroom closet), the small camping trailer behind her house (which belonged to the tribe, but which Daisy claimed she wanted to keep for extra storage space but which was actually used for another purpose altogether). Finally, he removed a two-by-two-foot section of plywood and stuck his head through the opening under the kitchen sink which provided access to the crawl space. A flashlight beam illuminated clear evidence that no one had been crawling in the dusty place. *I guess she must've been telling the truth.*

The cattle rancher appeared by the fire, looking moderately sheepish.

"Hah!"

He squatted beside her rocking chair. "I heard that 'hah.' "

"You was supposed to hear it, you big jug-head. Just imagine—coming into an honest, law-abiding woman's home, accusing her of hiding a runaway girl who's wanted for . . ." She could not bring herself to say *murder.*

"I can't think of any reason Deputy Packard would've been in this neck of the woods unless he come to see you. And the only reason he'd want to see you would be to inquire about Sarah's current whereabouts."

Daisy responded with a grunt.

"But since he didn't show up here, I guess he never managed to find your place."

*And he never managed to find Sarah.* Pleased with this thought, she rocked a little faster. "Lots of people get lost out here."

Moon picked up an iron poker, stirred the smoking embers. "Packard was probably on his way to Ignacio, to get some directions." He frowned at a sudden spurt of flame. "Or more likely, to get somebody at SUPD to show him the way to your house."

*I hope he's not coming back.* Realizing that God was always listening, she added: *Not that I hope the poor man's drowned in the river. Just that he won't come snooping around here.* Having made that clear, she slowed her rocking to a more tranquil pace. "You never told me what happened to this Utah deputy. Did he get banged up some when he wrecked his car?"

Moon leaned the poker against the stone fireplace. "It does not look good for Deputy Packard—when he drove his Bronco into the Piedra, both doors popped open. The eyewitness told Danny Bignight that he tried to pull the driver out of the water, but he slipped loose and got swept downriver. Packard might have made it to the bank somewhere downstream, but when I left the bridge about an hour ago the search party still hadn't found him." He added grimly: "What with all the snowmelt runoff we've had this spring, the river's running fast enough to roll big boulders away."

The old woman had seen more Piedra floods than she could remember. This year's was one of the most impressive. Daisy shook her head. "It may take a few days, but they'll find his body a few miles downstream."

The tribal investigator did not dispute this prediction.

For some minutes, the fire crackled merrily, seemingly laughing at those manifold troubles that plague the lives of human beings.

When the clock struck nine, Moon got up from his chair. "I'll be away from the Columbine for a few days, taking care of some business."

Daisy stopped rocking, looked up at this man who stood straight and tall as a lodge-pole pine. "What kind of business?"

"Sheriff Popper—he's Packard's boss—is coming in from Utah to find out what his deputy was doing on the

Southern Ute reservation, and what's happened to him. I expect he wants to be present when they pull Packard's body out of the Piedra. And we'll be having some meetings with the FBI and the SUPD. Sheriff Popper and me, I mean."

"Oh." She returned her gaze to the fire.

He hesitated. "If you hear anything from Sarah, let me know right away."

The old woman showed no sign of hearing this request.

*I still think she knows something she don't want to tell me.* "If you have any problems while I'm busy, call my foreman. Pete Bushman's got standing orders to see that whatever's broken here gets fixed. If he can't come himself, he'll send a couple of the cowboys down to take care of it." The Columbine was largely independent of the outside world. Whether the job required skills in plumbing, electrical wiring, welding wrought-iron, or mending a leaky roof, the hired help managed to get the job done.

Moon stood before a mirror mounted on the closet door, adjusted the damp hat, cocked his head this way and that. "Funny thing, how people can surprise you."

"What people?"

"You remember Yadkin Dixon—the fella who comes begging at your back door?"

"I'd rather forget him." She snorted. "The good-for-nothing thief."

"Well, turns out he's good for something."

Another snort. "So is pig manure."

"Mr. Dixon was the eyewitness to Deputy Packard's accident at the Piedra bridge." Moon adjusted the Stetson just a tad. "And he risked his life in an attempt to save the deputy. Which makes him a hero of sorts."

Daisy thought about this, came to an uncharitable conclusion. "I bet ol' Yad risked his life to try to loot the drowning man's car." But this news had quite taken the wind out of her sails. *Maybe—like my mother always said—there is some good in everybody. Even that beady-eyed* matukach *moocher.* But for the set-in-her-ways old woman, this was an unsettling thought. So she dismissed it.

• • •

NOT long after Charlie Moon's departure, Daisy Perika got herself ready for bed. Once under the colorful quilt, she lay very still. For a long time, she tried to think of *nothing*. This was not possible. For a longer time, she watched countless beads of rain beat against the windowpane. But her old ears could not hear the rain. Not on the double-pane window, not on the roof. Her almost-new house was too well-insulated to admit the soothing sounds of Nature's lullaby.

Somewhere on the far side of midnight, Daisy got out of her warm bed, pulled on her slippers and a heavy overcoat that had been the property of her third husband. It was of the type and vintage popular during the 1940s in cities like Chicago and Detroit. The inside breast pocket on the left side—placed to be convenient to a gunman's right hand—was just the right size and shape to hold a short-barreled .38 Special. Daisy did not own such a weapon. As has been mentioned, she was a 12-gauge shotgun sort of personality, and the up-front kind of shooter who would never think of concealing a weapon.

She left her house by the back door, padded through wet sand to the tiny camping trailer. Once inside, she shed the overcoat and slippers, plopped her weary body onto a chilly cot, pulled a coarse woolen blanket up to her nose.

*Ahh . . . that's much better.*

What was much better was that she could distinctly hear distant rumbles, and rain pattering on the metal shell—Grandmother Thunder's soporific spell. Within minutes, she had taken leave for that world-without-laws where anything can happen. At first, it was a peaceful slumber.

Then, it was not.

*In the shadow of Three Sisters Mesa, Daisy laboriously made her way up the trail on the rocky slope. When she arrived at the shelf, she saw him. Only a few paces away, a young-looking white man was standing by the lightning-scarred ponderosa, staring at the small cave. Without knowing how she knew (for this is what dreamers do) the old woman was certain this was that very same man who had driven his car into the Piedra. The deputy was saying something to Sarah Frank, who was huddled in the cavern's dark recess. The man had Sarah's cat cradled in his arms, and though Daisy could not quite make out his words, he was clearly making a threat.*

*With a suddenness that took the shaman's breath away, Sarah emerged from her hiding place, the matukach lawman grabbed the girl, there was a violent struggle—*

*The dreamer tried with all her strength to hurry to the defense of Provo Frank's frail daughter, but her feet were rooted to the earth. Daisy tried to scream; was mute as the stones.*

*The man flung Sarah over the edge of the shelf, down the talus slope! In impotent horror, the tribal elder watched the doll-like body bounce and roll down the rocky incline, heard the girl's brittle little bones snapping like dry twigs.*

When the dreamer awakened on the cot, a driving rain was rattling on the camping trailer's thin metal shell, sudden gusts of wind rocked the flimsy structure, riveted joints squeaked and creaked, and Daisy's old frame was shaking like she had caught a hard chill. While she stared up into the noisy blackness the trembling of her limbs gradually subsided, but the heavy message of the night-vision pressed on her chest like a massive stone.

*Sarah Frank is dead.*

Unwilling to accept what her fears *knew* to be true, the shaman reminded herself that her visions were not always perfectly accurate projections of the future. Most of them provided warnings of some calamity that *might* occur unless someone (usually herself) took bold action to prevent it, and she grudgingly admitted that a very few of these "revelations" managed to get things upside-down and backward. These uncharacteristically modest thoughts Daisy-chained her to another, even more demeaning possibility: *Maybe it wasn't a vision at all—just a bad dream.* Which reminded the tribal elder of her nephew, who (so it seemed) took the view *all* of her visions were merely dreams. *The big gourd-*

*head!* She imagined herself whacking the unbelieving relative across the knees with her oak walking stick, and—when the imaginary nephew winced with intense pain—this revenge on the skeptic gave the offended party a measure of satisfaction. Before her conscience could slip a word in edgewise, Daisy cut it off: *Charlie Moon had it coming—if he hadn't told me about that Utah deputy driving his car into the Piedra, and how he must've come here looking for Sarah, I'd never have dreamed about him going to the place where I told the girl to hide.* Daisy Perika turned on her side, nudged her face into the lumpy little pillow. Of their own accord, her eyes closed. *If it was just a nightmare, it was all Charlie Moon's fault—if it wasn't for him, I'd have dreamed about something else.* A weary yawn. *Something nice, maybe. Like fields full of purple asters and them olden times when I was young and pretty and my little son was still alive and happy and . . .* She was whisked away into that dusky, timeless land where past and future stroll hand in hand. On this occasion, the dreams were sweeter and joy filled the hours.

Chubby little boy, chasing a frisky brown puppy through fields thick with flowers.

Pretty Daisy, running after him, laughing—black hair flying in a perfumed breeze.

But it seemed odd (her youthful version thought) that in the vast blue sky, there were no birds on the wing—only a single butterfly.

When she finally drifted up from this field of dreams, to skim along the interface with Middle World—this thought passed through her mind: *Soon as the sun comes up, I'll go find Sarah and tell her about that cop from Utah. If he didn't drown in the Piedra—not that I'm hoping he did, God—he might come back and cause us some trouble.*

# TWENTY-EIGHT

## *IN THE CANYON*

THE morning that followed the shaman's nightmare was not of that exhilarating sort where a valiant sun, gleaming sword unsheathed, charges boldly over the horizon to obliterate the lingering remnants of last night's noisy storm troopers. This blushing dawn was held at bay by a thugish mob of rumbling thunderheads. To the shaman's ears, it seemed the brawny gathering was tumbling boulders into the canyon—and mumbling ominous warnings of worse to come.

These rude demonstrations did not deter Daisy Perika.

Before the first crack of dawn had echoed off the towering cliffs, she was filling a hemp bag with food, a quart Thermos of honeyed coffee, wooden kitchen matches, warm woolen socks, and other such necessities as a girl in hiding might require.

With the sturdy oak staff clenched in her hand and the bulging sack looped over her shoulder, Charlie Moon's aunt entered the gaping mouth of the canyon—only to discover that the year-round stream that typically trickled lightly along the sandy bottom of *Cañón del Espíritu* had swollen overnight into a muddy, roiling creek. In places, it was knee-deep. Leaning on her walking stick, the intrepid hiker proceeded to get her feet wet. The water she waded in was numbingly cold, and choked with silt from far up the canyon. It occurred to Daisy that fording this stream might turn out to be a serious mistake; perhaps her final one. *If I was to fall down, I might not be able to get up again.* She quaked with a bone-rattling shudder. *I don't want Charlie Moon to find my body stuck in some bank, me with my mouth full of mud and ravens pecking at my entrails and my eyes staring wide open like a pair of poached eggs!* Daisy's long list of shortcomings did not include a lack of imagination. But the image of perishing in these rushing waters—much like that deputy from Utah who had ended up in the far deeper and more dangerous waters of the Piedra—was a picture that brought all her native stubbornness to the surface. The tribal elder set her jaw like iron, made up her mind. She would simply refuse to die in this place. *When my spirit crosses over that last river, I intend for my body to be in bed. I'll be decked out in my best polka-dot nightgown and my long white stockings and have my hair done up in a braid. But if it happens outside, I won't give up the ghost unless I'm on dry earth.*

And having decided to stand, she did not fall.

Once across the stream, Daisy set her face toward the barely discernible path that snaked its sinuous way up the steep slope where, for thousands upon thousands of winters, water trapped in the cracks and fissures of Three Sisters Mesa had frozen, thawed, and frozen in endless cycles. With the infinite patience of Nature's tireless rhythms, the recurring contractions and expansions had gradually loosened great slabs of sandstone. These were compelled by Gravity's decree to tumble down and reside alongside those of their kin already resting in the haphazard jumble. This process eventually fitted the broad waist of the mesa with an enormous skirt of stony rubble.

The aged woman moved along the precipitous path with considerable caution. One false step could end in a fall, possibly a broken hip or leg. In this wilderness, where an injured person might not be discovered for days, even a sprained ankle might result in a lonely, lingering death. She could clearly see the gory scene: *If I took a slip and broke something, come nightfall the foxes and coyotes would be all over me. Snapping and biting and fighting over the pitiful little bit of meat left on my bones.* As she watched the spectacle develop, a cougar arrived, chased the coyotes and foxes away. She was about to cheer the tawny brute, when the big cat picked up the remains of her corpse in its jaws, dragged it away for a private feast. Daisy scowled at the imagined affront, gripped her oak staff like the club it was, readied herself in case a mountain lion dared such a discourtesy while she still had a breath of life in her. *If he so much as shows his fuzzy face, I'll give him such a whack that he'll forget his name and next of kin!*

## *IN THE CAVERN*

AFTER pausing a dozen times to huff and puff like a worn-out old workhorse, Daisy Perika finally arrived at the narrow bench that separated the talus slope from the sheer cliff that rose up to the crest of Three Sisters Mesa. Standing near the dead ponderosa, whose lightning-splintered branch still smoldered with resinous smoke, she gazed hopefully at the little hole-in-the-wall. As if someone who should not hear might be lurking nearby, she spoke in a hissing whisper: "Sarah—it's me. Daisy."

An unsavory serving of silence fed the old woman's fears.

Pegging at the stony earth with her walking stick, Daisy approached the dark slot, raised her voice in a quaking plea. "Sarah—you in there?"

Still no response.

Daisy unhitched the hemp bag from her shoulder, rummaged around in it until she found the box of wooden matches. The aged woman bent her already bowed back, stepped into the darkness, struck a sulfurous tip on the gritty wall. She held the miniature torch in front of her face; the flickering flame was mirrored in the shaman's eyes. On the sandstone walls, pale yellow light-wraiths danced with sinister shadows. Whatever other presences might reside in this place, Provo Frank's orphaned daughter was not among them. And there was no sign of the blanket Daisy had given Sarah, or the girl's backpack—or for that matter, the cat. When the match burned down to scorch her fingertips, Daisy dropped it, struck a fresh one, held it knee-high to inspect the floor of the small cavern. There were a few girl-sized footprints in the sand, and a small plastic bag filled with something that looked like candy. The Ute woman bent her aching knees, snatched up the candy bag, held the match flame close to the label. *Gummy bears. My goodness, what will they think of next?* She absentmindedly dropped the sticky, sugary food into her coat pocket. *Maybe she had enough of sleeping in caves and decided to go back to my house, where it's warm and dry.* Daisy nibbled at her lower lip. *But there's only one way down from here, and out of the canyon. If Sarah had left before I set out to find her, she'd have already been at the house this morning. And if she left any later than that, I would've met her on my way into the canyon. And I didn't see her tracks in the wet sand. So she's still somewhere in Spirit Canyon.* Somewhere covered a lot of space. *You could hide a herd of buffalo in this place.*

When Daisy emerged from the darkness, the cloud-filtered daylight made her squint. As she stood under a gaunt, outstretched ponderosa limb, the Ute elder saw a black something in the sky above the canyon. It was circling, rising and falling in a capricious thermal. *It's too big to be a raven.* She lifted a hand to shade her eyes. *What is it—an eagle, or a hawk? If I could see the tips of the wings, I'd know.* As the self-propelled aviator suddenly swooped lower, she realized that it was neither. *That stinky buzzard probably figures I'm the next best thing to dead meat.*

But when she dropped her gaze to look down the talus slope, Daisy caught her breath. Far below, at the very bottom of the jumble of angular boulders, was the soul-chilling residue of last night's nightmare. Daisy's legs wobbled; she leaned against the lightning-scarred ponderosa, closed her eyes, relived the terrible vision as if it were happening at this very moment. As before, she saw Sarah emerge from the cave, scream at the white man who was holding Mr. Zig-Zag close to his chest.

But on this occasion, there was more detail.

*The man dropped the cat, grabbed the skinny Ute-Papago girl. He said something the dreamer could not hear, then laughed.*

*Sarah bit him on the wrist.*

*The matukach cursed, slapped her. Hard.*

*The girl shrieked, kicked him on the shin.*

*The furious man tossed the girl aside like a spoiled child discarding a broken toy.*

*The shaman watched the frail body tumble down the rocky slope; cringed as little bones cracked and snapped.*

Because Daisy knew what she would find, the descent along the narrow path proved considerably more difficult than the arduous climb. As she took one step at a time, foreboding thoughts nibbled at her mind like rats gnawing in the walls of an old house. *How did that deputy know where Sarah was hiding? Maybe he was watching my house and saw her go into Spirit Canyon and followed her up to the cave. He must've wanted to arrest her and take her back to Utah. I don't think he had intended to kill her—that was practically an accident. But he must've been feeling awfully guilty about what he'd done and wanted to get away as fast as he could—that's why he was driving so fast and missed the bridge. And now he's dead too—drowned in the Piedra.* Barely recovering from a stumble that almost made her tumble, Daisy's thoughts shifted to Sarah Frank's death. *Poor little thing must have suffered a lot, rolling down that rocky slope, her bones breaking like dry sticks. Oh, God—I hope I get to her before that scabby buzzard does!* But even without the depredations of the scavenger, it would be terrible enough. During her time on this earth, the tribal elder had seen dozens of corpses, and knew that this experience would be among the worst.

When Daisy finally arrived, she was furious to discover that the circling vulture and a pair of his famished mates had arrived ahead of her. "*Paga-nukwi!*" she shouted, "Go away!"

Unfazed by these rude commands, the feathered scavengers continued to feed.

Shedding the thin veneer of her civilized ways, the Ute woman let out a barbarous whoop and attacked—flailing at the startled diners with her walking stick.

The vultures withdrew—though only a few awkward hop-steps away, where they strutted about indignantly, flapping dusty wings, croaking throaty protests at the wild-eyed biped.

Knowing she must now face the corpse close at hand, Daisy steeled herself. *What I'll do is tell myself over and over: "This isn't Sarah—this is just the left-behinds."* Clenching her teeth as she approached the corpse, Daisy rehearsed the comforting words. *This isn't Sarah . . . this isn't Sarah . . .*

But the tough old woman was stunned by what she saw on the stones: pink flesh ripped to shreds, a tangle of broken limbs, the sickening silvery shine of exposed bones, a slack-jawed skull staring from empty sockets. . . . Daisy held her breath; this unspeakable horror bore not the slightest resemblance to the little girl with the enormous brown eyes. Indeed, if it were not for the human skull and the torn clothing, this might be mistaken for the mangled carcass of some wild animal.

She heard herself whispering: "This isn't Sarah . . . this isn't Sarah . . ."

But Daisy's world had been turned upside down. Head spinning, knees quaking, she leaned on her oak staff until the earth stopped moving under her feet. When it did, the backsliding Catholic crossed herself. *Oh, God—help me to understand.*

Understanding was granted. Other, more precious gifts were also forthcoming.

For the first time in many days, Daisy closed her eyes and prayed—addressing her petition to *my Lord Jesus Christ.* For an indeterminate time, she was at peace.

Alas, the sweetest moments pass most swiftly.

And though a few questions remained unanswered, mulling over these lesser mysteries could wait until those cold, gray days of Dead Leaves Falling, when she would sit near the fire with a mug of steaming coffee, and muse about hidden things. At the moment, there were important decisions to make.

A part of Daisy was eager to hurry home, telephone Charlie Moon, and tell him what she had discovered in *Cañón del Espíritu*. Her nephew always knew exactly what to do. That would be the sensible course of action. But with some problems, the "sensible" path was not the best one to take. In this instance, it might be better simply to wait, and at least for a season—let the dead lie quietly.

The tribal elder seated herself by the grisly remains.

It was terribly difficult work, but this woman had the Old People's blood coursing through her veins. For her ancestors, life had been a hard business. Something bad happens, you deal with it, then look forward to the next sunrise. By the time the sun was behind the mesa, she had covered the broken body with slabs of sandstone. The barely perceptible mound was camouflaged with bits of dry sticks, even transplanted tufts of grass.

When she had completed her labors, Daisy Perika was confident that the buzzards would never feast on what was left of *this* flesh. Moreover, she had concealed the remains so well that no one would ever find them. She frowned. No one except Charlie Moon—that man could find a pea-sized brown pebble in a bushel of pinto beans. *But only if he was looking for it.* She would have to make sure her nephew had no reason to start snooping around in Spirit Canyon. When the right day came—if it ever did—she would bring him to the makeshift burial. In the meantime, there were serious matters to think about; plans to be made and carried out. Pushing herself to her feet, she stood by the grave, scanned the canyon walls, listened. Her eyes saw nothing. Her ears heard nothing—except for harsh protests from the deprived buzzards, who circled overhead, croaking their righteous complaints.

• • •

On her way home, the Ute shaman had the queerest sensation that she was being watched by a pair of hollow eyes. She was not entirely surprised. It was common for spirits of the recently dead to show an intense interest in the living. Quite often, these confused souls did not realize they had been separated from their flesh. On several occasions, such phantoms had approached Daisy with questions—like what day it was, or for directions to some familiar place. Most of these displaced entities ached for a few words of comfort. More disturbing, it sometimes happened that the shadow would follow a living person home, to linger there for days, weeks—even months. This had happened to the Ute elder more often than she liked to remember. When she was a younger woman, Daisy had managed to endure these occasional invasions of her privacy. But as the years passed, she had become more solitary and also more picky about with whom she would share those precious few days she had left in Middle World. Ghosts do not make good houseguests. Very few were invisible to the shaman's eyes, and many of them had voices. Loud, demanding voices. Raspy, gossipy voices. Thin, whining, complaining voices. And those who were able generally felt compelled to talk, oftentimes in some ancient tongue she did not understand. Some spoke only rarely, others chattered from sunset 'til dawn—during those twilight hours when flesh and blood must have its rest. The notion of a spirit pacing about her home, rattling dishes, switching lights on and off, jabbering for hours on end was not a prospect she greeted with hearty enthusiasm. On the contrary, it rankled. And it was not merely a matter of being an annoyance, a ghost could be downright dangerous. Daisy recalled the sad case of a Hopi woman who had been paralyzed from the hips down by the vengeful spirit of a niece who was displeased with the meager burial offerings left by her poverty-stricken relative.

As she trod along, Daisy attempted to ignore the sense that she was being watched. *Stalked.* She resorted to denial: *Maybe it's just my imagination.*

A familiar raven landed on a juniper snag, caw-cawed a warning to the shaman. Daisy turned quickly, saw the diaphanous apparition not twenty paces behind her!

With a terrible intensity, it stared back.

Suddenly, without the least warning, Daisy's body stiffened. Her arms shot straight out, giving her the appearance of a short, stubby telephone pole. The tribal elder's eyes rolled in the sockets, presented white orbs—her head tilted back, so that the ghastly eyeballs stared straight up. Her throat began to make a noise that resembled gargling. Spittle dripped from the corner of her mouth, dribbled down her cheek.

This might have been enough to frighten all the creatures who watched, which included the raven, of course—plus a pair of chipmunks, a tuft-eared squirrel clinging to a cottonwood limb, a red fox concealed behind a dwarf oak, a masked badger scowling from its den, a blue-striped "racer" lizard, a venomous little scorpion that was capable of glowing when illuminated by ultraviolet light, an off-key quartet of fat Mormon crickets, plus various and sundry other insects whose considerable number precludes the listing of every one.

But Daisy was not done. Her performance had barely begun.

She hobbled (she could not run) around a prickly huckleberry bush, mumbling (she was past shouting): "Oh-oh-oh! I'd give my last greenback dollar for a one-eyed pinto pony. Wa-hoo! Tippecanoe and Tyler too! Oh, somebody please take me home and feed me vinegar tea and grasshopper stew!" She paused for a breath of air. "Ahhh . . . ahhh . . . I'm a poor old woman who don't have a roof to keep out the rain! Oh-oh-oh! What I'd give for a hollow log to sleep in . . . and a dry cow pie for a pillow!"

After six more passes around the huckleberry bush, the aged woman was about ready to pass out. She paused, took a terribly long time to get her wind back.

When she had partially recovered, Daisy turned, took a quick look at the path to the fresh grave. *I don't see nothing.*

*Maybe it worked.* In her considerable experience, spirits of the newly dead were already in a nervous state, and fearful of encountering any kind of trouble. No matter how much the inexperienced haunt might want to follow a person home, they tended to avoid the company of lunatics. Especially homeless lunatics who slept in hollow logs.

Hoping to spend the evening without any ghostly company, Daisy set her face toward hearth and home. But as she waded the stream, even above its gurgling and warbling the shaman thought she heard a mournful wailing. She stopped in the middle of the muddy torrent, braced herself on the oak staff, cocked her ear to listen.

It seemed there was a second call, but a blustery gust of the canyon's breath swept it away with a scattering of last autumn's dead leaves, prickly tumbleweeds, and miscellaneous other flotsam and jetsam.

Adding her melancholy sigh to the breeze, and with the sense of one recrossing the cold, deep Jordan, the weary woman waded her way toward the homeward bank. But as soon as she stepped onto dry land, the sense of being *followed* overwhelmed her—it was apparent that this particular spirit had not been deceived by her impromptu performance. Though disappointed, Daisy was not defeated by the realization that *It* apparently intended to follow her right into her parlor. If the tough old woman had had a motto engraved on her mantelpiece, it would have been something in the vein of NEVER GIVE UP or GO DOWN FIGHTING. Furthermore, she was not without resources. The shaman knew that when a person's home became infested by a troublesome ghost, there were certain remedies available. After shaking the water off her feet, she began to tick off the top three methods of evicting unwanted ghostly guests.

A few cloves of garlic hung in every room might do the trick. *But that stinks up a house something awful. I'd probably have to give up my home before the spirit did.*

She could call Father Raes Delfino, and request an exorcism. *But for three years, I've been mad at that priest for retiring from St. Ignatius and moving to that little cabin on*

*Charlie Moon's ranch. And if you're mad at someone, you can't ask him for favor.*

That left number three. It was possible to lure a ghost out of your house. The most effective method was to get hold of something the haunt treasured, and hide it in somebody else's home. If the earthly possession was something the spirit simply couldn't do without, like a favorite pocket watch or a diamond engagement ring—the disembodied presence would feel compelled to follow it, and the formerly haunted person would return home to a ghost-free house. All you needed was something special that had belonged to the dead person. Having arrived at her door, Daisy leaned her walking stick against the wall and frowned. *But I don't have nothing like that. And I don't have any chance of getting it. Not unless I go back and take the stones off and—* She was distracted from this gruesome thought by a thin, feline whine.

Mr. Zig-Zag was sitting at her feet. Seemingly oblivious to the fact that he was bloody, missing several tufts of fur, and curiously decorated with clinging cockleburs, the creature licked fastidiously at a front paw, then looked up expectantly at the human being—the species from whence all blessings came—as if to say: "Where's the food?"

"Well, well—would you look at that!" She exchanged thoughtful stares with the cat. *I wonder how long it'll be before Little Bo Peep comes looking for her lost kitty.*

European nursery rhymes were not Daisy's strong suit.

# TWENTY-NINE

## *THE PROBLEM*

EXHAUSTED by the ordeal in *Cañón del Espíritu* and despair*ing* over the memory of the grisly discovery she had concealed in a makeshift grave, Daisy Perika headed into her parlor, collapsed on the couch into a weary heap.

Mr. Zig-Zag had also had a difficult day. After a thorough search for an ideal spot to recline, the bedraggled cat finally decided to stretch out beside the Ute woman.

"Go away," she mumbled.

Mr. Zig-Zag yawned in her face.

Daisy was simply too tired to take a swat at the cheeky creature.

After nodding off into a fitful nap that was knotted with a tangled string of troublesome images, Daisy awakened to blink at the animal whose peaceful sleep was an affront to her. She nudged the furry creature. "Hey you—wake up!"

The cat did as bid, blinked at this wrinkled creature who had disturbed his *siesta*.

Daisy turned on the scowl. "You don't fool me for a minute, Fuzz-Face." She knew that a cat who'd had free eats and shelter would not be satisfied—not until the moocher had taken over title to the property, including mineral rights—and subjugated the former owner to the position of Adoring Attendant, hurrying to satisfy his every whim. In several case histories with which she was familiar, this role reversal had been accomplished with such ingenious smoothness that the human victim was completely oblivious to the crime. Aware of his deceitful plans, she eyed the cunning creature with a knowing curl of the lip. *Within a day or two, Mr. Rag-Bag will pick out his favorite chair, decide when he wants to be fed, and when he wants me to tuck his little carcass into bed.* But the crusty old woman had no intention of becoming a feline's fawning servant; Daisy Perika had another plan in mind. The tribal elder was dead certain that before the night was over, *someone* would come calling. Someone who was wandering around in the outer darkness, searching for her stray pet. Having no human company to converse with, Daisy spoke to the animal on her couch. "With you here, Sarah's bound to show up."

The creature focused ambivalent amber eyes on the human being.

"And when she comes looking for you—what do you think I'll do?" Daisy knew. She would see to it that the cat departed. And where the cat went, Sarah would be sure to follow. Like in "Mary Had a Little Cat," or something like that. But where should they go—and how could Daisy manage the delicate transfer? That was the problem.

While she waited for the unfortunate girl's appearance, Daisy did not intend to spend the evening in idleness. *What I need is some work to do. That'll help me think.* After an examination of the cat's split ear, the medicine woman gathered some of the instruments of her trade, which were a mix of the ordinary and arcane variety. She used a cotton swab soaked with wood alcohol to clean splotches of blackened blood off the animal's shoulder and head, then added a few precious dabs of Navajo Hisiiyháaníí oil to his wounds. "Looks like you met up with Mr. Teeth," she muttered, "and he put the bite on you."

In a boastful "You should have seen the other guy" gesture, the battered cat presented her with a claws-extended paw.

"Oh, sure." She chuckled. "I guess you got in a lick or two of your own."

When the first aid was completed, she turned her attention to about two dozen cockleburs that were firmly enmeshed into the black-and-white fur. Removing them was a tedious process. While holding a tuft of hair between finger and thumb, she used a mustache comb to remove the offending seedpod. This act of mercy occupied much of her evening.

When she had removed several dozen burrs, the cat began to whine. Gave her the big-eyed look.

"*Now* what is it?" And then it dawned on her. *It's started already.* "You want me to get you something to eat." She shook a finger at the beast. "Okay, but don't think I'm gonna make a habit of waiting on you." Having made her point, she got up, headed for the kitchen. Halfway there, remembered that there was no tuna left in the pantry. *I wonder if cats like Velveeta cheese?*

As it turned out, this one did.

While Daisy watched Mr. Zig-Zag consume his supper, the devious old woman began to think. Almost as soon as she would consider a plot, a flaw would appear, and she would drop it to pursue another crooked line of thought. During this process, Daisy stared at empty space, nervously patted a hand on her knee, occasionally nodded to agree with herself on some critical point. After several hundred ticks and tocks of the clock, the experienced tactician concluded that she had come up with just the right plan. The solution went something like this: When you have something you don't want, give it to someone else. And she knew just who *someone else* was. A deserving party. The problem was solved—if only a few circumstances and a couple of knuckle-headed people would cooperate. She set her jaw. If they didn't, she would just grab them by the neck and shake them until they did!

The time for action had come.

She picked up the telephone, punched in the familiar number for Charlie Moon's Columbine Ranch. After four rings, she heard the pleasant voice of Dolly Bushman, who—in Daisy's opinion—had the severe misfortune of being bonded in holy matrimony to the foreman. Pete Bushman was (in Daisy's opinion) a blight and a plague. "It's me," Daisy said.

"Oh, Mrs. Perika—how are you?"

"I'm all right." The hostile Indian tried to sound civil. "Is my nephew at home?"

"Oh, no. Charlie's off somewhere with that sheriff from Utah. We don't expect him back 'til Saturday, at least."

*Good.* "Well isn't that just like him—taking off for days at a time without saying a word to his closest relative."

"You could call him on his cell phone."

"He generally keeps it turned off. And I don't like to leave messages on that silly machine."

"Daisy, dear—Charlie told me that if you had any kind of problem, we was to take care of it. If something needs fixing at your place, I'll just send Pete down there and—"

"No, thank you—there's nothing here that needs fixing." *Well, that's not exactly true. But even if this was something he could help me with, I wouldn't want that hairy-faced old white man in my house. He smells like a fresh cow pie and he's always spitting tobacco juice.* "Is Father Raes holed up in his little cabin, reading the Bible and praying six times every day?"

"He's gone off someplace or other." Though she was a Baptist, Dolly Bushman's tone let it be known that she did not appreciate the Indian woman's rude way of speaking about the Catholic priest who was—in her view—as holy a man as had ever set foot in Colorado. "I don't know when he'll be back."

Daisy smiled. "Well, I've got some things I need to bring to the ranch." This was the literal truth. "Soon's I can get somebody to drive me, I'll show up."

"Daisy, I'd be glad to send Pete down to get you. Or one of the cowboys—"

"No, don't bother." The Ute woman breathed her patented martyr's sigh. "I wouldn't want to put you people to any trouble on *my* account."

"But it wouldn't be no—" Dolly heard a click in her ear.

Having disconnected Dolly Bushman from her thoughts, Daisy Perika was already dialing another number.

Her male cousin answered promptly. "H'lo. Who's this?"

"You're Gorman Sweetwater," she said with exaggerated patience. "And whenever you forget, just check your driver's license—if you still have one. Your name's printed on it." She cackled out a passable imitation of the Witch of the West, which was pretty close to what some of the more superstitious folk on the reservation had her pegged for. "And so's your picture, in case you don't remember what you look like, which might be a blessing now that I think of it, so maybe you'd best leave the thing in your wallet."

"Daisy?"

"No, this is Marilyn Monroe, struttin' around the swimmin' pool in a pink bathing suit."

The seductive picture posed before him, Gorman sighed with the regret of an old man who remembered the carnal pleasures of the mid-twentieth century only too well. "No you ain't. You're Daisy."

"So how are you doing, you old wart-head?"

"Oh, pretty good. Did I tell you I bought me a new pickup?"

*Only about ten times.* "Is that a fact—what make is it?" She mouthed the expected words: *It's a GMC—the onliest pickup a man should—*

"It's a GMC—the onliest pickup a man should spend his hard-earned money on."

"Now that you mention it, I think maybe I heard something about it. Is it a red truck?"

"Well, yeah—only GM calls it something like Carmine Sunset, or Strawberry Dream." He thought about it. "No, Strawberry Dream is the color of that red ice cream."

"Well, whatever they call it, it must be real pretty. And didn't I hear it had a fine white camper shell on the back?"

"Genuine fiberglass," Gorman said with more than a smidgen of pride. "And it's got four-wheel drive and an air bag on the driver's side and the biggest V-8 of any truck in its class—"

"Sounds like something special. Why don't you bring it out here for me to see?"

"Well . . . I dunno." There was a clicking sound as he applied a toothpick to an incisor. "It's a longish drive to your place, and gas is awful pricey these days."

"Tell you what—you drive that shiny new red truck out here tomorrow morning and take me for a ride, and I'll fix you a breakfast like you ain't had since old dogs was fussy puppies. And I'm talking three brown-shell eggs."

"With some crispy bacon?"

"Six slices. And a big slab of ham and sliced potatoes—all fried in lard." Sensing his hesitation to commit, the wily old gamester rolled loaded dice. "And I'll buy you a tank of gas."

Gorman Sweetwater's tone reflected his doubts about such a grand promise from a woman who pinched pennies hard enough to make Honest Abe grimace. "A full tank?"

"Right up to the brim."

"High octane?"

"Sure. But you show up by nine." Daisy Perika scowled at her unseen cousin. "And I don't mean Indian Time."

After the discussion of a few additional details, the deal was done.

Daisy said good-bye and hung up. The wheels were turning. Now she could relax, and she did.

As the clock chimed eleven, she was drifting off toward that gray land where old women become young again, where trees sing and stones speak and shamans fly high over mountain peaks. Not halfway there, she met a thin little girl, who was standing in the shade of a mulberry tree.

*Sarah Frank was wearing a pink satin dress. Her hands, dripping blood, were holding a wooden club. The lonely little soul seemed not to notice the tribal elder. Sarah was calling out, over and over: "Mr. Zig-Zag—where aaaarrrre you . . ."*

Daisy reached out to touch the child, and was awakened by a screechy yowling.

It was, of course, the self-centered cat. Mr. Zig-Zag was pawing at her leg.

She made a face at the pesky creature. "You've been fed. What is it now—you want to watch your favorite show on the TV?" Garfield Eats the Parakeet, *I expect.*

Not so. His gaze was fixed on the door.

"Oh, right. You want to go outside." *At least he's trained not to mess up the floor.* Grateful for this small blessing, Daisy got up, headed for the exit. About to turn the knob, she hesitated. *Maybe that's* not *why he wants out.* She switched off the lights, crept over to the window, opened it barely an inch. As was her lifelong habit, she listened intently to the sounds of night.

In a sagebrush thicket, an invisible cricket. *Clickety-clickit.*

A pie-eyed owl on a juniper snag. *Hut-hut-hooooooo . . .*

And wafted in from *somewhere* on the chilly breeze—"*Mr. Zig-Zag . . . where aaaarrrre you . . .*"

The cat heard it, too; he responded with a melancholy yowling.

Daisy waited a hundred heartbeats, heard the unspeakably mournful call again. But much closer now. *I knew it—she's come looking for her pet. It won't be long 'til she'll be pecking at my door. And She'll want to sit up and talk 'til the crack of dawn.*

But if the cunning old schemer had her way—and she generally did—this particular night visitor would not tarry for long. No, before the yellow-balloon moon floated over the mountain again, the homeless waif would be far away—in what Daisy Perika assured herself, would be a more suitable habitation. With her cat, of course.

And so she waited for the expected arrival.

While she waited, the shaman thought she saw a flickering shadow on the wall, then it was gone. *No, there it is again.* This tiny mystery was solved when she noticed the small, brown insect fluttering around the ceiling light fixture. She frowned. *I hate moths.*

It would never have occurred to Daisy Perika that this *moth* might be a butterfly. Nor was there any reason that she should have entertained such a thought. Butterflies flutter by when the sun is high; at night, they fold their wings and sigh and sleep and dream dreams that cannot be imagined, much less described. Everyone knows this.

So it was most likely a moth.

# THIRTY

## *A SIMPLE MATTER OF EXPERTLY APPLIED MANIPULATION*

WHEN Gorman Sweetwater drove up in his beloved new pickup, Daisy Perika was outside waiting for her cousin. *I hope he hasn't been drinking this early in the day.* After Gorman had soaked up a six-pack, he would gaze at her with the droopy-jaw, hollow-eyed look of a certified moron. A glance at the suspect relative convinced Daisy that he was about as sober and sensible as he ever got. *Which ain't saying all that much.*

Gorman lowered the window. "When did you get yourself a cat?"

Daisy glanced at Mr. Zig-Zag, who was sniffing at a tiny purple flower. "This ugly fuzz-ball don't belong to me—he's just a stray that wandered in the other day." That was close enough to the truth.

"Looks like he tangled with a coyote." The perpetually hungry man eyed a covered basket Daisy had slung over her shoulder. "What's in that?"

She shrugged under the weight. "Oh, just some things."

The expectant diner licked his lips. "I bet it's a picnic lunch."

Daisy offered an enigmatic smile. "You might be right." She inspected the camper shell. "Is the back of your truck unlocked?"

"Sure." He got out, slammed the door, relieved his cousin of her burden, sniffed at the aromatic hints. *Fried chicken. Baked beans. And some kinda fresh-baked pie.* Another sniff. *Peach cobbler.* He started to open the lid—

"Leave it shut!" Daisy slapped his hand. "That's for Father Raes."

He exhaled a melancholy sigh, said good-bye to the pie. "Don't he live up at Charlie Moon's ranch since he retired?"

"Sure. And that's where you're taking me."

"Oh." *Well, it'll be nice to see the priest again.* He stowed the basket in the back of his pickup, and was about to shut the camper shell door when Daisy shouted orders to the contrary.

"Leave it open."

"You want me to load some more stuff?"

"Not right now. You can have your breakfast first."

His spirits somewhat restored, Gorman followed Daisy and the cat into her home, all the while assuring himself that this would be a profitable day. In addition to the free meal, but he'd make sure Daisy didn't "forget" her promise to fill his gas tank. Almost an hour later, having enjoyed the excellent breakfast, the appreciative man thumped his chest and presented his host with a complimentary burp.

Because her cousin was an obnoxiously odorous man, as likely to expel gas from one orifice as another, Daisy was grateful for the limited nature of this expression of culinary approval.

"We'd better get goin'," Gorman said. "I got to be home before dark."

"Why's that?"

Realizing that he still had some room under his belt, Gorman buttered a made-from-scratch biscuit. Never one to avoid a tasteful pleasure, he added two heaping tablespoons of strawberry jam. "It's because of my eyes."

She stored a heavy skillet in the oven. "What's wrong with your eyes?"

Gorman took a bite of the biscuity confection, attempted to recall the technical term. *Cattle-racks? No, that's some-*

*thing you put on a truck. But it's got something to do with driving. Oh, now I remember.* "My eyes has the Cadillacs."

She slammed the oven door. "The *what*?"

He explained in that tolerant, though mildly condescending manner which the well-informed reserve for relatively ignorant relatives: "It's a eye-problem that makes it hard for me to drive at night. That's why I got to be home before dark."

Daisy blamed herself for asking. *After all these years of him spouting nonsense, I shouldn't expect the old knot-head to make any sense.* She grabbed a damp dish towel, gave the table a series of vicious swipes. *I hope whatever's wrong with his brain don't run in the family.*

He spooned sugar into the coffee cup. "But my optimist says he can fix it."

She stopped in mid-swipe, her mouth gaped guppy-fashion. "Your *what*?"

Though tolerant with those less blessed than himself, Gorman was beginning to run short on patience. "Why d'you keep saying 'what-what-what'?" He set his jaw. "Ain't you never heard of how some old people get Cadillacs in their eyes? And don't you know that a optimist is a eye doctor?"

"No, I didn't know those things." Daisy sighed. "I guess I'm just not as smart as you are."

Disarmed by this candid confession from a woman who never, ever admitted to having the least shortcoming, Gorman softened his tone. "It's not your fault, Daisy. Why, anybody else who lived out here all by theirself for years on end, with no way to keep up with what's goin' on in the world—they'd be even dumber than you."

Barely resisting the temptation to swat him with the dish cloth, she thought: *It's a good thing I didn't have that cast-iron frying pan in my hand.* "Thank you so much for understanding."

Out of sympathy for the deprived woman, Gorman changed the subject. "Anyway, like I said, my doctor's sure he can fix what's wrong with me."

"Then he is for sure."

About to take a sip of Daisy's famously strong coffee—which was rumored to have melted stainless steel spoons and caused strong men's eyeballs (Cadillacs and all) to eject from their sockets with a loud popping sound and hang limp on their cheeks—Gorman paused, stared at his cousin over the brim of the cup. "He is for sure *what*?"

She smiled. "Your doctor is a sure-enough optimist." *If he thinks he can fix what's wrong with you.*

*Well, at least we finally got* that *straight.* The family scholar downed a swallow of the shaman's potent brew.

Daisy pattered her cousin on the head. "You know what I think?" This being a rhetorical question, she did not wait for a response. "I think you oughta trade in that shiny new pickup truck." This being an ambush, the crafty old bushwhacker waited for him to ask for what.

"Trade it in for what?"

"Why one of them long, red Cataract convertibles!" Her body shook with laughter.

Gorman stared at the peculiar woman, made an instant diagnosis. *Al's Hammers—that's what it is.*

# THIRTY-ONE

## *THE SHAMAN'S GAME*

GORMAN took a gander at the things his elderly cousin had loaded into the bed of the GMC pickup while he was having his breakfast. A big canvas laundry bag, evidently stuffed with clothing. Several quilts and blankets, a fluffy feather pillow. And Daisy wasn't finished. At her instructions, he carried out three heavy cardboard boxes that were filled with canned goods, everything from vegetable-barley soup and great northern beans to peach halves (in heavy syrup), old-fashioned SPAM and candied yams. There was also a box of Saltine crackers and two bags of chocolate-chip cookies.

The better to look askance at this load of freight, the curious man cocked his head. "You figure the Father'll eat all of that?"

"Sure. That skinny little priest puts food away like a starved grizzly." She pushed a plastic grocery bag of miscellaneous items into the truck bed. "I've always had a suspicion that he's got a tapeworm." The self-assured diagnostician wiped her hands on a cotton apron. *And he especially likes cookies.* She added this to an already long list of medical clues. *Next time I get the chance, I'll fix him some of my tapeworm medicine. But first I'll need to get me some kerosene and about a pint of castor oil . . .*

Gorman glanced at his cousin. "Is that it?"

"No, but what's left I'll put up front."

Daisy's cousin lifted the heavy tailgate, slammed it into place. "I've heard some talk about Charlie Moon's big lake—they say it's so chock-full of trout that a man can walk across the water on their backs. Barefooted, without getting his ankles wet." He lowered the shell door, snapped it into place, shot Daisy a hopeful glance. "I got some fishin' tackle in the cab. You reckon Charlie might let me drop a hook in the water?"

"Maybe." She looked doubtful. "If I put in a good word for you."

Gorman watched her toddle back into the house.

Daisy returned with the cat cradled in her arms.

The driver looked down his nose at the creature. "You thinkin' of takin' that scabby-lookin' chewed-up animal with us—in my brand-new pickup?"

"I'm not just thinking about it—I'm *doing* it." She placed Mr. Zig-Zag in the cab, then got in herself. Once she was settled, Daisy turned her glare on the reluctant chauffeur. "Gorman, I got news for you—you'll have to crank this thing up. It won't go by itself."

During the long drive north, Daisy busied herself with removing a final few burrs from the cat's fur. It was a monotonous task, much like knitting a sweater or applying tiny colored beads to soft buckskin moccasins—the sort of work a woman does when she needs to think. And Daisy had quite a lot to think about. So much that she had no intention of wasting these precious minutes gabbing with her addle-brained cousin.

As mile markers passed like lonely soldiers retreating to the rear, Gorman endured the silent treatment—but he could not understand his relative's reticence to chat about this and that. The man had his feelings. And they were hurt. As they were entering the southern edge of Granite Creek, he could no longer contain the pent-up store of words that had been building up behind his lips, and decided to break the ice by bringing up a subject of wide and general interest. "GMC sure makes a first-class truck."

Daisy removed the last sticky seedpod, put it on her knee with the others.

"This one's got an after-market CD player. And satellite digital radio. And six speakers. And—" He winced as his cousin stuffed the cluster of cockleburs into the pickup's immaculate ashtray.

The grateful animal purred like a finely tuned model motorboat motor. And looked up at Daisy as if on the verge of making a thoughtful comment. Or, perhaps, to ask his benefactor a question.

"D'you want to hear some music?" (No, this was Gorman speaking.)

"If I do," Daisy snapped, "I'll let you know."

This response—which he took as negative—caused a gray cloud to pass over Gorman Sweetwater's craggy face. But a determined conversationalist does not throw in the towel when he has taken one on the chin. Bobbing and weaving past the sensitive subject of music, he readied a heavy counterpunch. Horsepower. "This model's got the finest V-8 engine ever to come out of Detroit City." Knowing she would be staggered by this, he followed up with a bone-jarring uppercut. "And computer-controlled all-wheel drive."

Daisy's face was like granite.

The driver slowed for a stoplight. "And high-tech brakes that—"

"And a big air bag at the wheel."

The lightweight glared at his passenger. "What?"

She offered him the wide-eyed innocent look. "An air bag on the driver's side—ain't that what you told me when we was talking on the phone last night?" She reached over to pat her relatively slow-witted relative on the arm. "I bet you thought I'd already forgot."

The light changed, he drove on—but with a nagging suspicion that he had been knocked off his pegs. He just couldn't figure out how she'd done it.

• • •

By high noon, Gorman Sweetwater had passed through the main Columbine gate, and was tooling along the miles-long ranch road.

As they approached the foreman's house, Daisy barked an instruction. "Slow down."

He meekly followed his cousin's order.

Dolly Bushman was on the front porch, mercilessly beating a dusty throw rug to death.

*I don't want her to get suspicious.* Daisy grinned crookedly, waved. "Hello, there!"

The foreman's kindly wife returned the gesture, smiled, yelled back: "Hello yourself, Daisy. It's nice to see you. Charlie's still not back yet but—"

"Then I guess I won't be staying long." She addressed Cousin Gorman out of the corner of her mouth. "I'm through talking to White-Eyes—step on the gas!"

Dolly watched the pickup lumber off, listened as it rumbled across the bridge over Too Late Creek. *Well now I've seen everything—Charlie Moon's grouchy old aunt is behaving almost like a normal human being. She must be feeling good today.*

Daisy Perika was feeling good. Today, things were definitely going her way.

Gorman slowed at the ranch headquarters—where Charlie Moon hung his hat and Daisy had a downstairs bedroom reserved for her occasional visits.

The tribal elder reached over to jerk at her cousin's sleeve, which caused the pickup to swerve. "Keep right on going." She pointed. "Take the dirt track around that big red barn—it goes over the ridge that has all the spruce, and then to the cabin. That's where Father Raes stays when he's not off running all over Europe or South America."

The fisherman had his own priorities. "Where's the lake?"

"Not too far from the cabin." Daisy watched the Columbine hound appear from under the wraparound porch, raise his nose to sniff the air. *I wonder if he can smell the cat.*

When they arrived at their destination, Father Raes's old

Buick was nowhere in sight. Daisy breathed a sigh of relief. *Thank goodness he's not back yet.* But she knew that he never locked his cabin door. On the Columbine, there was no need for the sort of precautions that town folk had to worry about.

Unless, of course, Daisy Perika came calling.

Having parked in the inky shade of a blue-black spruce, Gorman opened the camper shell, lowered the tailgate, unbuttoned his shirtsleeves.

"Just take in those heavy boxes, with the canned food—then you can go fishing." Daisy had the whining, squirming cat clutched in her arms. "I'll tote the rest of this stuff in myself."

His eyebrow arched itself. As if to say: *When you act all goody-goody nice, I am naturally skeptical.* The eyebrow was entirely justified in its suspicions.

After Gorman had completed his appointed task, Daisy pointed toward the alpine lake. "Now take your fishing pole over there—see if you can catch yourself a ten-pound trout." Having disposed of Mr. Zig-Zag, she reached for a small bag of groceries. "Fish for an hour, but not a minute more. By the time you get back, I'll be ready to go."

He did and she was.

When Gorman returned with a fourteen-inch rainbow, he found Daisy waiting in the pickup. The ecstatic angler waved the wriggling catch in her face. "Caught him on a red-eyed grasshopper!"

"That's a pretty fish." The old woman glanced at the cabin, where she saw the cat's face in the window. And, for a fleeting moment, that *other* face, which looked as if it might weep forever. Daisy turned away. "Let's get going." She added: "When we get to Durango, I'll top off your gas tank."

And so they drove away.

If it was not the best of days, it was certainly not the worst.

Consider Gorman Sweetwater. He had enjoyed a free, top-notch breakfast, pulled a fine trout from Charlie Moon's private lake, and drove home with a full tank of gasoline in his brand-new red GMC truck with the genuine fiberglass shell on the back. Per diem, the take had been more than adequate. A sensible man should not expect any more of a day than that.

Consider Daisy Perika. The tribal elder had accomplished her immediate objectives—laid down her burdens, one might rightly say. She had left that pesky cat in Father Raes's log cabin. And that wasn't all she'd left there, but the old woman tried not to think about that unfortunate aspect of the matter. Daisy was not proud of what she had done, but neither did she feel an overwhelming sense of guilt. Under the extraordinary circumstances, the Ute elder had very few options—none of them pleasant to contemplate. She consoled herself with the thought that this unfortunate business was now her nephew's problem.

• • •

It was well past midnight, and Daisy was tossing and turning in her bed as troublesome thoughts pounded in her head. She wondered what would happen when Charlie Moon found out what she'd done. And what would happen if Father Raes found out first. Daisy desperately wanted to confide in someone—someone who would understand why she had felt compelled to take this course of action. *I can't very well talk to Louise-Marie LaForte—that old biddy couldn't keep a secret if you sewed it onto her skin.* The sleepless woman wondered whether Marilee Attatochee was lying wide awake in her bed, worrying herself half to death over what had become of Sarah Frank. *I bet she's looking at the walls, just like me—and can't sleep a wink.* She rolled over for the thirty-third time, stared at the telephone by her bed. *I could call her up and tell her that Sarah . . .* But that made no sense at all. *I'd be a silly old woman to do such a thing.* Daisy was not silly. Far from it.

But she kept looking at the telephone.

# THIRTY-TWO

## *WRONG NUMBER*

*Without knowing how she had gotten there, Marilee Attatochee found herself inside a long, shadowy space. The chamber was enclosed by gray stone walls that were set with tall stained-glass windows; pink-eyed bats flitted about a darkly beamed loft. A new red carpet had been rolled out along a narrow aisle that separated an assortment of rough-hewn benches. The altar (if it was an altar) was illuminated by dozens of black tapers. The priest (if there was a priest) was nowhere to be seen, but illuminated by the flickering light of the candles, a pale, eight-year-old version of Al Harper was picking a five-string banjo, singing "If You've Got the Money, Papago Gal—I've Got the Time."*

*One moment, Marilee was seated on a bench—the next she was standing at the end of the line of mourners, which numbered precisely three. When the singer-musician began to pick a few licks of "Bluegrass Breakdown," Marilee began to tap her foot.*

*The man in front of her turned to present a long, horse-like face. "Please, madam—do not disturb the solemn nature of the ceremony!"*

*"Sorry—I guess I got carried away." She added: "I'm kinda mixed up."*

*He looked down a beak-like nose, cleared his throat. "Mixed up, you say?"*

*She explained: "I don't know where I am."*

*A broad smile. "Why you're at the Tonapah Flats Hi-Tone Funeral Home, Community Crematory, and Small Engine Repair Shop."*

*"But what am I doing here?"*

*He sighed, shook his head: "You are attending a jim-dandy memorial service—the jim-dandiest one we've had all year!" Long fingers clicking like castanets, he performed a quick little three-step jig, finishing with: "Cha-cha-cha!"*

*"Who died?"*

*After doing an expert backflip, the dancer-acrobat replied: "That barbarous little Indian girl, of course—the one who murdered pooooor old Mr. Silver." A thin brow arched to a suspicious height. "Are you a relative of the youthful criminal or otherwise responsible for the felony?"*

*Sarah's cousin shook her head. "No. I'm just . . . Mr. Silver's taxi driver."*

*"Oh. I see. Well, I suppose that's all right, then." He was distracted by a sudden warbling sound. "Excuse me, but it would appear that I have a chickadee concealed somewhere on my person." He searched his pockets, apologized for the error. "Sorry—it's a call on line four." There was another warble as he opened his coat. From the five pastel instruments attached firmly to his chest he selected the green one. An equally green spiral cord connected the telephone to a terminal just above his left shirt pocket. "Who is calling?" A pause. "If you do not wish to speak to me, why did you ring my private line?" He listened, then glared at Marilee. "This is quite irregular, Miss Attatochee."*

*"What?"*

*"The call—it's for you."*

The dreamer's eyes opened wide—she could still hear the telephone ringing from the other side. No, not *that* other side—the other side of the bed.

Marilee Attatochee blinked at an alarm clock's illuminated face. *Nobody in their right mind would call me after two A.M. It'll be some slobbering drunk who thinks I'm his best friend. Or it'll be Al, wanting me to bail him out of jail.* She listened to another ring. *No, it can't be Al, because I let him come back—which was really a stupid thing to do because he's such a jerk—but I was so lonesome.* She closed her eyes. *Maybe I didn't let him back in the house. Maybe that was just a bad dream too.* A groan. *I wish I hadn't but I know I did because he's here in the bed beside me. I can hear the half-wit snoring.* The annoyed Papago woman gave her live-in boyfriend a sharp elbow in the ribs. "Wake up!"

"Arrrgh . . . Eeeunngh . . ." Alphonse Harper also made a gargling sound.

She applied another elbow-dig.

"Wha . . . What?"

"Answer the phone."

He scowled at the plump lump beside him. "Why don't you answer it?"

"Because it's on your side of the bed, dipstick!"

"Oh. Awright, then." Al scrambled around until he got a hand on the noisy instrument, pressed it against his ear. Immediately he heard the whisper from somewhere faraway:

"*Marilee . . . Marilee?*"

*I knew it'd be for her.* "Whozis?"

Silence.

He switched on a light. "Dammit, who's woke me up in the middle a the night?"

*Dead* silence.

"Dammit!" Al banged the instrument down. "I hate it when people do that!" He turned his scowl on the telephone. "Ain't there some kind of law—"

"Shut up, Alphonse."

He switched off the light, muttered a vulgar curse at the caller, whined a lament to his girlfriend. "Now I won't be able to go back to sleep." The wide-awake complainant was talking to a woman who had already drifted off. Back to the funeral.

*The line was shuffling along slowly, but Marilee found herself beside the small white casket. "Why's it closed?"*

*She had not asked anyone in particular, but a little girl at her right elbow put a yellow daisy on the casket and said sweetly: "It's because Sarah is horribly, horribly mutilated."*

As he had predicted, Alphonse Harper did not go back to sleep. For ever so long, he lay flat on his back, staring at a dark place where the ceiling surely was. After ever-so-long plus a minute or two, a light came on. In his head. Figuratively speaking. This was quite a new experience for Mr. Harper—one that startled him. *I bet I know who that was on the phone!*

He slipped out of bed, taking considerable care not to waken Marilee. Which, if she had noticed, would have made her suspicious that Al was up to no good. Which he was. In the parlor, he switched on a lamp on a corner table, examined a second telephone. "Ah-ha," he said. This was a big "Ah-ha." It was, in fact—for the first and last time in Al's mostly inconsequential life—a true moment of discovery. And one that the small-time entrepreneur figured he might turn a tidy profit by.

# THIRTY-THREE

## *MAKING THE DEAL*

RAYMOND Oates gazed across his granite-top desk at the pathetic-looking character who had knocked on his office door a moment earlier. *Wonder what he's doing here?*

Slouch hat in hand, Al Harper was hunched slightly forward—like a bullfrog about to jump. This amphibian-metaphoric appearance was misleading; Marilee Attatochee's boyfriend was merely leaning toward his hope for a taste of prosperity, which was embodied in the physical person of this wealthy man.

The corpulent attorney pulled a six-hundred-dollar lighter from a tight vest pocket, touched it to the tip of a tightly wrapped *Arturo Fuente*. "Take a load off, Al."

Harper selected a fatly padded leather armchair. "Thanks, boss."

"I wish you wouldn't call me 'boss.' " Oates clenched his capped teeth on the cigar. "You are not in my employ."

"Uh, sorry." The sycophant grinned obsequiously, shifted his pelvis around until he found the optimum spot for comfort. "Didn't mean no harm, Mr. Oates. When I say 'boss,' it's just my way of showing respect."

Somewhat mollified by this clumsy flattery, Oates leaned back in his throne-like chair, eyeballed the clock on the wall.

"It's just a few minutes past ten." He allowed himself a sardonic grin. "I can't figure out what brings you out so early in the morning, but I'll make two guesses. Either Marilee kicked you out again, or Marilee kicked you out again. Which one is it?"

The most cowardly of men can finally have enough, and turn on his persecutor with all the fury of a cornered rabbit. Al Harper twitched his nose, waited for the grin to slip off Oates's pudgy face. When it did, he said: "I've been wide awake since two A.M."

Oates saw something new glinting in Harper's working eye. Something that made him feel uneasy. He shifted to a conciliatory tone: "You must be tired."

"Yes, I am." Al Harper looked longingly at the cigar. "I could sure do with a smoke."

Oates opened a desk drawer, withdrew a box that still had a dozen of the original twenty-five cigars. He shoved it across the polished granite. "Help yourself."

Al took a cigar, stuffed it into his mouth.

"Take another one for the road."

The nicotine-deprived fellow accepted the generous offer, carefully placed the second cigar over his left ear. As he searched his pockets for the ninety-eight-cent plastic butane lighter, Oates leaned across the desk, flicked the golden instrument under the tip of the Curly Head Deluxe. Harper took a long draw on the aromatic cylinder of Dominican Republic tobacco.

His curiosity whetted, Oates moved to the edge of his chair.

The visitor puffed out a tiny cumulous cloud, idly watched it waft toward an open window, to be sieved by the screen. "I'm here on important business."

Oates took a puff on his own stogie. "Thought you might be."

Al removed the cigar from his mouth, twaddled it between his fingers. "I got something you'll be interested in."

"Is that a fact?"

"Damn right." He restored the cigar to its rightful position; it jiggled as he talked around it. "I know you're lookin' for Sarah."

"Cops and bounty hunters in six states are looking for that little Indian gal. But not me—searching for fugitives is not in my line of business." Oates tapped his cigar on a massive granite ashtray that matched the slab on the desk. "But on behalf of my murdered half brother, I am naturally interested in seeing justice done."

"Naturally." Al Harper's good eye sparkled with a greedy glint. "And gettin' back what the kid stole from Ben Silver."

Oates's eyes narrowed. "What do you know about that?"

Harper shrugged. "Only what I hear—that after Sarah clubbed old Ben with that baseball bat, she stole some stuff."

Oates was growing weary of the game. "I've got a ten-thirty appointment with a real estate developer out of Salt Lake. What've you got that I might be interested in?"

"A phone number."

The chubby businessman smirked. "That's it—a phone number?"

The visitor mirrored the smirk. "Marilee got a call last night, and I picked it up."

The cigar went limp in Oates's liver-tinted lips. "So who was it?"

"Somebody who wanted to talk to Marilee." A pause while he took a long pull on the cigar. "She was whisperin', but I'm sure it was Sarah. And when the brat heard my voice, she wouldn't say another word."

"That's interesting, Al. But I don't see how—"

"You ain't heard the good part."

"Okay. Tell me the 'good part.' "

"After Marilee went back to sleep, I laid there in bed and thought about it. Then I remembered Marilee had got herself one of them caller-ID gadgets, which comes in handy in her taxi business. I went into the living room and read the number off it, and wrote it down." He inhaled again. "And you know what?"

"No, Al—I don't know what."

"That phone call was from an area code that's in Colorado."

It was Oates's turn to shrug. "I expect there's three or four million people in Colorado that's got telephones. Might have been any one of them. A wrong number, most likely."

"We both know Sarah Frank's daddy was a Southern Ute Indian. And his tribe has got a reservation in Colorado, right on the border with New Mexico." Al Harper got up from the overstuffed chair. "But if you're not interested, maybe I should just find the kid myself." He put out the cigar in Oates's spiffy ashtray, stuck the stub over his spare ear. "Then I could collect that big re-ward you put on her." He turned toward the door.

Oates managed an oafish smile. "Look, since you took the trouble to come and see me about it, tell you what I'll do. You leave the number with me, I'll check it out when I get the time and if it turns out to be interesting—"

Marilee's boyfriend reached for the doorknob. "You can have it for five hundred bucks."

Oates's eyes bulged. "You've got to be kidding!"

"Okay, you want to bargain—that's okey doke with me." He looked over his shoulder. "Make it seven-fifty."

"Now see here, Al—"

"A thousand."

Caught off guard by the man's unexpected show of grit, Oates raised both palms in surrender. "Done."

"Make it U.S. greenback dollars. Twenties'll do nicely."

Oates snorted. "I use twenties to light my cigars." He pulled a thick wallet from his hip pocket, riffled through a wad of greenbacks. "I got nothing smaller than a hundred."

"Then I guess that'll hafta do." He held out a hand that trembled, warily watched Oates count off ten hundreds, then passed him a scrap of paper.

After Al Harper had departed, Raymond Oates took a moment to fume, and finally to fulminate. Having vented his wrath, he began to mumble to himself. "That no-good piece of trash—coming in here, holding me up like some common robber!" He took a long look at the scrawl on the piece of paper. *It's a Colorado telephone number, all right—but probably one Al made up. If he's swindled me, I'll get somebody to break both his legs.* The president of Oates Enterprises, Inc. pressed the red button on his telephone pad, counted off six seconds until the door to his personal secretary's office opened and the big-boned, craggy-faced woman appeared. Rosey O'Riley wore her hair in a short, mannish cut, and she always dressed in black. Oates's face split in an oafish grin. *This woman always makes me think of Johnny Cash.* He began to strum an invisible guitar, hum "I Walk the Line."

The annoying man did this two or three times a week.

Mrs. O'Riley—who wore black because she had been mourning the death of her husband for some thirty-odd years—clasped her hands and waited with a pained expression until the strumming and humming had subsided.

*The Woman don't have no sense of humor.* "Crank up that confounded computer, see if you can find out whose telephone number this is."

She inspected the scrap of paper, memorized the ten digits. "Yes sir. It should only take a few minutes."

It did, in fact, require the efficient secretary precisely fifty-two seconds on the Internet to identify the Mountain West Telecommunications subscriber who held that number. But this was not a lady who was satisfied with half measures. It took another minute to determine the physical location of the telephone. *Now that's quite interesting. I wonder if there could be a connection to that Indian who arrived with the FBI agent to visit Sheriff Popper.* It took approximately three additional minutes to check out her hunch, another thirty seconds for her state-of-the-art color printer to disgorge several sheets of paper. If Mrs. O'Riley had been the sort of high-spirited exuberant who has a tendency to shout "Eureka" or "Wa-hoo," she certainly would have. As it was, the undemonstrative woman contented herself with a self-satisfied smile and a congratulatory thought: *This is really quite gratifying.*

Raymond Oates stared at the name, then furrowed his brows at his employee. "That's nobody I ever heard of."

She offered him a single sheet of paper.

Oates had a knack for stating the obvious. "Looks like a map."

"It is, sir." She pointed a perfectly manicured fingernail. "The residence where the telephone is located is indicated by the star in the center."

The cigar smoker studied the layout. "Looks like it's plunk out in the middle of nowhere."

"Yes, sir." Mrs. O'Riley, who savored the big punch line, had saved the best for last. "I did some cross-referencing. You may be interested to know that the person to whom the telephone is registered has a connection to that Ute Indian—Mr. Charles Moon."

"This is good stuff, Rosey." He rubbed his hands together. "Tell me more."

The secretary explained the relationship. She also provided her employer with an additional two pages from the printer. "One of these is a topographic map with twenty-foot contour intervals, the other is a satellite photograph of the same four-square-mile area. On each, I have inked in a small arrow to indicate the structure—presumably a private residence—where the telephone is located."

Oates was nodding faster than one of his oil-well pumps. *This could be where that Papago girl's hiding.*

The secretary prepared to withdraw. "Will that be all, sir?"

Her voice broke the spell. "No, it won't." He propped the heels of his fourteen-hundred-dollar ostrich-skin cowboy boots onto the immaculate desk, took a couple of aggressive chews on the cigar stub. "Give yourself a nice bonus, Rosey. Let's say . . . twenty bucks." *Don't want to spoil the woman.* He glanced at his wristwatch. "And take an early lunch."

"Very good, sir." The remarkable employee seemed to evaporate.

• • •

Mrs. O'Riley pulled her black Volvo up to the Sybil's Tea & Pastry Shop, switched off the ignition, removed a black cell phone from an equally black leather purse, pressed a programmed button. "Hello, cousin—how are you getting along?" She listened to the expected response, then: "Oh, I'm just fine." Ray Oates's secretary nodded. "Yes, I've been keeping my eyes open and ears pricked." She lowered her voice to a gossipy murmur: "Matter of fact, I have something that will interest you."

She provided a terse account of Al Harper's visit—it was hard not to hear *every word* when the door to Mr. Oates's office happened to be cracked a quarter-inch. The person on the other end of the line was silent as Rosey described the mysterious late-night call for Marilee Attatochee which was intercepted by her odious boyfriend, and the location in Colorado where the call had originated. She read the telephone subscriber's name to her relative, explained the connection to Charlie Moon. There was a brief pause in the conversation as a cattle truck rumbled by. "I have two computer-generated maps and a satellite composite photograph that pinpoints the dwelling where the caller's telephone is located. I'll leave a sealed manila envelope in the usual place."

Her cousin said that would be just fine, then brought up the old, familiar issue that mildly annoyed the efficient secretary.

"No, I still don't have any idea who Mr. Oates talks to on his private phone or what he says." She reminded her relative for the umpteenth time: "For one thing, the line isn't connected to the console on my desk. And when Mr. Oates intends to make a really hush-hush call, he always sends me out of the building on an errand—or like today, for an early lunch."

Cousin finally got down to the matter of payment.

"Oh, you know how I hate to talk about money." Rosey examined an immaculate set of fingernails. *This Sonoran Sunset tint is just a shade too light.* "But let's say twenty dollars."

• • •

WHILE chewing and smoking his cigar down to a stubby butt, Raymond Oates suffered a series of ulcer-provoking thoughts. This intense mental activity was accompanied by piggish little grunts and brow-furrowing frowns. After looking at the issue from this way and that, he concluded that the late-night telephone call to Marilee Attatochee was almost certainly made by Sarah Frank, and with that as a working hypothesis there could be no dillydallying around—the situation called for immediate and drastic action. *What I need is a couple of knuckle-draggers.* But for this particular piece of work, not just any run-of-the-mill knuckle-draggers would do. He ignited the tip of a fresh cigar, began to mull over a list of potential candidates, eventually narrowed it down to two. Number One was highly motivated. Number Two would strangle his sister for a carton of Lucky Strike cigarettes. This was not a mere figure of speech; when Two was twelve years old the beady-eyed little brute actually *had* strangled his sister. Her dual offense was (a) she had discovered Brother's secret cache of cigarettes and (b) she had told Grandma about the hiding place. Sis had not died from the strangling, but following the assault she had (as they used to say in those days) "never been quite right."

The attorney picked up his private line, punched in a call to Knuckle-Dragger Number One, got an answer on the second ring. "It's me—Ray Oates. Can you talk? Okay. Look, I came across a piece of information on that runaway Indian girl. Might turn out to be a hot lead, or nothing but fairy smoke and stump-water. But I want you and another fella to go check it out." He responded to the expected query with an impish grin. "Yeah, that's who I have in mind." Hurrying to ward off the expected objection, Oates added: "We'll discuss the details tomorrow night—usual time and place." Which translated: 11:00 P.M. sharp at the Oates residence. The house lights would be off.

The small-town wheeler-dealer thumbed the END button, placed another call, conducted a similar conversation with

Knuckle-Dragger Number Two. Similar, but with a sinister little twist. The man who had strangled his sister would have some extra work to do. Whether they found the Papago kid or not, Knuckle-Dragger Number Two would make sure Knuckle-Dragger Number One never came home again. Which would leave Oates with the surviving knuckle-dragger to deal with. But that was another problem, for another day. The thing was to always stay a few steps ahead of the game.

Quite pleased with himself, Raymond Oates sucked thoughtfully on his cigar, puffed a fluffy smoke ring. The coldhearted son-of-a-rustler had developed his own highly personalized brand. Of philosophy, that is. Which could be summed up more or less as follows: *If a man's got bushels of disposable income and has the right contacts, 99 percent of his problems can be solved with a couple of phone calls.*

Socrates, he was not.

# THIRTY-FOUR

## *CRIME AND PUNISHMENT*

CHARLIE Moon was cruising down copper street when he saw his best friend, who happened to be Granite Creek PD's chief of police. The Southern Ute tribal investigator deftly slipped his freshly washed Expedition into a cramped parking place. There were more spacious slots available, but he was a cattle rancher and beef prices had recently taken a dip and the meter on this post was showing forty-five minutes, which was worth six bits.

Moon cut the ignition, watched the broad-shouldered Scott Parris ambling along the opposite sidewalk like a clumsy young halfback. *I wonder if he played football in high school.* As the thought was passing through his mind, he watched Parris tip his cowboy hat at a pretty redhead who flashed him a semiseductive smile. Moon laughed as the chief of police turned to watch her pass, bumped headlong into a heavyset man in a bulky black raincoat who had been tagging along behind the hapless cop. The other party in the collision was even bigger and wider than Parris—he might have been a professional wrestler. Moon shook his head as his friend apologized to the oversized citizen, who appeared to take no offense at the minor mishap. As the big man went on his way, Parris craned his neck to watch the shapely redhead depart.

After a rusty old Dodge pickup had rattled past, Charlie

Moon crossed the street, waved at his friend. "Hey, where you headed?"

Scott Parris turned to regard the rail-thin, seven-foot-tall Ute. "The Sugar Bowl. In case you've already forgot, that's where we're supposed to meet for lunch."

"The Sugar Bowl—you sure?"

"Sure I'm sure." Parris cast a doubtful gaze on the Indian. "Where'd you think we was gonna have our midday meal?"

Moon was looking up the street, also at the redhead. "At Dukey's A-1 Texas Barbecue."

"Dukey's isn't a serious barbecue joint—just the bus station's lunch counter." Parris snorted. "And the place is a dump. It's a wonder the health department hasn't shut 'em down."

"Okay." Disappointment fairly dripped off the Ute's face. "But I sure had my heart set on a big, greasy, chopped-brisket sandwich. With a side of potato salad and a bowl of Dukey's smokehouse beans and—"

"Oh, all right." Parris fell in step beside his best buddy. "But don't go blaming me when you wake up dead from eatin' tainted grub."

"Okay." Moon slapped his friend on the back. "You can dance on my grave."

"That'll be just for starters." Parris told the Ute what else he would do on his grave, but this will be treated as an irrelevant detail.

Moon selected a booth by the fly-specked window, under the neon script that boasted Bud Lite with every electric flicker.

Parris squinted to see into the dark recesses of Dukey's A-1 establishment. "From what I hear, he eats leftovers right off the plates." He grinned at Moon. "If we're lucky, maybe Dukey has died from food poisoning."

It was not to be. The proprietor showed up, a cigarette dangling limply from his lips, a green order pad in his hand. "Hey, guys—I ain't seen either a you in a month a Sundays. I figgered maybe you both converted to veggie-tarianism." He followed this with a throaty "Har-har."

Sensing that his friend was reluctant to converse with Dukey, Moon ordered his sandwich and sides. "And a king-size Pepsi. With just enough ice to cool a sickly grasshopper's fevered brow."

"You got it, Big Chief." Dukey turned the full strength of his personality on the chief of police. "How about you, Dick Tracy?"

Scott Parris looked out the window, wondered where the pretty redhead had gone. *Probably to meet a nice young man at a decent restaurant. Or maybe she's dining alone. If I knew where she was, I could just saunter in and maybe bump into her again . . . Well, it wasn't exactly* her *I bumped into, but in a manner of speaking . . .*

"Hey—I ain't got all day!"

Parris blinked at the man behind the grease-stained apron. It was also stained with other things, but the details didn't bear thinking about. "Cup of coffee. Decaf."

As he scribbled on the pad, Dukey muttered: "Java—unleaded." He scowled at the hesitant customer. "What d'you want to eat?"

"Nothing."

"What—you on a diet or somethin'?"

"Look, the only reason I'm willing to risk drinking your coffee is that it's been boiled enough to kill off all the—"

"My friend is not feeling up to any spicy food, Dukey." Moon smiled at the homely face. "Just bring him the coffee."

After a brief eye-to-eye standoff with the beefy cop, the owner of the third-rate eatery stomped away toward a smoky kitchen, where he did the cooking and rinsed soiled dishes in filthy water.

Attempting to dislodge a dried-up smudge of barbecue sauce, Parris scratched his thumbnail on the table. "Charlie, if you drove for ninety-nine miles in any direction, I doubt you'd find a worse hole-in-the-wall than this."

The Ute flashed a childlike smile that would have disarmed a more reasonable man. "You've never tried Dukey's brisket."

Parris rolled his eyes. "I have also never drank plumber's

lye—or tasted a fresh cow pie. And just look at this place." To demonstrate the ocular procedure, he turned his head this way and that, gazed into the shadows. "I bet there's no customers here but us. Except for out-of-towners who come in on the bus, nobody would have little enough sense to eat in this—"

"Which is why the service is so prompt." Moon heard the squeaky door open, the coupled bell clang the arrival of a probable diner. It was the largish man Parris had bumped into on the street. Mr. Raincoat. "See," the Ute said, "there's another hungry gourmet who, after inspecting several local eateries, has wisely chosen Dukey's A-1 Texas Barbecue."

"Please, let's not say any more about Dukey's slop—let's talk about something less depressing." He gave his friend a knowing half-grin. "Like why you wanted to see me today. As if I didn't already know."

There was a pause in the conversation as Dukey arrived with coffee and a tall glass of Pepsi-Cola with a single ice cube floating thereupon.

When the proprietor was out of earshot, Moon took a sip of the fizzy beverage. "Okay. So why do I want to see you?"

"It'll have something to do with that killing in Tonapah Flats, and that Indian girl who's disappeared. Remember how we worked that case years ago, when her mother was murdered?" Parris made a painful grimace. "Dang, what's the kid's name?" He blushed and sighed at the same time. "Just yesterday, I saw it in an FBI report, but my brain is turning to cheese, Charlie. I mean, one minute I've got some information between my ears and then it just slips away—" He stopped dead still. "Wait a minute. Sarah. Sarah Frank—that's it."

"Did you read the FBI report?"

"I kinda scanned it. I was expecting you'd bring me up to date on the details—"

Dukey abruptly showed up with Charlie Moon's brisket sandwich plate, plopped it down with a bang, gave the other, reluctant diner a poisonous look, seemed not to notice when an inch-long length of ash fell from his cigarette into Parris's coffee.

As the owner of the establishment hurried away to offer service to the huge man who had recently arrived, Moon reached across the table to restrain his friend from getting up. "He didn't mean to do that."

Noting that Moon made the statement with little conviction, Parris replied through clenched teeth. "Yes, he did. And I ought to go break his head—"

"But you won't."

"I won't?"

"No."

"You sure about that?"

"Sure I'm sure."

"Tell me why, Charlie."

"Because you're a seasoned pro and a heavyweight to boot. Dukey's a dime-a-dozen back-alley brawler who'd tip the scales at maybe a hundred and sixty in his birthday suit." Moon put on a reproachful look. "It wouldn't be a fair match."

"Fair don't come into it. That lowlife hash slinger deliberately dropped cigarette ash into my coffee."

"Let me take care of it."

"What'll you do?"

"For starters, I'll get you a brand-new cup of coffee."

"I don't want any of Pukey-Dukey's stinkin' coffee, Charlie. I want to kick his butt right up between his shoulder blades."

"Okay. Whatever pleases you. But before you displace his pelvis, can we talk shop?"

Parris cooled a couple of degrees. "About that bad business in Utah?"

"Uh-huh." Moon took a bite of the sizable sandwich.

"Okay. Give me the executive summary."

The chopped brisket was delicious, but he dared not mention this to his still-overheated friend. "Tonapah Flats, Utah. Old man by the name of Ben Silver was supposed to be at a local clinic, seeing his doctor. The appointment gets canceled when Doc is called away to deal with a big pileup out on the interstate. Silver's taxi driver—who just happens to be Sarah Frank's Papago cousin—hauls Mr. Silver back home. When Silver shows up early, he figures out someone's been burgling his house, calls 911, gets the sheriff on the line. Before he can say anything useful, somebody yanks the phone cord out of the wall, bangs him on the head."

"Somebody *who*—Sarah Frank?" Parris watched Moon nod. "What's the evidence?"

The Ute managed to talk and eat at the same time. "A couple of minutes after the 911 call is interrupted, Sheriff Ned Popper shows up, discovers Sarah standing over the body—holding a baseball bat. She flings the Louisville Slugger at the sheriff, makes a run for it. Sheriff ducks but not fast enough. This Utah lawman ends up with a big lump on his noggin; Popper's lucky *he's* not dead. Soon as he gets to his feet, he goes inside and finds Mr. Silver on the floor, barely alive, bleeding from his head. Sheriff asks the victim what happened. With his dying breath, Silver implicates Sarah." At this point, Moon had a hard time swallowing. "And the blood on the bat was Silver's."

"Well, that's about as conclusive as it gets." Scott Parris had a mental picture of the tiny little girl who had lost both her parents. "How old is she now?"

"Fourteen."

The chief of police stared at the ashes dissolving in his coffee. Shook his head at the horror of it all. "Just fourteen. And she's already killed a man."

Having lost his appetite, Moon set the mouth-watering sandwich aside. "But we don't know for sure *why* she killed him. Might be self-defense."

"Yeah." Parris nodded hopefully. "Maybe when the old man saw her rummaging through his personal belongings, he got angry. Tried to grab her. And she fought back." He looked up. "She's just a dumb kid. Might get off with a couple of years in a juvenile facility."

"If she goes to trial."

"You don't think she'll be picked up?"

"I don't know what to think. One of the Utah sheriff's deputies—a nice young fellow by the name of Tate Packard—showed up on the east end of the reservation last week."

Parris remembered those days when a younger Sarah had spent months with Daisy Perika. "Near your aunt's place?"

"Near enough. During a big thunderstorm, Packard drove his car off the road and into the Piedra."

"I read a bulletin on that. Didn't connect it with the killing in Utah." He scratched again at the scab of dried barbecue sauce. "Was the deputy's body recovered?"

"Not the last I heard." Moon eyed the half-eaten sandwich. "Piedra's running fast and muddy this spring. Packard's remains may eventually float to the top of Navajo Lake. Or maybe not. Some of 'em, we never find." He tapped a plastic fork on the plastic plate. "BIA police have looked long and hard for Sarah on the Papago reservation, which is a fair-sized chunk of southern Arizona. They don't think she's there, and I'm not inclined to disagree with them." He looked up at his friend. "But for some reason I don't know—it's pretty clear that Deputy Packard believed she was on the Southern Ute reservation."

"What about ol' Ned Popper?"

The Ute didn't hide his surprise. "You know him?"

"Yeah," Parris said. "We used to hunt antelope, down by Raton."

"Popper claims he don't have any notion why his deputy was in Colorado, much less on the res." Moon pitched the plastic fork aside, locked eyes with his best friend. "This Popper—you trust him?"

"I don't know him all that well." Parris shrugged. "From what I hear, he's a sure-enough tough customer. There was some talk that he was mixed up a bit in local politics."

Moon frowned. "What does that mean?"

Another shrug. "Oh, I don't know for sure." Parris blushed. "He probably did a few favors for some influential folks. And they did some for him." The former Chicago cop spread his hands. "Sometimes, that's the only way to get things done."

The tribal investigator decided to let that pass.

The Granite Creek chief of police changed the subject: "This action is a long way from my jurisdiction, Charlie. What can I do to help?"

"Probably not much. I'm going to be doing some snooping around on the reservation. Ask some people some questions." *Especially my aunt Daisy.* "But just on the off chance that Sarah shows up here—"

"You figure she might make her way to Granite Creek, ask for directions to the Columbine?"

"It's a long shot. But if I don't pick up something on the res, it may be the only shot I've got."

"I'll circulate the FBI photos to all of my officers, put the word out to the bus station." Parris smiled at his friend. "If Miss Frank shows up in my town, I'll have her in custody before you can count to one."

"Thanks, pard."

"Let's get out of this dump."

"Okay." Charlie Moon watched a uniformed driver approach a Greyhound. "Soon as I take care of some business."

"Forget it, Charlie—you don't need to bother with Dukey on my account."

"I'll be back in a minute." Moon passed by Mr. Raincoat, found his way to a shadowy corner booth by the ladies' room. He tipped his black Stetson at the pretty lady.

She smiled at the long, lean cowboy. "What's up, Tex?"

"Could I sit down for just a minute?"

The redhead looked at her watch. "Sixty, fifty-nine, fifty-eight . . ."

Moon straddled a chair. "You're a very attractive woman."

"Thank you. Is that why you followed me into this fine restaurant?"

"Partly."

She pursed her pretty lips. "Only partly?"

He nodded. "I got a proposition for you."

"You certainly don't waste any time."

"Time is a highly valuable commodity."

"Your place or mine?"

"Ma'am, I don't believe you have a place in Granite Creek."

"What are you, big boy—some kind of clairvoyant?"

"Nope." Charlie Moon produced the gold shield from his shirt pocket, presented it. "I'm some kind of cop."

The brittle smile froze on her face, instantly aging it by a decade. "How very nice for you."

"But not for you."

She glanced over his shoulder.

"That big fella you're looking at—you just give him a signal to come over here and rescue you?"

"What if I did?"

"It's fine with me. Fact is, it's exactly what I was hoping you'd do."

Raincoat loomed near.

"That's close enough," Moon said.

The big man stopped. "Little lady, this fella botherin' you?"

"Yes, I am." The Ute got to his feet. "Now you sit down where I was at."

Raincoat's hands made ham-sized fists. "Why would I want to do that?"

Moon's eyes narrowed. "Because I told you to."

"That's pretty big talk for a—"

"He's a cop, Mick."

Raincoat, AKA Tricky Mick, blinked at the redhead. "What?"

"Last chance," Moon said. "Sit down."

Mick sat.

The tribal investigator placed both palms on the filthy table, leaned close enough to smell the man's sour breath. "I saw you work your dodge on my friend." He nodded to indicate Scott Parris, who had not gone unnoticed by the pair. "Good-looking lady gives him the big eye, which gets him all flustered. Gorilla-Mick bumps into him, picks his pocket."

The pair of grifters presented stony faces.

"It was a nice, clean job." Moon addressed the plug-ugly half of the team. "But you picked the wrong guy's pocket."

Redhead was beginning to get the drift of things. "He another cop?"

"Better than that." Moon grinned. "He's chief of police."

Mick groaned.

"You got two choices," the Ute said. "Number one, you go straight to jail." He watched their faces blanch. "Then there's number two. Mick peels off his raincoat, real slow and easy—and hands it over to me. I remove my friend's wallet from one of those oversized pockets, check to make sure his greenbacks and plastic are still inside. Then you two get up, take a stroll out to the bus and get on board."

Redhead and Mick exchanged looks.

"The coach that's warming up leaves for Colorado Springs in about two minutes. Maybe a tad less. You're not on it, I'll introduce you to the chief of police."

Redhead nodded at her partner. Mick shed the raincoat.

Moon went through the pockets, removed four wallets, an antique pocket watch, a brand-new Case pocket knife.

"The folding knife's mine," Mick grumbled.

The Ute pitched it on the table.

The bus driver tooted his horn.

Moon watched the pair hurry away to their appointed carrier.

Parris watched his friend approach. "What was that all about?"

"If I tell you, you got to swear you won't interfere."

"I'm not mad enough to swear, but okay."

Moon watched the Greyhound pull away. When it was out of sight, he passed the raincoat to his best friend.

"The sun's shining to beat the band—I don't need this."

"Neither did the other guy. Which was something an experienced copper should have noticed when Mick and Redhead staged that encounter with him on Copper Street."

Parris stared at the bulky raincoat. Reached for his hip pocket. "Oh no—don't tell me."

"Your wallet's in the inside coat pocket. Along with some other stuff you can return to several local citizens, who will be extremely grateful to their keen-eyed chief of police."

Parris examined his wallet, found everything in its proper place. "Charlie, we can't just let those two yahoos ride out of Granite Creek. Next town they hit, they'll be up to their usual tricks."

"Then put in a call to your cop friends in Colorado Springs. But you can't stop the bus."

"Why?"

"Because I gave both of 'em my word."

"Well, that throws a whole new light on the situation. A man's word is . . . his bond and all that whatnot." A hesitation. "But would you mind if I made an incisive observation?"

"Not at all."

"Now I don't want you to take this the wrong way, Charlie—but you seem to be awfully pleased with yourself."

"Pleased?"

The chief of police nodded. "Even if I said puffed-up, it would not be going too far."

"Well, maybe I got a reason to be pleased. Even puffed-up." Moon reminded him: "It was *you* that got stung. And *me* that noticed what those two was up to."

"I can't argue with that, Charlie. You were on the ball all right. But still—a little humility wouldn't hurt you."

"Yes, it would. Tell you what—I'll be humble tomorrow. Or maybe the day after that."

Parris gave his Indian friend an enigmatic look. "Well, we're done here so I guess we might as well be oozin' on down the street. I got a one-thirty meeting with the mayor and she hates it when I'm late." He cleared his throat. "You got the correct time?"

"Sure do." Moon looked at his wristwatch. It took the Ute a couple of disbelieving blinks to realize that his wrist was buck-naked. Mouth open, he looked in the direction the Greyhound had gone. "That sneaky redheaded woman—she must've slipped it off while I was—"

Scott Parris's huge laugh exploded, boomed across the

room, shook the cobwebs on the rafters, rattled the dirty windowpanes.

Startled by this unexpected hilarity, Dukey dropped a gallon pot of pinto beans.

# THIRTY-FIVE

## *THE TRAVELER RETURNS*

It was a few minutes before midnight when Father Raes Delfino turned off the paved highway, unlocked the Columbine gate, drove slowly along the hard-packed dirt-and-gravel road that would eventually bring him to the ranch headquarters where, he presumed, Charlie Moon would be sleeping on the second floor. The original moon—resembling the convexity of a silver spoon—was almost full, almost overhead. He glanced at the mildly tarnished satellite, mused that it could use some polishing, *Well, that was a silly thought. I've been up too long.* In an attempt to dislodge the encroaching spirit of slumber, the Jesuit shook his head. *I must stay wide awake until I'm home.* Home. The powerful word called up fond images of the log cabin Charlie Moon—a most generous soul—had made available to him upon his retirement from St. Ignatius and the active priesthood. The remote cabin was the perfect physical refuge from the tumult and troubles of this world; a place where he could withdraw without the least worry of being disturbed. Well, almost. From time to time, some cowhand would "drop by," always "just to see if you needed somethin'." A few of these men were practicing Christians, quite a few more were hardened sinners, but whether they were aware of it or not—all were souls whose ultimate desire and eternal purpose was union with God. This being so, Fr. Raes always had time for these visitors. And he loved them every one. *My obligation to feed the Lord's sheep will not end until I take my last breath. If then . . .* He watched an incandescent meteorite streak across the midnight velvet, expire in silence.

His buoyant thoughts and the faithful automobile carried him through the darkness, across the rolling high prairie, along the hem of the blue-gray mountain's pleated skirts, past the foreman's darkened house, over the Too Late Bridge, which spanned the Too Late Creek, which flowed into the big river—whose numbingly cold waters were currently rolling along toward a rendezvous with the immense Pacific.

The priest slowed as he passed Charlie's Moon's large house. The Columbine headquarters was dark, but did not sleep. When he saw a pair of red eyes glinting in his headlights, the driver realized that Sidewinder was on the job. He smiled, muttered a fond hello to the eccentric animal.

The Columbine hound had heard the sound of the automobile when it was still miles away, and recognized the familiar clackety-clacking of valves tapping in the aged Buick engine. The surly beast had emerged from under the long porch just in time to offer a solemn greeting to the ranch's most distinguished resident. On the other side of a long ridge, nestled in a glade of blackish-blue spruce, was the priest's small cabin. The hound would pay a visit there when the world was light again. The kindly man always had some tasty tidbit to offer a hungry visitor. And though no one had taken note of this curious fact, the holy man of God was the only person on the cattle ranch that Sidewinder—a highly accomplished thief—would not steal food from. The dog watched the cherry-red taillights recede and wink out, listened intently to the decaying sounds of the engine. Finally, when there was little more to see than the moonlit profile of the Buckhorn range, nothing to hear but the humming hymn of night wind in the pines, the dog yawned, retreated to his straw bed under the headquarters' porch.

## *THE PRIEST ENCOUNTERS A SMALL MYSTERY*

It was with considerable satisfaction that Father Raes Delfino emerged from his dusty automobile, removed a single suitcase from the trunk, and trudged down the flagstone path toward the cabin. *It is so good to be home again.* He opened the front door, flicked the switch, was temporarily blinded by the incandescent flash of a sixty-watt bulb in a copper-shaded lamp. Blinking, he placed the suitcase on a chair, walked across the small parlor—stopped dead still. He looked around. Nothing appeared to be amiss. He listened. Not a sound. Nevertheless . . . *Something is not quite right.*

The logical half of his brain kicked in. *Everything is just as it should be. It's merely my imagination. I'm exhausted from getting up before sunrise, enduring a long, tiresome drive. And I've not had a bite to eat since breakfast.* Taking note of this last assertion and wishing to express its hearty agreement, his empty stomach uttered a guttural growl. *Well, I know what to do about that.* The practical man headed for the kitchen, flipped another light switch—goggled at what he saw on the table. *What is this?*

*This,* upon closer examination, proved to be three cardboard boxes and two plastic grocery bags stuffed with stuff. Mostly food—in glass jars, steel cans, cellophane bags. *Who would have left me all of this?* Not Dolly Bushman; the foreman's wife thoughtfully provided such ready-to-eat treats as luscious lemon layer cakes and crispy apple fritters. When Charlie Moon dropped by with food, the victuals leaned toward massive beefsteaks, sugar-cured hams, quart jars of blackberry jam. He noticed a note, which was secured under the corner of a box, immediately recognized the mischievous old Ute woman's scrawl. *God help us all.* He held it under the light.

*about time you got back*
*where have you been this time*
*to see the new pope I bet*
*and kiss his ring*

*I figured you wasn't getting enough to eat*
*so I left you a few things to chew on*
*And that's not all I left you ha-ha*
*Daisy*
*PS don't say nothing to Charlie*
*you know what they say*

In case Father Raes did not know What They Say, she had penciled the proverb in for him:

*what a big jug-head don't know won't hurt him*

The scholarly man scanned the message again, found the second reading just as extraordinary as the first. The expression on his face testified to that sort of suspicion that a citizen experiences when a politician proclaims: "My only ambition is to be a public servant—send me to Washington (or Denver, or wherever) and I'll look after things for you." Indeed, he might well have said pshaw. Balderdash. Even hogwash.

Moreover, and in addition to harboring general misgivings, Father Raes Delfino felt just a touch of anxiety. *Daisy Perika—why the very name is a synonym for Trouble. And what is this "ha-ha" business—what else has she left here in my absence? Something to plague me, no doubt.* But only a few heartbeats passed before the old woman's gift of food made the man of God blush with shame. He bowed his head, closed his eyes, prayed: *Dear Father in Heaven—forgive me for entertaining such unworthy thoughts. Daisy may be a bit odd, and the note certainly has its mysterious qualities—but it appears that she has cleaned out her little pantry and brought the bounty all to me. I should be especially thankful for such a selfless act from a person whom one would hardly expect to give a crust of bread to a starving tramp on her doorstep even if she tripped over his body—Excuse me. I'm so sorry—I didn't really mean that. Daisy has many good qualities and I am thankful for what she has done.* A long pause. A penitential sigh. *As soon as I have had a few hours sleep, I shall call her up and thank her for this kindness. Amen.*

But while the priest felt absolved from his minor sin, he still did not feel comfortable. The thought nagged at him: *There is something more to this than meets the eye.* His keen eyes surveyed the kitchen for some clue. He listened. Even sniffed the air. *Yes. I'm absolutely certain—there's someone here!*

But who? And where?

He was of the opinion that there is an answer to every question. Though not always the one we are prepared to hear.

What he heard was a scuffing sound in the cellar. As if someone—or *something*—had bumped into a basket of red cabbages or a sack of sweet potatoes.

Father Raes called out, "Who's down there?"

Silence. Of the sort that inhabits a dusty, musty tomb.

The rightful resident was resolute. "You might as well show yourself."

He marched across the kitchen floor, jerked open the cellar door, assumed a stern demeanor as he addressed the blackness below: "Either you come up, or I'm coming down." For the third time that night, he toggled a light switch. There was no response from the single bulb that hung above the cellar stairs. *Must be burned out. I'll have to get a flashlight.*

As it happened, this turned out to be unnecessary.

The man of the house heard a feline whine, was startled to see a black-and-white bundle of fur toddle up the wooden stairs. Just as if they had been lifelong friends and belonged to the same political party, Mr. Zig-Zag purred—and rubbed his gaunt rib cage against the cleric's leg.

Father Raes chuckled, bent to rub the amiable animal. "Well, well—what do we have here?" *The solution to a small mystery, of course. For some reason known only to herself and God, Daisy Perika has brought me a cat.* "Come along, I'll find you something to eat." As he watched the creature lap up a saucer of milk, he wondered: *Why doesn't*

*Daisy want her nephew to know about this animal?* He consulted his wristwatch, yawned. *Well, it's far too late to be puzzling about such issues. When I talk to Daisy, I'll ask her.*

After Mr. Zig-Zag had had his fill, he wandered around and about the cabin, sniffing at table legs, old shoes, empty corners. Finally, giving the priest a rub on the shin, and mouthing a respectful "meow," the animal stepped softly over to the cellar door, looked back expectantly at the latest human being to be bent to his will.

"Ah, so you wish to sleep down there with the root vegetables?" *And stalk the wily mouse, I suppose.* "Very well, then. But just in case you wish to come back upstairs—or go outside, I'll leave both doors slightly ajar."

Having finished his business with the cat, Father Raes Delfino retired for the night.

Though sorely in need of rest, his sleep was troubled.

As the weary man tossed and turned, he dreamed about dozens of stray cats swarming over the cabin, an old Ute woman who was laughing at some private joke she'd played on him, and most disturbing of all—the presence of a ghostly presence in his bedroom. Once, he awakened to see the small, thin form standing near his bed. *It is a female. And she is staring at me.* Not the sort of man to be unduly alarmed by such an unpretentious apparition—he had seen truly frightful phantoms during his missionary work with primitive tribes in the Amazon—the priest reached to the night table for his spectacles, switched on the lamp by his bed. *Now I don't see a thing.* He switched off the light, fell back on a lumpy pillow. *It must have been a hallucination.* Following a satisfying yawn, he drifted away to a restful sleep. If there were other dreams, the dreamer did not remember them. But after a late-morning breakfast, he picked up the telephone, dialed the Ute woman's number that he knew so well. He also knew the woman very well. *I will thank her for the food, but I will also be very direct, and ask for an explanation about this cat that she doesn't want Charlie Moon to know about.* He knew the Ute elder would be evasive. *Daisy is up to something.* Which was like saying the governor was a politician. Or water is wet.

• • •

THOUGH she did not know the day or hour it might occur, Daisy Perika was expecting the call. When the telephone by her rocking chair rang, she leaned sideways to eye the thing. Particularly the caller ID. *Yeah, it's him all right.* The crafty old woman smiled, resumed her rocking. She also began to sing a favorite hymn:

"I come to the garden alone, while the dew is still on the ro-ses."

The telephone continued to ring, Daisy continued rock. And to sing.

"And the voice I hear, fall-ing on my ear . . ." *What's the rest of that line?*

A quick intake of breath.

"He walks with me, and he talks with me."

Back and forth in the chair.

"And he tells me that I am his own."

The telephone ceased its ringing.

The old woman did not cease her singing.

"And the joy we share, as we tar-ry there, none other has ev-er known."

Her happy song went right on, through the last two verses.

Her seesawing chair kindly provided the rhythm.

Creak-squeak.

Creak-squeak.

Creak-squeak.

The rocking felt very good. *It's what they call . . . something-or-other.* Daisy frowned. *What's the word?* It came to her.

*Therapeutic.*

# THIRTY-SIX

## *WHAT HAPPENED EARLY ON A DAMP MORNING IN THE SPRUCE WOODS*

DURING the past several months, Sidewinder had found himself a new friend, who went by the name of Sweet Alice. The Columbine hound often spent the predawn hour out on a run with the outlaw mare, as was the case on this particular morning, when they had taken their exercise along the shore of the alpine lake.

After a vigorous workout that made the horse sweat and the dog pant (dogs are not permitted to sweat), they were moving along at an easier gait. As the odd couple loped along the prairie past Father Raes's cabin and entered the dense strip of forest on the rocky ridge above the Columbine headquarters, the hound caught a whiff of a scent that went distinctly against the canine grain. Sweet Alice watched while Sidewinder paused in midstride, held a right front paw poised above a fallen aspen branch, which in death wore a shroud of bright green moss. Unlike the ferns, neither aspen branch nor green moss would have an important role in what was about to happen, but minor players deserve to be mentioned. What about the ferns?

Only yards away, something was rustling the ferns.

The horse's eyes were wide, but more with curiosity than alarm.

The descendant of wolves—who had twice tangled with

mountain lions—waited for the appearance of the age-old enemy. Sidewinder had never backed away from a fight.

With a suddenness that almost took the old dog's breath away, it appeared. Stared back at him with an impudent black-and-white face.

A low growl rumbled under the hound's ribs. A brush of coarse hair bristled along his neck.

The reckless cat arched his back—hissed like a snake about to strike.

Sidewinder lowered his head, bared yellowed teeth, made ready for the deadly lunge.

Something else appeared in the shadows. The presence was a few paces behind the cat, and barely visible in the morning mists. Though the lips did not move, her thin young face spoke to the hound. *Please don't hurt my cat.*

The formidable beast was completely disarmed.

Sensing an opportunity, Mr. Zig-Zag approached the dog with dainty, fastidious steps, rubbed his neck against the gentled adversary. Purred.

Sweet Alice—known for her equine sense of humor—snickered a derisive whinny.

Sidewinder groaned, looked away.

A perceptive observer would have concluded that the dog was embarrassed.

## *LATE THAT EVENING, AT THE PRIEST'S CABIN*

DURING his second night at home Father Raes Delfino had not heard a sound, but when he awoke with a start and sat straight up in bed—she was there. Close enough to reach out and touch. On this occasion, he did not reach for his spectacles or switch on the light. Neither did he speak. What this wise man did was wait. And listen.

The priest heard the most astonishing confession.

When she had finished her whispers, the judicious cleric weighed his words before responding. "You're absolutely certain that you have killed a man?"

A nod.

"Do you wish to explain the circumstances?"

She stared at the floor.

"Very well." Father Raes assumed the stern expression. "But you must understand—taking the life of another human is a *most* serious sin." He paused to gather his thoughts. "The first thing you must do is repent. Then, you must ask for God's forgiveness." He added: "And I will pray for your soul."

### *TONAPAH FLATS, UTAH*

KNUCKLE-dragger number Two was sitting in his truck, which was parked in the dark among a cluster of willows that also concealed an abandoned trailer home and the rotting carcass of a horse that a city hunter had mistaken for an elk. Having no one else to talk to, the chronic complainer muttered his grievances to himself: "Oates sure expects a helluva lot for his money. The cheap bastard starts out with 'Go and see if the Indian kid is holed up at such-and-such a place' and we agree on a price and then he commences to adding on chores like 'Oh, and by the way, there's a couple of other little things I'd like for you to take care of.' And so I end up sitting out here in the stinking boonies waiting for the man Oates wants killed and buried." *And he's a sure-enough* dangerous *man. I shoulda asked for an extra thousand.* After scowling at the gravel lane that dead-ended at a run-down apartment building, the malcontent checked the dashboard clock. *He oughta been here an hour ago.*

Having nothing else to do, the brutish man reached for the sawed-off shotgun, broke it down, ejected a pair of red shells, put them back in again, snapped the double barrels shut. Then did it again. And again. It helped to pass the time.

# THIRTY-SEVEN

## *SOME DAYS IT'S JUST ONE DANG THING RIGHT AFTER ANOTHER*

WHEN Miss Katcher tapped tentatively on his door, Sheriff Ned Popper was engrossed in a confidential wiretap report. "Come on in, Bertha."

The dispatcher, who had been losing weight, and looked more haggard with each passing day, stuck her sagging face into his office. "Shurf Pokker, there's an out-a-town lawyer here to see you."

He arched a bushy eyebrow. "He have a name?"

"I forgot to ask him." Being more or less a literalist, she added: "But I imagine he must have."

"Send him in." The duly elected sheriff of Tonapah Flats got to his feet.

The visitor's shoulders filled the doorway; his gray suit, pale-yellow silk shirt, sky-blue tie hinted at money and power. His beefy demeanor suggested an off-duty lumberjack masquerading as a man of business. The enigma presented a genuine smile, stuck out a bear-size paw. "I'm Bruce Staples. Of Arnette, Fagan, Jarvis, Staples, Gish, Bullock, and Armstrong. Our firm is in Salt Lake."

Popper smiled at the center of the totem pole, shook his hand. "Rest your bones, Mr. Staples."

"Thanks—don't mind if I do." The attorney plopped into an armchair, cuddled an alligator briefcase on his lap.

"And by the way, my name's Popper—with three *P*'s."

Bruce Staples chuckled. "I know your name, Sheriff. Ben Silver told me all about you."

*Uh-oh—what's this about?* "So you knew Ben?"

"Indeed I did. Both as a client, and a friend."

Sheriff Popper waited for the other boot to drop.

Mr. Staples was not a man to waste words or ticks of the clock. "Ben came to see me exactly six days before his death."

The size-fifteen footwear fell with a sizable thud.

"He had me draw up a new will. Being brief and to the point, it was keyed into the computer, printed out, signed, witnessed, and notarized before he left my office." The efficient attorney sensed the expected questions forming behind the lawman's craggy face, answered every one of them. "I would have contacted you immediately after his untimely demise, but the day after my meeting with Ben I left on a trip to Argentina. I returned yesterday, and read my client's obituary in the newspaper." There was a hesitation, as if Staples was searching for precisely the right words to string together. "Given the circumstances, it is necessary that you and I have a face-to-face."

The sheriff spoke softly under the handlebar mustache. "Was Ben expecting someone to make an attempt on his life?"

Staples shook his head. "But he did express some concern about his deteriorating health."

Popper popped the obvious question. "So who'd Ben leave his stuff to?"

"As for the bulk of his estate, I am not authorized to reveal that information at this time." The attorney removed a black plastic folder from his briefcase. "But I am instructed to inform you about the deceased's wishes concerning the disposition of a particular item of personal property." Turning to page two of the document, Staples cleared his throat, read Paragraph VI, lines sixteen through twenty-four.

Popper's jaw dropped, hung on its hinges.

Probably because the attorney owned a quarter-share in a

prosperous Caterpillar dealership, the sheriff's gaped mouth suggested a 966D Cat front-end loader about to scoop up a few cubic yards of rubble. Smiling at the high-horsepower metaphor, Mr. Staples snapped the briefcase shut, vaulted up from the chair, glanced at his wristwatch. "I'd like to stay and chat, but I have urgent business back in the city." On the way out of Popper's office, he rotated the lumberjack shoulders, looked back at the mute lawman. "I almost forgot. You are authorized—encouraged, in fact—to communicate the information about Ben's personal-property bequest to his half brother Raymond Oates." With that, he closed the door behind him.

For a long interval, Popper stared at the oak door. *I just don't believe it. Why on earth would Ben—*

The telephone on his desk jangled the lawman back to reality.

He heard himself say: "Hello."

"Who's this?"

"Uh—Sheriff Pokker." *Dammit, now she's got me doing it!* "I mean *Popper.*"

"Well, I wanted to speak to Deputy Packard, but I guess it's better to talk to the top dog." *Even if the dimwit ain't sure what his name is.*

"Who's calling?"

"This is Hank Bigbee, from Cut Bank, Colorado. But you can call me Buddy."

Sheriff Popper propped his elbows on his desk. "What can I do for you, Buddy?"

"Well, you can let me know if you was able to use that tip I passed on to Deputy Packard about the Indian girl."

Popper barely suppressed a groan, found a ballpoint pen. "What tip was that?" *We only had about a thousand.*

"Why me and Tillie—Tillie's my wife—we saw that kid in Cortez. Cat and all."

The sheriff doodled a stick-legged cat on his desk pad. "You did, huh?"

"Sure as July follows June." Bigbee repeated the story he'd told the deputy. "And if you pick her up at her Aunt

Daisy's place on the Southern Ute res, me and Tillie damn well expect to get that big re-ward."

*Aunt Daisy?* Popper paused in mid-doodle. There hadn't been anything in the news releases about Charlie Moon's aunt. "Would you please repeat that, Mr. Bigbee?"

"Hey, no need to Mister me—I'm just plain Buddy." But Just Plain Buddy repeated what he had said. About Aunt Daisy and the big re-ward.

"And the first time you called, you told Deputy Packard exactly what you just told me?"

"Sure did. Practically word for word."

*And Packard made a beeline straight for the Southern Ute reservation.*

"And your deputy said he'd put my name on the list." A rasping smoker's cough. "And we oughta be first in line for that big re-ward, 'cause I didn't fiddle-faddle around—I called on the same day we saw that Indian girl, which was on the morning after she murdered that old fella in Tonapah Flats." Buddy listened to a shouted reminder from his wife. "Will you check to see that our name's on the re-ward list—mine and Tillie's?"

"You can count on it." Popper made a note of the caller's telephone number. "If this information turns out to be useful in helping us locate this girl, I'll make certain you get whatever's coming to you."

"Thanks." Another yell from the wife. "Oh, one last thing—Tillie said to tell you the kid called her cat Zig-Zag."

Like any capable small-town politician, the sheriff knew the names of all of his constituents, and 90 percent of their pets. *Well, that puts the butter on the biscuit.* The Utah lawman thanked the helpful Colorado citizen and hung up. *Tate Packard withheld critical information related to a homicide investigation, which means if he ain't stone-cold dead when I find him, I'll make him wish he was.* The furious man was jamming his hat on his head when the dispatcher elbowed her way past him, plopped her massive self into an armchair. "Shurf Pokker, I gotta talk to you."

This happened about once every month. Bertha's worry-motor generally cranked up with a sputtering of rumors and complaints, finally chugged to a stop with a threat to quit and find a better job *somewheres else*. He eyeballed the clock on the wall. "I'm kinda busy right now. Could it keep for a little while?"

The woman shook her head in a defiant gesture, suggesting an innate stubbornness an Arkansas mule would have admired.

Popper pushed the hat back on his head, seated himself on the corner of his desk. "Okay, but don't take too long."

Looking over his shoulder, she frowned at a wall calendar that featured a color print of a lovable beagle puppy licking the face of an equally lovable kitten. "Shurf, we got troubles."

He watched the ceiling fan, which—like the second hand on the wall clock—seemed to be slowing. "What is it this time—somebody been pilfering nickels and dimes from the petty-cash jar?"

Another shake of her head. "It's lots worser'n that—we got *big* troubles."

Drop by drop, his reservoir of patience was leaking away. "Please don't keep me in suspense."

Katcher the Dispatcher turned her beady-eyed stare on the boss. "Bearcat didn't show up for work this mornin'."

He stared at the enigmatic woman. "Bertha, that happens at least a couple times a month. If that's all you're worried about—"

"Bearcat ain't just not here—he's dista-peered!"

"Come again?"

"I did some checkin'." She counted off one finger. "He didn't show up at his apartment last night." Another finger. "And the manager says his bed ain't been slept in."

"Well that just proves BC was out on an all-night toot. He'll probably wake up in a ditch somewhere with his head hurtin' so bad he'll wish he was dead and—"

"Shurf—Bearcat *is* dead!"

Despite her comical manner, this assertion jarred Popper. He assumed a gentler tone. "Why do you say that?"

"'Cause I *know* Bearcat's dead—I feel it in my bones."

Bertha hugged her considerable self, evidently confirming the message originating deep in her marrow. "And Tate Packard's dead too. Somebody drown-ded him in the river!" She closed her eyes, her massive body shook in a hideous shudder that threatened to wrench joint from limb.

"Now, now, Bertha." He patted her on the shoulder.

When she had recovered from the shakes, the dispatcher looked Popper straight in the eye. "Shurf, somebody is killin' off our depitties. And they ain't done with their killin'." She leaned toward the boss. "I figger I'm gonna be next!"

The sheriff recalled his late wife, and how the unfortunate woman had suffered every day of her life. *Poor Bertha must be having one of those peculiar problems women have with their innards.* He had no reliable knowledge of such matters and did not wish to be educated on the subject. "You worry too much." Another pat. "Tell you what, you take the rest of the day off. Get yourself some rest."

Another shake of the head. "That's what caused all this trouble in the first place." The dispatcher gave the sheriff a guilty look. "That day that ol' Ben Silver was killed, I wasn't tendin' to my duties like I should've been. If I hadn't been runnin' back and forth to the toilet, why Mr. Silver would be alive today."

"Bertha, we can all think of things we might've done that would have made a difference." He put on a smile that lifted the tips of the handlebar mustache. "Take me, for instance. If I'd got to Ben's place a couple of minutes sooner than I did, I might've been able to prevent the killing. And then there's the hand of Fate—if that big accident out on the interstate hadn't happened that morning, Ben would've been able to see his doctor at the clinic, and he wouldn't have come home early and surprised the girl." He waited for this to sink through his dispatcher's inch-thick skull, but it was apparent that she was not listening to a word he'd said. Popper's eyes narrowed. "Bertha, I'm going to ask you a simple question, and I want you to tell me the unvarnished truth."

To avoid the lawman's steely glaze, the dispatcher hung her head.

Popper was not deterred. "Have you been reading more of them crime-fiction books they sell down at the newsstand?"

"No." A shrug. "Well, maybe."

"Tell me the truth."

"Okay." A sniff. "Ever once in a while I might read one." She jutted her chin. "Maybe two or three a week. But that don't have nothin' to do with—"

"Yes it does, Bertha. The people that write that trash don't know a thing about actual crimes, or real police work. I've warned you before—you keep reading that awful stuff, it'll turn your brain to mush!"

The aficionado of excellent literary fiction was not to be intimidated. "This don't have a thing to do with what I read, Shurf Pokker." The obstinate woman's head continued to shake, as if some internal motor would not shut off. "Mr. Silver's killin' and our murdered depitties—that's all my fault. Why I might as well done it with my own hands!" She glared at her employer. "And you might as well take off that silly hat and sit your skinny butt down behind your desk, 'cause you're goin' to hear me out."

Defeated, Ned Popper hung up his hat, seated himself as directed. "Okay, Bertha. Get it off your chest."

"I'll do just that." In preparation for the task, she drew in a deep breath. "And after I tell you what I got to say, you'll understand why I can't work here anymore."

The weary man leaned back in his chair, clasped hands behind his head, closed his eyes. *I oughta make a recording, so next time Bertha gets ants in her pants I could just play it back and we both could listen to it and save her the trouble of talking a blue streak 'til the cows come home.*

Bertha Katcher made a slow start, gradually picked up the pace, finally got rolling under a full head of steam. The dispatcher didn't put on the brakes until she'd gotten to the end of the line.

The sheriff watched a brown beetle scuttling up the wall. *Compared to being a sworn officer of the law, I imagine them little bugs must live a fairly simple, peaceful life.*

"Shurf Pokker, I'm really awfully sorry about—"

He groaned. "Bertha, Bertha—what am I gonna do with you?" *I could draw my .45-caliber revolver right here and now, shoot you between the eyes. But that'd be sure to stir up a lot of fuss.* He sighed. *And there'd be no end to the paperwork.*

# THIRTY-EIGHT

## *INCIDENT AT THE COLUMBINE GATE*

STANDING straight as a post, she raised her nose, prickling bristly whiskers. Sniffed.

By nature and of necessity, prairie dogs are remarkably inquisitive creatures. Anything that approaches the boundary of their underground compound is considered a potential threat. This particular rodent's thriving little community was situated on prime real estate just across the highway from the entrance to the Columbine Ranch, and she was on lookout duty. The focus of her attention was a pickup truck concealed in a cluster of junipers.

Without a soul noticing, Time slipped by. Twilight crept ever closer.

Four miles overhead, a spray of waning sunlight inflamed a slice of icy cloud to opalescent incandescence. Much nearer to earth, a dusky hawk circled in search of his supper. Far enough away to mute a thundercloud's ominous mumble, a gray spray of rain washed the dusty prairie. In the passing storm's wake, a breeze ruffled and rippled a pea-green sea of tender grasses, stirred up fragrant scents of damp sage.

No one emerged from the pickup.

As a thickish gloom oozed down mountain slopes to fill the vast grassy basin between the Misery Range and the Buckhorns, the prairie dog lost interest in the wheeled vehicle, darted into a burrow to pursue whatever nighttime pastimes may occupy these spirited creatures, be it dreamless sleep or sleepless dreams . . . or wordless memories of former worlds.

Others—like the nervous millipedes, poisonous centipedes, hairy hook-tail scorpions, and various other categories of nasty night crawlers—were different kinds of animals altogether. They did not retreat from the onset of darkness; their sinister business was just beginning.

One of them started the pickup engine.

### *THE APPROACHING FLATBED TRUCK*

RUDOLPHO Lopez eased up on the gas, stomped his left boot onto the clutch pedal, shifted the gear down by one grinding notch.

The half-asleep cowboy on the passenger side opened a pair of bloodshot eyes, belched beer fumes. "What—we there yet?"

Lopez grinned. *He sounds like my four-year-old granddaughter.*

### *THE PICKUP*

KNUCKLE-dragger Number One watched the big truck slow. "Here comes our chance to get through the gate."

Knuckle-Dragger Number Two, who was seated on the passenger side, cleared his throat and voiced a concern: "From what I hear, these Utes are seriously dangerous people. If that big spear-chucker catches us messin' around on his property—"

"Don't fret about the Ute." Number One cast a scornful glance at this unwanted accomplice. "If push comes to shove, I'll take care of Charlie Moon."

Number Two grunted. *Before I head back to Utah, I'll take care of you.*

Number One experienced a sudden, cold premonition—like ice was freezing in his spine. *I don't trust this rattlesnake. Soon as the job's done, I'll put a bullet in his head.*

## *MEANWHILE, BACK IN THE FLATBED*

THE driver eased the big truck off the paved highway, onto the Columbine Ranch lane. "We're at the gate, Six." Six was short for Six-Toes, which was exactly how many the Anglo cowhand had on each of his feet. Lopez braked the vehicle to a rocking, creaking stop. "Take the padlock key outta the ashtray and go open the gate."

Six mumbled his customary grumble about ". . . always bein' the one who has to open the damn gate" but dutifully fumbled around until he found the designated key, stumbled out of the big truck, and got the job done within a minute, which was not bad for a congenitally clumsy bumbler who had recently drained seven longneck bottles of Milwaukee brew.

Lopez watched his tipsy partner swing the gate aside. *I'd better take him straight to the bunkhouse. Charlie Moon sees ol' Six drunk, he'll fire him right on the spot.* Somewhere under the moan of the wind, the driver thought he heard the low growl of a second engine, the squeak of worn brakes. He glanced at the rearview mirror, saw something back there in the moonlight. Something with no headlights. *Now that don't smell right.* He pulled the flatbed halfway through the open gate, stuck his head out the window. "Hey, Six—somebody's pulled in back a me. Go see who it is and what he wants."

Pleased to have something brand-new to complain about, Six-Toes staggered off muttering: "I hope Señor Lopez don't get a sudden appetite for one a them red-hot jalapeño peppers, 'cause I expect he'd want me to chew it for 'im before he swallered it and them Messican vittles gives me heartburn." He approached the unfamiliar vehicle, got a glimpse of the Utah plates in the moonlight, vainly strained to see inside the dark interior. "Howdy!"

Silence.

Six-Toes tried again. "Hey—whacha doin' here at the Columbine gate?"

The voice that responded, though gruff, was friendly enough. "Need to talk to Charlie Moon. Thought I'd follow you in."

"Well, I don't know 'bout that." Six-Toes scratched at a curly tuft of hair that was rooted in his ear. "The boss expectin' you?"

"Uh . . . no." A clearing of the throat. "Thought I'd surprise him."

Six-Toes hated to make the least decision, such as whether to put mustard or ketchup on his cheeseburger, or a dab of both. He shuffled his well-endowed feet. "Uh—just a minute whilst I go check with Lopez."

A coyote sitting at the edge of a deep arroyo performed a passable tenor solo.

Somewhere in the dark theater, an owl-critic hooted.

• • •

RUDOLPHO Lopez drummed his fingers on the steering wheel. *What's taking Six so long back there?* There could only be one answer to that. *I bet whoever it is has given him a drink. Which is just about the last thing he needs right now.* Leaving the engine running, he got out of the big truck, stomped along the lane toward the vehicle behind him. Lopez stopped to stare at the pickup. Both doors were open, the dome light on—but there was no one inside. To make the situation even more interesting, there was also no Six-Toes. "Hey—Six! Where you at?"

A yip-yippee from the coyote tenor.

A hoo-hoo-ti-hoo from the big-eyed mouse eater.

*Well if this ain't just the damnedest thing.* Lopez paced off an increasing spiral around the trucks, until he found what he was looking for. Which is to say, Six-Toes, who was not forked-end down, but flat on his back in a clump of rabbit bush. *Hah. I bet some yahoo with a fifth of Jim Beam gave Six a shot or two and he passed out.*

Someone had given Six-Toes a shot, but whisky was not what. That same someone tapped the flatbed driver on the shoulder.

Having been startled enough to bite his tongue, Lopez cursed, turned to see who had snuck up on him. He caught the iron-hard fist full on his chin.

## *AT THE PRIEST'S CABIN*

EXHAUSTED BY two almost-sleepless nights and long days of catching up with such work as was necessary to maintain even a small household, Father Raes Delfino had gone to bed early. While saying his prayers, the old man had fallen into the deepest of sleeps, was now drifting through the loveliest of dreams.

*Perfectly at peace, he strolled along a narrow path. Aside from a few splashes of sunlight, his way was shaded by branches clothed in leaves of burnished gold. On his left, heavy gray mists partially concealed a dense forest, where chatter of wren and sparrow cloaked the conversations of such other creatures as dwelt in its depths. To his right, just beyond a meandering honeysuckle hedge, grassy, flower-dappled hills rolled away to a distant horizon. Over his head, the darkening sky was larkspur-blue, ahead of him, it was aglow with rainbow fire and other glistening hues he could never have imagined. Singing softly to himself, the dreamer topped a knoll, and behold—in the valley below, a river rushed riotously over a jumble of glistening boulders. His long trail terminated at a stone bridge, and as the priest approached, he was dismayed to see a closed iron gate on the near side—and a large, muscular man standing guard. Assuming this formidable fellow to be the toll collector, the pilgrim began to search his pock-*

*ets, could not find a solitary dime. He was wondering who might loan him the cost of safe passage—when someone tugged at his sleeve.*

His pajama sleeve.

• • •

SUDDENLY aware of the now-familiar presence, Father Raes blinked at the semidarkness surrounding his bed, caught a glimpse of the shadowy form. "What is it?"

With admirable patience, he listened to excited whispers. *The bad men were coming.* She had seen it all through the *little window.* This had already happened two nights in a row, but tonight she was sure they were coming. *Really* sure.

The sleep-deprived man sighed. *Poor little thing.* He planted his bare feet onto the cold floor. *I'll make a pot coffee, and do some reading.* His left foot found his right slipper. *But shortly after sunrise, I shall make another call to Daisy. If she does not answer her telephone, I'll drive down to the reservation and knock on her door. And I won't leave until we have sorted this business out.* In response to additional urgent whispers, the Jesuit assumed an authoritarian tone: "I will sit up and keep watch—but I insist that you calm down." *God willing, you will be able to rest.*

# THIRTY-NINE

## *THE UNEXPECTED GUEST*

AFTER enjoying a late supper of broiled steak, boiled potatoes, and pinto beans, Charlie Moon was washing the dishes. When he heard an authoritative knock on the door, the rancher strode down a darkened hall, across a large parlor illuminated by flickering firelight. Passing under a cast-iron chandelier, he pulled a brass chain to switch on the lights, then opened the door onto the west porch.

The gaunt man in the bulky black raincoat grinned under the handlebar mustache, raised two fingers to touch the brim of his matching black hat. "I was just passing by, Charlie—thought I'd stop and say howdy."

"Howdy yourself." Moon made a gesture to invite Ned Popper in. "I'm surprised you got through the locked gate." There was a telephone at the Columbine entrance that was wired to the foreman's house, but after dark strangers had trouble finding the thing. And even if they made the call, there was no guarantee Pete Bushman would push the button to unlatch the gate. The mercurial foreman's hospitality depended on the particular mood he was in, which generally ranged somewhere between grumpy and downright nasty.

Sheriff Popper removed his raincoat and off-duty hat, which was a fine Golden Gate lid he'd laid down two hundred and ten dollars for, and that was during the annual half-price sale at Tonapah Flats Western Wear. "Well, your gate wasn't locked tonight."

Moon made a mental note to inform his foreman about this oversight. "If you're the least bit hungry, I'll fix you up a spot of supper."

"Thank you kindly, Charlie—but I had me a big hamburger sandwich just an hour ago."

*He looks worn out.* "How about a dose of caffeine?"

"I don't normally have any this late in the day, but something from the coffeepot would sure hit the spot."

"Then I'll make us a fresh batch. And while I'm tending to that, make yourself at home."

After the Ute had gone back to the kitchen, the Utah lawman wandered around the headquarters parlor. He stopped to admire a case of rifles and carbines. *Some of those are really fine pieces.* His aimless amblings continued until he came to a three-by-five-foot frame hung between a pair of north-facing windows. Under the glass was a meticulously made, hand-crafted map of the Columbine Ranch.

When Moon returned with a blue enamel pot and two cups, his guest was still studying the cartographer's product. "This is a really big spread you got."

"Columbine's been a working ranch since the early 1870s. I got that map last year, from the Granite Creek Historical Society." He couldn't help mentioning that he also owned the Big Hat, which was on the far side of the Buckhorn Range. "You want some milk or sugar?"

"No, black and bitter will suit me just fine." The guest took a long drink of the hot liquid, pointed at a blue oval on the map. "Charlie, I kinda got turned around in the dark—whichaway is this good-sized lake from your house?"

"Almost due south."

"Oh, yeah. Now I'm squared away." Popper half-smiled. "I swear—older I get, the harder time I have findin' my way home after dark. But either one of my deputies—" He paused at the thought that one of his sidekicks was almost certainly dead. "Bearcat could find a black beetle in a barrel of tar."

"You got Bearcat watching the shop for you?"

"Nah." He finished off the cup, poured another from the pot. "That big plug-ugly didn't show up for work this morning." His face flushed red. "But when I have to take off for a day or two, the state police cover for me." Popper tapped a blunt finger on the map, where the artist had drawn a tiny box with a pitched roof. "This little house ain't too far from the lake. Looks like it was put there for a fisherman."

Moon grinned at this kindred spirit. "You like to wet a hook now and then?"

"Oh, sure. Ever chance I get, I feed the trout some salmon eggs." A hesitation, then Popper did a bit of fishing. "If you'd be willing to rent that little place, I might want to take a week or two vacation there."

"Ned, you're welcome to cast a line in Lake Jesse whenever you want, and I'll put you up here in the headquarters. But that cabin is occupied by a friend of mine."

Popper managed to look envious. "Must be a real *good* friend."

The Ute nodded. "Ever since he retired, that's been Father Raes's place." This seemed to require an explanation. "For almost twenty years, he was the priest at St. Ignatius, down in Ignacio."

"Well, if I live to retire, I may just show up here with a fishin' pole in one hand and a can of worms in the other." At Moon's invitation, he took a seat in front of the massive stone fireplace.

Two and a half cups of black coffee later, Sheriff Popper stretched out his feet to the warmth of the flames. "You got a really nice place." *And I bet you're wondering why I'm taking up space in it.*

"Thanks." *I wonder when he'll tell me what he's doing here.* "It's quiet and peaceful." The Ute added: "Most of the time."

"I don't s'pose there's any news about my missing deputy."

"Not that I've heard of." Light from the prancing flames danced in the tribal investigator's dark eyes. "But SUPD and the Archuleta County Sheriff's Office are keeping a close eye on the river. Once the water drops a couple of feet, I expect he'll turn up."

Popper swirled his cup to make a small, dark whirlpool. "Poor fella's probably wrapped around a snag." He turned to frown at the Ute. "I'd rather find almost any kind of corpse than one that's been drowned."

Moon had encountered more than his share of soulless bodies. He nodded.

The sheriff turned his gaze on the fireplace. *I wonder how much this Indian knows that he ain't telling me.* "Were you surprised that Tate Packard showed up on the Southern Ute reservation?"

The tribal investigator deflected the question: "I was surprised your deputy came without telling you."

"Me too." Popper coughed up a throaty chuckle.

"With a fifty-thousand-dollar reward for inspiration, I guess Mr. Packard figured it was worth a shot." The Ute pitched a chunk of juniper onto the fire. "Sarah's father was a Southern Ute. Your deputy must've figured she'd be as likely to head for our res as seek shelter with her mother's Papago folks in Arizona."

"And you don't see it that way?"

Moon took a sip of syrupy-sweet coffee. "Provo Frank's parents died ages ago, and Sarah doesn't have any close kin left among us Utes. But she has about a dozen cousins on the Papago res. Plus some aunts and uncles." *And you know that as well as I do.*

For a pleasant interlude, they enjoyed the warmth of the fire.

Popper broke the silence. "What about Sarah's aunt Daisy?"

Moon told the Utah sheriff what Popper already knew: "Daisy's *my* aunt. Not Sarah's."

"Oh." A sheepish grin. "I have trouble keepin' my own kinfolk straight."

"But," the Ute admitted, "Sarah is pretty close to my aunt. If that little gal headed for our territory, Daisy's door is where she'd knock. And almost anybody in Ignacio could've told Packard about that connection. But I asked my aunt about your deputy on the same day he drove his Bronco into the Piedra. She hadn't seen the man."

Popper nodded slowly. *So she says . . .* "Since the last time we talked, I've found out a thing or two."

The tribal investigator waited to hear what.

The white lawman cleared his throat. "Day before Deputy Packard left for Colorado—and the Southern Ute reservation—he took calls from about eleven-dozen people who thought they'd spotted Sarah Frank." Popper paused. "Turns out one of 'em actually had. Seen Sarah, that is. I had a phone conversation with the fella yesterday. He told me how him and his wife had a talk with the girl."

"Where and when?"

"At a truck stop in Cortez. It was early in the morning—on the day after Ben Silver was murdered."

Charlie Moon watched hungry flames lick bark off the juniper log. "I stopped by my aunt's house that afternoon. If Sarah had been there, I'm sure I'd have known it." *Maybe she showed up later.* This thought was punctuated by a gunshot-like pop from the resinous wood. He turned toward his guest. "What makes you so sure this was a genuine sighting?"

"This particular girl mentioned she was on her way to see Aunt Daisy." Firelight danced in the Utah lawman's eyes. "And her cat's name was Mr. Zig-Zag."

The tribal investigator nodded slowly. *So Sarah did come to Colorado.*

Popper took a long drink of coffee, grimaced as the brew seared a dime-size ulcer in his stomach. "Way I figure it, my deputy knew he had a hot lead on the kid, and a good chance to collect the reward money. So to eliminate any chance of competition—like from me or Bearcat—he erased the message off of our new telephone system. If this Mr. Bigbee from Colorado hadn't called a second time and got me on the line, I'd still be in the dark."

Moon was busy talking to himself. *If Sarah showed up at*

*my aunt's place, Daisy's been hiding her. I'll go down there tomorrow morning and have a long, hard talk with that conniving old woman and—* His thoughts were interrupted by Popper's drawl.

"Charlie, I'd appreciate it if you'd introduce me to Mrs. Perika."

Moon turned to blink at the Utah lawman. "You figure she'll tell an out-of-state cop what she won't tell me?"

"Some women like to talk to me." *Some women like Bertha.* The older man grinned. "Anyway, it can't hurt to ask."

Daisy's nephew grunted. *You don't know her like I do.*

"Well?"

"Tomorrow morning, I'll take you down to Aunt Daisy's place. You can explain to her how it's in Sarah's best interest to turn herself in." Moon managed to keep a straight face. "And if that don't do the trick, you'll have to get tough—tell her it's against the law to harbor a fugitive from justice." *That'll be fun to watch.* He pushed himself up from the chair. "In the meantime, I'll fix you up with a room."

"Thank you kindly. These old bones don't travel as well as they used to."

"Upstairs or down?"

"Bottom floor will suit me just fine." Popper picked up his cup, tossed the last of the coffee down, grounds and all. "But all that caffeine I soaked up has got me wide awake."

"I could find you a good book." Moon nodded to indicate the well-stocked shelves: "I've got first editions of everything Will James ever wrote."

"Mr. James is a favorite of mine, and that would normally be just the ticket." Popper glanced at a feathered lance mounted above the mantelpiece. "But I'm kinda in the mood for some excitement."

"Well, we could go into town and pick a fight." Moon turned some possibilities over in his mind. "There's a gang of thugs that hang out at Tubby's Cantina. The least one of 'em tips the scales at two-forty-six, and the sissy of the bunch bites off rattlesnake heads for breakfast, has rattle soup for lunch, and boils the rest for supper—with okra."

Popper shuddered. "I *hate* boiled okra."

"And in between meals, he snacks on black widows."

"Well, I have to tell you—"

Moon raised a hand to silence his guest. "I know what you're about to say, and you're dead right. It wouldn't be an altogether fair fight—the two of us taking on a dozen of them. But I say let those roughnecks look out for themselves."

"Thanks anyway, Charlie." Popper sighed. "I'm not in the mood to injure anybody."

"Okay. But aside from a wholesome bar fight or sittin' down with a good book, I'm fresh out of suggestions."

Popper gave the Ute a sly look. "I've heard some tales about you—there's folks that say you're a man who likes to play poker."

The gambler grinned. "Those folks might be right."

## *THE SHERIFF'S GAME*

ELBOWS on the kitchen table, the men got down to the serious business of having some fun.

Charlie Moon removed the seal from a brand-new deck. "Let's make it low stakes."

The Utah player cocked an eyebrow. "Why?"

"Well, seeing as how you're my guest, I wouldn't want to bleed you dry."

Popper snorted. "If you want to play it safe, that's all right by me."

The first few hands went about fifty-fifty, with Moon ahead by about two bits. After that, it was the sheriff's game—Popper began to get the better of his host. Wistful tales of times gone by were exchanged, olden days and cowboy ways were duly praised. Stale chocolate donuts were consumed, also salty peanuts and pretzels. After taking an eighty-cent pot, the happy sheriff bawled out all he could recall of "Cotton-Eyed Joe." The Ute responded with "Prairie Lullaby"; Moon's yodeling coyote-call couldn't hold a candle to Don Edwards, but the performance brought a tear to the older man's eye. The Utah lawman put a cap on it with "Take Me Back to Tulsa."

By mutual agreement, the out-of-stater dealt that evening's final hand.

Moon eyed his cards. *Imagine that.*

"How many you want?"

"Uh—I'll just need one." *Wouldn't it be something if it was the five of diamonds.*

"Hah—you won't bluff me as easy as that!" Popper dealt Moon the Card.

The Ute's famous poker face was sorely tested. *I wonder if he's dealing from the bottom of the deck.*

The Utah man scowled at his hand. "Dealer takes three." Which he did. "Your bet."

Moon tossed a dime onto the table.

After it had wobbled to a stop, Popper laid out a shiny Jefferson nickel and five Lincoln cents. "I'll see you."

Moon put his cards on the table. "Two pair."

The sheriff of Tonapah Flats leaned, gave Moon's hand a queer look, then raised his gaze to the Indian's face. "I hope you're not one a them superstitious card players."

The Ute smiled. "So do I."

Popper pointed at Moon's hand. "Black aces over eights. And the kicker's a five of diamonds." He held his breath for a moment, barely suppressed a shudder. "You know what that is, don't you?"

Every poker player in the Western hemisphere knew what *that* was. But Moon gave the Utah cop an innocent look. "Something that'll beat what you've got?"

"I'm gonna let you have this pot." Popper folded his full house. "Least I can do for a player who's holding the Dead Man's Hand."

Moon looked at the fan of cards. "Well, now that you mention it, I thought there was something familiar about it—that's what Wild Bill Hickok was holding when that fella what's-his-name—"

"Jack McCall was the gunman. And he shot Mr. Hickok in the back of the head."

"With a forty-five-caliber, double-action six-shooter," Moon muttered.

"There's lots of hairy-chested, hell-for-leather players who'd get all green around the gills if they was to draw black aces over eights." Popper's grin sliced razor-thin. "It's a good thing that neither one of us puts any stock in such spooky stuff."

"Speak for yourself—us Utes take those *matukach* superstitions very seriously." His eyes twinkled with merriment. "Some bad-luck cowboy's bound to die tonight." Charlie Moon raked in the pot.

Popper stared across the table. *But who'll it be—you or me?* The Utah sheriff got up, stretched his long, lanky frame. "All you need to do is say 'good night, old-timer,' and point me toward my bunk."

# FORTY

## *THE WATCHER*

AFTER locating the priest's cabin, Knuckle-Dragger Number Two had observed the sturdy structure for quite some time—vainly hoping the girl might come outside. A single window spilled a spray of amber light onto the forest floor. *Looks like he ain't gone to bed yet.* His thoughts shifted to his primary target: *If the kid's here, maybe she's still up too.* All things considered, it would be best to corner the old man and the girl in the same room; it wouldn't do to have one of them slip away and bring that Ute and a gang of armed cowboys back to the cabin. *I'd better do this job with my bare hands.* Though the night stalker reckoned it was unlikely that gunshots would be heard back at the ranch headquarters, he preferred to make as little noise as possible. He took a few almost-silent steps across a crunchy carpet of pine and fir needles, warily approached the glowing window. He spotted the white-haired man immediately, but there was no sign of the runaway Papago girl. *Damn!*

## *THE READER*

WIDE awake now, Father Raes Delfino was in his bedroom, seated at a knotty-pine desk. The fat red volume illuminated by his reading lamp was large enough to be a Chicago telephone directory or an unabridged dictionary, but it was something far more precious. The book that occupied the attention of the retired Catholic priest was *St. Francis of Assisi—Omnibus of Sources.* For the past twenty-seven months, day by day, page by page, the devout scholar had been absorbing every detail on the life of the blessed little man who so loved his Lady Poverty. At the moment, his attention was focused on page 1253, and the section entitled Mirror of Perfection. The subject was the saint's special love for the hooded larks. When Francis died, a great multitude of his feathered friends had appeared above the spot where his body was. The assembly of *Lodola capellata* circled above, singing most sweetly.

Father Raes paused to wipe a tear away.

So engrossed was he in his reading that he had not heard the stealthy footsteps outside his home, or noticed the face framed in the window.

The knock on the front door surprised more than startled the reader. He marked his place with a scrap of scarlet ribbon, got up from his chair, headed into the small parlor. *Who can it be at this late hour?* Having dismissed the whispered warnings about what she had seen through the *little window,* he considered a few possibilities, quickly eliminated all but one. *Charlie Moon, of course. He must have been out walking, and noticed my light.* The innocent approached the cabin door—and his destiny—with a smile on his lips.

Father Raes opened the door, blinked at the unfamiliar face. *Charlie must've hired a new hand while I was away.* "Good evening—what can I do for you?"

"Charlie Moon sent me." In a friendly salute, the stranger touched a finger to the brim of his hat. "Boss wants me to bring the little Indian girl over to the ranch house. There's some news from Utah he wants to tell her about." He attempted a congenial smile. "What he's got to say won't take long. I'll bring the kid right back."

Father Raes stared at the late-night caller. It was absurd that Charlie Moon would send someone for Sarah. Impossible. *Charlie has no idea what his aunt deposited at the cabin . . . this man is lying.* He started to speak, hesitated.

The person who stood in darkness blinked at the little man with a halo of snow-white hair. "If she's asleep, just wake her up—"

The priest shook his head. "That is quite impossible."

The uninvited visitor assumed a mildly accusative tone: "You telling me she's not here?"

Father Raes began to close the door.

"I come for the kid." The stranger put his heavy boot across the threshold, leaned so close the priest could smell onions on his breath. "And I'm taking her with me."

"You are not taking anyone anywhere." The Jesuit scholar shifted to pool-hall vernacular: "That shot is not on the table."

The hard-muscled man's lips twisted into a brutish grin. "You don't know who you're dealing with, Padre."

Not so. The holy man of God knew precisely who he was dealing with. The faces were different, the threats varied, but they were all the same. "Do you have a name?"

"You can call me Smith." The trespasser saw a shadowy form slip down the hallway—and close behind it, a black-and-white cat. He stiff-armed the old man aside.

Father Raes stumbled toward the fireplace, tumbled hard onto the brick hearth, felt a stinging pain as his pelvis fractured.

Having dispensed with his diminutive opponent, the intruder took a stride toward the hallway. *She's headed for the back door. I'd better grab her before—*

The priest's right hand had found the sooty end of an iron poker. God's pinch-hitter clenched his teeth, made his swing—caught the intruder solidly on the shin. Not the most elegant blow ever landed.

But it got the job done.

# FORTY-ONE

## *THE COLUMBINE FOREMAN'S REPORT*

SHORTLY after Sheriff Popper had retired to his bedroom, Charlie Moon was—so he believed—just about finished with the day's work. He was setting up the pot for the next morning's coffee when he heard a distant roll of thunder. *That's over the Misery Range and the wind's westerly, so we might get some rain.* The rancher smiled at the thought of what a good downpour would do for the yellowing grass, plus what it would do for his sleep. The soothing lullaby of fat raindrops plopping onto the metal roof was the perfect soporific. These pleasant thoughts were interrupted by an urgent banging on the kitchen door. *At this time of night, this can't be good news.* Taking long strides across the room, he imagined the worst. *I bet that twelve-thousand-dollar polled Hereford bull we bought last week has taken sick. Or one of the cowboys has gotten himself killed in a bar fight.* As he opened the door, Pete Bushman stumbled in.

"Howdy, boss." The foreman removed his hat, clenched the brim in both hands. "Before you hit the sack I thought you oughta know that a couple a the boys got bunged up some."

Moon groaned. "Which ones?"

"Lopez and Six-Toes. They was on the way back from town in the flatbed. It musta started right after they passed through the main gate."

For the first time since Popper's arrival, Moon remembered the Utah sheriff mentioning the unlocked gate.

The foreman cocked his head like a man who was about to reveal a special insight. "One of 'em—and I expect it musta been Six, 'cause Lopez is a careful driver—drove the track off'n the lane and into that little dry wash. You can imagine how that woulda started up a big argument betwixt 'em, and fussin' came to cussin' and first thing you know those two hotheads started poppin' off like two-dollar firecrackers." He pulled a deep breath, started up again: "And then they commenced to takin' swings at one another."

"Is that what they say?"

"Well, they ain't actually *said* a solitary word."

"Then how do you know—"

"I don't exactly *know,* it's what you call a spec'lation." The hairy-faced foreman scratched at his scraggly beard. "I mean, there wasn't nobody else with 'em, so they *must've* knocked each other out."

"If they were unconscious when you found—"

"I didn't find 'em. It was Little Butch that come across 'em when he went out a while ago to check the gate, make sure it was locked. And it's a wonder he spotted 'em—as far off'n the lane as they was. Anyways, Butch says they was laid out pretty as you please, like two sides a beef."

"Pete, I don't see how two men could knock each other unconscious."

"That's because you ain't given it much thought." Bushman's eyes were bulging with the strain of his own thinking. "Here's how it happens—all it takes is that both of 'em throws his Sunday punch at the *same time,* and they connects within a fraction of a second—pow-pow! Both men is coldcocked, both of 'em go down."

Moon shook his head at this improbability.

The supporter of the Theory of Simultaneous Pugilism did not conceal his chagrin. "Well, if you've got a better idea, don't hold back—I'd be pleased to hear it."

"Okay, try this. They're marked up because they got into a brawl in town. After they got through the gate, they drove off the lane into the dry wash, got out of the truck to drink up what was left of the liquor they'd brought with 'em—and passed out cold as kraut." He added with a grin: "But not necessarily at the same instant."

The foreman rolled the competing conjecture over in his mind. "Well, I s'pose it *mighta* happened like that." His face assumed its typical stubborn expression. "But I still like my notion better."

"Send 'em around after sunrise," the Ute said. "I'm gonna have a serious powwow with that pair."

"Okay." Bushman inhaled another long breath through his whiskers. "I don't mind so much if you send ol' Six-Toes down the road, he ain't good for nothin' much but ridin' fence and chopping kindlin' wood. But I hope you won't fire Lopez—he's one a the best hands we got."

The Ute rancher had a faraway look in his eye. "There's just an off chance that somebody else busted up our cowboys before they could lock the gate." *Somebody who showed up before Sheriff Popper found the gate unlocked.*

The foreman pulled at an earlobe. "I never thought a that."

"Get Six-Toes and Lopez talking soon as you can. If they met up with some hard cases, I'll want a description. And just in case the Columbine's got some unwanted visitors, post a half-dozen armed guards."

"I'll do that right now." Entertaining visions of rustlers and other such lowlifes, Bushman stalked off toward the door. He stopped, turned on his boot heel. "I almost forgot to ask, but who does that pickup outside belong to—the one with the Utah license plate?"

"Sheriff Popper, from Tonapah Flats." Smiling at the suspicious expression on his foreman's perpetually worried face, Moon added: "He's a friend of mine." He pointed toward a corner bedroom. "If you'd like to go wake him up, I'll introduce you two."

Bushman eyed the closed door as if he just might call the boss's bluff. But the foreman departed, leaving an eloquent "hmmph" behind.

Moon listened to the heavy door slam. *It's late, but I better give Father Raes a call, ask him to lock his cabin door.* The owner of the outfit went into the parlor, picked up the telephone, punched in the number. There was a brief silence, followed by a recorded message from the telephone company's computer, monotonically asserting that the line was ". . . not in service at this time." Moon stared at the instrument in his hand without seeing it. In the window, a flash of light. Four counts later, a rumble of thunder came to rattle the windowpanes. *There's two dozen different reasons for a line to go dead, and twenty-three of 'em are nothing to worry about.* He placed the telephone back in its cradle. *But just to be on the safe side, I'll go over to the cabin and have a look.* Rather than drive, he decided to take a flashlight, walk along the telephone line. *With a little bit of luck, I might spot a break.*

• • •

SOME sixty miles to the south in Durango, in the snug little brick house on Buttonwood Lane, Special Agent Lila Mae McTeague could not get a wink of sleep. She was perched on the edge of her bed, toes curled under bare feet, violet eyes staring at yellow daffodils sprouting on faded wallpaper. For weeks, it had been a mere possibility, but today the official memorandum had trickled down to the Denver Field Office, from whence it was forwarded to her fax machine in Granite Creek. The ambitious woman had a serious decision to make. And suspected that she had already made it. *But I won't be able to rest until I call Charlie and tell him about the job offer. I'll ask him what he thinks I should do.* She clenched her hands into fists. *Oh, I am such a hypocrite! I should just tell him the Bureau has made me an offer I can't refuse.* She reached for the telephone, hesitated. It occurred to the lady that she should think of some excuse to call the tribal investigator, chat awhile about this and that. *Then, when it feels like the right moment, I'll mention my chance for a big promotion, see what Charlie has to say about it.* She wanted him to say: "Don't ever leave me, Lila Mae." But she knew what the Ute would mumble in that deep, sad voice. "Well . . . do whatever you think is best." Her brow knitted into an angry scowl. *A damn lot of help you are, Charlie Moon—you and your worthless platitudes. You're about as sensitive and romantic as a—as a glacier!* The gorgeous woman ground her perfect teeth. *But I'll call you anyway, and get this over with.*

Problem was, she couldn't think of an excuse to call him this late in the evening. Miss McTeague finally gave up, fell back onto the pillow. As she was playing with a pearl button on the collar of her nightgown, the answer to a question she was not even thinking about came straight out of nowhere, jolted her brain like an electric shock.

She sat straight up.

The forensics photograph of Ben Silver's prone body seemed to shimmer before her eyes. She could see the buttons ripped from his shirt—the boot on the floor by his knee. Her mouth opened—"Oh my God!" After a minute of going over the facts, she knew she was right.

The FBI agent snatched the telephone, punched in the Columbine number, listened to the dial tone drone. *Ring!* It did. She banged a fist against her knee, willed him to answer. *Pick up, Charlie. Now!* Four rings. She begged. *Please-please-please!* After seven rings, she got the answering machine, listened to the programmed message, waited for the beep.

"It's me." *Well, that sounds dumb.* "Uh—Charlie, this is McTeague. Look, I think I've figured something out about the Silver homicide in Tonapah Flats. Something *very* important." She paused to take a breath. "I don't want to leave the details on your machine, but call me the *very minute* you hear this message." She started to hang up, hesitated. "I don't know if I can prove it, but I'm absolutely certain that at least one of those Utah cops is dirty." The fed felt the pulse throbbing in her neck. "Maybe *all* of them."

• • •

AFTER lowering all the automobile's windows, Knuckle-Dragger Number Two shifted into low, jammed his boot heel on the accelerator pedal. The priest's Buick picked up speed, bounced over a slab of basalt, brushed aside a few spindly willows. An instant before the front tires splashed into the lake, the driver leaped from the old sedan, stumbled, almost fell, muttered an earthy curse. He backed up the pebbled bank, heard the hot exhaust manifold hiss in the icy waters. The engine shuddered, coughed, died. The chassis began to settle into the murky depths. He had assumed the lake was deeper. The wide-eyed spectator chewed on his lower lip. *I hope it's got a soft, muddy bottom.*

Almost a yard deep now, the General Motors product listed slightly toward the driver's side, sank until water flowed into the open windows. It settled more quickly, then oh-so-slowly. Hesitated. Stopped.

He ground his teeth. *Sink, damn you!*

As if energized by this rude command, the Buick responded with a lurch forward. Like a Mesozoic amphibian fossil reincarnated—only to perish again, the massive black turtleback slipped beneath the surface.

Harboring a superstitious fear that the aggravating vehicle might (by some sinister automotive physics?) float back to the surface, he held his breath—only to witness a sudden burp of bubbles. Then another. *Must've been air caught in the trunk.*

As if all were well, moonlight rippled serenely on the waters.

He exhaled a grateful sigh. *Well, that's over and done with.*

Not so.

*And nobody saw me do it.*

Ditto.

This particular descendant of Cain had not noticed the winged witnesses circling above the shore. His eye was blind to their flitting forms, his ear deaf to their clear, sweet song.

Larks?

A romantic might dare to *hope* so.

But hooded as well?

Given the locale and habitat, such a visitation seems quite unlikely.

# FORTY-TWO

## *ACES OVER EIGHTS*

ON this night, the forest was full of peering eyes. By way of example—on a rocky knoll above the priest's cabin, in a smallish, grassy glade, a still figure was immersed in inky nightshade. Sheriff Popper watched the Ute's approach. Tried to decide what to do.

• • •

HAVING found no break in the telephone line, Charlie Moon approached the cabin. He was mildly surprised to discover that the priest's old Buick was not parked in the usual spot. *Looks like he's took off on another one of his trips.* Following a distant cannonade of thunder, a few raindrops peppered onto the brim of his black Stetson. The beam of his flashlight traced the line from the final pole to the west wall. *Well no wonder his phone didn't ring—the wire's fallen off the terminal box.* An inner voice whispered: *Or somebody* pulled *it off.* The sober-minded man smiled at his morbid imagination. He picked up the section of cable, examined it in the bright glare of the flashlight—rubbed his thumb over the broken end. *Looks like it was pulled loose, all right.* He suppressed the inner voice, substituted a commonplace explanation: *Probably an elk or something bumped into it.* He tossed the line aside.

*I'll come back later with some tools, get it reconnected.* One thought led to another. *But just in case Father Raes gets back before I do, I'll leave a note to let him know his phone isn't working.* He went to the front door, started to turn the knob. The door opened. *Now that's funny—it wasn't even latched. I guess that priest is getting a little absentminded.*

He stepped inside the small parlor.

The atmosphere was eloquently taut, as if the fabric of night might rip under the strain. The Ute felt a *presence.* He called out: "Hey—anybody home?" *Well, that was a dumb question.* Moon grinned at himself, switched on a lamp. *I'll leave a note on the kitchen table.*

• • •

HEAVY pistol in hand, Sheriff Popper entered the cabin softly as a kitten walking on moss. It happened in the blink of an eye—the Utah lawman saw his man, squeezed the trigger, the hammer dropped on a center-fire cartridge, a lump of copper-jacketed lead went spinning toward the intended target.

The outcome was inevitable.

Even if the lawman had not been an expert marksman—and he could shoot an acorn off a scrub oak at twenty paces—it would have been hard to miss at this range. The poker player lowered his revolver so the barrel pointed at the floor, felt a plum-size lump in his throat. *I'd as soon have shot my own brother.* But like thunder follows lightning, this had been bound to happen. On a night when a player got dealt the Dead Man's Hand, somebody was bound to cash in his chips.

And the big Indian was most certainly dead. The .45-caliber hollow-point had taken off the top of his head.

## *A MINOR DIFFERENCE OF OPINION IN THE BUNKHOUSE*

JEROME Kydmann cocked an ear. "Pete—did you hear that?"

Having what is commonly known as a one-track mind,

Pete Bushman could not conduct two trains of thought at the same time. Busy with a futile attempt to shake and slap the pair of beat-up cowboys to some semblance of consciousness, the Columbine foreman did not appreciate this distraction from the Wyoming Kyd. "Hear what?"

"Sounded to me like a gunshot."

Bushman smacked Six-Toes hard enough to knock his dentures loose. "I didn't hear no gunshot."

The cowboy was not surprised. *Grumpy old man couldn't hear it thunder.*

There was a flash of lightning, an ear-splitting *BOOM!*

Bushman snorted. "Kyd, what you heard was thunder."

# FORTY-THREE

## *LILA MAE TRIES AGAIN*

FBI special agent McTeague called the Columbine for the third time. Slammed her telephone down when she got Charlie Moon's answering machine.

## *THE COLUMBINE FOREMAN'S STRINGENT REMEDY*

PETE Bushman regarded the pair of bunged-up, half-conscious cowboys with an expression of utter disgust. *I ain't gonna wait all night for you two sleeping beauties to wake up and start talking*. Having made this decision, he unscrewed the cap from a plastic bottle, poured a generous helping of ammonia-based cleaning fluid on a wad of cotton. The foreman was not a stickler when it came to chemical persuasion—and Safety was not Mr. Bushman's middle name. Results were what mattered and he intended to have his *right now*. He stuck the noxious preparation directly under Six-Toes's nose. Waited for the inevitable effect.

The wait was just shy of three hundred milliseconds, which in human experience passes for instantaneous.

The unfortunate man, who had already had an absolutely terrible day, jerked his head away from this latest outrage.

To fend off any subsequent assault, Mr. Toes also flung a forearm in front of his face, and mouthed a piteous moan.

"Heh-heh." *I knew that'd do the trick.* "Now start spittin' out words, Six." The heartless foreman yanked at his victim's earlobe. "Who was it that lowered the boom on you?"

Six-Toes opened his left eye, perceived a fuzzy vision of Pete Bushman's fuzzy face, then ventured to peel the right orb. "Wadder yer say?"

Charlie Moon's second-in-command leaned close to the cowboy's sunburned face. "I said—who knocked your block off?"

The injured party gingerly touched a hairy paw to his bruised jaw, winced at the sting. The last few hours were a fog, but as he pondered the day's several misadventures in chronological order, the final disagreeable memory surged up like stomach acid after a platter of *chili rellenos* and jalapeño-enhanced refried *frijoles.* "It musta been that yahoo out yonder at the front gate—the one that pulled up behind our flatbed."

The foreman's eyes narrowed to thin slits. "Who was this yahoo?"

"I don't 'zacktly know his Christian name," Six-Toes whined. "But that low-down sucker-puncher must've been one a them Mormons!"

Bushman's blank expression conveyed the impression that he did not get it.

The bruised cowboy explained. "I got a gander at the plate on his pickup. That big-fisted bushwhacker was from Utah!"

Bushman was not overly surprised. *Well just imagine the man's brass—after fisticuffin' two Columbine hands half to death, he's sleeping in the boss's house like he was Charlie Moon's next-a-kin!* Being a go-getter who esteemed audacity in other men, Bushman felt a certain measure of admiration for the cheeky Utah sheriff. But this would not deter the foreman from doing his bounden duty. Sober as a Quaker schoolmarm on Easter Sunday morn, he turned to address that good-looking young cowboy known as the Wyoming

Kyd. Which he did. "Mr. Kydmann, go round up them armed guards we put out awhile ago. I want 'em all at the boss's house *right now.*"

"You got it." The steely-eyed spur-jingler from Wyoming, Rhode Island, vanished in a flash. *I still say what I heard was a gunshot.*

The foreman pulled a Winchester carbine off the rack in his pickup, marched off toward the darkened Columbine headquarters. His intention was to inform Charlie Moon that he was harboring a crazed man who had—for no apparent reason—assaulted two Columbine cowboys. Bushman cocked the carbine. *And I don't care if he is a big-shot sheriff over in Utah—he could be a full bishop in the Mormon church, but here in Colorado he's just a damned out-a-state tourist.*

• • •

PETE Bushman, the Wyoming Kyd, the loaded-for-bear cowboys—would search the headquarters from basement to attic, find it empty of human life. After which, all hands were roused. Sleep-deprived men were sent out in twos and threes to mount a methodical search of the Columbine. Every bunkhouse, hay barn, horse barn, tack room, and toolshed would be checked—plus the vacant blacksmith's quarters, the heavy-equipment shed where the tractors, combine, and bulldozer were housed, even the abandoned line shack on the north fence. And as an afterthought, the priest's log cabin. But Charlie Moon's employees would arrive—as Mr. Bushman would later tell his distraught wife, "way too late to do any good."

## *THE SHAMAN'S TERRIBLE DREAM*

DAISY Perika's head was resting on the feathered pillow, her sleep-spirit adrift in a frothy sea of mists, memories, and myths. As the tribal elder slipped through the mystical dimensions, she came face-to-face with the Ute shepherd who had crossed that river a dozen years ago. The dreamer was pleased at the unexpected appearance of her old friend. "Nahum Yaciiti," she said. "How long has it been since—"

The holy presence raised a palm for silence, his voice rumbled like boulders rolling off Shellhammer Ridge. "I have been sent to you with a message."

This was not the cheerful Nahum she was used to. But with dead people, you never knew what to expect. The old woman steeled herself for the revelation.

"Someone you know has left his body," Nahum said. "He is here with me."

Being old as a tall ponderosa, Daisy was neither surprised nor alarmed. From among the few remaining survivors of her antiquated generation, someone she knew died almost every month. She expected to behold a familiar soul hovering near the messenger. "I don't see any—"

"You do not see, because your eyes are dim."

Somewhat chagrined, Daisy snapped: "Then tell me who it is!"

"Of all those souls you've known in Middle World, who have you loved the most?"

The tribal elder felt a sudden surge of panic. "Oh no . . ."

# FORTY-FOUR

## *ABSENT*

*The essential residue of Charlie Moon was suspended within a peaceful no-where, no-when of utter emptiness. Aside from a tenuous suspicion of self-presence, there was little evidence that he existed—no intake of breath, no thumping of heart, only darkness to fill the eyes. He was even denied the familiar elbow room of space, three-dimensional or otherwise. But because his soul was unencumbered by elbows, lungs, eyes, heart—or other fleshly parts, this absence of stimulation and sensation was largely irrelevant.*

*He was at peace.*

*And might have been content to remain there forever. But for a shadow cloaked by the Void, there is no there. There is no ever. Even the subtle illusion of time is exposed as a part of the Conjurer's art.*

## *IN MIDDLE WORLD*

AT the touch of someone's hand, a shaking of his shoulder—Charlie Moon became aware of his left arm, elbow and all.

His ears heard someone faraway say: "Hey!"

He opened his eyes. The first thing he saw was a burnished copper lamp suspended from a beamed ceiling. The next thing he saw was Popper the Copper's homely face, looking down through a fuzzy tunnel. "Hullo, champ—you still with us?"

With a monumental effort, he replied: "Uhhnng." Moon imagined a nine-pound John Henry sledgehammer pounding railroad spikes into his head. But a piece at a time, he remembered who he was. Where he was. *Why* he was. He raised a hand, touched a finger to his temple. "Ouch!"

Popper's voice boomed: "You took a good knock on your gourd." A frown as he looked around. "Where's that priest who hangs his hat here?"

The Ute raised himself on an elbow, watched the room spin down and stop. "Father Raes's car's gone. So I guess he's away somewhere." A relevant question occurred to Moon. "Who whacked me with a telephone pole?"

"Bearcat." The sheriff helped the Ute into a straightback chair, pointed his chin at the man he'd shot dead—much like Jack McCall had popped Wild Bill Hickok. "I bet you didn't know the big Choctaw's name was Leland Redstone."

Charlie Moon did know. He turned his head, caught a first glimpse of the massive figure on the floor, was momentarily mesmerized by the horrific spectacle. Like Popper, Moon did not notice—a hand's breadth below the dead man's right knee—the small bloodstained rip in Bearcat's trouser leg where Father Raes's poker had made painful connection with flesh and bone. The Ute stared at the space where the Utah deputy's head had been. Aside from a fragmented rim of white skull, a few jutting tufts of coal-black hair, nothing remained from the ears up. Bits and pieces of skull and brain were plastered on the paneled walls, the propane range, the refrigerator door. A gallon of blood had pooled on the cracked linoleum floor; this crimson tide was congealing darkly at the edges. The Ute choked back the uppermost portion of his supper, fixed his gaze on the checkered oilcloth—saw a dozen-dozen bloody crimson squares, paired with a gross of bone-white partners.

"Leland Redstone," Popper said again, as if repeating the

name might undo what was done. Tears welled up in the flint-hard lawman's eyes. "Ever since he was a little boy, Leland was a world-class woolly-booger. Not afraid of nothin' or nobody." With the back of his hand, he wiped salty beads off his face. "His mamma started callin' him Bearcat on his sixth birthday—which was when the neighbor's dog chomped Leland on the ankle." He smiled affectionately at the big-shouldered corpse. "The feisty little boy grabbed that mutt on the hind leg—and he chomped it right back!" He coughed away a lump in his throat. "And little Leland, he wouldn't let go. No sir, not even when they throwed a pitcher of ice water on him and the dog. They say it took both his daddy and his big brother to pry him loose, and all the time that dog was a-howlin' bloody murder." He turned his face away from the grisly remains. "I expect you'd like to know what my deputy was doin' here in the priest's cabin."

"First," Moon muttered, "I'd like to know what *you're* doing here—I thought you was in bed."

"That's what I wanted you to think, Charlie." The sheriff hesitated. "But truth be told, I never intended to do any snoozin'—that's why I swigged down such a load of that strong coffee." Smiling at Charlie Moon's quizzical expression, Popper continued. "Call me Mr. Suspicious, but I'd have laid three-to-one odds you was hiding Sarah Frank on the Columbine."

"Why would you think—"

Popper interrupted the question. "I also figured some of the things I'd told you might make you want to go and check on the girl—after you thought I was sound asleep. So I set there on the edge of the bed with ears pricked and eyes peeled, and waited to see what'd happen."

The Ute recalled Bushman's visit. "And you didn't have to wait very long."

"No, that's a fact. Wasn't more'n a few minutes when I heard your foreman come stompin' into the kitchen, yelling his head off about some of your cowboys that'd been found unconscious at the front gate. After old Loud-Mouth left, I cracked the bedroom door and saw you making a telephone call. From the way things looked, nobody answered."

"The line was dead."

"Right after that, you left the house and headed off through the woods, and I just naturally followed you." Apologetically, he added: "With you carrying that flashlight, I was able to stay quite a ways behind. Otherwise, I expect you'd have heard me." Popper grinned. "Now you want to know why Deputy Bearcat was in the cabin?"

At a sudden searing pain, Charlie Moon closed his eyes, grimaced.

Taking this as a "Yes," Popper started up again: "Even after being banged hard on the bean, I expect you can call to mind Ben Silver's half brother Ray Oates, and Sarah Frank's cousin Marilee, and Marilee's boyfriend Al Harper."

A grunt from the tribal investigator.

"Well, Al Harper told Ray Oates a tale about a late-night phone call to Marilee. According to Mr. Harper, the call was from little Sarah herself."

Charlie Moon opened his eyes. "Did Harper get the caller's ID?"

A nod from Popper. "It was a Colorado number. But the phone was registered to a person none of us had ever heard of."

"Who—"

"Don't get ahead of me, or I'll forget where I was." Popper presented a brushy-browed scowl. "What you *should* be askin' is: 'How did a backward old lawman like Ned Popper happen to find out about this highly confidential conversation between Harper and Oates?' "

"Okay," the Indian said: "How?"

The wily lawman twisted a waxed tip of the spiffy mustache. "I'm not at liberty to reveal that highly sensitive information." His mouth made a prideful smirk. "Let's just say that I've got my sources." The way the Utah lawman saw things, Charlie Moon (being an outsider to Tonapah Flats) did not have The Need To Know that Ray Oates's personal secretary was also the sheriff's second cousin, or that Rosey

O'Riley provided a tidbit of useful information now and again. But Popper was miffed that his cousin's harvest of information had been so sparse. *It's a pity Rosey didn't find out that Oates had the whole damn sheriff's office staff on the take. Except for my honorable self, of course. And now that I come to think of it, it's been years since Mr. Money-Bags has offered me so much as a thin dime to fix a parking ticket.* The public servant didn't know whether he should feel flattered or insulted. Or what he *might* have done had a sizable bribe been proposed . . .

Popper seemed to have drifted off into some private space. The Ute waited patiently for the white man to return.

Sheriff Popper eventually did. "I'm about ninety-nine percent sure that Ray Oates got in touch with Bearcat—and told him about the phone call Sarah supposedly made to her Papago cousin. And Bearcat was what you call 'highly motivated.' See, my deputy not only wanted to collect Oates's reward for getting the 'stolen property' back—the big Choctaw had an urgent personal reason to find the girl." Seeing the Ute's slightly raised eyebrow, Popper decided to get the embarrassment over with. "You remember my dispatcher—Bertha Katcher?"

At a painful cost, Moon nodded his aching head.

"Well, it's still hard for me to believe ol' Bertha had the energy—but for years she's been moonlightin' for Ray Oates."

Hoping to clarify his foggy vision, Moon rubbed at his eyes. "Doing what?"

"Oh, destroying police records, removing physical evidence from the vault, passing on confidential information—stuff like that." Popper collapsed into a chair, glared across the kitchen table at the Ute. "Now I ask you—what sort of a sad excuse for a human being would stoop so low as to turn another man's faithful employee into a paid spy?"

"That is going pretty far down the dark path."

A grim-faced Popper nodded. "Bertha Katcher was an outright traitor." But he also blamed his cousin, who had shown insufficient initiative. *Rosey just never had enough get-up-and-go. If she'd worked out some way to listen in on Ray Oates's telephone calls, none of this would've happened.*

As the throbbing behind his eyes subsided, the tribal investigator gently prodded the older lawman along. "So what has your dispatcher been up to lately?"

"I'd say she's had enough business to keep her busy." The sheriff felt a sudden hunger for something sweet. "When Oates realized that Sarah Frank wasn't going to steal what he wanted from Ben's house, he decided he'd hire somebody who would."

"So Sarah's not a thief."

"That's right. And she didn't murder Ben Silver."

"That's welcome news." Charlie Moon smiled. "But I have a hard time imagining Miss Katcher burgling Mr. Silver's home, much less murdering the old man. Besides—wasn't she tending to her dispatching duties that particular morning?"

Popper put his hand in a candy jar, found a lemon drop. "Oh, Bertha was at the station all right—but she was busy managing the break-in for Ray Oates." He popped the hard candy into his mouth, propped his elbows on the table. "See, the setup was for Bearcat to slip through Hatchet Gap, and do the breaking and entering at Ben Silver's house. And while Bearcat was busy looking for Ben Silver's whatzit, Bertha had posted Deputy Packard at Dinty's Grill. Packard's job was to keep an eye on the private lane to Silver's house—and phone a warning to Bearcat if anybody turned in."

"It was a simple plan," Moon said. "The kind that generally works."

"It was. And would've. Only I sent Packard to help the state troopers with that accident over on the interstate, which was also why Ben's appointment with his doctor got canceled, which was why Marilee brought the old grouch back home early. What happened after that, I learned from Bertha who got it straight from Bearcat. Ben Silver walked into his parlor and realized somebody'd been messing around in his house. He called 911 right about the time my dispatcher had run off to the ladies' room, which is why the call got automatically forwarded to my cell phone and I ended up taking Ben's emergency call while I was on the way into town." Winded by this lengthy statement, he paused to take a breath, also to wonder what Bertha would have done if she *had* picked up on Ben's call for help. *Talk about your moral dilemmas.* "It was too bad Bearcat was still in the house when Ben showed up. And Sarah must've been there, too—hiding from my deputy. Anyway, while Ben was trying to tell me something was wrong, Bearcat jerked the phone cord outta the socket and grabbed ol' Ben like he was a sack of onions. The big Choctaw gave Ben a choice—'Either cough up what I want or I'll shake it outta you.' "

This quote triggered the recollection circuitry in Charlie Moon's brain, which called up the memory of that lively afternoon in the Gimpy Dog Saloon. The scene played by like a flickering old black-and-white film; it was transformed into Technicolor as Deputy Bearcat administered the shake-treatment to Cowboy Roy. *That explains why Mr. Silver's shirt buttons and boots were on the floor.* The tribal investigator's face burned. *I should've picked up on that right away.* But he comforted himself with this thought: *Clever Lila Mae McTeague never made that connection neither.* This mistaken consolation would be short-lived.

Unaware of the Ute's regretful insights, Popper continued: "Ben was always a stiff-backed old varmint—he told Bearcat where he could go straight to, which wasn't Helena—or any other place in Montana."

Moon stared at the wall, frowning at the hand-hewn, cement-chinked logs. "Mr. Silver must've known your deputy wouldn't leave him there alive."

Ned Popper nodded. "Once Bearcat broke the phone connection, Ben knew he was already a dead man." The Utah lawman picked up a forty-nine-cent salt shaker, examined the dispenser as if it was the most fascinating plastic fabrication he'd ever seen. "Bearcat was always a little slow making up his mind, and about the time he was trying to decide what to do with the old man, his cell phone jangled. It was Bertha, telling him I was on the way to Ben's place and he'd better get outta there lickety-split. Before he left, Bearcat bashed Ben in the face two or three times—he thought he'd killed the old man, but Silver wasn't one to give up the ghost 'til he was damn good and ready. Not knowing there was a witness, Bearcat commenced to backtracking his way back through Hatchet Gap. Sarah must've come out from wherever she'd been hiding and tried to help ol' Ben. That's how she got his blood on her hands, and from her hands onto that ball-bat she flung through the window at me." A thoughtful pause. "I expect she either thought I was Bearcat come back—we wear the same kind of county-issue hat—or maybe she figured the whole sheriff's office was in cahoots on the burglary." He shook his head. "She wasn't far wrong. Three bad-hats out of four—that's a pretty sorry score." Tired of this dismal neighborhood, he shifted gears and headed for a more sunny destination. "I imagine you'd like to know what Mr. Silver had that his half brother wanted so bad."

Moon seemed to be somewhere else.

The compulsive conversationalist is not discouraged by such minor issues as a disinterested audience. "Well, I can tell you." A slight frown. "Or at least how Ben Silver described it in his will."

This got the Ute's attention. "Will?"

Pleased at having a live audience, Popper nodded. "That's right." Another twist on the mustache tip. "Funny thing—you'd never guess what it was, not in ten thousand years."

Moon made a run of it. "A gold nugget big as your fist."

"Good try, but you're not even close." The sheriff described the treasure.

Moon said: "A small thing, to be the cause of so much trouble."

The Utah sheriff nodded. "Now, guess who he left it to."

"I'm all out of guesses."

Popper told him.

The Ute felt his head start spinning again. "Why would he do that?"

The sheriff shrugged. "Why not?"

Moon was all out of answers. And questions.

A clock on the wall swept up precious seconds, dust-panned them into the past.

The taciturn Indian was a strain on the sheriff's compelling urge to finish his tale. "Aren't you going to ask me how I come to find out what my employees was up to?"

Moon sighed. "Consider yourself asked."

Sheriff Popper needed no further encouragement. "Bertha didn't know Bearcat had hightailed it off to Colorado to find Sarah Frank—she thought he'd been murdered, along with Deputy Packard. Way she saw it, Ray Oates had hired some thug to kill off everybody that could tie him to the burglary, and the unplanned murder of his half brother. With Packard drowned and Bearcat vanished, my dispatcher figured she was number three on the hit list. So hoping I would protect her, Bertha confessed." Recalling an unresolved suspicion, he scowled at the tribal investigator. "So I thought I ought to pay you a call. See how deep the mud was at the Columbine." Seeing the puzzled expression on Moon's face, he explained: "That late-night call to Marilee Attatochee came from your ranch."

The Ute blinked at the Utah sheriff. "There are six phone lines on the Columbine. Which one—"

The Tonapah Flats sheriff was pointing at Father Raes's telephone.

Moon considered this news for a few heartbeats. "If Sarah Frank was anywhere on the Columbine, I'd know it."

Popper's eyes spoke for him. *Maybe you* do *know it.*

# FORTY-FIVE

## *UNFINISHED BUSINESS*

As Charlie Moon's strength returned, his senses sharpened. Catching the scent of Bearcat's blood, he fought off a surge of nausea, pushed himself up from the chair.

The Tonapah Flats sheriff followed the owner of the Columbine through the cabin's front door, into the chilly night.

The storm had broken up and dispersed to distant neighborhoods. Lagging behind were a few disorderly toughs who flexed puffy muscles, threatened thunderous mayhem and cataclysmic disaster—but these were merely the noisy bluffs of boisterous bullies. But yonder, pooled like molten glass on the grassy prairie, was a quiescent presence that deserved serious attention. Aloofly silent, supremely serene, Lake Jesse concealed her dark secret beneath a surface of shimmering moonshine.

At peace in his ignorance, the Ute helped himself to a deep breath of mountain air that had never been so charged with invigorating energy. *It's a lucky thing Father Raes wasn't here when Bearcat showed up.* He wondered where the priest might have gone off to this time, hoped it was someplace far away from the Columbine. It would take a while to clean up the mess.

## *ON THE SHORE OF LAKE JESSE*

A masked shrew darts to and fro along a fallen piñon, pausing here and there to sniff for victuals, occasionally inserting a long, pointed snout under the wrinkled bark. Though the tiny creature's diet includes a variety of tasty items, this particular *Sorex cinereus* prefers fatty, high-calorie treats like the plump pine beetle larvae, and her clever nose knows this favorite delicacy is close at hand.

As a few last-breath bubbles percolate to the lake's surface, the perpetually famished diner is distracted from her task—but only momentarily. After a blink of beady eyes, the hyperactive rodent gets back to the urgent business of finding a late-night snack—but she is startled to see a bright *something* take flight from the watery interface with night; soar upward toward some unseen destination.

What was this?

A snowy-winged night-fowl on the prowl?

A flash of moonshine reflecting off the water?

Or . . . something altogether *other*?

## *AN EXERCISE OF THE INTELLECT*

As Knuckle-Dragger Number Two trudged along betwixt lake and cabin, his mind had time to generate a few thoughts, some lacking in clarity:

*Hah—that's one blackbird priest that won't be preachin' no more sermons.*

*I wonder if Sarah What's-her-name has still got Mr. Oates's thingamajig.*

*I wonder if Bearcat ever found that skinny little Papago brat.*

*I wonder where I should shoot Bearcat at.* (The thinker may refer either to an anatomical or a geographic location.)

*Maybe just this side of the Utah line.* (The issue is clarified.)

*I'm hungry.*
*I could eat a porky-pine, hide and all.*
*I wonder how far it is to a Burger King.*

## *THE SHERIFF'S CONCERN*

"CALL me a worrier," Ned Popper murmured to Charlie Moon, "but I am plagued by a nagging spot of botheration." He cast a furtive glance at the cabin, where his deputy's semi-headless body was sprawled on the kitchen floor. "I know how Raymond Oates's mind works, and I can't see him sending one man here to find Sarah Frank. I'd be surprised if Bearcat came all the way to Colorado without any backup."

Except for a clicking of aspen leaves in the breeze, the silence was perfect.

In this world, Perfection does not tarry long.

The Ute heard a slight rustling in the tall grasses. An animal, he thought. *But not the four-legged kind.* Moon wished he'd brought a weapon.

Popper heard it a moment later; his hand instinctively moved toward the holstered .45.

"Huh-uh." The hoarse voice rattled in the darkness. "Don't put a finger on that hand-cannon, Sheriff. And don't neither a you move a inch or I'll let you have both barrels."

"Groundhog," Popper muttered. "One of Ray Oates's hired bootlickers." The surviving Tonapah Flats lawman called out: "What brings a greasy, pea-brained hash slinger like you so far from home?"

"Business, Popper—*that's* what." The barrel-like form appeared at the ragged edge of the gloom. Groundhog had a sawed-off 12-gauge cradled in his arm. The weapon was pointed in the general direction of his intended victims, and he was coming nearer, one deliberate step at a time. Enjoying his meaty role as Hard Case with Deadly Weapon, Groundhog directed his next line to the Ute. "Tell me where you got that little Injun gal stashed—an' I promise not to gut-shoot you."

The walk-on was upstaged by a blinding flash of white-hot fire that tap-danced along the Buckhorn peaks. This performance was followed by a thunderous applause.

Knuckle-Dragger Number Two paused, looked around, yelled for Knuckle-Dragger Number One: "Hey, Bearcat—where you at, Hoss?" *I'll kill the Choctaw later, but right now I wouldn't mind havin' me some backup.*

Popper and Moon comprehended the situation with a terrible clarity:

Groundhog would take down the armed man first. But he was at the margin of the scatter-gun's effective range; the shotgun toter had to come closer.

Popper drew in a deep breath. "Your call, Charlie."

"Count off six more paces, shoot him dead."

"You figure I can pop off a shot before he unloads?" *One.*

"Nope."

Groundhog advanced another step.

*Two.* "Well thank you for the vote of confidence, Charlie."

"Don't mention it, Ned."

Groundhog was walking faster now.

*Three.* Popper flexed the fingers on his right hand. *Ah, what the hell—I never expected to live this long. Four. And I always prayed I wouldn't end up in one of them nursing homes.*

Moon noted with some pleasure that Sheriff Popper's BUY YOUR TROUBLE HERE shop was open and ready to commence with business.

*Five.* The old lawman's grin arched under the dandy handlebar. *Thank you, God—for letting me be here, doing this. Six.* His right hand went for the revolver.

Things got hectic.

Groundhog's finger tightened on the trigger—

Popper's heavy pistol cleared leather—

The Ute let out a heart-stopping war whoop—

For a fraction of a second, Groundhog couldn't decide which one to shoot—

Popper boomed off a slug that snipped a nip off the fat man's ear—

The left shotgun barrel belched pellets and flame—

The sheriff caught a spray of red-hot buckshot, stumbled backward, tumbled to his knees—

Moon was making a dead-on run at the shooter—

Groundhog swung the shotgun, fired the right barrel—

A pestilent swarm of BB's stung the Ute's flesh—

As he broke the shotgun, ejected the still-smoking empties, Oates's hireling was astonished to see the Ute still coming . . . *a dead man running*? Hands trembling, he fumbled in his pocket for fresh loads—

Charlie Moon was nine strides away—

Groundhog thumbed in the new ammo, deftly snapped the barrel shut—

Popper blinked away blood streaming down from his forehead—

Knuckle-Dragger Number Two aimed point-blank at the Indian—*Adios, blanket-ass!*

The sheriff tried to steady the wavering .45—

And then—

Time began to s l o o o w . . . . .

Abruptly, the clock stopped.

*See the still picture—*

*A levitated Moon, frozen in mid-stride—*

*Popper petrified, an oath lodged in his throat—*

*Groundhog, teeth clenched, finger tight on the trigger—*

Then, the chronometer started up again, with a frenzy of gears-a-clicking, hands-a-whirling—Tickety-tock, tickety-tock, tickety-tock—

A heavy thumpity-thump of unshod hooves, a guttural growling—

Sidewinder hit the shotgun-toter low, took him down hard—wolfishly went for the throat.

Snorting and pawing, Sweet Alice moved in for her fair share of the kill.

Transfixed by this pair of practically paralyzing surprises, Popper and Moon watched the victim's arms and legs flopping and flailing, the Columbine hound ripping and gnawing—the outlaw horse kicking and stomping her portion into a bloody pulp.

The brutish assassination took perhaps a half-dozen heartbeats.

When the grisly deed was done, silence returned.

The Ute stood mute.

But it was one of those occasions when something *had* to be said.

The Tonapah Flats sheriff said it. "I don't mean to complain, Charlie—but this peaceful ranch of yours is a mite too lively for a man of my disposition." He cleared his throat and elaborated: "I could sure do with a few minutes of peace and quiet." Still on his knees, but with revolver at the ready and blood in his eye, he squinted suspiciously at the darkness. "So I sure hope there ain't nobody else hidin' yonder in the woods."

A man is entitled to his hopes. But not the fulfillment of his every wish.

*See the wispy figure of the frail orphan, concealed deep in the thicket of spruce and pine, lightly entwined in the bloodberry vine. Watch the gaunt-faced girl close her eyes—tremble at the terrible knowledge concealed within. See what she sees, over and over again—the heartless men going about their brutal business:*

*Furious at the painful blow inflicted by the poker-wielding priest, Bearcat beats Father Raes until the elderly man's face is a mass of blood-soaked bruises.*

*Groundhog arrives from his search of the forest, reports no sign of the Indian girl.*

*As they stuff the priest's body into the trunk of his worn-out automobile, the surly assassins exchange curses and accusations.*

*Weep with her as the makeshift hearse bumps and lurches across the prairie cemetery, share Sarah's shudder as the steel tomb sinks slowly into the alpine grave, feel her shiver as chill waters draw out the last trace of warmth from Father Raes Delfino's still body—even to the very marrow in his bones.*

*But now, the shared vision ceases.*
*What she sees after this is Sarah's secret.*

The Buick-coffin would not be discovered until the sun was high over the Buckhorns.

# FORTY-SIX

## *SIX DAYS LATER IN CAÑÓN DEL ESPÍRITU*

*STAND with your back to Three Sisters Mesa, your heels on the hem of the Pueblo women's tattered talus skirt, your toes pointing at the unmarked grave Daisy Perika made. Now raise your face, cast your gaze toward the opposite wall of the canyon. Look closely—almost concealed behind the cluster of white-limbed aspen is a dark horizontal slot. This cleft in the wall is called, in the Ute tongue—Supáy Aváagani—Quiet Shade House.*

*This lonely dwelling has only a single room, but that chamber commands a singular view. From this vantage point, a keen-eyed sentry can see anything that moves along the canyon floor. And the watcher can see without being seen; the inner sanctum is a place of perpetual shadows, where etched stick-figure wizards stand entranced on fire-blackened walls and fantastic animal pictographs dance and prance across a dozen millennia. And quiet it is. Whether the silence is the result of some ancient sorcerer's spell or merely an acoustic delusion, neither strident raven-call nor mournful wind-hymn will disturb those who enter in.*

*At this moment, Quiet Shade House shelters a pair of recent arrivals. They are not strangers in the Canyon of the Spirits; this is a return visit. A homecoming, one might say.*

*Though it is difficult to make out their forms, this much can be said: The cat is spotted black and white, the girl is small and frail, and for a product of her twofold tribes—remarkably pale.*

*There is a sudden, chilling breeze; she trembles with the aspen leaves. This being the place it has always been, she being what she has become, Sarah has learned the virtue and value of silence. But if mute, she is not blind—her gaze is hypnotically fixed on that terrible place across the canyon. What she sees there—almost a hundred yards away—are three persons. One of them, Sarah dearly loves—another she is jealous of. The third is an ancient, hunched-over woman whose leathery skin has been varnished by many summers of scorching sun. Burdened with a lifetime of trials and troubles, the tribal elder leans on an oak staff—stares at a barely discernible mound of rocks and rubble.*

•••

THE woman at Daisy Perika's side was slim and willowy-graceful, neither spot nor wrinkle blemished her ivory skin.

Standing behind the women was a tall, slender man.

All three were gazing at the slightest of bulges in a helter-skelter landscape of ice-fractured rocks and monumental blocks of stone that had tumbled down from the heights. The disturbance in the disorder appeared ever so slightly *unnatural* among the random jumble of boulders.

During these past few days, Daisy had thanked God a thousand times that she had not lost her nephew. Charlie—whose lean body had been probed, sutured, and bandaged from heel to crown—still carried a few pellets of buckshot. She groaned inwardly at the memory of Father Raes Delfino's funeral, which had been attended by hundreds of his flock, at least two dozen priests, and three bishops. Moreover, the Ute elder had also seen holy angels there. *Precious in the sight of the Lord is the death of his saints.* Daisy could not imagine life without the little priest who had loved her soul so very much. "I am tired to death of standing by graves." Blinking tears away, she pointed the walking stick. "Especially one I put together myself."

Special Agent Lila Mae McTeague looked up the slope. Here and there among the sandstone rubble, a forlorn little dwarf oak or a plucky tumbleweed had taken opportunistic root and enjoyed such temporary residence as nature allows. The strikingly handsome woman shaded her violet eyes from the midafternoon sun. "The place where Sarah Frank was hiding—it's up there?"

Daisy nodded. "After you have a look at what's under these rocks, I'll show you that little cave."

"The forensics team will examine the grave." The federal law enforcement officer glanced at her wristwatch. "The helicopter should be here shortly."

Charlie Moon turned, painfully walked a dozen paces away, paused—stared off into empty space.

As if unaware of his silent departure, Lila Mae McTeague continued her conversation with Daisy. "I'll want to examine the site where Sarah encountered the deputy, but you needn't take the trouble to make the climb. I'm sure I can find the place—"

"Oh, I'll take you up there." Daisy gripped her staff with both hands, took a squinty-eyed look at the high shelf. "I'll have to stop from time to time to get my wind, but I can make it all right."

The white woman knew that the Ute elder had never liked her. *She always thought I was going to steal her nephew away from her.* "While we're waiting for the forensics team, perhaps you would like to tell me about that morning."

Daisy looked blankly at the white woman. "What morning?"

*Her mind certainly does wander.* "The morning when you entered the canyon to find Sarah Frank, and make certain that she was—"

"And what I found was what's under this." The Ute elder rapped her walking stick on the cairn of rocks, sharp clicks bounced off Dog Leg Mesa's mottled wall, returned to ricochet off the Three Sisters cliff. "I'll tell you all about it." Her black eyes sparkled at the young woman who carried a Glock 9-mm automatic in her black leather purse. "But first, you tell me something."

Not accustomed to being interrogated by mere civilians, the FBI agent hesitated. "Like what?"

"That feud between those two white men in Utah—what's the story on that?"

McTeague chanced a sideways glance at Charlie Moon, who had meandered even farther away. "Your nephew hasn't told you?"

Daisy shook her head. "Lately, he's been awfully close-mouthed." *Even when Charlie's in the same room with me, its like he's someplace else. I guess Father Raes's murder is as hard on Charlie as it is on me.* But Daisy suspected that was not the entire story. *Something's gone sour between Charlie and this* matukach *woman.* The tribal elder watched a mountain bluebird flutter by, land on a spindly juniper limb. The impudent little bird stared back at Daisy with tiny black-bead eyes. The feathered creature seemed almost ready to speak, but what Daisy heard was the FBI agent's voice.

"Being in poor health, Ben Silver believed himself unlikely to survive another year. He was determined that his half brother Raymond Oates should not inherit any of his property, particularly the object which had originally belonged to their mother. I refer, of course, to the remarkable Native American artifact—a quartz effigy of a butterfly. Since the death of his stepfather, Mr. Silver had kept the family treasure concealed under his shirt, in a canvas wallet suspended from his neck. His intent was to will the family heirloom to the University of Alabama, but before he visited his attorney, Sarah Frank did something that upset all his plans."

With an expression of overwhelming sadness, the tribal elder nodded. "She snitched it."

"Certainly not." *So Charlie really hasn't told her.* "What Sarah did was confess."

Daisy's expression reflected her confusion. "Confess what?"

"The girl revealed the sordid truth to Mr. Silver—that Raymond Oates had urged her to steal the quartz butterfly, and that she was sorely tempted. Sarah not only apologized for even considering such a wretched act, she also gave Mr. Silver the cash that Mr. Oates had paid her to commit the theft, and asked him to return it to his half brother. Mr. Silver was not surprised that his sibling would stoop to corrupting a child, but he was astonished to hear Sarah's confession—and immensely impressed with the poverty-stricken girl's integrity. He insisted that she keep Oates's cash, and made quite a bold decision—he gave her the artifact right on the spot, along with the canvas neck wallet."

Not sure she had heard right, Daisy cocked her head. "He *gave* it to Sarah?"

McTeague nodded. "As a reward for her honesty, and on the firm condition that she must *never* let the family heirloom fall into Mr. Oates's hands. Subsequently, Mr. Silver visited his attorney in Salt Lake and had a will prepared, which stipulated that the stone butterfly was bequeathed to Sarah Frank, and already in her possession." She recalled an important detail. "The wallet also contained several hundred dollars in cash."

The elderly Ute took a deep breath. "That's a pile of money—especially for a little girl who hardly ever had two dimes to rub together."

The fed watched a hawk circle, rise gracefully in a thermal. "Sarah had always dreamed of moving back to Colorado, and the Southern Ute reservation. Now, thanks to conniving Mr. Oates and generous Mr. Silver, she finally had sufficient travel money."

The shaman turned her head, aimed her eye at Dog Leg Mesa, and the shadowy sanctum of Quiet Shade House. "So she was all set to come and move in with me." *And I guess she still is.*

"That was her immediate objective." *But I believe Sarah's ultimate goal was to move in with Charlie Moon. As if he didn't have troubles enough.* A sigh. *Poor, dear Charlie.*

Daisy shook her head. "It's hard to imagine them two white men fighting like cats and dogs over a piece of rock."

Having done her homework, McTeague felt compelled to share her recently acquired knowledge: "The butterfly effigy—not to be confused with the so-called 'butterfly bannerstone'—was crafted from what is commonly called rose quartz because of the color, which varies from a delicate pink to deep crimson. Technically, the mineral is known as ferruginous quartzite."

Daisy muttered something in her native tongue. Something rude.

"According to explanatory text in Mr. Silver's will, when his mother was a small child, she found the prehistoric artifact in Alabama, on what was probably a riverside Indian campsite. Archaeologists, who examined the object while his mother was still alive, estimated the pink butterfly to be between five and seven thousand years old."

*She talks like one of them uppity professors at Fort Lewis College.* Daisy's voice fairly dripped with sarcasm: "Thank you for explaining that."

"You are quite welcome." The fed recalled a pithy proverb that warned of the folly of casting one's pearls before the swine.

The swine in question had an avaricious glint in her eye. "Is this stone butterfly worth anything?"

McTeague pretended to misunderstand. "Such out-of-context surface finds have virtually no archaeological value."

The frugal old woman clarified her question. "I was talking about cash money."

The erudite young lady suppressed a smile. "A wealthy collector of antiquities might pay quite a large sum for the ferruginous quartzite butterfly effigy—which is probably a unique specimen." McTeague was determined to get back on track. "Now perhaps you would like to tell me about your discovery of the corpse—"

Daisy cut her short: "What's going on between you and my nephew?"

Lila Mae caught her breath, paled. "Why—what do you mean?"

The tribal elder shook a crooked finger in the white woman's face. "Listen—I'm older'n these piñon trees and I could die before I draw another breath! So don't you waste what little time I got left asking silly questions like"—she pursed her lips and mimicked the white woman's innocent tone—" 'What d'you mean?' " Daisy snorted. "I may be a little slow, but I ain't mole-blind or stone-deaf. For the last hour, you two ain't hardly said a word to one another." She cocked an iron-gray eyebrow. "So what's up—you and him had a spat?"

Miss McTeague jutted her chin. "I really don't see how that's any business of—"

"Well it *is* my business!" Daisy banged her walking stick on the ground. "I'm Charlie's closest living kin, and it's my job to look after him." She pointed the stick at McTeague's knee. "You two been hanging around together for a long time, and most likely doin' a lot more than just holding hands and the way I see things—"

"Well, *really*!" The pale face was blushing pink.

"Don't interrupt me—it's bad manners!" Daisy's brow wrinkles deepened into perplexed furrows. "What was I saying when you made me forget?"

McTeague rolled her pretty eyes. "Something about 'the way you see things.' "

"Oh, right. Thank you." Daisy reached out to pat the *matukach* woman's arm. "The way I see things, it's high time you and Charlie Moon got married. Settled down. Had yourselves some children. Two girls and a boy."

It was McTeague's turn to arch a brow.

Sensing that she was making some headway, Daisy pressed on: "You ain't been a teenager for quite a few summers, and take it from somebody who knows—the more years you put on, the harder it'll be to find yourself a halfway decent man." She stared at the woman's neck, added darkly: "You already got some skin hangin' loose under your chin."

Of its own accord, McTeague's chin lifted, her right hand went to examine the alleged sag.

"Ha-ha—I was just teasing you." Daisy's knobby little frame jiggled with merriment. "Don't worry, your skin's still tight as rawhide on a drum." Reverting to form, she shook the finger again. "But it won't be long—next winter, maybe the one after that—some cold, gray morning you'll pick up the looking glass and won't like what you see. So now's the time to marry yourself a good man and start making babies!"

McTeague tried to smile. "My—you make it all sound so terribly romantic."

"You listen to me, young lady—I've outlived three husbands and what matters is these things." Daisy counted them off on her fingers: "One—does he earn a decent living. Two—does he stay sober most of the time. Three—does he leave other women alone. Four—does he take a bath at least once a week. Five—does he understand that if he ever hits you, he'll wake up dead the next morning." Having folded up fingers and thumb, she raised a fist for the punch line: "Romance is for storybooks and picture shows."

The white woman drew in a long breath. "If I was willing to discuss such a personal matter with you, I might begin by saying that I am rather surprised."

"Surprised at what?"

"At your matchmaker's choice—I have always been under the impression that you did not approve of me."

"Well, I'd naturally rather Charlie married a nice Ute girl, or even one of them peculiar Pueblo women." *And one of them Mexican* señoritas *might be okay.* Daisy glared at the white woman. "But for whatever reason, my nephew seems to be stuck on you." She shook her head at this impenetrable mystery. "So I guess I'll have to go along with it."

"That is very generous of you, I'm sure." McTeague prepared to score a point. "But you seem to have overlooked a critical issue."

"What's that?"

"Charlie has not asked me to marry him."

Daisy was quick as a flash. "Well of course he hasn't."

Charlie's aunt explained with an air of weary patience: "Amongst us Utes, it's the woman that asks the man." She looked up to heaven. *I ain't exactly lying—more like joking.*

McTeague blinked. Twice. "Do you actually mean to tell me that—"

"Sure." The way Daisy saw it, once a person told a whopper she might as well get as much mileage out of it as possible. "You might not know it, but Charlie's more of a traditional Ute than he lets on—especially when it comes to serious things like buying horses and getting married." Not one to deny herself the protection of a *matukach* superstition, the Ute storyteller crossed her fingers. "My nephew's been waiting for you to pop the question."

McTeague stole a quick glance at the tall, silent man who had by now wandered halfway across the canyon. "Has Charlie actually *told* you that he's . . . I mean, waiting for me to bring up the subject of . . ." She could not make herself say the word.

Daisy's little-used conscience was beginning to prickle. Going on the assumption that a deceptive gesture was not so sinful as a spoken-out-loud lie, she settled for a nod.

*The old trickster's probably making all of this up, hoping I'll say something to her nephew and make a perfect fool of myself. Then again . . . Charlie is an uncommonly shy man. Perhaps it wouldn't hurt if I were to simply mention—No, that's absurd. On the other hand . . .* Uncomfortable with being Lila Mae, she assumed her Special Agent McTeague demeanor, addressed the Ute woman in a stern tone: "Let's drop this subject."

"Suit yourself." Daisy shrugged. "But someday when you're an old maid living with some fuzzy poodles and Charlie's got a dozen children and grandchildren playin' on his cabin floor, don't say I didn't warn you."

The victim closed her eyes, started counting to ten. Settled for seven. "Tell me how you discovered the corpse."

Knowing she had gotten under the white woman's skin, Daisy took a deep breath and began.

The FBI agent held a microcassette recorder under

Daisy's chin while the woman gave a detailed account of her experiences on that grim morning.

The witness completed her narrative with a scowl: "And after I chased them ugly buzzards away, I covered up the body with some rocks and sticks and stuff." There was nothing left to say.

A damp breeze brought a pungent scent of juniper-spiced rain from the upper reaches of the canyon, paused to rustle about in the willows as if searching for something lost, whispered a melancholy sigh, drifted away.

•••

*In quiet Shade House . . .*

*The silent figure has neither moved, nor altered her gaze.*

*Her spotted cat dozes in the shadows, beholds visions of spotted leopards stalking prey in steaming equatorial jungles.*

*The chuff-chuff of an approaching helicopter awakens the feline dreamer.*

•••

WHILE Charlie Moon remained on the canyon floor, and the skilled technicians meticulously dismantled the grave the Ute elder had so cunningly constructed, Daisy Perika led Special Agent McTeague up the long path to the shelf at the crest of the talus slope. The federal agent spent almost an hour poking around, making measurements with a steel tape measure, recording various coordinates with a miniature GPS receiver, penciling numerous entries into her notebook, and, of course—taking dozens of digitized color photos.

As inky shadows poured out of fissures and crevasses, Daisy and McTeague retraced their steps to the canyon floor, arriving in time to witness the shattered corpse being removed from its lonely place of rest.

After a hushed exchange with forensic experts, the FBI agent set her face toward Charlie Moon.

From the corner of her eye, Daisy Perika watched her

nephew and the white woman. For some time, they stood at arm's length, evidently engaged in earnest conversation. *I wonder if Miss Fancy-Pants'll ask Charlie to marry her.* Hoping to count such a coup, the Ute shaman strained all of her senses to hear. The effort was in vain. Daisy winced as they laughed and glanced her way—*I bet McFigg told Charlie what I said about Ute women asking the men to marry them.* The old woman's annoyance faded as the couple drifted ever closer. Suddenly, there was a brief embrace and the *matukach* woman departed. Daisy muttered to herself: "I wonder what happened between those two. Not that Charlie Moon would ever tell me anything." *But by and by, I'll figure it out.*

In the meantime, she stood by the empty grave, waiting as only the very old can wait.

# FORTY-SEVEN

## *THE ORPHAN*

OBSERVING Charlie Moon's limping gait, Sarah Frank realized the time had come to depart from the place of shadows. When he ducked his head under the rock shelter's overhang, the thin girl reached out, took the tall man's hand.

The Ute looked down at her. "You doing okay?"

She nodded, grimaced at a sudden flicker of pain on his face. "Where Groundhog shot you—does it hurt awfully bad?"

He grinned. "Only when I do cartwheels."

Sarah bit her lip to keep from smiling. "Charlie, I'm *really* sorry I called Marilee from Father Raes's cabin—that was a dumb thing to do." She waited for him to insist that it wasn't really so dumb. He did not.

Moon was occupied with his thoughts. *Aunt Daisy should've never left you at the ranch without telling me. I probably ought to have a hard talk with her.* He grunted. *Right. Lot of good that would do.*

Believing the grunt was meant for her, Sarah tried to explain: "I just wanted to let Marilee know I was all right. I knew she would be worried about me."

The Ute assumed a stern look. "I was worried about you, too."

The unspoken question hung in the air between them.

"I wanted to tell you I was there, Charlie." The girl looked at her dusty shoes. "But Aunt Daisy told me not to talk to *anybody* except Father Raes."

"Don't give it another thought." Moon's expression softened. "You didn't get hurt—that's what matters."

The forgiveness Sarah had been seeking did not satisfy her. "But if I hadn't used the priest's telephone, Al Harper wouldn't have found out I was hiding on the Columbine and Mr. Oates wouldn't have sent Groundhog and Bearcat to find me and if Father Raes hadn't hit Bearcat with the poker, he would still be . . ." *Alive.* The word had caught on the lump in her throat. *But the priest is dead. And all because of me.*

Sarah was right, of course.

And wrong.

And therein is concealed a fragment of the eternal mystery.

Moon saw the haunt of guilt in her eyes, felt its dreadful weight. "You're not responsible for what happened to Father Raes." *Raymond Oates will have to answer for that. And before another Judge, Groundhog and Bearcat.*

The Ute was *almost* right. But not quite.

"Charlie . . ."

"Mm-hmm?"

"If Bearcat had found me, do you think he would've *killed* me?"

As the tribal investigator considered this innocent question from the sole witness to Bearcat's murder of Ben Silver, Sheriff Popper's words echoed in the dark corridors of his memory: *No matter how nasty the job is—you can always depend on Bearcat to get it done.* "There's no point in thinking about things like that."

She jerked at his hand. "But I can't *help* thinking about it."

Moon pretended to shrug it off. "Let's go get a dose of sunshine."

Still hand in hand, they left the gloom of Quiet Shade House.

Though reluctant to abandon the stalking of a fat black

cricket, Mr. Zig-Zag gave up the game and followed the human beings into the light.

•••

THE tribal elder watched her nephew approach with Sarah Frank. "All them government people are gone." As if it hardly mattered, she added: "Including that FBI lady." At the mention of the pretty white woman, Daisy Perika thought she saw a sparkle in Moon's eye. *Aha—I knew it! But I'll let on like I don't suspect a thing.* "I don't know why you two had to be so standoffish." Eyeing the girl, Daisy said: "Charlie wanders off like he's lost, and you go hide in the shadows."

"I was afraid of the grave," Sarah murmured. "That man in it tried to throw me off the cliff." *And if I hadn't kicked him, Aunt Daisy would've buried* me *under those rocks.*

"Well, I can understand how you'd feel that way." The shaman patted Sarah's thin shoulder. "His spirit decided to follow me home." Realizing that this was an opportunity to provide the half-Ute girl with some useful information, Daisy proceeded with the lesson: "Once a day-old ghost gets inside your house, getting rid of it is like trying to wash sorghum molasses out of your hair. What you want to do is to keep 'em from crossing the threshold in the first place. So I tried to act like I'd lost my mind." A sideways glance at her nephew dared Charlie Moon to smile. "Sometimes that'll scare a ghost away." At the puff of a clammy breeze, Daisy pulled her woolen shawl tightly around her shoulders. "But it didn't work. That white man's spirit has been hanging around my house ever since. Rattling pots and pans. Turning lights on and off." She released a hopeful sigh. "But now that they've hauled his sorry carcass away, I don't expect he'll be bothering me anymore."

Moon's expression made it clear that he disapproved of such talk in front of the girl.

When Daisy became aware that her overly tall nephew was looking down his nose at her, she tilted her head back, glared up her nose at him. "Well, what's your excuse, Kaw-Liga?" Catching Charlie off-guard was her specialty.

"What?"

"Kaw-Liga was a wooden Indian in an antique store." She smirked. "Us *real* Utes know stuff like that."

Moon smirked back at the Real Ute. "Kaw-Liga wasn't in the antique store."

"Don't correct me—I'm older than you and I know what I'm talking about!"

The alleged Wooden Indian asked: "What exactly are you talking about?"

It took Daisy a moment to gather her thoughts. "Ol' Kaw-Liga never did ask that white woman whether she'd like to be the mother of his—"

"There wasn't any white woman." Knowing it would irk his aunt, he launched into the lesson with a combination of patience and courtesy. "Way it happened, was like this: Kaw-Liga never could get up the nerve to speak to that Indian maiden—who was the one in the antique store—and it was too late when a rich man came and bought her and—"

"Listen to me, you big gourd-head—I was singing along with that Hank Williams song years before you were born and I know every word in every song he ever sung. So don't you go correcting me—I'm not interested in anything you have to say!"

"Then I might as well be 'Howlin' at the Moon.'"

Daisy was in no mood to let the subject drop. Unconditional surrender was what she wanted. "Then admit you know I was right!"

"'I Saw the Light.'" He hung his head. "'You Win Again.'"

Emboldened by this unexpected capitulation, Daisy raised her oak staff. "Charlie Moon—tell me *right now* what plans you and Lola Fay McFigg worked out, or I'll whack you across the shin with this stick!"

Looking like a man suffering from the "Lovesick Blues," he muttered: "'I've Just Told Mama Good-bye.'"

Daisy's petals wilted. *And I'd hoped they'd name their first daughter after me.* "Does that mean there won't be no—"

" 'Wedding Bells'?" He exhaled a wistful sigh. "Looks like 'I'll Be a Bachelor Until I Die.' "

"Well, it'll be your own fault."

He nodded. " 'I'm So Lonesome I Could Cry.' "

*Charlie don't sound quite like himself.* The elder's overworked brow furrowed with concern. *And he's got a kind of glassy look in his eye.* "Don't let that high-tone white woman bother you overly much, Charlie. You know what they say—'There's lots of other fish in the ocean.' "

Moon shook his head with an uncharacteristic vehemence that alarmed his aunt. "There's other fish in the *bucket.*"

"Okay, have it your way." The concerned relative reached out to touch his hand. "Them other fish are all in a *bucket.*"

*Gotcha!* "But '*My* Bucket's Got a Hole in It.' "

Barely suppressing a shudder, Doctor Daisy made her grim diagnosis: *Charlie's losing his mind. But I shouldn't be all that surprised—most of the men on his daddy's side of the family was a little peculiar.* She tried to recall an appropriate herbal preparation for treating his mental malady. *I could make him some yarrow tea. No, that's for a toothache. What I need is some peony or valerian roots. I wonder if I've got any left over from last year's batch.*

Moon was trying to think of a way to work 'I'm a Long Gone Daddy' into the conversation, when his concentration was interrupted by a squeeze from Sarah's hand.

She was smiling at him. Reassuringly. *Poor Charlie—you've still got me.*

Assuming Sarah had caught on to his game, he returned the smile.

Assuming her nephew was about to mutter another absurdity, Daisy thought she might distract him by changing the subject. "Something's been bothering me ever since I buried that Utah deputy here in Spirit Canyon."

Moon had anticipated that his aunt would raise this issue. "You've been wondering: 'If the deputy's under the sod, who drove his Bronco into the Piedra? Was it some person who came to the reservation with Packard, then hightailed it when things went sour? Or was the reckless driver a third party, whose identity and motive remain a mystery?' "

Grateful for this apparent return to normality, she waited to see how long it would last. *Well, do you know and are you gonna tell me?*

He did and did. "The driver of the ill-fated Bronco was Yadkin Dixon."

"That *matukach* good-for-nothing who walked off with my ax!"

Moon nodded. "Seems Mr. Dixon stumbled onto the spot where Deputy Packard had stashed his car, hot-wired it and took off like a bat outta—" He remembered the little girl who was holding his hand. "Uh—outta a barn loft." The tribal investigator went on to describe how the enthusiastic felon was driving too fast in the rainstorm, missed the bridge, ended up in the river, barely managed to get out before Packard's Bronco washed downstream. "When some kindly motorists stopped to help, Dixon thought it was not in his best interests to admit he was a car thief." He shook his head, grinned. "So he told 'em he'd almost drowned himself trying to save the driver."

Daisy grudgingly admitted that as thinking-quick-on-the-spot lies went, this one was up there in the top 10 percent.

Her nephew agreed. "And Mr. Dixon might've gotten away with it, but yesterday he borrowed a fancy red Jaguar from a tourist who'd stopped in Pagosa to buy herself a T-shirt. The lady saw him drive away, called 911 on her cell phone, and SUPD was notified by the state police dispatcher. Just as Dixon hung a left at Capote Lake, Officer Danny Bignight pulled him over. When Danny recognized the hero of the Piedra Bridge incident, he got suspicious and started asking some hard questions. After our SUPD cop leaned on him for a while, the truth came out." Moon raised a hand to forestall the venting of his aunt's pent-up I Told You So. "Dixon told Officer Bignight that he wasn't responsible for his actions—all his life, he's suffered from an overpowering compulsion to test-drive other people's automobiles. You can read the details in next week's *Drum.*"

Daisy had puffed up like a tree frog about to chirp. "I told you that rascal would steal anything that wasn't nailed down."

"Yes, you did." Moon gave his aunt a gentle pat on the back, which she thought was well deserved.

Having resolved the who-was-the-Bronco-driver puzzle, Daisy turned to Sarah with another query: "So why didn't you tell me that white man gave you his pink butterfly?"

Sarah put her hand over Ben Silver's canvas neck wallet, which made a slight bulge under her blue cotton blouse. "He made me promise not to tell anybody about it while he was alive." His exact words had been *until my corpse is six feet under the sod.*

Daisy detected a sizable flaw in this argument. "He was dead before you got here."

The girl nodded. "But by then, lots of people thought I'd killed him. If you'd found out I had his stone butterfly . . ." Her words trailed off into the twilight.

Daisy understood. *I'd have been* sure *you murdered that* matukach. "So what're you gonna do now?" Before the girl had a chance to respond, the tribal elder gave her the Look. "I don't think you should go back to Utah and live with your Papago cousin and her boyfriend."

Sarah tossed a shy glance at the tall man, squeezed his hand. "Maybe Charlie would like for me and Mr. Zig-Zag stay at the Columbine."

Moon was about to extend the invitation when he looked down at the hopeful fourteen-year-old—and realized he was staring Serious Trouble straight in the eye. *I'm a Long Gone Daddy.*

The phrase is admittedly overused, but—"There was a taut silence." *Extremely* taut. Indeed, if a mischievous musician had reached out and plucked it, the resultant *TWANG!* might have fractured the brittle atmosphere into shards.

Daisy Perika found herself on that proverbial spot. She knew that the best cure for what ailed her nephew was not tea brewed from the tincture of peony or valerian roots, but a brand-new sweetheart—and here was Sarah Frank, applying for the job! *But she's young enough to be Charlie's daughter.* On the other hand—*The girl is half-Ute.* Which reminded the Ute elder: *But her other half is Papago.* Daisy shook her head and snapped: "Charlie's ranch is no place for a young lady—it's full of half-wit, cow-pie kickers." In a gentler tone, she added: "You'll be better off here with me." Noting that Sarah was still giving her nephew the cow-eyes, the crafty old woman added a spicy enticement. "There's lots of important things I could teach you—like how to use nutmeg and dill weed to kill fleas and centipedes." *The silly girl's not listening to a single word I'm saying.* The sly old woman tried another approach. "And on days when I get all lonesome and blue, it'd be nice to have somebody to talk to." *I might as well be talking to a tree.* At a pleading look from her nephew, the tribal elder ground her remaining teeth, mumbled: "I've been having some troubles with my hip joints. If I was to fall down and couldn't get up, you could phone for help." This final humiliation almost did Daisy in.

Confronted with duty, Sarah effected a girlish little shrug. "Okay. I'll stay with you for a while." *Until Charlie realizes that he needs me.*

Charlie Moon released the breath he had been holding. *Thank you, Aunt Daisy.* He looked to the heavens. *And thanks be to God.*

*Keep reading for an excerpt from the upcoming Charlie Moon novel*

# THREE SISTERS

*Now available from St. Martin's Minotaur Paperbacks*

## ONE

### *WEST-CENTRAL COLORADO— THE COLUMBINE RANCH*

IN this grassy, glacier-sculpted valley sheltered by the shining Mountains, one man celebrates Thanksgiving every day of the year. Around about midnight, when he pulls the covers up to his chin, Charlie Moon is reminded of the multitude of blessings that enrich his life. Mulling over a few favorites helps him smile his way to sleep. Consider this evening's excellent selection.

Crisp, high-country air that fairly crackles with energy.

Soaring granite peaks that drip with dawn's golden honey, blush rose and crimson at twilight.

Hardly a stone's throw from his bedroom window, the rushing, murmuring, sing-me-to-sleep river—rolling along on its journey to the salty sea.

Ah—the lullaby has accomplished its soporific task.

He'll sleep like a log all night, wake up with a lumberjack's appetite, jump on whatever job needs doing, and get it done *right now.* Before the sun sets on another day, he will shoe a fractious quarter horse, arc-weld a fractured windmill axle, install a new starting motor on a John Deere tractor. In addition to these workaday skills, the resourceful man has a few other talents that come in handy from time to time. Not entirely clear? Okay, let's put it this way: On those occasions when business gets deadly serious, Mr. Moon knows how to tend to it—and he does. By doing *whatever is necessary.*

You'd expect a man like this to have plenty of friends, and you'd be right. There's no shortage of "Howdy Charlie!" backslappers and fair-weather sweet-talkers. But really *good* friends? You never know for sure till you hit bottom, but Moon reckons he can count the ones he can count on—on the fingers of one hand. His best buddy, Scott Parris (the thumb!), is right up there at Number One. Numbers Two and Three—on account of something bad that happened here last year—are an enigmatic hound dog and a man-killing horse.

As far as close family goes, they're all gone. Well, except Aunt Daisy—his "favorite living relative."

All things considered (even Daisy), Charlie Moon is an uncommonly fortunate man.

So, is he completely satisfied in his little slice of paradise? Afraid not. Close to his heart, there is an empty spot. What the lonely man hankers for is a special *someone*. Sad to say, the ardent angler's attempts at courting the ladies mirrors his experience at pursuing the wily trout. One way or another, the best one, the keeper—the *catch of the day*—she always gets away. But Moon has neither the time nor the inclination to dwell upon unhappy thoughts. So he doesn't. Flat-out *refuses* to.

## *MORNING*

AWAKENED by a pale silver glow in his window, Charlie Moon rolls out of bed, soaps up under a hot shower, slips into a lined canvas shirt, pulls on heavy over-the-calf woolen socks, faded jeans, comfortable old cowboy boots—and stomps down the stairs to get some meat frying in the iron skillet, a batch of fresh-ground coffee perking in the pot. Doesn't that smell *good*? And listen to the radio—the announcer on the *Farm and Ranch Show* is predicting an upturn in beef prices. Encouraged by the hope of turning a good profit, the stockman fortifies himself with a thick slab of sugar-cured ham, three eggs scrambled in genuine butter, a half-dozen hot-from-the-oven biscuits and two mugs of sweet black coffee. Good news, stick-to-your-ribs grub, and a double shot of caffeine—his day is off to a dandy start.

Moon steps out onto the east porch to greet the rising sun. The Indian gives each dawn a name. He stands in awed silence. Calls this one *Glorious*.

Slipping across the river, a breeze approaches to whisper a tale of snow in his ear. Not a surprise, especially during a deceptive late-winter thaw that is luring vast pastures of wildflowers into early bloom. Here in the highlands between the Misery and Buckhorn Ranges, snow is never far away. Even on the Fourth of July there's generally a dab of frosting left on the top of Sugarloaf Mountain, and foreman Pete Bushman likes to tell about a mid-June blizzard in '82 that buried his pickup right up to the windshield. While considering the chilling rumor, Moon hears a startled cloud mumble about something that's amiss. He blinks at the sun. What is this—the amber orb is caught fast on the jagged teeth of Wolf-Jaw Peak! Not to worry; it is a stellar jest. From a distance of one astronomical unit (93 million miles), the heavenly body smiles warmly upon the mortal's face.

Moon returns the smile. *Thank you, God—for everything.*

From somewhere *up yonder* booms a thunderously joyful response.

He hears this as a hearty "You're welcome, Charlie."

No, he is not superstitious. Far from it. Charlie Moon is a practical, down-to-earth, well-educated man who understands that the thunder was produced by those white-hot lightning legs tap-dancing across the Buckhorn Ballroom. Even so, over the years he has become aware of a deeper Reality, of which this flint-hard world is but a fleeting shadow—an infinitely magnificent thought in the mind of the *I Am*.

But *talking thunder*?

Certainly. The Ute has come to expect such courtesies from the Father.

## *TWO OF THE WOMEN IN CHARLIE MOON'S LIFE*

SOME miles to the south of the Columbine—on the Southern Ute reservation—the wind also huffs and puffs, but the breath exhaled from the mouth of *Cañón del Espíritu* is not so chilly, which is a good thing, because Daisy Perika (who has buried three husbands) is older than most of the towering, pink-barked ponderosas atop Three Sisters Mesa. In addition to those ailments common to the geriatric set, the damp cold makes every joint in her body ache. Plus her toenails. An exaggeration? Perhaps. But this is what the lady claims and so it must be reported.

Sarah Frank (who has a crush on Charlie Moon) cannot imagine Aunt Daisy as anything but what she sees—an ever-shrinking, bent-backed, black-eyed, wrinkled old husk of a woman with a tongue sharp as a sliver of obsidian. But what does this mere slip of a girl know? Not so many winters ago, Daisy was a cheerful, slender, pretty lass who danced to thrumming guitars, sang wistful love songs, and rode her black pony bareback, thrilling to the tug of the wind in her long, dark locks. Now she spends most of her time indoors, crouched close to the warm hearth, where during the entire circle of a year a piñon fire crackles and pops. And there, just on the other side of the Ute shaman's window pane, the harsh wilderness remains—ready to freeze the flesh, bleach the bone. There is much more to tell about this cantankerous old soul, involving cunning, conniving, self-serving schemes that cause no end of trouble for her amiable nephew, the brewing of overpriced, often dangerous potions from flora gathered near her home, plus an unwholesome liaison with the *pitukupf,* that dwarf spirit who (allegedly) lives in an abandoned badger hole in *Cañón del Espíritu.* If all this were not enough, there is also the tribal elder's alarming tendency to—No. For the moment, enough said. When Daisy is "of a mind to," she will make herself heard. Count on it.

## *THE THREE SISTERS*

TOWERING up from the eternal twilight of *Cañón del Espíritu* to dominate the austere skyline above Daisy Perika's remote home is a miles-long mesa whose summit (unlike those tabletop structures depicted in glossy picture postcards) is not flat. It is, due to a peculiar geologic history, quite the opposite of that. Residing on its crest is a trio of humpity bumps, the smallest dwarfing the largest man-made structure in La Plata County and Archuleta Co. to boot. According to a tale told by older Utes, the origin of these sandstone formations is rooted in violence. Once upon a time, only a few hundreds of years ago, there was a thriving Anasazi community in the vicinity. This is a fact, verifiable by remnants of venerable cliff-clinging ruins and thousands of distinctive black-on-white potsherds scattered along the canyon floor. It is also true that Old Ones' village was destroyed by a marauding band of thieves and murderers, but these were not necessarily Apaches—that is a lurid tale cooked up by the Utes. The Apaches assert that the crime was committed by a roving gang of Navajo, who in turn blame a rowdy band of West Texas Comanche, who point accusing fingers at the haughty Arapahos, who attribute the atrocity to those shifty-eyed Shoshone, who claim the thing was done by the Utes, and so the venomous slander-snake swallows its tail. The truth is—none of these tribes was involved.

But back to those bumps on the mesa. Not surprisingly, the few facts have become thoroughly mixed with myth, and Daisy Perika will tell you that the only members of the Anasazi village who escaped (if *escape* is an appropriate term) were a trio of young sisters who climbed a precipitous path to the top of the mesa, which in those olden days was smooth and level enough to shoot pool on. The terrified women hoped to hide among the piñon and scrub-oak thickets until the brutal foreigners had departed, but before reaching the summit they were detected by a keen-eyed warrior who alerted his comrades. While the bloodthirsty enemy with filed-to-a-point teeth and hideously tattooed faces ascended the mesa with exultant whoops and terrifying war cries, the sisters prayed to Man-in-the-Sky to protect them. He did. They were (so Daisy's story goes) instantly turned into stone by the merciful deity. Hence, we have Three Sisters Mesa.

It is hoped that this technical information on instantaneous petrification is appreciated—in spite of the fact that Three Sisters Mesa has nothing whatever to do with those particular Three Sisters with whom the following account is concerned. This being the case, let us leave the ancient stone women atop their mesa.

We now return to the twenty-first century, where we shall (in due course) encounter the relevant trio of female siblings—Astrid, Beatrice, and Cassandra Spencer.

But first we must pay a call on Daisy Perika.

# TWO

## *SOUTHERN UTE RESERVATION*

### What Cassandra Saw

*Hunched like an old toad in her rocking chair, eyes half shut, hands folded in her lap, knees toasting before the stone fireplace, Daisy Perika appears to be asleep. Or dead. She is neither.*

Since supper, the Ute tribal elder had hardly stirred, and was very close to dozing—when she heard the patter of feet.

These particular feet belonged to Sarah Frank, the fifteen-year-old Ute-Papago orphan who had lived with Daisy for almost a year, and loved Charlie Moon for as long as she could remember. Having completed her algebra and American-history homework assignments, Sarah switched on Daisy's television, inserted a blank disc into the DVD's thin mouth, and set the controls to begin recording at one minute before the hour. The devoted viewer had every single episode of *Cassandra Sees* in her collection.

Daisy did not spend many of her precious remaining hours purchasing what the medium had to offer. On a lonely weekday morning, while the girl was away at school in Ignacio, the Ute elder might watch a talk show for a few minutes before falling asleep, and on a Friday night she would tell Sarah it was "all right if you want to turn on that *Country Music Jamboree* you like so much and watch them silly hillbillies." Though she would pretend to have no particular interest in the energetic *matukach* entertainment, Daisy waited all week for the high-stepping, foot-stomping clog dancers, thunder-chested yodelers, nimble-fingered guitar pickers, and whoopin'-it-up hoedown fiddlers whose sounds and images traveled (at the speed of light!) all the way from gritty, spit-on-the-sawdusted-floor Texas honky-tonks, pine-studded Arkansas ridges, and mist-shrouded Kentucky hollers—into her cozy parlor. Their merry exuberance would curl Daisy's mouth into a little possum grin and set the old woman's shoe toe to tappity-tapping on the floor. But no matter how good the beginning and the middle were, the end was the best part. After all the crooning about Momma, railroad trains, prison, adultery, fornication, drunkenness, theft, lies, slander, and murder were finished, the closing was invariably an old-time gospel song. *Hidden deep in the heart of every sinner is a yearning for God.* Last week, when an ancient, snowy-capped black man had called upon those angels to Swing Low in that Sweet Chariot, tears had dripped from the old woman's eyes. Daisy was ready to hitch a ride and go arolling up yonder—last stop, that unspeakably lovely mansion her Lord was preparing in His Father's House. Home at last! It could not come too soon.

Daisy raised her chin, looked over the thin girl's shoulder. "What's coming on?"

"*Cassandra.*" Sarah was clicking through the satellite channels.

"Oh." *That's pretty good.* She turned the rocking chair to face the expensive "entertainment center" Charlie Moon had contributed, along with other furnishings for her new home.

Sarah was perched on a footstool, her face close to the television screen. She would not miss a thing.

Mr. Zig-Zag (Sarah's spotted cat) padded in from the kitchen, stretched out on the floor beside her, yawned at the flickering picture.

The broadcast began with a sooty-black screen, and an eerie strain of organ music that was the psychic's trademark.

Then, on the dark electronic velvet, a bloodred script was traced by invisible pen: Cassandra Sees.

"Yes!" The girl clapped her hands.

Having had its say, the title bled away. As the last crimson drop fell into an unseen reservoir, the psychic's all-seeing eye appeared, filling the screen. Iridescent it was, and opalescent—the platter-size iris mimicking a blooming cluster of multicolored petals, turquoise blue, twilight gray, spring-grass green!

*That is* so *cool,* Sarah whispered to herself. "But I don't know how she keeps from blinking."

The enormous eye faded, Cassandra Spencer's pale, masklike face appeared. The oval countenance, at once strikingly sinister and hypnotically attractive, was framed in long locks of raven hair, artfully tucked behind her ears. The psychic's eyes were aglow with terrible secrets, arcane knowledge. They seemed to say: *We not only See; we Know.*

"Oh," Sarah breathed. "Cassandra just gives me *goose pimples.*" As she held out a skinny arm so Daisy might see the proof of this claim, her frail little frame shuddered with a delicious fear. "I wonder if she'll talk to a dead person tonight."

The Ute shaman, who was certain she talked to more ghosts and spirits in a month than this uppity young white woman had encountered in her entire lifetime, offered a "Hmmpf." But Daisy was leaning ever-so-slightly forward in her chair.

Mr. Zig-Zag, who had his own visions to pursue, drifted off to sleep.

As the psychic uttered her usual greeting, Sarah silently mouthed the words: *Dear friends . . . welcome to my home.*

Her face faded off the screen. A camera panned the walnut-paneled parlor in the star's Granite Creek mansion, sharing with the audience a cherry cupboard housing delicate bisque figurines of ballerinas on tiptoe, a miniature flock of crystal swans, a cranberry vase that held a single, gold-plated rose. Then, as an unseen technician threw a switch, viewers were transported out of the parlor-studio to a scene in the host's dining room, where several enraptured guests were seated, smiling at images of themselves on a cluster of video monitors.

"What a bunch of dopey half-wits," Daisy muttered. *You'd never get me on a dumb show like that.*

The psychic's face appeared again, the lovely lips speaking: "This evening, we deal with the controversial subject of reincarnation. Our special guest is Raman Sajhi, a citizen of India, who is touring the United States to discuss his best-selling new book—*My Five Thousand Lives.*"

*Five thousand lives my hind leg!* Daisy snorted at such nonsense.

Camera 3 picked up the turbaned guest's pleasant face. He responded to his host with a polite, semiprayerful gesture—delicate fingers touched at the tips, a modest bowing of the head.

Daisy Perika eyed the bespectacled foreigner with no little suspicion. "Raymond Soggy don't look a day over a half-dozen lives to me."

Sarah giggled.

Mr. Zig-Zag, who still had eight to go, dozed on.

Mr. Sajhi commenced to pitch his book with thumbnail sketches of selected previous lives. In addition to his miserable stint as a convict on Devil's Island, the poor soul had also done time as a golden carp in a Shanghai pond, an Ethiopian dung beetle, a camel (of no particular ethnicity or distinction), a wealthy rajah's hunting elephant, and a ferocious female Bengal tiger who had devoured several citizens, including a British subaltern who was a close friend of Mr. Kipling. Though a combination of jet lag, TV appearances, and signings at mall bookstores may have been contributing factors, the author reported that he was tired-to-the-bone from the hard labors of his many incarnations, the current of which was, by his meticulous calculations, appearance number four thousand nine hundred and ninety-nine.

Mr. Zig-Zag abruptly awakened, gaped his toothy mouth to whine.

During a commercial break, Sarah Frank addressed Daisy Perika: "Do you think people can really come back to live more than one time?" The girl, who had once dreamed of returning as a butterfly, glanced at the cat. "Do you think we could come back as animals?" Before the Ute elder could respond, Sarah asked: "If we could, what kind of animal would you want to be?"

Three questions too many.

Resembling a ruffled old owl, Daisy scowled at the impertinent girl. Which settled the issue.

Cassandra appeared on the screen. "Now we will discuss a particularly fascinating category of spirits—those who return for the sole purpose of communicating an important message to the living."

Daisy and Sarah watched the psychic introduce a second guest, who provided a fascinating account of how her deceased grandfather had, once upon a certain snowy night in December "nineteen-and-eighty-two," appeared by her bed and told her where to find a Havana perfectos cigar box stuffed with rare and valuable nineteenth-century coins. The box was there, of course, under the loose floorboard in the smokehouse where the old fellow had stashed it, half full of coins. But that was not all. The mournful specter had also confessed several youthful misdeeds to his astonished granddaughter—including a colorful account of how he had dealt with a Tennessee sharpster who had made a pass at his first wife. Granddad had, so he said, used a scythe to remove the unfortunate fellow's head from his shoulders. The lady explained to a rapt television audience that this was "very unsettling to hear." No one in the family had the least notion that Grandpa had been married but once, to Grandma. The fact that he had "killed his man" was of little consequence. "Back in those days in the Ozarks, that was just the way things was." The guest was about to enlarge on how things was back in those days in the Ozarks, when—

With an alarming suddenness, Cassandra dropped her chin.

The psychic's eyes seemed to be gazing blankly at her knees, which were modestly concealed under a black silk skirt—or, as the many viewers assumed, at something (other than her knees) that they were *not able to see.*

"Murder." This was what Cassandra saw, and what she said.